"BUCK SNORT" TONI AND "WIND HORSE", MOUNTAIN MEN

TERRY GROSZ

WOLFPACK PUBLISHING

WOLFPACK
PUBLISHING
— EST 2013 —

Print Edition

Wolfpack Publishing
6032 Wheat Penny Avenue
Las Vegas, NV 89122

ISBN: 978-1-64119-549-2

Library of Congress Control Number: 2018965569

DEDICATION

This book is dedicated to my three Arizona grandchildren: Bria Jackson, Bryce Jackson and Bryant Jackson, one and all. These children, born from our adopted Vietnamese airlift baby, Kimberlee, have been nothing short of extraordinary given their circumstances. Kimberlee, divorced and without a college education and ill most of her adult life because of exposure to Agent Orange as an infant in Vietnam, many times has worked two jobs while living at poverty's edge, and has managed to raise three of the most remarkable kids my wife and I have ever known.

Bria, Bryce and Bryant, even though deprived of many of life's basics because of Kim's health and living situations, are wonderful. None of them smoke, drink or do drugs. They have always been very respectful to their mother and any other adults they come into contact with. They are multi-skilled, high level students and athletes in and of their own right.

Bria, Kim's daughter, is putting herself through college by working two jobs and utilizing grants whenever available while maintaining an "A" average in college. Additionally, she is an exceptionally skilled hip-hop dancer, a "beautiful person" to everyone around her with her sweet and caring disposition, and gives the best hugs in the world to her grandfather!

Bryce, Kim's older son, is a high level, multi-skilled athlete currently attending the University of Nevada at Las Vegas on a full-ride football scholarship. He is a leader both on and off the field. Throughout his schooling, he has consistently maintained a very high GPA and is one of the politest and well-mannered young men my wife, Donna, and I have ever had the honor to be associated with.

Bryant, Kim's younger son, is a quiet and well-mannered young man. He has the build of a remarkable athlete, takes very good care of his body, and maintains a high GPA in high school. Several colleges have already shown an interest in Bryant who is just a high school junior this year. He has rallied back from several injuries with grit and determination. He is on his way to becoming a role model for other athletes at school.

These three children, even in the face of many financial and familial adversities with Kim having to be both mother and father to them, have matured into outstanding strong human beings, Christians in thought and deed, honest, respectful and representing the highest qualities of what any grandparent would want in his grandchildren as American citizens.

It is to these three grandchildren that I very proudly dedicate this book in their honor...

CONTENTS

Chapter Sixteen

CHAPTER ONE

―――――――――――――――――――――――――――――――――――――

HEAVEN, FIRE, "HELL" AND "WIND HORSE"

FIFTEEN-YEAR-OLD VINCE TONI stirred in his second-story bedroom as his biological clock ticked and the vestiges of the morning's sun crept into his room through his lone window awakening him. For a few minutes, Vince just lay there in his bed enjoying the warmth from his blankets and the comfort of his bed. Then faced with the fact that he had to run his trap line and get back in time to milk the cows and then help his Missouri sharecropper farmer stepdad Al Johnson, he bailed out of bed. The coolness of the air in his unheated bedroom and the cold felt through the bottom of his feet when they hit the wooden floor jolted him awake if he wasn't awake before! Feeling nature's urge, he hurried over to the 'thunder-mug' by the back wall in his

1

bedroom and relieved himself. Then quickly dressing, Vince threw on his old coat that his real dad had always worn and then quietly crept down the wooden stairs and out the back door so he wouldn't wake his parents sleeping in their first-floor bedroom.

Quietly opening up the back door and feeling the blast of the late fall's cold on his face, he hurried over to the barn. There he let his stepdad's three horses out so they could feed and water in the pasture but kept his favorite riding horse in the stall. Grabbing a curry comb, Vince curried down his horse, put the bit into the horse's mouth and led him out into the center of the barn. There he hooked his horse up to the one-horse shay, checked the back of the wagon to make sure all of his trapping gear was present and then headed back into the house for one more item that he needed. Sneaking back into the house once again so he wouldn't wake his sleeping parents, he grabbed his father's flintlock rifle and a carry bag full of flints, two powder horns, greased patches and balls, and then slipped back out from the farmhouse and trotted back to the one-horse shay.

Moments later, Vince was on his way to several small creeks and beaver ponds three miles away on a friend's farm. Arriving at the creeks and waterways, Vince tied off his horse, grabbed a carry bag full of trapping gear, slung it over his shoulder and trotted towards his first trap in his long trap line. He found nothing in his first three traps but in trap four he found a young beaver. Taking off his pants and shoes, Vince waded out into the icy cold waters, retrieved his beaver and trap and returned to the shoreline. There he removed the beaver from the trap and reset it and then dipped his lure stick into a small bottle of castor, stuck it back into the bank where the end of the lure stick was over the now reset trap and continued on along his trap line hoping for more furbearers to be in his traps. (Author's Note: An oily brown odorous substance obtained from the glands in the groin area of a beaver and commonly used by beaver trappers to lure beaver to a trap. Beaver are very territorial and are readily lured to the scent from another beaver's castors. In the days of the early fur trade, castor was also commonly called 'castoreum'. Castor is commonly applied to a small limb or twig hanging over the open jaws of a trap in such a manner that when a beaver comes over to investigate another beaver's scent on the end of the twig or limb, it will stand up, grab the twig or end of the limb hanging over the pan of a trap to get a better smell and will find himself with one or both feet in the trap.)

One hour later found a half-frozen Vince Toni slipping back into his warm pants, socks and shoes. At his feet lay four muskrats, two beaver and a surprise catch, namely a very large river otter! Happy over his day's catch, Vince slung his carry bag over his shoulder full of muskrats, beaver and river otter and struggled up the bank and headed back the mile or so to his one-horse shay. Arriving about a half-hour later, Vince was surprised to see his farmer friend Chuck Curry standing by his horse and wagon. Struggling under his load of animal carcasses and trapping gear, Vince did not right away see the look of concern on his friend's face. Finally arriving at his wagon, Vince piled all of his gear and animal carcasses into the back and then looked up into his friend's face only to see a serious look on the man's face.

Vince said happily, "Good morning, Chuck. Did you see the load of muskrats and beaver I brought back this morning? We will have some good eats in the beaver and 'rats', not to mention I can make some more money once I pelt out these critters and sell them to the fur buyers at the St. Louis Missouri Fur Company in St. Louis."

That was when Vince saw that the deep look of concern on his friend's face never changed after being greeted! "Why are you looking at me like that, Chuck? What is the matter?" asked Vince.

"Vince, you had better get home. There has been trouble at your home place," said Chuck with a heavy sounding voice.

"What are you talking about? What has happened, Chuck?" asked Vince, as a cold feeling began gripping his heart and sweeping over his body.

"There has been a fire at your place," said Chuck quietly, "and Sheriff Dickens, figuring you were probably running your trap line over on my farm, has asked me to fetch you and have you get on home."

Vince realizing that something was really wrong back at his home, threw his rifle into the front seat of the shay, untied his horse and was soon racing for home. About 30 minutes later a very concerned Vince Toni and a well lathered-up horse sped into the front yard of his home. There he found a number of neighbors, the sheriff and THE SMOKING RUINS OF HIS HOME!

"Sheriff, what happened? Where are my folks, where are my folks?" yelled Vince, as he ran up to the smoking ruins of what once had been his home!

Moments later, Vince felt the hand of the sheriff being placed on his shoulder and then saying, "Vince, they are gone! Apparently they were asleep when their cat must have knocked over a whale oil lamp and set the house afire. Then either the smoke or the flames got your folks, they not being aware their house was clear a-fire until it was too late," said Sheriff Dickens.

Then Vince found the arms of several neighbor ladies being wrapped around his badly shaking body as the emotions of his loss swept over and through his 15-year-old body. Shortly thereafter, Vince got control of his emotions and then the realization began sinking in. He had lost his much loved real father to an angry mule's kick when he tried cleaning one of its rear hooves when Vince was younger. Now he had lost his much loved mother, the only other person in the world he really loved. As for his stepdad, there was no love there. His stepdad had beaten him regularly no matter how well he finished a job or project. So as far as Vince was concerned, there was no loss in losing someone who had regularly beaten him at every turn in the trail for little or no reason. In fact, that is why Vince ran his trap line. He had realized there was no place in his home under the new father so he ran a trap line in order to make some money and once he had enough saved, he would take the money earned from his fur sales and strike out on his own.

Now all Vince had was the family's four milk cows, their four horses, a chicken house full of chickens and a barn in which to live! Vince's heart just sank over the realities of life he was now facing at just 15 years old! Then things got worse if they weren't already bad enough…

"Vince," said Sheriff Dickens, "do you have anybody else who can come and get you and take you in so you have a place in which to live?"

For the longest moment, Vince did not truly understand what the sheriff had just asked him. Finally, Vince said, "Sheriff, I know of no one else in my family. My mom was an orphan when she was younger and I know of no other living relative"…

"Vince, unless you have someone else in your family who can come and take you since you are a minor under state law, you will have to be turned over to Cal Jenkins's orphanage to live until you are at least 16!" said Sheriff Dickens.

Upon hearing those words, Vince's already heavily taxed heart took another blow! Cal Jenkins's orphanage was known as a 'hellhole'! It was common knowledge that Cal only ran what he called an orphanage just so he could gather in lost and homeless children and then work them almost to death on his local 1,000-acre corn farm! Vince had heard all of the horror stories of the beatings, bad food, hard work, in fact almost slavery and even how some children had just up and quietly, mysteriously disappeared while under Cal's 'care', never to be seen again!

"Sheriff, I ain't a-going! Cal Jenkins runs a 'hellhole' and everyone around here knows it. But he has his brother, the local judge, on his side and there ain't nothing one can do about it once you are in Cal's clutches!" said Vince steadfastly.

"Vince, you know the law. That is just how it works. I can let you stay in your folks' barn for a few days until you can get things in order but after that, it's off to the Jenkins orphanage and that is that!" said the sheriff. Upon hearing those words, Vince 'roostered-up' and shook his head saying, "No!"

"You heard me, Young Fella! You have ten days to get your things in order and then that is that! Your stepdad was a sharecropper on the land. If he can't farm it like the landowner wants it farmed, and since he is dead that is a moot point. That means the landowner is going to reclaim his property and put someone else on it to farm it. So that is that, Vince. You are going to have to move and since you are underage, the orphanage is your only option under State of Missouri law! That is until you reach 16 years of age and then by law you can be out on your own. I don't make the laws, I just enforce them," said Sheriff Dickens…

That night, Vince cried himself to sleep as he lay wrapped in a smelly horse blanket in a hay mow in their old barn! The next morning with a broken heart over the loss of his beloved mother, Vince carried on. He milked the cows, fed the horses and chickens and took the milk into their small town of New Haven located along the Missouri River to sell. Then coming back home and after looking all around to make sure no one was watching him, Vince began digging into the manure pile next to the barn. Soon he had uncovered a three-gallon stoneware crock. Looking all around once again to make sure no one was watching him, he removed its lid and placed all of his milk sale money into the crock and reburied it back under the manure pile where he hoped no one would ever look.

That afternoon, Vince herded his four horses and four milk cows down the country lanes towards his friend's home. Bringing the stock and his shay full of chickens in a cage into the front yard, there he met Chuck Curry and his eight children.

"What can I do for you, Vince?" asked Curry.

"Mr. Curry, as you well know by now, I have to leave the farm and live at the orphanage because of my age according to the sheriff. I am here to make you a deal. I will leave my four horses, four milk cows, chickens and one-horse shay for you and your family to use as you see fit. However, just as soon as I turn 16, I can legally leave the orphanage and be out on my own. I would like to then come back and take my four horses and move on to greener pastures. However, as your pay for caring for my property, you can keep the cows, chickens and my shay. I also will leave my dad's rifle and my trapping gear here with you as well, but would like to have those back when I turn 16. How does that sound?" asked Vince.

"Well, if that is what you want to do, Vince, then that is alright with me as well," said Curry, as he took Vince's extended hand and shook on the deal. Then Vince walked back to his barn because he still had some work that he needed to do before the sheriff threw him off the farm…

That night, Vince returned to his manure pile and dug up his stoneware crock. He then carried it off the property and over to a nearby creek and buried the crock under a green ash tree growing near a large boulder alongside the creek.

By last count, Vince had $327.88 in coin in that crock, which was a small fortune in those days. (Author's Note: Most common working men made about $300-500 per year in the early 1800's!) Vince had saved up his money from working odd jobs around the farming community mostly helping in the butchering of hogs, from his deer, bear, muskrat and beaver fur sales, from selling snapping turtle meat removed from snapping turtles he had caught around the local waterways in his turtle traps, from winning $20 in a local turkey shoot by outshooting 33 adults, and selling deer, elk, feral hog and black bear meat from animals he had shot in the local forests with his father's rifle. He also sold the eggs and squabs he had removed from nesting passenger pigeons that frequented the oak forests in the area, as well as meat from the adult passenger pigeons and wild turkeys that he had taken with his father's shotgun. This he did starting from age ten until the day his home had burned to the ground and he had lost his parents and most everything else to the fire!

Come day ten after the fire, Vince waited outside his barn for Sheriff Dickens to arrive. Around noon the sheriff arrived and riding behind the sheriff on his saddle horse rode a very quiet Vince Toni. A very determined Vince Toni who would survive the rigors and hardships he now was facing living at an orphanage known for its harsh treatment of its charges or he would know the reason why. Then once he turned age 16, he would be out of there, on his own and then make his way and see what the world had waiting for him. After all, he lived in America and to his way of thinking, the wilderness just across the Missouri River was opportunity waiting for whoever found it...

Half an hour later, the sheriff rode his horse into the front yard of a rundown old farmhouse and several outbuildings making do as the area's local orphanage for the homeless. With a shout, out from the farmhouse walked a 'death warmed over' looking man wearing a dirty apron and a big grin surrounded by a six-day growth of whiskers.

The man walked over to the sheriff and said, "Howdy, Sheriff. So this is the lad you have been telling me about. Well, young fella, get your ass off that horse and get inside so I can show you around and then you can start earning your keep! Thanks, Sheriff, I think I can take care of this from here on."

Without another word, Cal Jenkins walked back inside the old farmhouse and Vince was carrying his only possession other than the clothes on his back, namely a smelly old horse blanket from his barn. As it turned out, his 'inheritance' from a previous life of hardship was about to get one hell of a lot harder! He was soon to discover that his new life was to be one filled with terror come nightfall, filth, beatings and starvation, along with a wonderful learning experience provided by a man named Cliff Fulton and then meeting a fellow castaway and 'brother-in-arms' was 'blowing in the wind'…

Walking inside the orphanage, Vince found it overrun with about a dozen cats, and the strong acrid smell of fresh cat urine and feces hung heavy in the air! Vince was then led upstairs to the second floor by Cal where he was shown a large bare room with13 mattresses spread out along the floor and three unwashed and smelling of urine and poop 'thunder-mugs' located along a back wall.

"Here is where you sleep on the floor. Pick a mattress over next to that wall that isn't being used. That will be your mattress. Breakfast is at five in the morning, there is no lunch, and supper is around eight at night after you get back from working in the fields. If you don't work and work hard, you don't eat. It is just that simple. You piss me off and you will feel this horse quirt across your lazy ass and back! Really piss me off and expect to get belted in the mouth just like I would do any man. Use the 'thunder-mugs' at the end of the room and since you are the most recent one to arrive, you get the job of cleaning them out and washing them daily before you eat breakfast every morning. If you don't take care of them, expect me to dump the crap and piss on your head and onto your sleeping mattress! You will also skip breakfast and supper that day and lay in your own pew come nightfall! Those are the rules!" growled Cal.

"Now follow me downstairs after you dump off that smelly horse blanket on the mattress you chose. Make haste, young fella, because I have work for you right now and I don't tolerate slackers," said Cal as he left the bedroom.

Throwing his horse blanket down on a mattress, Vince ran down the stairs behind Cal, out the front door and over to a long building that was showing a lot of smoky haze being emitted from its one open side door and windows. Walking through the open end of the building behind Cal, Vince saw the long building was a huge blacksmith shop with glowing iron working furnaces, open forges, monster in size anvils, stacks of pig iron plate, and one tall man in the rear of the building hammering away on a piece of red-hot iron on an anvil. As Vince walked behind Cal who smelled of sour sweat and cat crap, he noticed a long bricked-up area holding burning firewood. Then upon closer examination, Vince saw several cast iron Dutch ovens and one large bean pot cooking away in the bricked-up area over the firepit.

Cal walked up to the rather large blacksmith hammering away on the metal jaws of a beaver trap. That caught Vince's eyes right off the bat and now he was all 'eyes, ears and false teeth' over what he was seeing since it was something he recognized. Then Cal said, "Here is your new

man. Since you didn't like any of the other kids
I brought by to be your assistant, this here kid is
your last option. He is a new kid who just lost his
parents and I have no idea if he is a worker or not.
That is for you to find out. But if he is a slacker
like all of the rest, I will find him a place working
out in the fields. Now by dammit, Vince, you fail
out here, you will find your lazy ass working out
in the fields with the rest of the useless kids who
are living here in this orphanage. This here man
is my blacksmith and his name is Cliff Fulton.
He is a hard taskmaster but I expect you will find
that out fast enough. Now, I have some work
to do over at the house so I will leave the two of
you to get acquainted and don't tolerate any fuss
or feathers from this here snot-nosed kid. Work
him hard so he can earn his keep." With that Cal
stomped off back to the orphanage smelling of
cat urine and poop…

"Can you cook, kid?" asked Cliff as he 'squint-
eyed' his new helper.

"Yes Sir, Mr. Fulton. But I will need some help
teaching me on how you want it done so I don't
cross Mr. Jenkins," said Vince quietly.

"Good! Now just so you know the ropes
around here, work hard and we will get along.
End up useless like those last three boys I had
and it is out into the fields with the rest of the
lads staying here. Now I noticed you looking at
all of the cooking pots as you walked by when
you came in. Just for your information, there are

13 boys living here at the big house and they are all eager eaters. Since Cal's kitchen is too small to cook in for such a large group of young men, we do most of the heavy cooking out here in the blacksmith shop. Here, let me show you," said Fulton, as he laid down the metal trap he had been working on and walked off.

With that, Cliff walked Vince back to the bricked-in ovens and cooking pits. There Vince saw hanging irons used to hang kettles and pots over the fire or hot coals, as well as a pit full of coals holding several large cast iron cooking pots cooking away. "This whole bricked-in area is where we do all the cooking for you kids at the orphanage. As you can see, this is a major cooking area by all the pots, hot coals and hanging irons. This will be your responsibility. If you can't cook and lots of it, the rest of the boys in this here place will kick your ass. That is because they get little for breakfast and really depend on a big supper, so you had better learn to cook and cook fast and well," said Fulton.

Then Cliff paused and looked over at Vince to see if what he had just said had registered. There he could see Vince's eyes looking everything over carefully like he was not only interested in the cooking detail but looking forward to it. Then Cliff started up once again, "Vince, you will also be responsible for not only cutting and hauling all of the wood for these cooking fires but the preparation and cooking of all the food. Mess up and

Cal will lather up your backside with that horse quirt he always carries! Now over there is the root cellar where all the fresh vegetables grown on the place are kept. Over along that wall in those cupboards is where the spices and cooking oils are kept and underneath those shelves are all the extra cooking cast iron pots and pans anyone would ever want. I have already set up tonight's supper but starting tomorrow, that will be your responsibility. Usually there will be a bean dish of some sort, Dutch oven biscuits, coffee and a stew of some sort with lots of mystery meat. I say mystery meat because Cal is pretty cheap, so meat around here can be raccoon, wild hog, turkey, snapping turtle, dog and anything else Cal happens to kill. He ain't much on manners so best you learn how to make a skunk taste good or those boys from the fields will beat your ass something awful when they come in for chow and it is not up to their expectations!"

Then pausing once again, Cliff looked at Vince to see if he had 'lost' him and was pleased to see the young man was apparently all eyes and ears when it came to learning. "Now once all of your cooking duties are up and a-going for the morning, you will be expected to help me. That means I will be teaching you the finer points of working iron, running forges, heat treating the metal without 'burning' it and making traps of every make and kind for the retail market and fur trade. For you see, ever since that Manuel Lisa fellow got into the fur trapping business in 1807 on the Upper Missouri and now in Nebraska, Cal has been his major supplier of traps, primarily the St. Louis-style of beaver trap which is a favorite of the West's fur trappers and the local fur companies. So we have a standing order for all we can produce and afore long, I will have you helping make those traps in addition to your cooking duties. There, now I have said it. The axes and saws are there over in that corner and I suggest you go out back and begin cutting tomorrow's wood for your cooking fires. In the meantime I have to get back to my trap making or I will get my ass chewed by Cal as well. However, if he wants to live another day, you will never see him use that damn horse quirt that he uses on the boys who live here, on me. If he does, he may damn well end up in one of your cooking pots and if that is the case, you had best use lots of onions and garlic on his miserable carcass, otherwise he won't be eatable…"

The rest of that afternoon, Vince slaved over the woodpile until he figured he had enough for the next day's cooking fires. Additionally, he had to maintain the right temperature fires under his cooking pots full of food and come dark, in from the field came a gang of very hungry young men. Then they swarmed into the eating area in the blacksmith shop and Vince found himself feeding a noisy and hungry crowd. As he did, he quickly discovered that three of the older boys 'ruled the roost' when it came to all of the unfortunate kids having to live at the orphanage. That was when Vince discovered rather quickly, after being struck from behind by one of those older boys, that they were to be fed first and with as much as they wanted… Little did he realize that was just a 'love tap', because the worst was yet to come!

Later that night up in the sleeping area for all of the younger men, Vince quickly discovered what hell he and his new life had descended into. Walking through the sleeping area after he had cleaned up the eating area and treated all of his cast iron cooking implements, he finally got to go to bed. As he picked his way among the now resting young men in the sleeping area, he all of a sudden found his legs swept out from under him, sending him crashing to the floor! Then he found one of the three older boys on top of him smashing him in his face with his fists!

"There, 'new kid', that will teach you who is boss in this here house and best you remember or you will get more of the same!" said a kid named Darrell as he climbed off a badly beaten Vince.

Hurt, surprised, badly bleeding and scared, Vince crawled out from under the bully and hid under his smelly horse blanket nursing his wounds. Then several times during the night, he could hear some of the younger boys crying out as the three larger and older boys were doing something to those smaller kids in the dark of the night which caused them to cry out in terror and pain! The next morning before daylight, everyone upstairs was rousted out from their sleeping mattresses and fed a breakfast of just oatmeal and then sent out into the fields to work all day with nothing for their lunches...

That next morning Cliff asked Vince, "What happened to cause your black eye and large bruise under that eye?"

Vince just mumbled something and then headed out to his wood detail that he had not finished from the day before. Later finished with his wood detail, Vince began peeling potatoes and preparing other foods for the supper to come. Once he got his supper for everyone prepared and cooking, Vince then found he was being taught the finer points of blacksmithing by Cliff. Thus went Vince's daily regimen of woodchopping, supper preparations, cooking and tending to his cooking. Then being taught more and more about basic blacksmithing like making horseshoes, being a farrier for the farm's livestock, learning how to make the right kinds of fires in the forges and maintaining them so the metal would take the right temper. Over the months as he improved in his skills as a result of Cliff's teachings, Vince began making parts of the St. Louis-style of beaver trap for sale in Manuel Lisa's Emporium located in nearby St. Louis.

However, he dreaded the nights even though he was bone-tired after his daylong labors running from around 5:30 in the morning until around 9:30 at night! Every night he found himself being abused, busted in the face and forced to defend himself in the presence of the three older boys who were terrorizing all the rest of the younger kids at the orphanage! And when he tried to fight back and defend himself, all three of the older boys would join in at the same time and beat him senseless. Then each day, he found himself trying to hide the nightly beating fact from Cliff, who he was really developing a great relationship with. That was because under Cliff's tutelage, Vince found himself a natural when it came to blacksmithing and cooking for gangs of folks. And the better he got over the year, the more responsibility Cliff gave Vince until he was making from raw pigs of iron, horseshoes, St. Louis-style beaver traps, some rifle and pistol parts, knives, axes and shovel heads!

But come nightfall when the darkness in the upstairs bedroom swallowed up the sleeping area, the night's raids on the younger boys by the three older boys became more and more rampant and violent! One night as Vince lay curled up under his smelly horse blanket, he all of a sudden realized the three dark shadows standing by his mattress were those of the legs of the three older boys! Turning to face the threat of another beating, he received a boot in the face for his defensive efforts, which knocked him almost senseless!

"Take your clothes off, Vince, or stand to be beaten beyond belief!" said Curtis, one of the three older boys standing at arm's length.

Upon hearing those blood curdling words, Vince tensed up and then lashed out with his legs and dropped Darrell who was standing near at hand to the floor! However when he did, he quickly found the other two boys dropping down upon him and beating him with their fists and then being kicked until he passed out! The next morning, Vince awoke to find himself naked on his mattress and bleeding from his anus! He then realized what all the other desperate sounds had meant that he had heard over the last six months of his living in the orphanage! Desperate sounds at night under the cover of the darkness coming from the younger kids as a result of what was being done physically to them by the older boys! It was at that moment in time, lying there with both eyes almost closed from the previous evening's beating, hardly being able to breathe because of his kicked-in ribs and now the realization that he had been violently raped and damaged from the rape, that Vince found his heart hardening and his mind made up...

The next day, Vince found that he could hardly walk, could barely see and found it hard to take in a deep breath or swing an ax during his wood-chopping detail because of very sore ribs! Cliff, upon seeing his young assistant stomped almost into the ground and seeing in his eyes a deadly look of revenge, grew alarmed. However, when he confronted Vince as to what had happened, he could see that Vince had changed. Changed because almost overnight as a result of what had happened to him Vince found himself hardening into manhood. The months of hard work at the field kitchen and at the foundry had turned him from a tough kid without parents to a rock hard man now on a mission. Little did Vince realize the visit that day by the sheriff with another young and homeless man about the same age as Vince deposited at the orphanage's doorstep would create a "sea change" in his life living in 'hell'...

That night at suppertime there was a new member at the orphanage. He was a tall Omaha Indian young man of stocky stature and a quiet presence about him that was hard to read. He sat by himself during supper and right off the bat, the three hoodlums running roughshod over the rest of the younger boys made sure they 'introduced' themselves to the Omaha Indian who told the boys his name when asked, which was "Wind Horse". Upon hearing that name, the three toughs laughed over the young man's name and made sure by their intemperate gestures that they were in charge and that he best toe the line. As they did, Vince saw that Wind Horse's face and temperament did not change. He just turned away from the bullies and continued quietly eating his supper. The looks on the faces of the three toughs when observing Wind Horse's quiet action of defiance, showed a building vicious anger developing over being ignored and Vince could see that Wind Horse was in for a rough night…

But Vince had changed after his night of being beaten senseless and then raped. He no longer was a young boy but as of that morning, a 'man of his own making'! Moments later, Vince walked over with his plate of food and quietly sat down alongside Wind Horse. "Howdy, my name is Vince. I overheard you say your name was Wind Horse. Welcome to "Hell", Wind Horse."

Wind Horse just looked over at Vince with an impassive-looking face and then said, "I am pleased to make your acquaintance. Yes, my name is Wind Horse and I am an Omaha Indian. My parents drowned on the Mississippi and I was the only one who survived from our overturned canoe. Since I had nowhere to go, I have been living on the streets of St. Louis for the last month eating what other people threw in the garbage. Then the sheriff caught me and since I was homeless, he brought me here."

When Wind Horse spoke in perfectly good clipped English, Vince looked amazed. That was when Wind Horse read the amazement in Vince's eyes and laughed an easy laugh saying, "Vince, the "Black Robes" (Catholic Priests) came to my people many moons ago. They taught us their language and told us the story of the man the rest of the white men hung on a cross of wood until he died. My father was a great man and a chief and insisted that we learn the white man's tongue, because he figured that the whites would soon cover the land like the grasshoppers do on the prairie come late summer. He was right and it was good he did, otherwise, you and I could not speak together." With that, Wind Horse stuck out his hand and he and Vince shook hands. However, as Vince did and aware of what the three older boys more than likely had planned for Wind Horse that evening, excused himself after he had eaten by letting his newfound friend know he was the orphanage's cook and still had some work to do. Then back to serving the last of supper went Vince but with an unusual determination of will and spirit…

Later that night as Vince picked his way through the boys and their sleeping mattresses, he did so with a determination he never knew he had. Lying down on his mattress, he was aware that the three bullies were all huddled near the door quietly talking among each other. Moments later, Vince saw three dark shadows silently moving ominously his way!

"All right, Vince, we hope you have learned your lesson. Now take your clothes off and lay on your belly or else," said an older boy named Harry.

Vince rose from his mattress and began undoing his pants but as he did, his hand dropped down to his pocket and in so doing in the darkness, withdrew an unseen 4"-long carriage bolt he had made late in the afternoon at the forge. Then without warning, he swung it at where he figured Curtis's head was with all of his might and a satisfying solid bone-crunching "THUNK" told him he had figured and aimed correctly! Curtis dropped to the floor only making a slight groan as the heavy carriage bolt struck him just below his right eye! Then all hell broke loose as the other two bullies jumped on Vince cussing and swearing in anger as they flattened him out onto the floor! Soon the darkness was filled with swinging fists, flying knees and a carriage bolt, as all FOUR of the men now fought it out on the floor!

By now, the bedroom was in an uproar as the other younger boys cleared out from the tremendous battle now ongoing in the middle of their sleeping quarters! There was such a commotion that it woke Cal, who moments later came running for the stairways leading from the first floor to the boys' sleeping quarters upstairs! When he did, he turned and just started up the stairway when he was 'flummoxed' by three flying bodies being hurled down the stairs and on top of him just as he started up!

"They are not welcome up here ever again!" yelled Vince. "And if they ever come up here again or hurt any of these younger boys ever again, they will not live to see another sunrise," continued Vince, as he placed a bloody 4"-long heavy carriage bolt back into his pocket for future use if it became necessary. Then he turned and thanked Wind Horse for the surprising help rendered in violently ridding the three older boys from the upstairs general sleeping area.

Wind Horse just smiled in the darkness of the upstairs sleeping quarters saying, "Vince, the Black Robes always taught us we should turn the other cheek to that of our enemies. I don't think they ever thought of enemies like those three and what they did to other less fortunate boys. I think they will forgive me for not following their Christian words… Now I need to move my mattress next to yours in case those three 'did not get the word' and come back for more of the same."

As a result of the previous night's battle, Cliff now discovered he had two assistants in the blacksmithing and cooking 'business'… Shortly thereafter, the three older boys reached the age of 16 and were dismissed from the orphanage because reaching such an age allowed for them to be out on their own. The day they were able to lawfully leave the orphanage, Curtis, Darrell and Harry walked over to the blacksmith shop and entered with 'blood in their eyes'! That was when Curtis advised both Vince and Wind Horse that if they ever met again, they had better come armed because the three of them were going to kill them outright!

Cliff, upon hearing those words, picked up

a piece of iron, walked over to the three still-fuming young men and advised unless they left immediately, he was going to lay the iron to their hides in such a manner that they wouldn't be able to kill even a piss-ant when he got through with them! That put the run on the three bullies when confronted by the burly and strong as an angry mule's kick, blacksmith. Once that threat was gone, Cliff turned to Vince who was still fingering his 4"-long carriage bolt in his pants pocket and Wind Horse saying, "Best you boys pay heed to what Curtis just said. I think he is a killer in his own right and if the two of you ever meet up with that bunch again, best you keep your powder dry. Now, we got another order in for more of my recently invented St. Louis-style beaver traps and best we get to it."

However, unbeknownst to everyone, Curtis, Darrell and Harry had already struck! Just before they had left the orphanage, the three had mixed rat poison into the dry oats used to make every-one's daily breakfast of oatmeal! Not enough of the poison to kill anyone but just enough to make everyone deathly sick! The next morning right after breakfast, everyone at the orphanage including Cal and Cliff almost immediately after eating the contaminated oatmeal, began throwing up, suffering violent stomach cramps, blackouts, leg cramps and bloody, uncontrollable black bowel movements! By the time Cal figured out what had happened and notified the sheriff, the three culprits had already departed on a keelboat heading up the Missouri River as trappers for a fur company heading into the Upper Missouri wilderness beaver trapping grounds.

However for the next week, not much got done around the orphanage and its blacksmith shop as everyone finally metabolized the rat poison put into their oatmeal out from their digestive systems. That was except for Vince! He apparently had gotten a heavier dose of the poison and it took the better part of a month before he was weakly up on his feet and back at work in the blacksmith shop and kitchen! But the almost fatal dose of poison that he received changed him for the longest time! Intestinally, the poison had really negatively impacted and messed his digestive system up big-time! After that near fatal poisoning, Vince discovered that there were many kinds of foods his system could not tolerate, especially foods that were wheat- or oat-based. He soon discovered that if he ate anything that was wheat- or oat-based, he developed tremendous intestinal methane gasses that when released did so with tremendous force, odor and **EFFECT!** So much so that one time while working on an open flame forge tempering iron for the springs of a beaver trap, he had a fit of gas attack problems. Without thinking about the huge gas attack and in the moment of getting his immediate work finished, Vince passed a large amount of methane gas near that open fire forge. When he did, there was a tremendous explosion and blast of flame from his hind end that blew out the rear end of his pants and singed all the hair off his hind end and upper legs! Not to mention, stunk up that end of the blacksmith shop something fierce!

When that incident occurred, Cliff Fulton and Wind Horse happened to be working nearby and observed the entire event. When that explosion occurred, that caused Cliff and Wind Horse to fall to the ground and roll around on the floor of the blacksmith shop in extreme mirth as they watched Vince running around and around with a singed smoking butt. A smoking bottom that was only extinguished after Vince was able to extinguish the flaming rear end of his pants by sitting his bottom into a drum of water used to cool freshly forged horseshoes. When those series of events occurred, history was made! Still holding his side from laughing so hard over Vince's unfortunate experience, Cliff said, "Vince, henceforth you shall be known as "Buck Snort" because when you farted, that sounded just like the sound a white-tailed buck makes when surprised..."

Once word of that comical event at the blacksmith shop had gotten out and told to the rest of the kids at the orphanage, Vince was known henceforth in great embarrassment to everyone thereafter as Buck Snort! That was until, in order to get back at his fellow kids at the orphanage for teasing him, Vince 'turned the air blue' with one of his classic gas attacks, sending everyone within 'gun range' running for the cleaner air found out on the open range…

CHAPTER TWO

"ASHLEY'S HUNDRED" AND A SURPRISE

One morning after Buck Snort and Wind Horse had arrived for work at the blacksmith shop located just next door to the main orphanage on the farm, they saw Cliff already hard at work firing up the forges so they would be ready for the day's work in beaver trap making. When Cliff saw his two young assistants arriving, he vigorously waved them over to where he was working. When they arrived at his side, Cliff looked at Buck Snort and said, "I know you are getting on in age and one of these days you will be out of this 'hellhole'. With that, have you thought about what you would like to do or where you would be going when that time arrives?"

Surprised at being asked such a question because he had not thought much about what he would do and still had some time in which to make up his mind, Buck Snort shook his head in the negative. With that and not saying a word, Cliff reached over onto a nearby shelf, removed a newspaper and handed it to Buck Snort. When he did and with Wind Horse looking over his shoulder, Cliff pointed to an article on the front page of the Missouri *Republican* newspaper for Buck Snort to read.

There in bold print were the words, "To enterprising young men. The subscriber wishes to engage 100 men to ascend the river Missouri to its sources, there to be employed, one, two or three years to work as trappers. Interested parties are to report to Major Andrew Henry near the lead mines in Washington County." For a moment Buck Snort could hardly believe what he was seeing. He loved the adventure of trapping for furbearers and now here before his eyes was an opportunity for him to be gainfully employed doing what he loved out in the dangerous and largely unexplored West! Especially since he no longer had a home to return to or any other relatives he could go and live with...

Then without saying a word, Buck Snort quietly handed the newspaper to his new friend Wind Horse to read with a grin of adventure spelled clear across his face. Being educated by the Black Robes to read and write in English, Wind Horse had no trouble reading what was in the newspaper. When Wind Horse had finished reading the article in the paper, he handed the paper back to

Buck Snort saying, "I will be 16 in one moon. I trapped with my father when he was alive and we sold the furs to the white traders who came into our village and purchased them. I no longer have any family and nowhere to return since they all drowned when our canoe overturned. If you are interested in becoming a trapper, I would go with my new friend and 'brother' and do so as well."

Cliff Fulton, now seeing the eager looks on both young men's faces over the chance for adventure and making it a livelihood as well, and pleased with the great relationship he now had with the two young men said, "I don't know how long this offer will be open to interested young men. But if you two would be interested in inquiring, I will cover for you while you do. The two of you can use my horses and leave tomorrow right after breakfast and I will cover for you with the cooking, woodcutting and all. However, the two of you had best be home by suppertime otherwise Call will see that you are missing and both of you know if that happens, he can be as mean as a snake in the hot sun covered with red ants."

In order to get an even earlier start, both Buck Snort and Wind Horse made arrangements with Cliff and then arose way before dawn and quietly rode off as they headed for the lead mines in nearby Washington County in order to meet with Major Henry and see if they could qualify and be selected as trappers. Later that morning, the two young men rode into a campsite near the lead mines that had been set up to interview interested parties who had read the newspaper article in the Missouri Republican, ascertain if they would be qualified and explain the terms and conditions of acceptance and employment if they chose to join up.

Having arrived shortly after daylight and before a long line of other hopefuls had arrived to be interviewed by Major Henry, the two young men were admitted into Henry's tent forthwith. Nervously standing like a couple of statues in front of such a well-known, respected and important military man, Buck Snort and Wind Horse said nary a word after the introductions had been made. Said nary a word especially when Major Henry just critically and quietly looked both young men up and down with an experienced and appraising eye. Then Major Henry, satisfied that the two men appeared to be good physical specimens and prospects said, "Just so the two you know what you would be facing if accepted as trappers for General Ashley's 100 men, let me expound. As trappers for this new company titled "Ashley-Henry Fur Trade Company", both of you can expect to come down with arthritis after trapping for a year or more in the icy cold beaver trapping waters. Where we would be going you will find that the grizzly bears fear no man nor do a number of the hostile Indian tribes residing in and along the Upper Missouri.

To become a successful "Mountain Man", you will need to possess an innate set of personal as well as learned wilderness skills and attributes. Additionally, you must show mastery of rifle and pistol skills, and be able to swim and climb rugged mountains on foot or on horseback. You must be ready and capable for armed combat with gun, knife and tomahawk at the drop of a hat! You must be able to skillfully hunt for your food, read signs and become excellent horsemen and familiar with furbearer trapping techniques. Lastly, you both must be able to survive for long periods of time under extreme conditions. That being said and by virtue that neither of you even blinked when I outlined the needs and conditions of becoming one of our company's trappers, do either of you have any questions over what has been said so far?"

"No Sir," quietly replied Buck Snort and Wind Horse in tandem.

"Good," replied Major Henry, "now here are our conditions of employment as a company trapper for the Ashley-Henry Fur Trade Company. As a condition of employment, you will sign up for a period of anywhere from one to three years depending on a grizzly bear eating either of you, you are killed by hostile Indians, you drowned or a speeding lead ball finds either of your slow moving carcasses when you aren't looking. The Ashley-Henry Fur Trade Company, as a provided condition of your employment, will provide each of you with a good horse, saddle, tack, a rifle, six beaver traps and a camp ax. You will be expected to provide any more horses you think you will need and any other camp equipment needed to survive in the wilderness by yourselves. Each trapper will be paid in 'halves'. That means of any furbearers you trap, process and bring to our soon to be built fort, half will automatically go to the company and you get to keep and sell the remaining half for yourselves. But you will be required to sell your portion of furs to the company and purchase your needed annual supplies from the company. Now do either of you have any questions with what I have discussed so far?" asked Major Henry as he critically peered at both men for their reactions, like a robin would do when looking at a nearby worm.

By now, both Buck Snort and Wind Horse's heads were spinning over all of the information covered. Plus they could now hear a crowd of other hopefuls gathering up outside the Major's tent anxiously awaiting their turn to pass inspection and seek employment as well.

"Wait, I have one question," said Buck Snort. "When will all of us be leaving for these beaver trapping grounds?"

"Barring any problems, General Ashley and I would like to be on our way by no later than the tenth of May. That is because we have several thousand miles of travel through Indian country to caravan, build our fort and trading post in

Indian country, and get you company trappers
on your way so you can establish your winter
camps prior to the beginning of the fall beaver
trapping season which should start sometime
around the end of September. I say the end of
September because that is the approximate time
when the beaver should be starting to come into
their 'prime' as furbearers and are the most valuable to the fur industry to which they will be
supplied."

"Then I take it you have accepted the two of
us for part of the number of your requested 100
men?" asked Buck Snort with his heart up in his
throat and hardly daring to breathe awaiting the
Major's response.

"That I have," said Major Henry, as he thrust
several papers across his portable desk for
the two men to affix their signatures or make
their mark as the newest company men for the
Ashley-Henry Fur Trade Company. Moments
later with their signatures affixed to their company contracts (when it came to reading and
writing, Buck Snort had been home schooled by
his mother and Wind Horse had been taught by
the Black Robes), both men shook Major Henry's
hand and then beat a hasty retreat out from his
tent before he could change his mind and decide
they were too young to be company trappers.
Well, that and Buck Snort had a load of gas built
up in his system and didn't want to pass any
of his noxious and evil smelling gas which had

become an issue ever since being poisoned back at the orphanage, especially in the confines of the Major's tent with more than disastrous results! However, just as soon as the two young men and now General Ashley's company trappers passed the long line of other hopefuls looking to sign on, Buck Snort let a silent but deadly load of gas fly as the two of them hurriedly exited the area to avoid being blamed by the long line of hopefuls for ruining Missouri's morning air!

"JESUS!" said one grizzled old-looking trapper named Jim Bridger, "who the hell just shit their pants and then rolled in it?" he bellowed as he critically looked around at all the other hopeful trappers standing in line, looking for the guilty party! That 'look' from the grizzled old trapper 'froze' everyone waiting in line in their tracks so as not to be blamed for such an offense in public...

Upon hearing those gagging words being uttered, a number of hopeful trappers to be quickly stepped away from the area of the gaseous cloud Buck Snort had left behind. With that huge fart, Wind Horse just grinned over his choice of partner, hoping he never let one like that slip inside their cabin once they were living together out in the wilderness... Then Wind Horse and Buck Snort lost it over the 'surprise' just left behind and started chuckling among themselves when they heard Major Henry loudly exclaim, "Which one of you uncouth son-of-a-bitches outside my tent just died? I certainly hope there isn't a grizzly bear living nearby. If that is the case and he winds that smell, he will come a-running looking for what just died and rotted so he has something to eat!"

Buck Snort and Wind Horse hurried back to the orphanage remembering Cliff Fulton's words about being back before suppertime to avoid Cal's wrath. Slipping back in behind the blacksmith shop, the two young men hurriedly unsaddled Cliff's horses and turned them loose so they could pasture and water. Then sneaking into the blacksmith shop through a seldom used back door, the two 'new trappers to be' were greeted with a knowing and conspiratorial grin from Cliff as he put the finishing touches to another of his specially made and in high demand, St. Louis-style beaver traps. Soon Buck Snort and Wind Horse had their heavy leather aprons strapped on and the blacksmith shop literally rang with the sounds of 'hammers to hot metal' as the men went about their business of forging and creating beaver traps like nothing out of the ordinary had just occurred.

Supper that evening came off like clockwork since Cliff had covered for the two young men while they were absent beginning their journey into an adventure of a lifetime. That night as the two young men lay side by side on their sleeping mattresses in the corner of the sleeping loft, the air was alive with additional plans they hoped to achieve before heading off into the largely unknown Frontier. That evening sleep finally sneaked up on the two adventurers to be and morning came too suddenly for two young men who had stayed up too late the evening before, excitedly talking up a storm.

The next two weeks slowly never seemed to arrive but when they did, all of a sudden there were still things to do that needed to be done. First when Buck Snort turned 16, he advised Cal he would no longer be required to stay confined to his 'hellhole' orphanage. However, he advised Cal that he would stay for another ten days and work for his 'board and room' until Wind Horse had reached his 16th birthday and then the two would leave together. Cal was not happy that Buck Snort had remembered when his birthday was because he was doing such a great job as one of the orphanage's cooks and as a blacksmith helping Cliff in the making of such in high demand beaver traps. But there was nothing he could do so he just 'grumped off' and beat two younger kids for slacking off in their duties. Then Buck Snort approached Cliff and asked if he could cover for him in his absence once again. When Cliff asked why, Buck Snort replied, "I need to visit my friend Chuck Curry and see if he would sell two of my horses back to me. I have four horses that he is holding for me but Wind Horse and I figure we will need at least two more horses in order to pack all of our needed gear and provisions once we are out and on our own, in addition to the two horses the Ashley-Henry Fur Trade Company will provide us."

For the longest moment in time Cliff just looked at Buck Snort as if trying to make up his mind as to how to address Buck Snort's question. Then Cliff said, "Well, 'hell's bells' Buck Snort, I will sell you two of my horses! I have three and don't really need the other two, so as a gift to you and Wind Horse for being my friends and such great workers, I will sell both of them to you for a total of just $20 if you would be interested!"

For the longest time Buck Snort just stood there in shock over such a great offer! As he did, Wind Horse finally tugged on Buck Snort's shirt sleeve saying, "Buck Snort, that is a great deal. If Cliff is willing to sell us those horses for just $20, take him up on his offer because any good horse will sell for more than that on any given day."

"You have a deal, Cliff. We two really appreciate what you are doing for us and I for one will never forget what you are doing. Yes, I will take those two horses off your hands for $20. But you will have to wait until I go to my 'hole in the ground bank' and get my money so I can pay you," said Buck Snort.

"Oh, I can wait. I ain't a-going nowhere. I am too "broked-up" and getting too old to be of much use to anyone else, so I will be here when you come back with my money," said Cliff with a good-natured grin spread clear across his face because he was able to help two young and deserving men.

The next day when Cal was out in the field fixing some broken down equipment, Buck Snort using one of Cliff's horses rode over to his creekside bank and retrieved his stoneware crock full of money he had saved for years for just such an opportunity of the kind that General Ashley had offered. Then it was back to the blacksmith shop where he removed $20 and paid Cliff for his horses. Then afterwards he hid his crock in the blacksmith shop in a place Cliff suggested. It was then that both he and Wind Horse got another surprise they were not expecting coming from their friend Cliff Fulton!

"You two boys come on over here. I have a going away gift for the two of you for being such good workers and my only two friends around this here orphanage," said Cliff. With that and a hand gesture meant for them to follow him, the two boys looked at each other in surprise and then followed their friend into his bare and rather Spartan sleeping quarters in the back of the blacksmith shop. Once they arrived in Cliff's sleeping quarters and office, Cliff moved over to a pile of something covered with an old blanket meant to hide the contents contained underneath. Throwing back the old dirty blanket, there lay 30 brand new St. Louis-style beaver traps made personally by the old blacksmith! "There you go, Boys. Them is another going away gift once

I found out the two of you might be going off into the wilderness to trap them beaver," said a broadly grinning Cliff, pleased over a gift he had labored over long and hard just for his two friends!

Upon seeing such a great and now timely gift, both Buck Snort and Wind Horse just stood there with their mouths wide open in surprise and disbelief hardly believing what they were seeing! Here was a gift of great expense at any emporium selling such items, and now here were 30 of the very valuable beaver traps being given to them as a parting gift when they left the 'hellhole' loosely called an orphanage. Simultaneously both Buck Snort and Wind Horse reached out and together hugged the old and kindly blacksmith, who was by then more of a father figure and mentor than their boss in the blacksmith shop!

Then Cliff tiredly sat his old frame down in a broken down chair and beckoned for the two boys to sit on the floor by his feet. Then taking time to fill his pipe with tobacco and put a match to it, he paused after taking a deep drag on the stem of his pipe and then slowly let the smoke almost magically swirl and curl out around him. As he did, Buck Snort and Wind Horse could plainly see that Cliff had something important to say to the both of them and neither young man dared to hardly breathe because it was now apparent the old man was drifting back in time into the world of his memories. As Cliff let himself be propelled into a favored time now long past, Buck Snort remembered what his mother had read to him years earlier. In that book, Buck Snort remembered a passage that said, "Memory is the scribe to one's soul" and closely watching Cliff at that moment in time, it was apparent that he was now recalling memories from deep within his soul… At that same moment in time, Wind Horse's 20,000 years of Native American heritage and genetics kicked in, "telling" him the old blacksmith that he was now closely watching was in what his People called "The Spirit World". Respecting that sacred moment in time his friend was experiencing and reliving, Wind Horse waited for him to 'come back'…

Finally, Cliff returned from 'his visit to his spirit world' saying, "Boys, I have a story to share with you. Few people know of what I am about to share with the two of you. Years ago, 1810 to be exact, I was a blacksmith and trapper working for a man from back east named John Jacob Astor. I don't expect for you two to remember him because that was twelve years ago and you were just little at the time. But he came here to St. Louis with a number of us on a fur trapping expedition heading out west. He was a very far-seeing and wealthy fur merchant and had come west to explore and see what the Frontier had to offer in fur riches being trapped by the Indians and sold to fur merchants in this area and the British in Canada of the Hudson's

Bay Fur Company and the Northwest Fur Company. During that expedition, we trapped our ways west as members of Astor's American Fur Company and met with a number of tribes in order to ascertain what the fur market would be were he to establish his own fur trading business. During those days I learned all about the trapping and pelt processing of the various fur-bearers, mainly beaver, that we ran across. As such, I learned all about what was required to be a fur trapper living out on the Frontier with little chance for resupply of provisions. I learned about the various tribes, both those that were friendly to the white man and those who were not. This I did until I injured my back in a bad horse wreck. After Astor and his American Fur Company men returned and I was unable to ride horses for any length of time, I retired from the fur trade and went into blacksmithing for a living. That landed me here on this orphanage because Cal had need for a full-time blacksmith to keep the farm and its equipment running. I have been here ever since. It ain't much of a life but it is a living, and I am thankful to the good Lord above for those blessings that I have a roof over my head and a place to eat."

Then since Cliff's pipe had gone out, he paused to re-light it and when he did, he realized Buck Snort and Wind Horse had hardly moved since he had revealed a surprising part of his fur trapping life and experiences to his two young friends. Cliff just grinned over how that revelation was being received and then grinned even more over the next revelation that he was planning on presenting to the two boys. "Boys, since neither of you have ever been faced with what is needed by one trapping for long periods of time out in the wilderness I have a proposal for the two of you. If you would like, since I have been there and experienced the needs and wants of one who found himself trapping out on the hostile Frontier, I could accompany the two of you when you go to select what provisions you will need and help you purchase what is more than likely required for such an adventure by the two of you."

Then Cliff sat back in his chair and puffed on his pipe waiting for a response from either of the two now wide-eyed young men with funny expressions spelled across their faces over hearing such a wonderful offer being offered to the two of them. Finally Buck Snort broke the spell that had enveloped both him and Wind Horse over hearing Cliff's surprising story and now, even more magnanimous offer!

"Cliff, we don't know quite what to say. We just figured you were just a blacksmith who had invented one of the best beaver traps around and was working for a mean son-of-a-bitch in Cal. Yes, we would love to have you help us in deciding what kind and how many provisions we would need for this trip we are about to undertake with General Ashley and Major Henry!"

Then it dawned on Buck Snort, who was just getting over the surprise of finding out about their friend the blacksmith and the magnanimous offer he had just made, when he realized he had a partner in this coming adventure. Then quickly looking over at Wind Horse and seeing the look of surprise still registering on his face over what he had just heard and then realizing he could speak for both men, said once again, "Yes! Yes, me and Wind Horse would love it if you would help us in deciding what we would need for living a year out on the Frontier!" continued a now very excited Buck Snort. Then all of a sudden Buck Snort realized they were still at the orphanage and how could they work out such a length of time away from the facility when they went looking for the needed provisions in nearby St. Louis saying, "But how could we do that? There is no way Cal will let all of us go for a full day. After all, he needs us here to keep making traps for sale by the local emporiums and cooking meals for everyone else living back here at the orphanage."

"I will take care of that. If he does not let us go for a day of shopping for the provisions you fellas need, then I will tell him that I will quit and just move on," said Cliff, in such a tone and tenor of voice that both Buck Snort and Wind Horse realized they would have no problem in doing what needed to be done in the way of provision acquisitions before they headed up into the

Upper Missouri with Major Henry and General Ashley.

The very next day, Cliff approached Cal and advised him as to what he wanted to do for Buck Snort and Wind Horse in helping them in their acquisition of provisions for their trip out onto the Frontier as trappers. Cal was not happy but clearly understood from the tone and tenor in Cliff's voice 'that it was a done deal' or else! Cal, in order to get what Cliff wanted to do over with just as fast as possible, volunteered the use of his wagon so the two boys could bring back the supplies they purchased all in one trip!

The next morning, with Cliff driving Cal's wagon and with Buck Snort and Wind Horse on the seat beside him, drove into St. Louis and stopped in front of "Manuel Lisa's Emporium". With a wave of a blacksmith's typically muscular arm, Cliff said, "Alright, Boys, this here emporium is one of the best in the country for the supplies the two of you will be a-needing. It was established by a Spanish fellow named "Manuel Lisa", who at one time was a pioneer fur trader and merchant on the Frontier, kind of like my old friend John Astor, who I originally went west with in 1810. Manuel is now dead, having died a few years back. However, thank Heavens, his company is still in business and one of the biggest and best suppliers in the area for those venturing into the largely unexplored American West and is currently operated by an old friend of mine named Joshua Pilcher. So I suspect that if we need anything special, my old friend will see to it that we shall have it and in short order at a reduced cost."

Moving on with his team and wagon, Cliff headed them around behind the emporium's warehouse to the area of the building's loading docks. There he tied their team of horses off at the back of the warehouse. Then Cliff, Wind Horse and Buck Snort, still firmly clutching his precious stoneware crock with his life's savings, entered the wonderland of a warehouse stocked with everything imaginable and needed by those living on the edge of the known at that time Frontier. Upon entering the warehouse, Buck Snort saw Cliff's manner of walking picking up and he could see in the old man's eyes a look and walk into a land of adventure like he had never seen before in his friend's eyes…

"I need a couple of you Company Clerks!" bellowed out Cliff at a couple of men just standing around 'jawboning'. Instantly the two company men just visiting seconds earlier broke out into a trot and headed Cliff's way, recognizing they had a customer 'ready and raring to go'.

"Alright, You Two Boys, listen up! We have a heap of buying to do and not a lot of time to do it before Cal gets pissed at the three of us, so we best get 'cracking'!" As Cliff spoke, both Wind Horse and Buck Snort looked over at each other realizing that this was the very first time they had seen Cliff so animated and excited over what he was about to do! Realizing they had a 'winner' in 'lead', both boys perked right up and were all "assholes, eyeballs and false teeth" when it came to being at attention, ready, willing and able...

"Alright, listen up! I am a-going to head out across this here warehouse like a golden eagle flying over a prairie dog town and not wasting a single moment. I am going to be all eyes and a-selectin' everything I feel I would need if I were in you two boys' boots. So pay close attention as I make selections on what you will need and pay heed to what I am a-saying as I do so. Because to save time, I am a-going to select what you need and tell you why I am doing what I am a-doing as we go along. If you have any questions as to what I am a-doing, bellow it out. Otherwise keep your mouths shut and your ears and eyes open as we go along," said a very much animated and obviously excited to be back in an aspect of the fur business Cliff Fulton... Then pausing in what he was saying, Cliff said, "I am doing it this-a-way because there will soon be a time when I won't be around to assist the two of you. Then it will be up to the two of you to make wise provision selections and if you don't and the right amount needed, it may be the death of you because of starvation, not being properly clothed and freezing to death or lack of ability to defend yourselves. That happens and only the turkey vultures will then pay heed if you make wrong decisions, stumble and fall within the range of their beaks!"

Then turning and facing the two Company Clerks, Cliff said, "But first of all, you two Clerks try and stay up with me. We are short on time so when a selection is made just stack it off to one side and we can figure out what it costs later. I am good friends with Pilcher, so my word and credit is good. Alright, let's go. Take me to the rifle and pistol sections of this here warehouse first," said Cliff.

Moments later, the five men were at a section of the emporium that smelled of gun oil and cleaning solvents along with standing in front of a long glistening wall of nothing but the latest rifles and shotguns America had to offer. Fast walking down the glistening line of various makes and models of rifles, Cliff finally stopped by one kind of flintlock rifles and began removing them from their stands and handing them back to the two highly amused Company Clerks over the older man's active way of going about business. However, when he handed FOUR of said selected rifles back to the Clerks at $16.50 each, Buck Snort with his crock of coins amounting to just a little over $300, gulped deeply! "Cliff!" exclaimed Buck Snort in panic. "I am not sure I have that much money to pay for all of those many rifles and why do we have to have four rifles when there are only two of us doing any shooting anyway?"

"Good question, Buck Snort," said Cliff, "now you are thinking like a fur trapper in Indian country should be thinking. First of all, don't worry about the costs of what will be selected here today. I say that because what you and Wind Horse take out from here today is all that you will have to survive with in the face of blizzards, flying arrows, speeding lead balls, grizzly bear attacks, falling into deep icy cold waters or facing off with other mean-assed and crooked trappers wanting to take what is yours. So your choices had best be good and the right kind and amount or you will find yourselves "going under", if you get the gist of my meaning! Where the two of you are a-going, you will need firepower and lots of it! Be aware, the grizzly bear fears no man, Blackfeet will kill you in an instant, a mountain lion will rip your guts out with his claws from his hind feet, a mean-assed trapper stealing what is yours will do so in order for him to survive and you not, and when Indians attack, they will come at you in superior numbers or not at all! So best be ready with the "best" and the "most" or you will leave your bones a-bleaching out on the prairie..." With that, Buck Snort had just received a world of Frontier knowledge and wisdom at that moment in time as did Wind Horse, regarding the fur trapping adventure they had just signed up for along the Upper Missouri that could also be a lesson in life and death as well. Both young men at that same moment in time decided among themselves they would now truly listen and learn from a man who had been "there" and had not left his bones bleaching out in the sun simply because he had not been prepared...

"These four rifles I just removed are the U.S. Military, Model 1803, flintlock rifle with a 34" barrel. They are caliber .52, which is more than capable for dropping a charging buffalo in rut, a mean-assed grizzly bear if the shot is placed correctly, a bull elk or moose or blowing a hard-charging Indian out from his saddle who is more than hellbent on removing your scalp. Observe that they are half-stocked with a heavier "wrist" made from black walnut, which is a stronger wood that will hold up to the rougher use normally found and many times required out on the Frontier. Also notice they have a steel shoulder-fitting butt plate and a single set trigger. It also has an iron rib from tail pipe to the end of the muzzle to hold and protect the ramrod and has an overall sporting balance. Lastly, with the shorter barrel, one can ride 'hellbent for leather' through the dense timber when the Indians are after him without hanging up a longer barreled rifle, which is the problem with the longer barreled Pennsylvania rifles. Well, that and a Pennsylvania rifle is one hell of a lot harder to reload while riding for your life on a hopefully fast horse," said Cliff. "Oh, before I forget, with a good eye and a steady hand one can easily drop a buffalo or an Indian out to 150 yards with these rifles just selected. And as for your second or reserve rifle, I always carried mine in a scabbard on my riding horse or the first horse in my pack string for fast retrieval when the odds were stacked against me and I had already fired my personally carried rifle and still had more killing to do if I wanted to keep my hair!"

It was then that Buck Snort realized the two Company Clerks were both quiet 'as a pair of mice pissin' on a ball of cotton'. It was readily apparent they were also listening to an old "Man of the Mountains" who had personally experienced what the Frontier had to throw at him and having learned such very clearly and cleverly, knew what the hell he was talking about!

Then stepping over to a number of wooden bins adjacent the long line of rifles lined up along a long wall of the emporium, Cliff called the two Clerks over and handed them a number of large and smaller powder horns to hold two different grades of powder, several bullet molds, ramrods for the rifles, wipers or gun worms, ball screws, extra parts to repair the locks and triggers as needed, sacks full of rifle and pistol flints, bags of greased wadding and two sets of tools for repairing said firearms. Then reaching over into another bin, Cliff pulled out two cast iron smelting kettles with ladles for melting lead for the making of balls for their rifles and pistols soon to come. By now, both Clerks were beginning to sweat and before the day was over, they would quickly discover that the old man and Man of the Mountains doing the selecting was going to almost run their legs off, especially if they missed a step!

Then without hesitation, Cliff walked over to another section of the warehouse holding firearms and selected FOUR horse pistols that were the same caliber .52 as were the previously selected rifles. When he did, he turned saying, "You two boys note that these four pistols just selected are also caliber .52, the same as are your rifles. That is so your balls are interchangeable in either weapon making them more versatile. And once again, I chose four. If you ever need to use your pistols, it is because you are being overrun by whatever is attacking you! At that moment in time, you best have a heavy caliber weapon capable of doing the job with one shot and two, because in damp weather if one misfires, you still have a second weapon in which to hopefully keep you or your partner from being killed or badly injured during the threat!"

Turning and facing the two now heavily sweating Company Clerks, Cliff said, "Take us to the section of the emporium holding all of the types of powders, pigs of lead (lead bars) and the like." Moments later, the five men stood in front of a number of pallets and bins, all stacked and stocked full of a number of items. Walking over to a small mountain of lead pigs, Cliff had

the Clerks set aside 100 pounds of the soft bullet making metal. Then he selected out several
canvas sacks of lead balls of caliber .52 and had
those set aside as well. When he did, Buck Snort,
just politely returning from another section of the
warehouse where he had left one of his signature
'gaseous blue clouds' and upon seeing the stack
of lead pigs and the purchasing of two additional
sacks of pre-cast lead balls as well, and remembering his shrinking collection of coins held in
his crock said, "Why the sacks of lead balls when
we have a pile of lead pigs already set aside for
us to make bullets from?" asked Buck Snort, with
Wind Horse nodding his head acknowledging
the validity of Buck Snort's question as well.

"I doubt you two boys are going to have any
time between now and when you leave to cast a
number of lead balls for your rifles and pistols.
Hence I had the Clerks set aside 400 of the pre-
cast lead balls so you will have something to
defend yourselves with on the several thousand-
mile trip the two of you are looking at undertaking and all of that through Indian country!" said
Cliff quietly…

Once again, Buck Snort and now Wind Horse
felt their faces burning in embarrassment over
the just asked dumb question in front of not only
Cliff but the two snickering Company Clerks as
well. It was painfully obvious to the two soon to
be trappers that they had a lot to learn, especially
in the common sense survival Frontier ways of
thinking department!

Then without saying another word, Cliff moved over to the section of the warehouse holding all of the different kinds and grades of black powders. There he quickly selected 20 one-pound tins of DuPont "FFg" powder for their large bore rifles and pistols (DuPont was considered by the Army and men of the Frontier as the premium black powder maker of the day in the United States). When Cliff made those tins of powder selections, the greatly concerned Buck Snort over his rapidly diminishing supply of coins in his crock to pay for such items said, "Cliff, why so many tins of powder? Why not just purchase a wooden keg of FFg powder instead of all those expensive tins of powder? That would be far cheaper looking at their listed prices."

"Buck Snort and you too, Wind Horse, listen up. Sure, a wooden keg of powder would be cheaper. But let's say for some reason, your keg of powder somehow got wet or split open during a horse wreck with the horse rolling over the wooden keg? As both of you know, wet black powder is useless and then what are you going to do when it comes to supplying yourselves with fresh meat or defending against an Indian attack? What then are the two of you going to do with just wet and useless powder that will not fire, huh? Now, take a close look at these other tins of powder that I just selected. Each tin weighs eight pounds because in part, the container is made of soft lead. As such, each container holds four pounds of black powder, is 'corked' tight and the cork has been dipped in wax to prevent your tin of powder from getting wet or damp. So now you are assured of always having dry powder in which to help in procuring food and using for protection. Additionally as I said, each container is made from four pounds of soft lead. Once you have emptied out each container, it can be melted down and you can cast additional balls from the container. Lastly, it is harder and less safe to pack a large keg of powder on a packhorse than it is to just place your tins of powder in a pannier for transport to wherever you are going." Then without further explanation, Cliff walked back to the original powder display of one-pound tins of DuPont's Best FFg powder and selected another 20 one-pound tins almost as an afterthought. Realizing there might be another flood of questions of why so much powder, Cliff pointed out to the two men that the one-pound tins of FFg powder could be more easily carried in their 'possibles' bags while afoot or on horseback. Then pausing, Cliff turned and said, "Besides, either of you get into a battle for your lives with 20 or so Blackfeet, you will be damn glad you have plenty of powder. That way, you can give a good accounting of yourself by being able to fill the air with lead before they overrun you, scalp your mangy heads and leave what is left of your carcasses out on the prairie for the wolves and grizzly bears to dine upon…"

Once again, Buck Snort and Wind Horse discovered another bit of Frontier wisdom that could possibly preclude them from having to leave their bones bleaching out in the sun somewhere in the forest or out on the prairie...

Realizing another valuable point had been made, Cliff proceeded to select a smaller number of lead tins of DuPont "FFFFg" powder for the flintlock pistols and rifle priming mechanisms (striker pans). As he did, there were no further questions posed from either Buck Snort or Wind Horse who had learned an earlier lesson and now were distracted and quietly laughing. They were quietly laughing because in the section of the emporium where Buck Snort had earlier and politely slipped off into in order to pass a gutful of odiferous gas, several other shoppers had just walked. Soon gagging and snorting after they had discovered Buck Snort's 'calling card' was 'the word of the day' in that portion of the emporium, sending the two budding trappers into fits of laughter over a secret they both shared...

Finished with that section of the warehouse, Cliff turned to the Company Clerks saying, "Lead me to the knife section of this here emporium." Immediately the Clerks headed for the knife section of the warehouse and as they did, Cliff gave a lesson on the value of good knives to his two 'greenhorns' new to the fur trapping business as they walked along. "You two need to remember, the second most important article needed by anyone living out on the Frontier next to a good rifle and pistol is a damn good and always sharp knife! There is always a need for a good and sharp knife which without, you will be lost every day of your life while out in the wilderness."

About then the Clerks arrived at their more than ample cutlery, ax and tomahawk sections of their warehouse. Walking out into the center of the numerous display setups of knives, Cliff just stood there for a few moments looking long and hard all around as if he was looking for one type or brand of knife that he was familiar with. Then all of a sudden Cliff said, "THERE THEY ARE, BOYS! Look at that bunch of knives over there! Those are the ones I was looking for, namely, Thomas Wilson sheer steel knives made in Sheffield, England. Those are some of the best butcher and scalper knives ever made from the finest steel the English have to offer. Remember, Boys, a trapper always has need for a knife or knives that are style-wise country made, heavy enough for chopping yet small enough to be used as a 'scalper' or general purpose knife. These Thomas Wilson knives have some of the best blades going. Boys, we are going to pick up a number of these, namely some skinning knives, butcher knives, what I call general cooking knives and some smaller assorted ones as well. Knives are essential to a trapper and if the truth be known, hardly less valid to an Indian as well. Whoa, 'lookee-here'! I am going to take three of this type of knife as well! See here, Boys, we will take this type of knife back to our blacksmith shop and I will re-grind this type of knife for use when you are skinning out any beaver you catch. I will re-grind these knives so the bevel is only on one side of the knife. That way, when you are skinning out your beaver or any other kind of valuable furbearer, that type of knife will reduce the danger of any of you slashing a hole in the pelt by mistake which will cost you at least a dollar for every 'slash-hole' you put into your pelt. Oh, we also need to pick up three butcher steels, several fine-toothed files and four whetstones in order to help keep the edges on our knives as well," said Cliff, who was acting like a kid in a St. Louis candy store while he was looking in the knife section of the warehouse. Additionally, that same level of excitement and their intrinsic values were also being infused into the memory banks of the two 'greenhorns' learning 'the tips of the fur and survival trade', namely Buck Snort and Wind Horse. With that moment in time concluded, the Company Clerks were handed an assortment of cutlery to be placed into the 'buy' piles of the other selected provisions as well.

"Now let us take a good look at them axes," said Cliff walking over to the ax, saw and tomahawk sections of the warehouse. Pausing and looking over the assortments of iron implements, Cliff finally selected two long-handled, square-bladed felling axes, two square-nosed shovels, six metal files, a twelve-pound keg of long nail spikes, a 20'-long logging chain and couplers, four smaller one-pound axes to be used in driving the traps' anchor poles into the mud of a beaver pond, two three-pound axes for driving nails or spikes when building a cabin, two smaller limbing axes, a six-pound splitting mall, a 'pull knife', a 4'-long single buck saw and a 'rip' saw. As Cliff quickly made those selections 'like he had been there and done that', he also took the time to point out to Buck Snort and Wind Horse the individual uses for each tool when building a cabin or cutting and splitting firewood. Then Cliff took the time to make sure the two young men clearly understood that only firearms and good high class rum rivaled the value of a good ax to those living out on the Frontier!

Then walking over to the English-made style of tomahawks, he gestured for the two young men to come closer so he could discuss what he felt each man needed to know about such weapons. In those discussions, Cliff covered the values of weight, size, balance and quality in workmanship. Then Cliff quietly said, "You get down to having to use this, it had better work for you or the critters will eat well on what is left of your carcasses..." Soon each man had selected the type of tomahawk they wanted to carry as a weapon of last resort, as Cliff carefully checked out their handles making sure they were made from 'ironwood'. That way in any kind of battle when only down to tomahawks, that style of weapon would not fail due to having a handle break during the stresses of violent combat. Cliff was pleased when after the tomahawk selections had been made based on the weapons' ultimate utility, he could see the seriousness now more than registering in each of the faces of Buck Snort and Wind Horse regarding the new lives they had chosen to live in a sometimes violent and deadly world…

Right next to the section of the warehouse holding bladed tools and weapons were bins and bins filled with different sized traps for all sorts of furbearers. Walking by the bins full of St. Louis-style beaver traps, Cliff and the boys just grinned. The boys grinned because they did not have to purchase any such expensive beaver traps since Cliff had already made a gift of 30 such great and highly sought after beaver traps to them earlier. But then Cliff paused by the bins, turned and said, "Boys, it's true that you already have 30 of these traps back at the orphanage. But keep in mind that most trappers will only run six to eight traps a day. That is because first, there are a lot of beaver out in the Frontier's waterways just yearning to be caught by even the poorest of trappers. Second, a good beaver trapper can fill each of his six to eight traps daily. Then the real work begins because those beaver have to be skinned and then later in the day, every one of those beaver pelts needs to be de-fatted or they will eventually spoil. (Author's Note: Healthy beaver have a heavy coat of fat just below their skin and above the rest of their body's tissue. That layer of fat is what keeps the beaver warm, even when living and swimming just under the ice during the winter months.) Then those now de-fatted pelts need to be stretched out with small slits cut along the edge of their fur and tied to a hoop made from green willow to fit the size of the pelt so it can dry. And by drying each and every one of those pelts, that keeps the infestations of insects down, makes them lighter, prepares them for bundling when dry and later transport to a trading post for grading, sorting and sale. So as both of you can see, if you choose to run in your trap line all 30 of the traps I have given you, you will have one hell of a lot of work ahead of you every day in just caring for those number of beaver caught."

"However," said Cliff as he walked by another bin of toothed and wicked-looking traps, "we need about ten to twelve of these Newhouse #14 wolf traps. I say that because by the deep months of the winter, because of the thickness of the ice and the difficulty of beaver trapping underneath it, you will not be trapping beaver. You will have already pulled your traps before freeze-up so you don't lose any of your valuable beaver traps and you will have then moved on to the trapping of wolves. By the 'deep of winter', the wolves will be in their 'prime' and that is when you will run a wolf trapping line because wolf pelts will bring you a high dollar back at the trading post come summertime. So, Boys, grab up about twelve of them wolf traps and put them over by that other stack of the goods and provisions that have been selected so far.

After twelve traps had been selected and placed alongside the stack of other provisions previously selected, Cliff walked on to the next section of the warehouse that caught his eye. By now, Buck Snort's heart was clear up in his throat because he knew he did not have enough money in his crock to pay for what had already been selected, much less for any more items! But Cliff was on a mission and Buck Snort just felt himself being dragged along for better or worse… However, a reckoning was coming when they had finished, and the only way Buck Snort figured he could pay the bill for all of the selected items was to sell his horses being held by his friend Chuck Curry. But that created another problem in that he and Wind Horse would now need those four horses to carry all of the goods currently being selected by their friend Cliff… And without all of those packhorses carrying all of the just selected provisions, they weren't going anywhere.

Stopping in front of a huge cooking section just a few feet from the last bin of animal traps, Cliff paused and just let his eyes survey the array of cast iron cooking implements. Then turning, he said, "Are you guys eager eaters or 'piss-ants' when it comes to being chow hounds?"

Both Buck Snort and Wind Horse looked at each other for a second and then turning and facing Cliff, said simultaneously, "Chow hounds, if the food is better than that being served at our orphanage."

"Do either of you know how to cook while out on the trail and if so, how well?" asked Cliff.

"My folks taught me how to cook," said Buck Snort. "That was all part of the 'home schooling' I received from my mother," said Buck Snort, as tears welled up in his eyes as he remembered the many good times he had with his mother over the years and they were quickly wiped away so no one saw his anguish over his great personal loss.

"Good," said Cliff. Then he walked over and without a single word being said, selected two large Dutch ovens and laid them off to one side, then two 16" three-legged frying pans for cooking over the coals, two large bean pots that could be used for making stews, bean and rice dishes, two two-gallon coffee pots, cooking irons to place over a firepit upon which coffee pots and the like could hang from while boiling or cooking, meat roasting rods for spitting meat, two 16" cast iron heavy duty pots, eating utensils, plates, coffee cups, wash pans, cooking and stirring spoons and forks. Then breaking a sweat himself, Cliff told the Company Clerks to carefully stack those items over by the other piles of selected items because cast iron was easily cracked or broken and that went double for their lids. Then remembering his old times on the trail and the trouble they had in keeping the cast iron lids together and in working order, ordered three more just cast iron lids.

Following that, Cliff requested of the two Company Clerks and soon found the group standing in front of a HUGE clothing section of Lisa's warehouse! Then without a word and like a man now REALLY on a mission, Cliff soon had not only the Company Clerks on the move running items over to the previously selected pile but Buck Snort and Wind Horse as well! Diving right into the middle of the clothing and cloth section of the warehouse, Cliff first picked out six 2½-point blankets at $7 each, twelve horse blankets at $6 each, four heavy woolen capotes at $5 each for use during the coldest of weather by the men, blue cloth at $4 a yard for clothing repairs, two dozen pairs of heavy woolen socks at $1 a pair (made in Europe) and made sure they fit the two young men, two pairs of heavy gloves at $4 each pair, and two pairs of heavy woolen pants made in Europe for each man and tried on for fit for $20. Then Cliff surprised both young men by having them try on several pair of buckskin leggings for fit for each man as well. That surprise came after each man had obligingly tried on the buckskin leggings. "Those leggings are what each of you will wear when setting out your beaver traps in the water. Then at the end of the day when you are through running your trap line, you will change out from your wet leggings into your woolen pants for the extra added warmth they will add when riding back to your camp from the trap line." Lastly, Cliff had each man pick out four "linsey-woolsey" shirts and try them on to make sure they fit.

Buck Snort, knowing from his many days working on the farm before it burned down, gave questioning looks over at Cliff when the English-made shirts were selected. Buck Snort damn sure realized that English-made shirts were expensive and wore out fast under heavy use. That being the case, why select such a material when living out on the Frontier which sure as hell was rough on everything, including mankind?

Seeing the new questioning looks he was getting from Buck Snort, Cliff laughed easily and then said, "These shirts will be worn during the summer months when the wearing of buckskin shirts will be too hot to wear. Those same shirts will be worn underneath your buckskin shirts during the winter weather for the added warmth it will bring." With those words of explanation, Cliff could see the acceptance over what he had just said was being understood as gospel and with those explanations, the two men relaxed. Then Cliff went over to a long line of shelves holding all kinds of hats. There at his bidding, he had each young man select and try on for the right fit a wide brimmed felt hat to wear to help keep the sun out from one's eyes, in addition to a heavy fur hat with ear flaps for winter use when trapping wolves in the northern latitudes.

Then Cliff had the Company Clerks hustle all of them off to another section of the warehouse holding the foodstuffs. There Buck Snort, Wind Horse and Cliff began selecting the foodstuffs they collectively figured they would need for living a year out in the back country. A year of trapping out in the back country where if they made the wrong guess on what they needed for food, there would be no chance for resupply because of the remoteness of their style of living.

There they selected bags of flour for making biscuits, gravy and as a thickening agent for stews, sacks of pinto beans, sacks of rice, several gallon jugs of rendered bear oil for their Dutch ovens when making biscuits, three one-gallon jugs of honey for their biscuits, 40 pounds of brown sugar cones for Dutch oven cobblers, tins of dried yeast for making biscuits and cobbler dough, dried apple slices, raisins, hard candy (both men had a sweet tooth), 200 pounds of green coffee beans that needed to be roasted and crushed in a Dutch before boiling to make coffee, black pepper, salt, red pepper flakes (suggested by Cliff to be used when constipated over having such a heavy meat diet), cinnamon, dried prunes, white pepper, nutmeg for cobblers and on it went. And as those selections continued, Buck Snort, who had been raised to always pay his bills, had a heavy heart! Had a heavy heart because he knew what few coins he had left in his stoneware crock had been spent over and over several times already that morning, and soon he was going to have to admit he could not pay for all of those items recently selected in front of the hardworking Company Clerks…

Then as if it would never stop, Cliff led the men over to several other sections of the warehouse for assorted items he figured they had missed earlier and would need at some time or another throughout the year while afield trapping. Then once again Cliff, like a man on a mission because they were 'burning daylight' and needed to pay for all of the things selected and get them loaded and back to the orphanage, seemed to hit an even higher gear in the selection process!

In several other sections of the warehouse Cliff selected and soon had on the run Buck Snort, Wind Horse and the two company men running items over to their 'selected' piles. Items such as iron moccasin awls for clothing repair, repair twine, spools of brass wire to repair cracked gunstocks, four kegs of Fourth Proof rum, horse hobbles, extra bridles, iron buckles, leather strapping for repairing packs and saddles, packsaddles, panniers, a 100'-long spool of cotton lead and picket rope, extra fire starting steels which had a 'habit' of being easily lost or broken, washing soap, shaving soap and straight razors for shaving. (Author's Note: Contrary to popular belief, many Mountain Men shaved and kept their locks of hair short. In that day and age, there was a head lice epidemic throughout the general population and by shaving that helped in keeping the head louse habitat on one's body to a minimum. Additionally, most Mountain Men realized that short, closely cropped hair made less of a grand scalp to show off back at an Indian's encampment...)

Lastly, Cliff saw to it that there were four tins of bag balm added (to help treat sores and skin tears on horses and human alike), extra leather strapping for pack and saddle repairs, a wooden keg of extra horseshoes, extra bridles and buckles, two good riding saddles, four sets of packs, four panniers, six additional whetstones for keeping shovels and axes sharp, and finally six carrots of James River chewing and smoking tobacco. (Author's Note: Tobacco in those early days in order to facilitate easy measurement for evaluation and safer travel when packed on horse or mule packs, was tightly rolled and wrapped with a heavy twine until the lump of rolled tobacco resembled that of a giant 'carrot' weighing approximately three pounds.)

When Cliff was all through selecting what he figured his two young friends would need for the year trapping afield on the Frontier, the senior Company Clerk after a lot of 'ciphering' came up with the figure of $879.33½ cents! Upon hearing that final figure, Buck Snort's heart sank with the realization that as he had suspected, he did not have enough money in his stoneware crock that he had been saving for a number of years to pay for all the goods that had been selected for him and Wind Horse!

That was when both he and Wind Horse got the surprise of their young lives. "You boys wait right here. I am walking over to the bank where I have been keeping my extra money for years. It ain't doing me any good over there at 3rd and Franklin at the bank so that is where I am heading. You company men let Pilcher know that is where I am a-going to withdraw the money these boys need for these provisions and will be right back so we can settle up with him. In the meantime, all four of you lads get to loading up all of those provisions into our wagon so we can get going back to the orphanage once I settle up with Pilcher."

With that, Cliff headed out the door en route his bank leaving Buck Snort and Wind Horse standing there with their mouths hanging wide open in surprise over what had just occurred! Then getting their wits about them over the surprise of Cliff footing the bill for a year's provisions and following Cliff's orders, the four men got busy toting all of those selected goods out to their waiting wagon at the warehouse's loading docks. Just about the time the four men had the wagon loaded with all of the previously selected provisions, weapons, cookware and the like, Cliff came hustling back with a bulging canvas bag full of Spanish silver coins. (Author's Note: At one time, the area occupied by the State of Missouri belonged to Spain and was administered accordingly, which included their coin of the realm, namely oversize Spanish silver dollars. Once the lands under the Louisiana Purchase were transferred over to the fledgling United States, the U.S. Mint at Philadelphia was responsible for minting coins and sending them to the far-flung borders of the United States. However, it took a few years for the U.S. Mint to be able to print up enough money so that the new western states like Missouri would have sufficient numbers of U.S. coins to go around. Since the Spanish silver dollar was made from silver, the local folks considered them good in all transactions, hence Cliff's use of Spanish coin to settle up the debt owed Lisa's Emporium for Buck Snort and Wind Horse's provisions.) Then on a handy desk, Cliff counted out what was needed including giving each of the company men a Spanish silver dollar for all their hard work and help in selecting and hauling out and around what was needed by Buck Snort and Wind Horse.

As the Clerks and Wind Horse finished loading up into their wagon, Buck Snort said, "Cliff, I don't know what to say or how to even thank or pay you for buying all of our supplies. You spent more money here today doing that than most men make in a year of hard labor. I just don't know what to say..."

Cliff, taking the reins in hand and 'clucking' the horses into pulling the wagon on down the road said, "You two boys just remember what I said and make sure after you get a gutful of living dangerously, being wet and cold most of the time and fighting off Indians trying to lift your hair, just come home safely. Then if you do, come out and see old Cliff at the orphanage and let him know how it went. As for paying me back, you need to remember that Men of the Mountains were always more than ready to get back to the forests, mountains and prairies where conventionalities like being paid back never stood in their way. That goes double for ever thinking about paying me back. Since I can no longer return to the mountains and forests that I love because my body will not allow it, I can at least help those who wish to experience what I loved and once did. Just bring your carcasses back with a full head of hair and that will be payment enough for old Cliff." With those words, Cliff just headed the team of horses on down the road and said no more regarding the wonderful surprise he had just bestowed upon two young men about to start out on their adventure of a lifetime into a largely unexplored and dangerous Frontier...

Also with those words, it got quiet in the wagon except for the groaning of the wagon's wood and metal joints as it lurched and hauled one hell of a load of provisions, foodstuffs and weaponry across rutted Missouri dirt roads as the three men headed for the 'hellhole' known as the orphanage. Later that afternoon on the way back, Buck Snort had Cliff swing the horses and wagon by Chuck Curry's farm where Buck Snort picked up his four horses that he had earlier loaned Chuck while he was a 'prisoner' at the local orphanage until reaching the age of 16. While there and taking some of his money from his stoneware crock, Buck Snort purchased three more horses from his friend. Those seven horses, plus the two purchased earlier from Cliff and the two the Ashley-Henry Fur Trade Company was going to supply the two men with on their day of departure, gave Buck Snort and Wind Horse a total of eleven horses. That meant the two young men had more than enough horses to carry them the several thousand miles up to where Fort Henry was to be built, as well as being able to carry all of their much-needed and valuable supplies for a year afield trapping beaver and wolves.

For the next two days, Buck Snort, Cliff and Wind Horse quietly when Cal was not around to 'grumble them', loaded all of their supplies onto packsaddles and into panniers so they would be ready to head up along the Missouri River to the mouth of the Yellowstone River no later than on Major Henry's planned departure date, which was to be just as soon as the winter's ice left the river. That way, Major Henry would have the spring runoff and its high waters in which to safely navigate his single, heavily loaded keel-boat up the Missouri River. That he would do while his over 300 horse and mule supply train, accompanied by approximately 100 Ashley-Henry Fur Trade Company trappers, mirrored the keelboat's slow progress upstream as they rode along the western bank of the Missouri River.

CHAPTER THREE

FORT HENRY, "MUSKRAT AND CLEM"

COME DAYLIGHT ON THE MORNING of departure, while the keelboat fully loaded with supplies and its crew lifted anchor and began pulling the boat upstream, the hundred or so trappers amidst huge clouds of dust kicked up by many horse and mule hooves got underway as well. As was to be expected, the boat and trappers' caravan averaged around 15-18 miles per day while traveling in and along the Missouri River. By day three of their travels, operational organization had pretty much set in and a routine among the land-based travelers and the keelboat crew had been established. Each day, a team of hunters moved out ahead from the slow-moving caravan and forged upriver approximately 15 or so miles per day. There they selected a safe campsite, killed four to six buffalo from the numerous nearby feeding herds, butchered out the animals and had the meat roasting over several large campfires by the time the keelboat with its hardworking 'cordelling' crew and the following trappers' horse and mule caravan arrived. There the entire contingent of men fed and rested overnight only to begin the routine all over the next day. (Author's Note: *Cordelling* is a French word describing how a keelboat was moved slowly upstream against the current of a river. Keelboats were 40-80' long with a 15-20' beam and were shallow draft. They were propelled by human muscle either with the use of poles by poling from the keelboat in shallower waters or by being pulled or 'cordelling' by 20-30 men towing the keelboat by a cable up to 300 yards long attached to the boat's main mast, making from 15-18 miles per day when the boat was in deeper waters. During this process, a man manning the tiller of the keelboat kept the boat in the mainstream, while the men pulling the boat along fought the brush and riverside hazards in order to make upstream progress.)

After many days of travel in which Buck Snort and Wind Horse got lots of practice in how to correctly pack and unpack their horses starting way before daylight so they would be ready to go in the morning's first light, they finally had it down pat and functioned as a practiced team.

Of course what made it easier was that someone else had been designated their camp's cooks and clean-up men, so all the two young men had to worry about was the packing and unpacking of the animals on a daily basis. Then came the day Major Henry and the trappers dreaded after many long days on the trail, when the caravan was to pass close by an Arikara Indian village located right on the eastern shore of the Missouri River. Fortunately the fierce and white man-hating Arikaras were intimidated by the presence of the two loaded and manned swivel cannons on the keelboat, the 30-40 heavily armed keelboat-men and the equally heavily armed fur trappers and their extensive caravan on the nearby western side of the river. As the keelboat slowly moved by the now much alerted Arikara, all they did was quietly watch the boat and huge horse and mule caravan slowly move on by on the far riverbank, full well realizing that to attack such a force of heavily armed men would be disastrous for the attackers. However, for the next two days of upriver travel, double guards were kept posted because of the small bands of Arikara who were following the contingent of boat and men looking for any kind of a weakness that could be exploited, especially the opportunity to steal any valuable horses or mules.

Days later the keelboat arrived where the Yellowstone River entered the mighty Missouri River and anchored on the western side of the

Missouri, much to the relief of Major Henry and his contingent of trappers. After the keelboat was anchored on the western side of the Missouri in a deep channel and a guard posted, the rest of the men set up a semi-permanent camp from which to work from when hunting for food, cutting timber and constructing the new fort and supply post. Additionally, Major Henry took a small group of men, located a high ground site for the future Fort Henry near the mouth of the Yellowstone and staked out the construction area. That night a great celebration was held by all of the men realizing the hard work in establishing the fort and trading post would begin the next day because they were 'burning daylight' and the fall trapping season was soon to be upon the group's teams of trappers.

The next day, Major Henry designated which groups of men would be responsible for leveling the ground upon which was to sit the new fort, those crews who would do the 'logging' of the fort's timbers for the palisades and buildings within the walls of the fort and those designated teamsters who would be using horses and dragging the logs to the building site. Additionally back at camp, hunting and cooking crews were so designated so the hardworking men would have good meals. Lastly, several smaller groups of men were designated for guard duty around the working men and the huge horse and mule herd now happily feeding in the nearby meadows adjacent the new fort's construction site.

As it turned out, Buck Snort and Wind Horse were two of those chosen as 'loggers', assigned a double buck saw and spent the next three weeks along with other like in kind 'loggers' cutting down trees and 'bucking' them to length for the walls of the fort and its interior buildings. On April the 22nd, 1822, Fort Henry was completed and christened as such. On April the 23rd, that day was designated a moving day and all of the supplies were unloaded from the keelboat and hauled over and placed safely inside the fort's walls. Collaterally nearby, a log barn and series of corrals were constructed for those horses and mules which would be left behind for the fort's occupants to have and use once the trapping teams had disbursed into the field. By April the 25th, a day of rest was declared by Major Henry, four buffalo from a nearby herd were slaughtered and set to roasting over an open pit fire, while designated camp cooks prepared a supper to celebrate the completion and opening of Fort Henry. That evening, the rum flowed and a heady celebration was had by all of "General Ashley's 100"!

The following morning, in order to have time to be on one's trapping site, have a cabin built, and have the beaver waters scoped out and traps ready to go for the 1822 fall beaver trapping season, Major Henry set to designating trapping crews. Because so many small groups of curious Indians had been observed during the month of

April while the fort was being built and none of them appeared to be very friendly, Major Henry decreed that all trapper teams would be comprised of at least four men for the safety in numbers that offered. For those groups of four or more trappers already established, Major Henry let those groups stand. For those groups of less than four men wanting to work closely together, he formed those not needed to stay back at the fort for protection and as traders with the local Indians, into groups of four trappers for their own protection while afield.

As fate would have it, Buck Snort and Wind Horse were lumped in with two older men they did not really know. One of those trappers selected as a team member towering over all of the rest of the Major's men at 6'-5" tall, was named Calvin "Muskrat" Johnson. (Author's Note: Most men of that day and age were on the average of 5'-6" to 5'-8" in height.) The other man of the newly formed group of trappers was one named Clem Watkins. As it turned out, both men in their previous lives had been partners as buffalo hide hunters. Both men as Buck Snort and Wind Horse soon discovered, had trapped muskrat, mink, raccoons and a few beaver as kids. However, both had been recent hunters for the Major's group of men and had reputations for being excellent shooters, killing most of the buffalo they shot for the group's daily meals with just one shot every time!

When the Major had introduced the four men among themselves, it was apparent that Muskrat and Clem were not too sure over the very young appearing men they had been partnered up with. But they realized that the pairing of men into four-man teams was for their own good and safety, especially since they were now deep into hostile Blackfeet, Arikara and Gros Ventre Indian Territory. That pairing also made for four sets of hands to help out instead of just two, and four heavily armed men would be more of a challenge to engage when it came to white man-Indian conflicts. Besides, some of the other more experienced men in the Major's group of trappers had lived and survived while out on the Frontier and had recognized the identities of some of the Indians the men had seen and identified as Arikara, Blackfeet, Lakota, Gros Ventre and Assiniboine, none of whom had a reputation of being historically too 'white man friendly' when the two very different cultures met.

Then as the four men became more familiar with each other over the following days, they all discovered each pairing of men was very well-armed, well-seated when it came to their riding stock, and had good pack stock as well as plenty of them. Additionally, it soon came to light that both parties were either well-provisioned or very capable of purchasing what they needed from the Major even at "Mountain Prices" because of their economic successes as buffalo hunters before joining up with the Major and General Ashley. (Author's Note: "Mountain Prices" was a term given by the Mountain Men for the prices they had to pay their suppliers for needed provisions when afield. Mountain Prices meant the trappers afield paid anywhere from 700-1,000% more for an item in the field than they would have had to pay for that same item back in St. Louis. Additionally, many times the goods provided for the Mountain Men in the field by their suppliers were found to be of lesser quality as well. The suppliers in turn cried 'foul' when their trappers complained over the high prices (Mountain Prices) by pointing out the risks and losses they had undergone in bringing the supplies through the rugged mountains, through hostile Indian country, braving horse wrecks or risking their cargos by bringing them up the dangerous shallow and snag-ridden Missouri River in keelboats.)

Those first nights after being paired up with Muskrat and Clem, the men sat around one of their many campfires getting to know each other better and planning their fall beaver trapping operations. Since none of the men had ever been in the country they now occupied, Buck Snort came up with an idea. He suggested that since there was such a large number of trappers in camp, his two partners get all of their provisions together just as soon as they could. Buck Snort felt that once everyone began getting all of their provisions together, the Major might soon run out of many vital items. Especially since he had only brought one fully loaded keelboat upstream plus what the horses and mules had carried. So best they get what they needed now before the mad rush to provision up was on. Then Buck Snort and Wind Horse outlined what they had brought along as provisions, and soon Muskrat and Clem had a pretty good idea as to what they needed so they didn't needlessly 'double provision'. Lastly, Buck Snort advised the two men not to buy any beaver or wolf traps because they already had acquired plenty. That surprised the two older men and they began quietly and positively reassessing the abilities and common sense attitudes of the two young men they had been paired up with as trapping partners...

Then Wind Horse came up with an idea after watching several rather large groups of men walking by their campfire. After seeing and becoming concerned over the size and number of such groups of fellow trappers walking by, Wind Horse said, "I suggest we leave as soon as we can so we can get on the best beaver producing ground before someone else beats us to it. I also suggest we not take the first ground we come to because some of these other men may want to do the same and then we will have too many trappers all in the same area trapping those same waters. I suggest we pass up the first number of rivers we come to and head up the Yellowstone

until we come to a river system that is far removed from this here fort. That way when the
others are wrangling over which group will be
trapping the best waters on the first couple of
rivers, we will be staking out the best territory
on the more distant and less trapper-populated
river and won't have all kinds of company causing us problems."

Upon hearing those 'wise sounding' words
coming from one of their newest and youngest
partners, Clem and Muskrat were now really reassessing the quality of their new partners. What
they were suggesting really made sense and
was far thinking. Then one evening Clem really
broke the ice by saying, "Say, Buck Snort, how
the hell did you get such a damn goofy sounding
'handle' like 'Buck Snort'?" When Buck Snort's
story came out about being poisoned with rat
poison at the orphanage by the three older kids
and it screwing up his intestinal system with
terrible gaseous results, especially after eating
anything made from wheat or oats, that story left
Clem, Muskrat and Wind Horse laughing until
the tears just rolled down their cheeks. But those
tears of laughter stopped when Buck Snort, upon
intestinal command, gave everyone laughing at
his unfortunate disability a 'taste' of what he had
just been describing! And in so doing, scattered
the men from around their campfire once their
noses had alerted them to what was coming like
'quail will do when they spy a low overhead

hungry flying hawk'! After that and a cup of rum apiece sharing funny stories about each other, the age barriers and overall suspicions began falling away and by their third cups of rum, the four trappers found peace in and among themselves as a 'team' soon to be reckoned with.

The next day as Buck Snort and Wind Horse had Major Henry's three blacksmiths examine and replace any horseshoes on their riding and packhorses, Clem and Muskrat went into the fort's supply warehouses and excluding cookware and traps at Buck Snort's suggestion since he and Wind Horse had plenty for the four of them, procured what supplies they figured needed to be added to what their newfound friends and partners already had so all four men could comfortably survive a year trapping afield. The next evening, the packs and panniers that needed loading were loaded as the men prepared to leave as early as they could the next day after they had packed all of their livestock for the trip ahead taking them into the unknown. Once again, Buck Snort had convinced the rest of the team that by leaving earlier than the rest of the hundred or so trappers at the fort, they could locate and stake out the better beaver trapping grounds before being overrun with all the other competition. Buck Snort also figured that by leaving earlier, since they did not know the country they would soon find themselves in, that would give all four of them the time needed to bypass the easier and closer beaver trapping waters for those further along the Yellowstone that would be less crowded. Plus, that would also give them a jump on finding a suitable building spot for their cabin and corrals so they could get going into building those structures before the 'snows flew' as well.

By noontime, Muskrat, Clem, Wind Horse and Buck Snort were 'mounted a-horse' and gathered in front of Fort Henry's front gate talking with Major Henry. There he cautioned the men to be extra careful around any Indians and that he would be waiting for their four returns come the summer of 1823, with a cup of good quality of rum for each of them and a smile because they would have many packs of beaver for him to purchase. With a wave of their hands and since it was his idea, Buck Snort led their caravan of trappers westerly up the Yellowstone towards the faraway mountains partially hidden in a haze many miles distant. To Buck Snort and Wind Horse, their great adventure in life had truly begun...

Several days later they camped along the first big river they came to leading to the south off the Yellowstone (later named the O'Fallon Creek). Shortly after daylight the next morning the four men proceeded on their westerly course up the Yellowstone in order to make sure they were far enough away from the horde of trappers soon to follow. Several days later they camped along the next big river they came across that headed south off the Yellowstone (later named the Tongue River). After much discussion about stopping and trapping along that river, the men thought about the number of trappers still back at the fort that would soon be flooding out across the country into the first two rivers and adjacent waters they had crossed. With that thought in mind, they decided they would ride even further to the west and see if those waters they came across looked like better beaver country. Then they would decide if they should stop and set up their camp figuring they were now far away from those teams of trappers to follow.

Two days later, the four men arrived at another river leading south off the Yellowstone (later named the Powder River). That evening there was once again much discussion among the four men about stopping and making their main camp along that river so they could build a cabin and a set of corrals for the coming year of beaver trapping. That was when Wind Horse who typically Indian-like, had remained quiet while the white men argued among themselves about if they were far enough away from the hundred or so trappers heading their way to trap beaver as well.

"I think we need to go even further if we want to trap beaver in peace," said Wind Horse as he tended the fire. "Plus, we have crossed many unshod pony tracks which lets me know that there are many Indians living in this area and I am not so sure that is something we would want. That coupled with all the herds of buffalo in the area makes me concerned that our chances of running across these Indians is greatly increased because there is such a good local food source. Again, something I am not so sure we would really need or want. I just have a feeling this is not the place for us. I think we need to go one river even further to the west," said Wind Horse and then having said his piece, went back to his fire tending.

"Indians usually have not only good common sense but many times they listen to the spirits as well," said Muskrat quietly, a man who had been raised among Indians back at his home place and knew of some of their cultural ways according to some of the stories he had shared with his group of trappers earlier.

Three days later, the men stopped overlooking a great river (later named the Bighorn River) that led south off the Yellowstone River. Without so much as a word among them like they all realized this was the one for them, they spent several hours later exploring what that river had to offer in the way of beaver trapping possibilities and cabin sites. In so doing, the men discovered just about every waterway both adjacent the main river and along the main river itself was heavily evidenced with beaver sign! With that, it seemed that every patch of water was bordered by growing willow thickets, groves of aspens or stands of cottonwoods, all showing extensive signs of heavy beaver use and cuttings. Every larger body of water seemed to be holding freshly tended conically shaped beaver houses, long and newly made or repaired mud and stick beaver dams and upon closer examination, the men discovered the watered areas were literally dotted everywhere with freshly utilized beaver slides! Additionally, many beaver were seen swimming around the watered areas in broad daylight in the middle of the day, which was rather unusual for that species.

"I feel this is the place the spirits are telling me where we need to build our cabin and trap beaver. Everywhere I am looking I see beaver sign, I see herds of buffalo scattered across the land with elk and antelope everywhere as a fresh meat source for us. This is the place," said Wind Horse quietly and with a conviction born of his breed.

Several miles below where the Bighorn entered into the Yellowstone, the men reined up and looked over a wooded area that ran down to the river's edge. Closer examination revealed a rather large opening into the wooded area from whence gushed a small creek whose vigorous running waters spilled down and into the Bighorn. Slow-walking their horses up into the open area within the surrounding pine and fir forests, the trappers discovered a horseshoe-shaped area of meadow and timber that was out of sight from anyone traveling along the main river course. At the northwest corner of the opening was a small grove of very welcoming aspens that bordered the small creek. Moving their eyes further to the west of the small grove of aspen laid a flat whose north, west and southern edges were bordered by timber. Looking all around, Buck Snort could see closely accessible timber in which to build a cabin, Wind Horse saw that the suspect cabin-flat would be out from the direction of the north wind, Clem liked the water source nearby and Muskrat liked that the spot was hidden from view from anyone riding along the riverside to the east. No two ways about it, the day was looking good…

For the longest time all four men just sat there quietly on their impatient horses wanting to feed and water, while looking all around the area. That was when Muskrat with a more than serious look on his face said, "This looks like home to me providing Wind Horse feels only good spirits abound in this area."

Wind Horse upon hearing Muskrat's tone of voice being of a serious nature when he had posed his question out loud, just grinned and finally said, "I think this would be a good place for our new home and the 'spirits' think so as well. That is just as long as Buck Snort does not do what he is capable of doing when he wants to get everyone's attention by 'breaking wind'…"

With those words and remembering back to that first night they had met and Buck Snort ran everyone away from the campfire with one of his gaseous 'treats', everyone laughed over Wind Horse's words of caution…

Shortly thereafter, the men dismounted and led their horses over to the grove of welcoming aspens surrounding the creek. There they un-packed all of their packhorses and arranged their packs in a circle under a thick stand of old-growth aspen for the shade the tree canopy offered and protection from being soaked by an early sum-mer thunderstorm if one was to happen by. That packsaddle arrangement was also an old trap-per's trick according to Muskrat, which provided some protection as a barrier against Indian attack when in a new and unknown area that held the possibility of attack. As Buck Snort rifled through a number of packs until he came across a number of hobbles, the rest of the men finished unpack-ing and then unsaddling their riding horses. As Buck Snort hobbled all of the horses, the rest of the men then led all of them over to water and after watering, removed their bridles and turned them out to feed in the nearby meadow where they could also be closely watched. Then being in unfamiliar territory, with rifles in hand, the men walked over to the piece of level ground that held promise and potential as a future cabin building site.

After more discussion on the qualities of the

site, the men split up to accomplish different assignments. Clem, a southern boy by breeding, had opted to be the group's camp cook. This he did because of having a lot of cooking experience gained when back on his family's farm in North Carolina. There having to cook for a cabin full of kids after his mother had been killed upon being 'arrowed' by a drunken local Indian who came to their cabin and demanded to be fed. In the process of shooing off the drunken Indian with her broom, he had turned and killed Clem's mother with an arrow to her heart. Nine-year-old Clem, upon seeing the killing of his mother, removed his father's always loaded double barreled shotgun from over their fireplace mantle and letting both barrels 'fly' at the same time, made sure that Indian never killed a defenseless woman ever again! However as a result of that fatal act by the Indian, his father had appointed him the family's cook because he was the oldest of the children and his father's labors were needed in the fields. So for ten years until he came west, Clem was his family's cook for a family of seven and apparently a damn good one according to Muskrat who had 'fed numerous times over the years at his table'!

So being the designated cook for the trappers, Clem headed over to the packs carrying the cooking gear and began hauling Dutch ovens, frying pans, cast iron pots, hanging irons and the like over to a centrally located firepit location adjacent to the proposed cabin site and began setting up his outside cooking area. Secondly, after having returned with a shovel from one of the packs, Clem began digging out his firepit and coal making area for his Dutch oven use to come. When that chore was completed, he 'set' the hanging irons over the new firepit area. Then walking over to their nearby creek, Clem filled the group's coffee pot, returned to the firepit and hung it on the hanging iron over where their first outdoor fire was soon to be. Moments later, Clem returned to another set of packs and removed some mixing bowls and from another set of packs, a bag of flower, sugar, salt and a tin of dried yeast. With those in hand, he returned to the firepit and began mixing up some flour, yeast, sugar and water and set it off to one side in the sun next to the firepit so it would have time to 'rise' so he could make his brand of Dutch oven biscuits.

In the meantime, Buck Snort, Wind Horse and Muskrat retrieved several long-handled axes from another set of packs, walked a short distance up into the timber and began gathering up dry limb wood and cutting off dead pine limbs for their campfire soon to be. With armloads of dry firewood in hand and arm, those three men began hauling the wood down to the firepit area and stacking it closely at hand for easy access by Clem when he began his cooking duties. Shortly thereafter, a small mountain of dry limb wood had been gathered and stacked for Clem's use which made him happy to no end.

As the 'wood gatherers' hauled down armloads of wood, Clem in the meantime hauled the men's riding saddles over to the firepit area so the men would have something to sit upon while eating the coming supper to be. Then he returned to the aspen grove and began unloading several other packs carrying the men's sleeping blankets and laid them out in each man's sleeping area under the protective cover offered by the thicket of aspen trees.

Then with the first fire on their new homesite in the outdoor firepit blazing away, Clem began roasting their green coffee beans in the bottom of a cast iron bean pot so they were roasted, later crushed and eventually put into a boiling coffee pot to make the men his style of strong 'trappers' coffee'. Then bringing over a gallon jug of their rendered bear oil that Buck Snort and Wind Horse had purchased earlier at Lisa's Emporium at Cliff's insistence for Dutch oven baking, Clem began greasing the bottom of the group's two Dutch ovens for his biscuit making that was to come. Since that and coffee would be their supper that evening because they had no fresh meat, he was planning on making a double batch of biscuits for the hungry men. With that in mind, Clem returned to the assortment of packs in the aspens and brought forth a gallon jug of their honey and brought that to the firepit and laid it close to the fire so it would warm up for use on their biscuits come suppertime as well.

By then, the sun was beginning to set in the west and with that in mind, all of the men went forth into the meadow and brought all of their 21 hobbled horses back into camp. While Clem and Muskrat bridled all of the horses and led them to their stream so they could water once again, Wind Horse and Buck Snort unloaded their spool of cotton picket rope from one of the pack-saddles and then wove it throughout the aspens so their valuable horses could be safely picketed close at hand to the sleeping men for the night. After watering, the horses were brought back, picketed and had their hobbles removed for the night. Putting the horses' hobbles back into their packs so no wandering porcupine would come by and nibble on the leather of the hobbles for the salt contained therein, the men then headed for their firepit and their soon to be supper.

That evening the tired men had Dutch oven biscuits smothered in honey, along with several cups of hot coffee. As they sat on their saddles eating and drinking, the men discussed and pri-oritized among themselves the next few days of work that lay ahead. The first item of business they all agreed upon since they were deep in Indian country, would be the construction of a corral for their horses. For without their valu-able horses if they were stolen by any Indians, the trappers would be afoot and deep in Indian country and that would mean they would be no better than 'dead men walking'. Then once the horses were safely inside a good and stout corral, the men would turn their attention to building a 'hell-for-stout' cabin that would stand the worst of the weather that could be suffered there in the northern latitudes they now occupied as well as any determined Indian attacks. Finally it was decided that from all the beaver sign they had observed riding along the river and in a number of its adjacent waterways, a storage shed would also have to be built as well for all the soon to be many bundles of beaver *'Plus'* (pronounced "plew", as beaver pelts were commonly called by those in the fur trade in that day and age). With that bit of business completed, a cup of rum in their bellies and the hordes of vicious biting mountain mosquitoes hovering in the air around each man in what seemed to be pillars of the always hungry winged critters, the men decided to head for their sleeping furs and call it a day. As they did, however, each man made sure once he laid his head down for a night's sleep, his rifle and pistols also lay within quick grabbing distance as well since they knew little of the Indian menace surrounding them but were determined to survive whatever came their way.

Clem was up early the next morning with a coffee pot boiling merrily away and a big pan of biscuit dough laid near the warmth of the fire to aid it in the needed rising before being made into Dutch oven biscuits. Off to one side of their nearby fast-flowing creek, the rest of the men were taking care of a call of nature and washing up or shaving in their grove of aspens. Once the men decided they were now 'beautiful', they began once again hobbling all of their horses and letting them go into the nearby meadow full of lush grasses to feed and get used to their main grazing area.

Since it was still before breakfast, Wind Horse, Buck Snort and Muskrat grabbed a saw and a couple of broad-headed axes and headed up onto the hillside. Soon the morning's air rang to the sounds of a ringing ax and the sound of a crosscut saw cutting down pole-sized pine trees to later be used in constructing the horses' corral. Shortly thereafter, Clem yelled out and the men came down from the nearby hillside and a breakfast of biscuits, honey and coffee was had by all.

After breakfast, Buck Snort and Wind Horse saddled up their riding mounts and placed a set of panniers on one of their packhorses. Then with a wave of their hands, they headed off down towards the Bighorn River flats where they had observed numerous buffalo grazing the day before. As Clem and Muskrat somewhat later put the finishing touches on building a meat pole next to the cooking area in their aspen grove, a single shot was heard ringing out down by the Bighorn. Two hours later, Buck Snort and Wind Horse rode back into their campsite trailing a

fully loaded packhorse carrying all the quar-
tered-out buffalo meat it could carry. Moments
later, all of the men began hauling up with ropes
onto the meat pole the quarters of the just-killed
buffalo so it could cool out and glaze in the cool
mountain air.

After washing all of the blood, snot and slime
off their hands, Buck Snort, because he was
having gas problems again since he had eaten a
mess of biscuits for breakfast made from a wheat
product and needed to get out into the open air,
Wind Horse and Muskrat headed off into the
timber with axes and saw, to once again begin
cutting pole-sized timbers for their new horse
corral. In the meantime, Clem taking one of their
shovels began digging postholes for the horse
corral soon to be constructed.

Stopping to wipe the sweat from his brow,
Clem happened to look out across their new horse
meadow at their horse herd making sure they were
safe. When he did, HE SAW TWO MOUNTED
INDIANS AND TWO INDIANS WHO HAD
DISMOUNTED IN AMONG THEIR HOBBLED
HORSE HERD! THE TWO DISMOUNTED
INDIANS ON THE GROUND WERE HOLDING
ONE OF THE TRAPPERS' HORSES BY THE
HEAD! THEN ONE OF THE INDIANS KNELT
DOWN ON THE GROUND BY THE HORSE'S
FRONT FEET AND HURRIEDLY CUT AWAY
THE HORSE'S HEAVY LEATHER HOBBLES
WITH HIS SHEATH KNIFE! MEANWHILE,

THE TWO MOUNTED INDIANS HERDED TWO MORE HORSES OVER TO THE INDIANS ON THE GROUND SO THOSE HORSES' HOBBLES COULD BE CUT OFF AS WELL. THAT WAY, THE THREE HORSES COULD THEN BE QUICKLY HERDED OFF BEFORE THE TRAPPERS WHO WOULD BE ON FOOT, COULD INTERFERE WITH THE HORSE THIEVES OR CATCH THEIR STOLEN HORSES. IN A FLASH, THE HOBBLES ON THOSE TWO HORSES WERE CUT OFF AS WELL…

BOOM! WENT CLEM'S RIFLE AND FROM 100 YARDS AWAY, THE SHARPSHOOTING OLD BUFFALO HUNTER SHOT ONE INDIAN CLEAR OUT FROM HIS SADDLE WITH A 'CHEST SHOT', LANDING HIM ONTO THE GROUND IN A CLOUD OF DUST! NOW THE SCRAMBLE WAS ON AS THE REMAINING THREE INDIANS COULD SEE THE TRAPPER RUNNING RIGHT AT THEM AND YELLING NOW WITH A PISTOL IN EACH HAND! THE TWO REMAINING INDIANS ON THE GROUND HURRIEDLY GRABBED THE REINS AND SADDLE HORNS ON THEIR HORSES AND QUICKLY SPRANG UP INTO THEIR SADDLES. LEAVING THEIR DEAD COMRADE WHERE HE FELL AFTER BEING SHOT FROM HIS SADDLE BY CLEM WITH HIS RIFLE, THE REMAINING THREE INDIANS PREPARED TO QUICKLY LEAVE THE AREA WITH THEIR PRIZES OF THREE OF THE

TRAPPERS' VALUABLE HORSES. HOWEVER, THE INDIANS' "GODS" WERE NOT WITH THEM THAT DAY. THE FAST-FOOTED CLEM HAD SPRINTED ACROSS THE MEADOW AND HAD CLOSED THE DISTANCE BETWEEN HIMSELF AND THE INDIAN HORSE THIEVES CONSIDERABLY. SEEING THE THREE INDIANS ALL BUNCHED UP AND PREPARING TO QUICKLY MOVE OFF WITH THE TRAPPERS' HORSES, CLEM STOPPED IN HIS TRACKS, AIMED ONE PISTOL AT A TIME AND ALTHOUGH KNOWN FOR THEIR INACCURACY AT LONG DISTANCES, MANAGED UPON SHOOTING TO KILL ONE FLEEING INDIAN'S HORSE AND SHOOT ANOTHER HORSE THIEF FROM HIS SADDLE!

BY THEN THE THREE HEAVILY ARMED WOODCUTTERS HAD RACED DOWN OFF THE HILLSIDE TOWARD THE SCENE OF ACTION, CARRYING THEIR EVER-PRESENT RIFLES AS THEY CAME. SOON THE AIR AROUND THE REMAINING TWO INDIANS WAS FULL OF HOT LEAD AS THEIR RIFLE SHOTS WERE HAVING AN IMMEDIATE EFFECT. ONE INDIAN HORSE THIEF FELL FORWARD UPON HIS SADDLE HORN, AS ONE OF THE SPEEDING LEAD BALLS FIRED FROM BUCK SNORT, WIND HORSE AND MUSKTRAT'S RIFLES STRUCK HIM IN THE HIP AND HE WAS MORTALLY WOUNDED! THE OTHER INDIAN WHO HAD HIS HORSE

JUST KILLED, HIT THE GROUND RUNNING! HITTING THE GROUND ON HIS FEET AFTER HAVING HIS HORSE SHOT OUT FROM UNDER HIM, THAT INDIAN QUICKLY LEAPT BACK INTO ANOTHER EMPTY INDIAN'S HORSE'S SADDLE AND FLED THE SCENE WITH HIS MORTALLY WOUNDED FELLOW HORSE THIEF BENT OVER HIS SADDLE IN AGONY FROM HIS DEEP HIP WOUND ATTEMPTING TO RIDE OFF AS WELL…

Within moments, the four trappers were gathered all together and hurriedly reloading their rifles and pistols in case other Indians were close at hand. Then with their rifles and pistols reloaded and 'ready for bear', the men slowly walked forward and surveyed the scene. As they did, Muskrat walked over to one of the dead Indians and after a moment of looking down at him said, "Damn, that dead Indian is a Crow! He is just a kid and damn it, the Crow are supposed to be our friends according to the Major!" Then Muskrat walked over to the other dead Indian and once again said under his breath, "Another Crow and like the other one, this one is just a kid as well. Hell, this one can't be over 13 or 14 years old!"

About then, one Indian's horse come running back to where the other two Indians' horses lay dead. Typical of some horses, they hated to be left alone and would always try to remain with others of their kind if possible. Such was the case with the returning Indian's horse. That horse, not wanting to be left alone out in the country, after losing its wounded rider, had turned around and had come back to where it knew the other horses it had come into the area with were last seen. Grabbing that horse's reins as it trotted back to the killing field, Muskrat pointed out the great amount of bright red blood all down the side of the horse and saddle. Nodding at his friend Clem, the two trappers took off at a typical ground-eating trot known to be used by many of their kind and soon disappeared into the timber in the direction from whence the lone Indian's horse had come.

As they did, Buck Snort and Wind Horse herded all the rest of the trappers' horses back to where they were once again picketed in the aspen grove before anything else happened to them. Half an hour later, Muskrat and Clem returned with smiles upon their faces. "We found where the wounded Indian had fallen off his horse and died from the loss of blood from his hip wound. He had been shot in the hip just below his guts. He was a dead man riding when that lead ball hit him," said Muskrat in a matter of fact tone of voice. Then he said, "That dead Crow was another damn kid, not more than 13 or 14. I can't figure it out. They must have gotten a wild hair up their asses and figured they would go out and count coup on some damn old trapper by stealing his horses. That was a fatal mistake on their parts. Now I wonder what is going to happen when that one lone survivor returns to his camp without the others and lets everyone know the trappers done killed off all his young friends! I sure don't cotton to having all of their kin arming themselves and coming this way looking for us with blood in their eyes. Even worse, taking out all of their 'bile' on every other trapper they run across in the coming days thinking they are at fault for all of the killing of their young kin."

"Not much we can do about that except remain extra vigilant," said Wind Horse. "Well, that and get this corral constructed as soon as possible so we can control what happens to our horse herd more closely in the future." With that, the dead Indians' horses and the dead Indians were dragged off and placed in a gully in a finger of timber. As for the live Indian horse, it was unsaddled and let loose to run with the wind. Two days later upon examination, all that was left after the wolves and bears had finished with the dead horses and Indians were the long bones, pelvic girdles and rib cages of the dead. Then several days later, even those bones had been scattered throughout the stand of timber, making their original cause of death a mystery. As luck would have it, no Crow Indians ever came looking for their lost kids. The trappers figured since nothing happened over the killing of the young Crows that maybe the lone Crow escapee did not make it home alive to report what had happened back at the trappers' cabin…

One week later, the horse corral was completed and the men had started on cutting all of the timbers needed to build a cabin large enough to hold all of the men comfortably, as well as many of their perishable provisions and provide the protections they needed come the winter's fury or any subsequent Indian attacks. Three weeks later, the four trappers had completed their cabin, its mud, stone and stick fireplace, split-log tables, chairs and window openings covered with shaved deer hides. Covered with shaved deer hides so some light could come in and yet could keep out most of the wet and cold come winter or the rains from the numerous summer thunderstorms that came their way in their neck of the woods. Last to be built was a 'hell-for-stout' log storage shed with a heavy log door meant to hold their extra non-perishable provisions, extra traps and bundles of hopefully soon to be caught and processed beaver furs. As an extra precaution, Muskrat had brought along a length of heavy chain, a bolt and nut that he figured they would use to keep the corral gate closed and locked so any Indians trying to raid the horses in the corral would have their hands full trying to undo the nut and bolt holding the corral gate closed. But now on second thought, that chain and bolt system was placed on the heavy log storage door since that shed held all of the trappers' valuable provisions and eventually bundles of valuable furs. That decision was made since the cabin now had a window opening facing the horse corral from whence to shoot if Indians were discovered raiding the horse corral.

Then for the next two weeks, the trappers built smoking racks next to their cabin so they could keep the bears away from the meat now being smoked, as the trappers smoked and bagged in tanned deerskin bags a plentiful supply of buffalo jerky for later use when out on the winter trail running wolf traps. Then the men set to cutting up a huge stack of dry wood for wintertime when cutting wood would be problematic due to the deep snows. Finally, the men smoked all of their beaver and wolf traps to rid them of the man and oil smells in preparation for their use during the coming trapping seasons. Lastly, as Wind Horse and Muskrat hunted and brought back quarters of buffalo for the meat pole, Buck Snort and Clem cast a small mountain of bullets for their pistols and rifles as well as disassembled all of their weapons. Then once disassembled, they removed the black powder and lead fouling so they would have better accuracy down range and then reassembled all of them for the much anticipated coming season of hard use.

Finally the men found themselves doing what they loved doing. For the next week, the men rode along the Bighorn scouting out the best beaver waters and making their plans for the beginning of their fall beaver trapping season. After a number of fruitful miles locating the better beaver trapping areas as was evidenced by all of the beaver sign of mud and stick dams, conical beaver houses and numerous fresh beaver slides, the men had decided they would begin their trapping where the Bighorn entered the Yellowstone and then trap their way south come the fall beaver trapping season. That way if they trapped out all the beaver just off the Yellowstone and immediately south, that would discourage any newly arriving trappers into thinking there were no beaver along that portion of the Bighorn or was already full of beaver trappers and cause them to move on elsewhere. Then the men would trap out the beaver south along the river, past their homesite and keep going in that direction until they ran out of beaver or were forced to move their campsite even further south as they followed the beaver sign and their trapping successes.

CHAPTER FOUR

⋄⋄⋄⋄⋄⋄⋄⋄⋄⋄⋄⋄⋄⋄⋄⋄⋄⋄⋄⋄⋄⋄⋄⋄⋄⋄⋄⋄⋄⋄⋄⋄⋄⋄⋄⋄⋄⋄⋄

"THE LURE OF THE FUR" AND TRAPPING THE "BIGHORN" — 1822 1823

EXITING THE CABIN EARLY one morning with his rifle in hand as he always did as a matter of precaution, Buck Snort made sure that he passed the gas that had built up in his system once he was outside and not inside. Then looking all around for any sign of danger as Cliff had always counseled when he was back at the orphanage, once the old blacksmith discovered the younger man had decided to become a trapper, and upon seeing none he relaxed. To his front was Clem busy around the outdoor cooking fire making breakfast. Continuing to look around, he saw his friend Wind Horse tending to a call of nature over in the nearby aspen grove. Continuing to sweep his eyes that late September morning with a cold chill in the air, he saw Muskrat standing off by himself looking skyward.

There he saw Muskrat checking for any weather signs, checking the area around the campsite for any signs of danger and then their two sets of eyes met. When their eyes met, Muskrat got a big grin on his face of embarrassment over being found out checking the weather and his surroundings, as any Mountain Man would do if he wanted to survive while living out on a sometimes savage and wild Frontier.

Cradling his rifle in the crook of his massive arm making the rifle look small in his 6'-5" tall giant of a frame, Muskrat walked over to Buck Snort saying, "By 'Gum', today is the day! Winter is on its way, the weather looks great for a day afield of beaver trapping and with these last few weeks of colder weather, the beaver should be starting to come into their prime. What say you, Buck Snort?"

"Back home when I ran my own beaver trapping line, this was exactly the kind of day and weather I would be looking for in which to begin running my fall season beaver traps. I agree with you. I have felt for the last few days we ought to be out running our fall trapping line and see what our hard work will bring us," said Buck Snort with a happy grin to finally be beginning what they came all this way out in the damn middle of nowhere to do.

Upon hearing support from Buck Snort regarding the start of their fall trapping season, Muskrat looked over at Clem as he began removing the

Dutch ovens from their beds of coals, dusting the coals and ash from off their lids, then lifting the lids and checking inside for the biscuit degree of 'doneness' he was looking for.

"Clem, you might add some extra buffalo meat on those spits. I say that because today we start running our fall beaver trapping line and that being the case, it may just be a long day for the lot of us," said a grinning Muskrat, also pleased to once again be doing what he loved doing.

Upon hearing those words, Clem put the lids of the Dutch ovens back down so the biscuits would stay warm, grabbed up a long-bladed butcher knife from off his nearby split-log cooking table and walked over to the camp's meat pole. There with a couple of deft swipes with his knife, Clem was on his way back holding up a long chunk of buffalo backstrap meat saying, "Will this do, Muskrat?"

Muskrat just grinned over his friend's antics and gave him a 'thumb's up'. Then Muskrat turned to look over to see if Buck Snort agreed over the size of the slab of buffalo meat now being cut up in preparation for being spitted over the fire, only to see his friend heading for the corral. There Buck Snort met Wind Horse coming out from the aspen grove and after a short conversation, both men headed for the nearby storage shed like two men on a mission.

Soon Buck Snort and Wind Horse were hauling down three sets of panniers, clanking armloads of steel St. Louis-style beaver traps made by their friend and blacksmith back at the orphanage Cliff Fulton, breechclouts and buckskin leggings and other gear needed to carry out their beaver trapping enterprise. Then as Wind Horse began filling two panniers with 4'-long dry willow poles that had been cut from a dense willow patch several weeks earlier, Buck Snort loaded all of their beaver traps into another pannier along with the rest of the needed beaver trapper gear, axes, bottles of castor and the like.

About then Clem yelled at the men that breakfast was ready and that brought the always hungry men to the firepit area without delay. There the men gathered up their metal plates, forks and coffee cups and sat down upon the 'sitting logs' that had been cut, hauled down from off the hillside and placed around the firepit for seating when the men had finished cutting all of the logs needed for building their cabin. Then as Clem cut off portions of the buffalo meat from the metal spit rods hanging over the open flame, the men eagerly extended their plates for the much anticipated medium-rare roasted meat and the several piping hot Dutch oven biscuits that followed. Then it was each man for himself when it came to pouring their own cups of dark black boiling hot liquid called 'trappers' coffee', and soon the only sounds heard were the men doing what hungry men did best when out in the wilds of the northern Frontier doing what they enjoyed…

Later that morning, led by the group's very accurate shooter, Muskrat was followed by Buck Snort and Wind Horse trailing three heavily loaded packhorses carrying panniers brimful of equipment, corked bottles of castor (an oily smelling liquid used to lure beaver to the trap — called 'castoreum' in the days of the fur trappers during the early to middle 1800's), 30 five-pound beaver traps, 4'-long dry wooden anchor poles to hold beaver traps in place, and clothing to be worn when moving into and out of the cold beaver trapping waters. Of note were two fully loaded extra rifles in the first horse's pannier just in case extra firepower was needed in case of an Indian attack. Rifles which were so placed as Cliff had instructed, after giving Buck Snort and Wind Horse a survival lecture back at Manuel Lisa's Emporium regarding Indians' penchant for attacking white trappers in superior numbers requiring more than just one shot or two to keep them at bay… Last in the caravan of fur trappers rode Clem. A previous buffalo hunter of note, who was like his long-time friend Muskrat, the kind of accurate rifle shooter a bad person only messed with one time! And by riding last in the line of trappers, provided just the right kind of protection needed in Indian country, especially when attacking Indians traditionally liked to strike the last in line in a caravan of trappers because of the historical confusion that always seemed to generate…

After about a 40-minute ride north along the Bighorn towards its mouth on the Yellowstone River, the men finally stopped. There with the Yellowstone in sight, the men stopped and after making sure there were no signs of danger close at hand, separated. Muskrat, the avowed best shooter in the group, rode off onto some high ground a short distance away from the rest of his fur trapper comrades. There holding the high ground where he could watch all around his compatriots and himself, he tossed his leg over the front of his saddle so he would be more comfortable and then cradling his rifle, kept a close watch over his friends busily laying out beaver traps below.

Down below along the Bighorn in among a series of beaver ponds, Buck Snort and Wind Horse dismounted and handing their riding horses' reins back to Clem who was also dismounted, walked over to one of their packhorses' panniers. There both men removed their warmer woolen pants and pistols and slipped into a breechclout and buckskin leggings to be worn when walking around in the cold beaver waters and muddy environments. Then each man grabbed a dried anchor pole, a heavy beaver trap, a small hammer and began walking along the muddy waterways looking for any signs of fresh beaver slides. As they did, Clem leading the men's horses followed along on foot so the panniers holding all of the needed trapping materials would be readily available to the two men doing all of the wet and cold work of beaver trapping.

Since Wind Horse had only accompanied and assisted his father who had done all of the beaver trapping in his family in earlier years, Buck Snort set about teaching him the correct way to trap beaver as he had been taught years earlier by his farmer neighbor, Chuck Curry. With Wind Horse in tow, Buck Snort stopped along a fresh beaver slide dotted with all kinds of recently made beaver tracks and numerous dropped leaves in the slide area from branches cut and dragged back into the water for consumption. "Watch what I do, Wind Horse, and I will teach you how is the best way to catch a beaver as was taught to me. This is the kind of beaver slide to look for with fresh wet mud, freshly dropped leaves from brush the beaver are dragging back to their houses or cache sites and plenty of fresh footprints in the muddy slide area. Then when you find a good example such as this one, find a good solid piece of bottom immediately adjacent the slide area in about four inches of water. Note how I set the trap by laying the jaws open by depressing the springs on the side and then set the 'dog' into this here piece called a 'pan'. Then I carefully set the open trap on the solid piece of ground that was just selected. Now hand me that wooden anchor pole. Note that it is dry and not a green stick or anchor pole. I use dry wooden anchor poles because sometimes a trapped and

desperate beaver will chew through a green anchor pole in order to escape. So far I have yet to
have a beaver chew his way through a dry pole
and that is why that is what I use. Now run the
end of the trap's chain out into the deeper water
and be careful not to drag the open and ready
to go trap off the solid piece of ground where it
is setting. Once I get to the end of this 6' chain
out into deeper water, I take my wooden anchor
pole and carefully thread it through the end of
the trap's chain in the "O" ring. Then taking my
hammer, drive the anchor pole into the bottom
of the pond."

Then walking back to the area where he had set
the trap on a solid bottom spot, Buck Snort continued his trap setting lesson by saying, "Now
watch what I am about to do." Taking his hand,
Buck Snort swirled the water vigorously around
the beaver trap until the water all around the
open-faced trap was swirling with muddy water.
"Now look," said Buck Snort, as he pointed to
a beaver trap perfectly hidden with a slight film
of mud from all of the muddy water just being
swirled around and above the trap. "Now see,
any arriving beaver will not see the trap and shy
away from it," continued Buck Snort with a devious grin.

"Now here is the slickest part when it comes
to trapping beaver," he continued, as he walked
over to a pannier and withdrew a corked glass
bottle full of a yellowish-looking liquid. Taking

his sheath knife, Buck Snort cut a 3'-long green willow limb from a nearby bush and then with the blade of his knife, carefully removed all of the green bark around the slender limb. "Note that I removed all of the green bark from this here willow limb which a beaver likes to eat. That way, all he sees is a bare limb and won't eat what he sees. Now, uncork the bottle of castor and just dip the end of this willow twig into the liquid. Then re-cork the bottle so this damn stuff does not spill because it is damn expensive. Notice that I now stick the other end of the willow twig into the bank so the end with the castor is just over the pan of your hidden trap. Now, beaver are very territorial and don't want any other beaver other than those of his own 'kin' in the same beaver pond. Plus, they have very good noses. Now you and I can't really smell this castor stuff but a beaver can smell it from many yards away because they have such great noses! When any beaver smells this castor which came from a different beaver, he will come right over in order to see who the new beaver is in his territory. In so doing, the beaver will swim right up to the end of this twig holding the castor on the end of it, drop his feet down, stand up, reach up and pull the twig with the strange castor on the end of it right to his nose for a better smell. When he drops his feet, hopefully one or both are in the trap. When that happens and the trap slams shut, the beaver in panic will swim away from where the trap caught him and will continue swimming away towards the deeper water until he gets to the end of the trap's chain held in place by our dried wooden pole anchor. Then he can go no further because he is caught in the trap and is at the end of the anchored trap's chain. However, he is still in pain and in a state of panic. As such, he will continue swimming until he is exhausted. Then the five-pound weight of this trap will eventually drag him under in the deeper water when he becomes too exhausted to keep swimming and then he will sink and drown. There you have it on how to set a beaver trap and hopefully you will have beaver in your trap sets at the end of the day," said Buck Snort with a big grin working with Wind Horse, who was more like a brother than just his best friend.

"Now, you take a trap and walk around this pond until you find a good and fresh beaver slide like the one I just showed you. Then you set your trap and I will watch and give you advice on how better to do it if it is required. Then once you have this beaver trapping 'thing' down pat, you will be on your own as will I and between the two of us, we will catch the hell out of the beaver. Then come summertime, hopefully we will have so many beaver *'Plus'* that when we get to Fort Henry and trade them in, we can make a lot of money," said a smiling Buck Snort.

Then turning, he said, "Now once we have a dead beaver, we will remove it from our traps, bring it to shore and since Clem and Muskrat have trapped beaver before, Clem will do the skinning right here on the spot as we continue running and checking the rest of our trap line. Now, for a change of pace, we will cook and eat some of the bigger beaver that we catch today because they are damn good eating. But for the most part, we will leave their carcasses right along this waterway for all the other critters to eat instead of taking all of them back to our cabin. Because if we haul all of these carcasses back to our cabin we are just inviting trouble. And when I say trouble, after a while having all of the black and grizzly bears in the country plus the wolves smelling all those carcasses, they will come a-calling and that will cause us a whole lot of trouble."

For the next hour or so, Buck Snort worked with Wind Horse as he put into practice the fine art of beaver trapping as Buck Snort had so shown and instructed. Finally seeing that Wind Horse had the beaver trapping 'thing' down pat, the two men continued 'leap-frogging' each other as they walked along the beaver waters locating fresh slide areas and setting their traps. By around noontime, the men had indeed set all 30 of their beaver traps. Then hailing in Muskrat from his 'distant perch' watching over the three trappers working along the beaver waters below with a yell and wave of his arm, the four men rode over to a distant aspen grove, dismounted and led their horses a short way inside the cover the grove offered. There the men let their horses graze as they sat down along the edge of the aspen grove so they could watch their back trail for any signs of discovery and subsequent danger. That they did because they were riding shod horses in a country where the Indians rode primarily unshod horses. And if the Indians ever rode across a shod horse's trail such as the trappers were leaving, they more than likely would track that trail out to see who the rider was. Then if the riders on the shod horses were those of white trappers deep in hostile Indian country, well, those trappers had better have fast horses or be accurate rifle shooters...

Finally after relaxing in the weak afternoon sun and eating a mess of great tasting and rich buffalo jerky, the men, one by one, found they were drifting off to sleep where they lay comfortably in a deep bed of dry aspen leaves. After a couple hours of sleep because the men had been up since before dawn, they were awakened after Buck Snort passed some of his signature gas from a messed-up digestive system which had been seriously damaged after being poisoned earlier back at the orphanage. When he did pass some gas, that awoke everyone with a start and when it did, Muskrat exclaimed with a big grin and an almost rolled-up nose, "Damn, I think a bull buffalo just crept into our campsite, crapped and then crept back out again!"

After the men's laughter had died down and an embarrassed Buck Snort tried apologizing, the men just kept on teasing him now that the air had cleared of the smell and then they gathered in their horses still laughing over the 'bull buffalo' statement made by Muskrat. As the men mounted up, Buck Snort thought back to that day at the orphanage when the three older boys led by Curtis put rat poison into everyone's breakfast oatmeal before they left the home to join the fur trade! Rat poison that almost killed Buck Snort after eating the oatmeal, leaving his insides so damaged that anytime he ate anything made from oats or wheat, like Clem's Dutch oven biscuits, it caused him to suffer great gas pains and created horrendous and almost stupefying smells. But here he was where he wanted to be and just figured 'there was more room on the outside than in his insides', so…

Being that the men were so far from their campsite and had seen so much beaver sign in the waters just trapped, they had decided to rest after setting so many traps and then checking them after a few hours after they had been set to see if they were successful. As they quickly discovered, it was a good thing that they had decided to check their traps on the way back to camp on the off chance they had caught a beaver or two…

Riding slowly back along their just set trap line, they discovered no beaver in their first eight traps set which were the last ones set in a 30-trap string. However, their next 22 traps each unbelievably held a beaver and most beaver found hanging dead in their traps proved out being what was called a "Made Beaver". (Author's Note: A "Made Beaver" in the fur trapping lingo of the day referred to an adult-sized beaver whose pelt was worth about $6!) The men could hardly believe their first morning's luck! True, they had seen a lot of fresh beaver sign and a goodly number of the critters swimming in the waters being currently trapped, but catching 22 beaver with just 30 traps was unheard of! In fact, they had so many large beaver to skin that every one of the trappers had to get involved in the skinning process or they were looking at riding home in the dark of night! Finally, by late afternoon, the men had finished skinning out all of their beaver except for the three they had kept for roasting come suppertime. Then Buck Snort reset all of their traps hoping for such a good day success-wise in the morrow. With that, the men washed their hands off in the beaver pond, mounted up onto their horses and then formed up into their usual protective fur trappers' caravan for the protection it offered for the return trip.

Somewhat later, the tired but damn happy men rode back into their campsite and while Clem skinned out the three remaining beaver they had brought back in the round to roast for their suppers, the other three men began de-fatting and hooping out the beaver pelts. When Clem finally had the trappers' supper ready of coffee, biscuits, beans and roasted beaver and had yelled out, "Suppertime", three very tired men emerged from their cabin covered in guard hairs, beaver fat and 'stink'!

After washing up in their nearby creek, the four tired men ate their supper in quiet silence, put their dirty dishes into the wash pan and re-treated back to their cabin to continue their monumental task of de-fatting and hooping the rest of their first day's catch of beaver pelts. When they did, Clem washed up the dishes, cleaned up and greased his precious cast iron, grabbed a full coffee pot of hot coffee because 'bedtime' looked like a long way off and headed for the cabin as well. For the remainder of that night and until first light, the four trappers under light from five beeswax candles and the light from the fire in their fireplace de-fatted and hooped the rest of the fresh beaver pelts!

Come daylight, a sleepy-eyed Clem staggered from the cabin, washed up in the creek and began making Dutch oven biscuit dough so it could rise and coffee for the men's breakfast. Just as the last man staggered out from the cabin after a long night of no sleep while they all had worked de-fatting and hooping all 22 beaver pelts, they all took care of a call of nature and then without washing their hands or faces, just headed for the cooking fire and a pot of more of Clem's strong coffee! By their second cup of strong 'trappers' coffee', coffee made stout enough to take the hide off an angry mule, the men collectively decided that running all 30 of their beaver traps was a bit much in light of the heavy beaver number found along their trap line! That being said, the men had decided they would only set 20 of their 30 beaver traps and pull the rest. Otherwise, none of them would be able to get any sleep and if any Indians attacked them when they were afield, all four trappers would just be killed as they slept in their saddles at the rate they were going having to stay up all night de-fatting and hooping beaver pelts! (Author's Note: In the "Journals of Lewis and Clark", it was mentioned that the number of beaver encountered during their long journey were so numerous, that their men if hungry could just grab a stick, walk over to any beaver water and knock a beaver in the head! This proved to almost be the case, especially in the area of the Rocky Mountains until about 1835, when signs of over-trapping were then being felt in the beaver populations and their number sadly had diminished to the point that they never again felt such greatness of numbers, not even to this day.)

That morning after breakfast, four damn sleepy trappers exited their campsite and headed for a large patch of willows along the Bighorn. As it turned out, that morning they were trailing a fourth packhorse with panniers, and a short time later found all four men cutting willow limbs from the willow patch so they would have more 'hooping' material for the anticipated evening's large haul of beaver pelts. By the end of day two, the trappers had discovered 25 beaver in their 30 beaver traps! Seeing those kinds of catch numbers, they pulled ten of their 30 traps. That they did to reduce the work needed de-fatting the skins and then having to hoop them so they could eventually dry out and be made ready for packing into bundles. That night it was just biscuits and coffee for their supper as it became necessary for 'all hands on deck' when it came to caring for all of that day's fresh pelts. Once again, the trappers found themselves up until the wee hours of morning before finally having cared for all of the 25 pelts just harvested the second day of fall beaver trapping!

By day three of their trapping efforts on the Bighorn, none of the men had recently shaved, washed up or even combed their hair. Once again after a rather skimpy breakfast of just buffalo jerky, the men rode out from their campsite in their usual order and headed once again for an already almost denuded willow patch. Filling up the spare packhorse's panniers with more willow limbs for the hooping process, the men headed for their trap line. By now, only Buck Snort was setting and checking the traps as Clem and Wind Horse now had skinning duties in order to keep up with the flow of beaver being harvested. And once again, the men decided that 20 traps were a bit much and that number was further reduced to just 15 traps being run because of the number of beaver in the areas being trapped and the trappers' successes in catching so many of the furry rodents every day!

Finally by the second week of trapping on the Bighorn, the number of trapped beaver dropped off as the trappers caught out the existing population in their first geographic area of trapping. Then the men moved further south along the Bighorn and laid out a new trap line with just 20 traps being used in another heavy in number beaver area. And once again, the four trappers found themselves up at all hours of the night in an attempt at staying ahead of the de-fatting and hooping process. Finally, the men 'sprang' all of their traps and just let them sit idle so they could take a day off and fold all of the previously dried beaver 'Plus' fur side in and bundle them 60 to a bundle, or about 90 pounds of dead weight per bundle. Then come summertime and the trip up to Fort Henry, the men would place two bundles on each packhorse or about 180 pounds of weight per animal for the trip. With all of the furs bundled up and placed into their storage shed, the men now had more living space back in their cabin now that the numerous hooped and drying furs had been removed, bundled and were now stored in their storage shed.

Following that, the men took another day away from trapping being tired of just biscuits and coffee for their breakfasts and went buffalo hunting. There they killed a young cow buffalo, butchered her out and brought her best parts back in the panniers. There minus what was needed for a special supper that evening, the rest was hung on the meat pole so it could cool out and glaze in the late fall air. Come that evening, Clem went all out when he prepared the men's supper. There was spitted buffalo meat (medium-rare of course, a trappers' favorite), coffee, Dutch oven biscuits, a big pot of beans loaded with red pepper flakes and lastly, a Dutch oven apple cobbler made from dried and soaked apple slices, loads of raisins, a cup of rum, a world of cinnamon and brown sugar! After supper that evening, the trappers broke out the rum and a carrot of tobacco and lounged around their campfire drinking and smoking their clay pipes in celebration of the good beaver trapping luck they had experienced to date. It was then in light of their trapping successes that Muskrat said, "I always did say them Indians had good sense and a touch of the spirits riding on their shoulders. Just think back to when we all came out this far and Wind Horse advised we needed to go one river further. Well, here we are and complaining about all the work we have been doing because we have caught so many beaver. Just goes to show them Indians aren't all wrong..."

There were lots of smiles over the wise words and truth just spoken about by Muskrat. Also,

Wind Horse just smiled inwardly over his wise choice of river systems as well. Later that night when the rum had its desired effect and the last pipefuls of tobacco had been smoked and their ashes knocked out from the bowls of their pipes, everyone went quietly to their sleeping furs and the darkened trappers' cabin shortly thereafter only sounded of four men of the wilderness in a deep and welcoming sleep...

Daylight the next morning found Clem hard at his breakfast making chores as the rest of the men washed up in the creek, shaved and took care of their calls of nature. Then the men, now rested up, looked forward to starting up their trap line once again to see what kind of luck they would once again have as they headed for their sitting logs around the campfire. After a breakfast of spitted buffalo steak, Dutch oven biscuits and coffee, the men saddled up and rode out from their campsite for a new willow patch. There they once again filled up a packhorse's two panniers full of fresh green willow limbs to be used in the coming evening's hooping activities and then headed out for their new trap line.

Arriving somewhat later, Buck Snort and Wind Horse went through their daily ritual of undressing and dressing into their breechclouts and buckskin leggings, grabbed up their needed trapping gear and headed for their previously sprung beaver traps. Once again, the men re-set their 20 beaver traps and re-scented their lure willows with castor and upon finishing, mounted up and then headed for a distant cottonwood grove. Upon their arrival, they rode their horses deep into the timber to avoid any chance discovery by Indians in the area. This they did because all morning long the trappers had been riding across a number of unshod pony tracks in and around where there had once been a small herd of buffalo. So to avoid any dangerous inadvertent discovery, the men had ridden into the cottonwoods deeply enough where they would remain unseen but still be able to watch their back trail from the cover of the trees just in case.

After eating a mess of their great tasting buffalo jerky and having a running conversation among each other, the trappers as was their routine, lay back and were soon fast asleep while their horses quietly grazed in and around them in the stand of cottonwoods. In the back of his mind in a dream world, Buck Snort, ever the light sleeper after being poisoned back at the orphanage, heard what sounded to him in the annals of his mind like the faraway recognition whinny of a horse. A recognition whinny of a horse more than likely smelling the nearness of the trappers' horses feeding in the cottonwood grove! Upon that, he awoke with a start figuring one of their horses had wandered off from the grove of cottonwoods and was now somewhere out on the open prairie 'in front of God and everybody'.

Looking all around but not moving his body until he decided it was safe to do so, Buck Snort all of a sudden heard the voices of distant Indians! When he did, out of the excitement of the moment and the cold gripping fear that came with the close in proximity sounds of Indians' voices, his intestines began doing flip flops. Soon, he found his body involuntarily releasing clouds of the worst kinds of gas possible! But that aside, he had now rolled over and looking out through the stand of cottonwood trees could see about a dozen mounted Indians curiously peering into the grove of trees holding the four trappers! To Buck Snort he could see that they were sitting on their horses on the same ground he and his fellow trappers had just ridden over with their shod horses! Then it became plain to Buck Snort that the Indians had discovered the shod tracks from the white man's horses and had followed them to the grove of trees looking for their riders!

"PSSSST, PSSSST," went Buck Snort, and soon he had awakened the rest of the trappers who all had now quietly rolled over onto their bellies and were nervously fingering their rifles from their hidden positions in the grove of cottonwoods as they watched the deadly and numerically superior Indian menace themselves now trying to figure out what to do next.

"Damn, Buck Snort. You sure picked a fine time to crap your pants," whispered Clem who was lying alongside the trapper making all the terrible smells! "Boy, if they can't smell that terrible smell, then those Indians are dead men riding!" continued Clem in a gagging whisper. Then Buck Snort could hear Clem gagging under his breath even more as he got a new sniff of Buck Snort's latest nervous passing of gas...

Buck Snort then heard Muskrat whisper, "Buck Snort, let us hope them Indians' horses get a whiff of that essence of dead skunk you are passing around and decide to move along. Otherwise with all of them finding us lying here, there soon will be one hell of a lot of killing!" With those words leaving Muskrat's lips and almost as if on command, one could hear four ominous metallic clicks as the trappers' flintlock rifles were brought to full "cock" and ready for 'business' should the need arise!

Then all of a sudden, it became obvious the Indians had just gotten a whiff of Buck Snort's gaseous 'masterpiece' as well! When they did, suddenly all of the Indians were holding their noses or rolling up their faces in disgust and their horses were now nervously moving around having taking in a great snootful of Buck Snort's 'Frontier Delight' as well! Then all of a sudden one Indian shouted out in alarm, "YAH TAH HAY! GREAT BEAR! I SMELL A GREAT BEAR IN THAT GROVE OF TREES!" With that and afraid of the killing power and the difficulty in bringing down an aroused grizzly bear with the weapons of the day, the Indians whirled their horses around and sped away from the cotton-wood grove realizing the bear when enraged could even outrun the fastest of their horses... So as not to disturb an obvious grizzly in its day bed in the trees based on the intense smell coming from that location and with the shod horse hoofprints they had been following earlier now forgotten, the terrible odor alone emanating from the trees managed to drive off the curious and highly superstitious Indians!

For the longest time the outnumbered trappers just lay in the cottonwoods waiting to see if the Indians would return. After about an hour and with no further sign of the Indians, the trappers mounted their horses and cautiously rode back along their previously set trap line of just 20 traps. And once again, a dead beaver hung in almost every trap when the trappers made a quick inspection of the recently set trap line! Kind of out in the open and with their latest 'scrape' with Indians still on their minds, Muskrat and Clem decided they would both stand guard with Wind Horse doing all of the skinning and Buck Snort, now having gotten over his gas events back in the grove of cottonwoods, checking all of the men's traps. Seventeen beaver later, the trappers tossed their last beaver pelt into a pannier. Still on high alert because of their earlier incident with the Indians, the trappers headed for their campsite using a handy treeline to ride along the edge of for the cover it offered and the defensive cover it would provide if discovered and attacked.

However, the 'Gods of Luck' were not on their side and the trappers never made it home that afternoon without a little 'excitement'... Somewhat later there before the trappers right in their line of travel, were about 100 Indians, men, women and children on the prairie with all of their horses and travois. They had just completed a buffalo hunt and were now in the process of skinning and butchering out about 40 downed animals. Quickly lying up in another grove of trees, this time aspens, the trappers dismounted, watched and waited until the last Indian pulling a travois loaded with fresh buffalo meat disappeared slowly off to the east. Waiting to make sure all of the Indians were now long gone, the trappers finally were able to continue on their line of travel back to their campsite. There once again under candlelight and the light from their fireplace, all four of the trappers de-fatted and hooped out their 17 fresh beaver pelts. Once again after a long night and into the morning, the trappers finally finished their de-fatting and hooping work and then tiredly and without any supper, retired to their sleeping furs for what few hours they could sleep before they had to check their trap line once again the coming day.

The following morning with the trappers being short on sleep, they all slept in. Awakening mid-morning and realizing they were late for checking their trap line, the men skipped a formal breakfast and began saddling their horses and pack animals while eating just buffalo jerky. Finally saddled up and in their usual protective caravan line, the men exited their campsite and with the narrow escape from the day before still fresh in everyone's minds, rode along the edge of a line of deep timber for the cover it offered en route the location of their distant trap line.

Somewhat later, the men left the covering treeline and headed for a distant line of willows growing alongside a huge beaver pond adjacent the Bighorn River. Once there, they dismounted and began hurriedly cutting willow limbs for the anticipated hooping of beaver pelts come evening time. However, not finding enough of the right-sized willow limbs used in hooping their usual harvest of Made Beaver pelts, the men moved on towards a distant and larger dense patch of willows. In so doing, the trappers rode along the previous day's buffalo kill site initiated by the Indians. As they did, the trappers observed a pack of wolves helping themselves to a buffalo's remains along with a huge number of coyotes, ravens, crows and black-billed magpies helping themselves to the meat scraps around a number of other buffalo carcasses as well.

Wanting to talk with Muskrat over what they were observing over at the recent buffalo kill site, Clem rode forward of the caravan and up to and alongside his friend. As those two rode along talking and keeping an eye on the nearby pack of wolves tearing into a buffalo's intestinal remains, Muskrat turned and with a broad grin said, "Buck Snort, did you crap in your buckskins once again?"

Following along behind the two riders in front of their little caravan, Buck Snort just shook his head quizzically over why Muskrat had just asked. First of all, he had not passed any gas seeing they only had jerky for breakfast which did not usually give him any gas and secondly, the wind was softly blowing out from the northwest and he and Wind Horse were in the rear of the caravan further to Muskrat's southern position. About then the trappers reined up alongside the patch of willows where they had been heading to finish filling the packhorse's remaining pannier with stouter willow limbs used for hooping the largest of their beaver pelts. Just as they stopped, Buck Snort could now smell a strong smell that Muskrat must have just smelled earlier. With that, Wind Horse said, "Muskrat, that strong smell is either coming from you or Clem because it is coming from your direction."

"URRRGHHH—URRRGHHHH!" roared a grizzly bear just awoken by the men's voices from his day bed in the willows, after having fed most of the night in the field of Indian-killed buffalo remains. "CRASH-CRASH-CRASH!" went the sounds of a willow thicket being torn asunder as the great bear, a huge boar weighing close to 900 pounds, exploded from the cover of the willows where he had been sleeping off a great dinner of freshly killed buffalo and SLAMMED RIGHT INTO THE SIDE OF CLEM'S HORSE AND CLEM! Instantly, already nervous over the earlier smells of the great bear that had wafted by the trappers' caravan of horses which had been mistakenly blamed upon Buck Snort, the trappers' entire horse caravan EXPLODED INTO AN INSTANT 'RODEO'! This they did upon seeing the enraged bear exploding out from the cover of the willow patch right alongside the trappers' caravan and attacking!

Wind Horse was bucked off and tossed under Buck Snort's horse's hooves as it too was exploding out of extreme fear from the CLOSE AT HAND angry charge of a monster in size grizzly bear! That was the last thing Wind Horse remembered after being kicked in the head by one of Buck Snort's horse's hooves! Buck Snort was luckily bucked off from his now terrified horse in such a manner that he was able to land on his feet and hit running away from the bear's violent charge. Muskrat on the other hand riding alongside Clem was instantly 'PAW SLAPPED' off his now in extreme terror rearing horse trying to get away from the grizzly bear, and was HURLED a good 20 feet before he hit the ground with a hard "THUMP"! However, Clem was directly in 'the line of fire' from the madly exploding grizzly bear moving with the speed of a hard charging bull buffalo and suffered the consequences!

Slamming into the side of Clem's horse, Clem

had the bear's huge jaws clamp down upon his right thigh and was 'HEAD-SLUNG' off his horse and into the patch of willows from whence the bear had emerged after being suddenly awakened by the sounds of men's voices! As for Clem's horse, a vicious 'PAW SLAP' from the great bear broke its neck with a LOUD BONE SNAPPING "CRACK" and down it went, with the bear immediately leaping upon it and then biting down upon the now dead horse's head with a 'LOUD CRUNCH'!

BOOM! went Buck Snort's rifle and a microsecond later, a round caliber .52 soft lead ball slammed into the back of the great bear's head, which was still in the process of mauling the head of Clem's horse! When Buck Snort fired, he was so close to the maddened grizzly that the flame from the end of the barrel from his flintlock rifle burned most of the hair off the bear's head and the speeding lead ball passed clear through the angry animal's head, then through the dead horse's head and finally into the ground on the other side! Now the smell in the air was that acrid smell of burned black powder, the strong smell of a panicked horse's urine, the often rank smell of a grizzly bear and now, Buck Snort could take the blame for another bad smell being emitted into the air because of the emotion of the moment...

Then for the next few moments, the only sounds that could be heard in the area were those of the calls from the frightened off flocks of ravens and crows that just moments earlier had been feeding contentedly on a number of dead buffalo remains... That and a sound of a ramrod being hurriedly used as it was in the reloading process of tamping down into a rifle barrel a greased rag and another caliber .52 lead ball! That was followed with the sounds of a powder horn hurriedly placing a powder charge in the priming pan just in case the willow patch held another dangerous surprise.

That was followed with the yell from Buck Snort over to a limping his way, all the while using his rifle as a walking stick, Muskrat. Seeing that Muskrat would more or less be alright, Buck Snort ran over to his dear friend Wind Horse, knelt down and laying his rifle down, picked up and cradled the man's head in his lap. A soft groan soon followed and then Wind Horse's eyes flew WIDE open and he said, "Who shot me?" Seeing and hearing that his friend was more or less going to be alright, he raised him up into a sitting position and then grabbing up his rifle, Buck Snort ran over to the willow patch into which he had earlier observed Clem being violently 'grizzly bear head-tossed'!

Crashing into the willow patch, Buck Snort soon found his friend Clem holding his thigh and loudly groaning and cussing all in the same breath in pain! Quickly kneeling by his friend, Buck Snort could see that Clem was in a lot of pain but aside from the deep and madly bleeding puncture wounds on his leg from the vicious bite of the angered bear, it was thankfully not broken. Helping Clem to his one good leg, Buck Snort helped him to stagger out from the willow patch and laid him on the ground on the other side. About then, Muskrat showed up with a look of concern for his madly bleeding friend as well. Fortunately, when Wind Horse had been bucked off and kicked in the head, his hand holding the lead rope on his two packhorses had been in a death grip and as a result, he still had ahold of his two very nervous packhorses. Seeing that, Buck Snort walked over to the two still very nervous and 'grizzly bear' scared horses and retrieved his buckskin leggings from one of the animal's panniers. Then after calming down the horse a bit, he walked back to Clem and using a leg of his leggings, tightly bound up Clem's madly bleeding leg. Looking over at his friend Muskrat, Buck Snort's look of concern got the response, "I am alright. I just have one hell of a sore hip where I hit the ground and my back hurts like hell but other than that, I am alright," said Muskrat upon thankfully seeing that his friend Clem was also going to live.

About then Wind Horse staggered over to the group of men, still leading his two horses saying, "Damn, my head says it sure could use a cup of rum about now." Upon hearing those words, all the men hurting or not and relieved that everyone was more or less alright, broke out into laughter… It was at that moment in time in which Buck Snort quietly said, "Gentlemen, we have just experienced the power of nature and the fragility of life one can experience, if he chooses to make his living out here on the Frontier…"

It took a dinged-up in the head Wind Horse and Buck Snort the rest of the day to round up their frightened off horses from when the bear had attacked and then get everyone safely back to their cabin. Then the work began. Buck Snort being the basically undamaged party, got to be the group's 'Frontier Doctor' and began patching everyone up as best as he could. As for Wind Horse, he was the easiest. A wet rag dipped into their creek and wrapped around his still throbbing head was about all that Buck Snort could do to help him. Well, that and two cups of rum and a 'lay-down' on his sleeping blankets and not moving for a couple of hours did the trick. However, it took over a week for the blue-black looking lump on his head where he had been kicked before that went away. As for Muskrat, it was amazing what three cups of rum did for all of his aches and pains after being 'paw slapped' off his horse by the enraged grizzly bear and hurled a number of feet to a rather hard landing on the ground… However, Clem was another matter. Buck Snort had to squeeze his puncture wounds in order to get all of the coagulated blood to squirt out from the holes in his thigh and until deep red blood began flowing and cleaning out the wound! Suffice to say, Clem was not happy over that painful part of the 'Frontier Doctoring'. Then a cup of rum was sloshed over the wounded puncture area, followed by a generous amount of bag balm thoroughly rubbed into the wounds. Following that, the leg was loosely bound up with a swatch of their gray cloth normally used by the group to repair torn clothing and propped up in a chair to help relieve some of the pain. Then two cups of rum were 'ordered' for the 'Frontier Doctor' as well… That evening, rum and jerky was ordered for the 'wounded' but only after Buck Snort had turned loose all of their horses in the corral and the others so they could graze and water. However, all were hobbled before they were let loose for the evening to continue feeding in the horses' nearby meadow.

Early the next morning found Buck Snort fixing the men coffee, Dutch oven biscuits and spitted elk meat from their meat pole. Elk meat that smelled a little 'strong' but that was all the meat that was quickly available, so onto the metal spits it went and was just cooked longer… That morning, the trappers sitting on their sitting logs were a sight to see. Wind Horse's side of his face was black and purple in color where Buck Snort's horse had kicked him in the head when he had fallen under that horse's hooves and he could only see out from one of his eyes! As for Clem, he had a leg that was swollen and oozing lymph from the puncture wounds that did not smell very good. Muskrat's back and right hip were black and blue after being 'paw slapped' off his horse and landing some 20 feet away with a hard 'thump' but other than that he claimed to be as 'fine as frog hair'! However, Buck Snort noticed that every time Muskrat went for another cup of coffee or to refill his plate, he was moving very slowly and carefully. So much for feeling as 'fine as frog hair'…

After breakfast, everyone saddled up with the exception of Clem. He was just too stove up to comfortably ride, much less walk, so it was decided that he would stay home for a few days until he had healed up some. Then with Muskrat sitting gingerly in the saddle and in the lead, Wind Horse leading the pack animals and trying not to move his head very much and Buck Snort bringing up the rear of the trappers' caravan for the protection a rear guard provided, out from their campsite the sorry-looking group headed for their trap line. All that group of trappers typified that morning were perfect examples of what Buck Snort had said the day before about the 'power of nature and the fragility of life…'

Somewhat later out on their trap line as Muskrat sat horsed and on guard, Buck Snort disrobed and climbed into his 'beaver water' trapping gear. Having missed a day in running their trap line because of the group's run-in with the grizzly bear, Buck Snort soon discovered they

had several problems. One beaver found float-
ing dead in a trap had been fed upon by a river
otter and its pelt destroyed. Another beaver had
been partially eaten by what appeared to be a
bald eagle, and another beaver's pelt had been
destroyed by several feeding sharp-billed ravens.
Other than that, the remaining 12 dead beaver
found in their traps that morning appeared to be
alright and were reclaimed.

That day after resetting all of the sprung traps,
the trappers changed their normal routine.
Instead of resting up at the end of their trap line,
the men just headed home for some more rest so
they could continue recovering from the damage done to their bodies the day previously and
Buck Snort could tend to Clem's leg wounds. Of
note though on the ride back to their cabin was
the fact that when riding by the carcass of the
grizzly killed the day before, the men got some
satisfaction in what they saw. There feeding
upon the great bear's carcass was a sow grizzly
and her two sub-adult cubs... As for Clem's
dead horse, it had been dragged away from the
previous day's battle scene by what appeared
to be another grizzly bear into the dense willow
patch. No one looked any further to see what
had happened to Clem's horse after that as the
men and their horses gave that deadly willow
patch a wide berth...

For the next two weeks, the trappers operated
on a somewhat relaxed trapping schedule. They

ran less traps, did not check them immediately after setting them and continued resting more and getting additional sleep. Besides, every man was finding that they had caught so many beaver and the de-fatting work had been so rigorous, that the skin on every man's fingers had begun to split wide open and became inflamed... So much so that the constant use of their bag balm treating those painful wounds had almost used up their entire year's supply. Finally by week three after the bear incident at the willow patch, the full complement of trappers was once again back in their saddles and back to their old trapping routine in a rush to catch everything they could before winter's freeze-up.

Freeze-up did not come until late in the winter of 1822, but when it came it arrived overnight. As it turned out, that last morning of beaver trapping on the Bighorn in 1822, provided a damn good lesson in weather reading. When Buck Snort exited the cabin that last morning of fall beaver trapping he received a 'weather surprise'. When he stepped out from the cabin that morning late in November, he was met with a blast of warm air unusual for wintertime in the northern latitudes. In fact, had he a temperature gauge, he would have seen that the November morning's air was a warm 76 degrees! Realizing that was not even close to a normal temperature for November, he paused and then looked skyward. Far to the northwest he observed a huge build-up of ugly blue-black looking clouds. Then he noticed that the air was unusually literally clear full of birds of every kind known to humankind in huge flocks and scattered bunches, all heading southward as if their lives depended upon it and their tails were on fire…

Standing there in front of their cabin, Buck Snort continued looking skyward in amazement over all of the aerial activity. The air was literally clear full of loons, ducks, geese, cranes, hawks, owls and every other kind of bird ever made by God! Then he noticed that the trees around their cabin were literally alive with every kind of little bird flitting from tree to tree but all were fleeing in a southward direction. Then catching himself, Buck Snort took a look around their camp and observed that everyone from his group was also standing there in awe looking skyward at all of God's winged critters fleeing south as if the Creator had emptied out all of the air from the northern climes and in so doing, forcing all of the birds south in one massive migration!

After breakfast that morning as the men headed out from their campsite, they noticed that it seemed that every bit of available open water around them as they rode was home to literally hundreds if not thousands of bobbing ducks, coots, loons, geese and every other kind of waterbird resting upon the waters! Then the men noticed the number of beaver swimming upon the waters pushing out ahead of them or dragging behind them huge bunches of limbs and treetops of green foliage. Then once near their conical-shaped house in deeper water where the local moose could not go and rob their caches of green limbs and branches, diving down with their clippings and stashing them into the muddy bottoms of the ponds. Then it seemed the beaver once that chore was finished, headed back for more green aspen, cottonwood or willows in which to cut off and carry to their caches with a never before seen urgency.

Then as Buck Snort dressed down for his water immersions in checking and setting traps, he noticed Wind Horse looking skyward more and more frequently as if something was bothering him. Realizing the 'Sons of the Prairies' carried in their souls 20,000 years of wisdom and memories of what had occurred around them before the arrival of the white man, Buck Snort said, "Wind Horse, what are you sensing?"

Wind Horse whipped his head around not realizing others of his party had been watching him and sensing in him his unusual behavior. Then seeing everyone else looking at him, Wind Horse said, "Bad weather is coming. When all of the birds leave from the north where The Great Spirit lives, that is His way of warning all of His People to leave because danger is coming." Then without another word, he too changed into his beaver trapping gear, grabbed up what he needed from a horse's pannier and headed up along the men's trap line like nothing was out of the ordinary.

Also sensing something unusual was close at hand, Buck Snort said to Wind Horse, "Wind Horse, after checking your traps for any beaver they may be holding, pull them. I feel now is the time to pull our traps before freeze-up and we end up losing them in the mud."

Without turning, Wind Horse waved his hand in acknowledgment over what Buck Snort had advised and soon both men were clearing their traps of dead beaver and bringing the heavy and valuable traps back to the horses' panniers along with their catch of the day. Soon, all 20 of their traps had been pulled along with the 16 beaver they had caught. As they did, Buck Snort noticed that the water's surface which had been 'mirror' flat when they had arrived on their trapping grounds, now had ripples of weather change running across it… Buck Snort also noticed that the warm air from earlier in the morning was now getting decidedly cooler! That was especially so against his wet clothing. Finally finishing up with the work running their trap line and changing back into his warmer clothing back at the horses as Clem continued skinning out the latest catch, Buck Snort felt an ever-increasing colder chill settling over the land and in the air.

Waving Muskrat in towards the rest of the men because they were finished, Buck Snort noticed that the very waters they were working in and around were really loading up with what appeared to be hundreds of exhausted water-birds happily flopping down in safety regardless of the presence of the nearby humans. Shortly thereafter, Clem had finished skinning out beaver number 16 and when he did he exclaimed, "Damn, I should have brought out a jacket and my skinning fingers are now like ice!"

Looking skyward once again and not having done so when he was busy checking the traps and removing them as well as their anchor poles, Buck Snort observed that the air above him was now even more heavily crowded with birds of every sort and kind and every one of them seemed to be frantically heading south. Then he saw why there was such anxiousness to head south. The blue-black clouds observed earlier hanging ugly in the sky very far away to the northwest, were now almost overhead. And those clouds were roiling around and dropping ominously closer and closer to the ground, and now the wind was picking up even more as the clouds neared and it had a cold bite to it!

"We best get our hind ends back to our camp-site and bring a load of firewood into the cabin, for I fear we are looking at one hell of a 'blow' coming our way and we best not get caught out in it," said Muskrat as he continued looking skyward at Mother Nature now showing her true winter 'colors'!

By the time the men arrived back at their cabin,

the early morning's calmness had turned into a gale of icy cold winds. The temperature had easily dropped until it was at least 60 degrees colder than it had been in the morning and the air was heavy with an almost skin numbing moisture. By now, the ugly blue-black clouds were rolling around in the Heavens not far overhead and even the horses in the corral were moving nervously around and around in their corral. By the time the men had put all of their trapping gear into their storage shed and had brought numerous armloads of wood into their cabin, closed down their window coverings, built a fire in their fireplace and had moved inside for the protection and warmth it offered, it was 'two shades of hell' outside...

The temperature had now dropped at least 70 degrees from the early morning's warmth, the wind was blowing at least 30 miles per hour, snow was flying horizontal to the ground and an unreal darkness had come over the land by around three in the afternoon! The men, now safely back in their cabin realized they were facing the first blizzard of the season, and it had been a good thing Buck Snort had decided to pull all of their beaver traps, otherwise they would have lost a number of them into the mud. That night the men under the light from a number of their candles and light from the fireplace de-fatted and hooped all of the last beaver they had caught during the 1822 fall beaver trapping season. Later that night after all their pelting work was done and after a supper of Dutch oven biscuits, beans and coffee, the men broke out their cups of rum and celebrated. Celebrated as the winter winds howled around their built 'hell-for-stout' cabin. Later that night, Clem stoked up their fire with several Douglas fir logs for the long burning they offered and everyone headed off to their sleeping furs and blankets. Soon because of the deep tiredness felt by all of the men and the effects from the several cups of rum drunk earlier, they one by one drifted off into a deep sleep while the winds howled around the eaves of their cabin with reckless abandon.

The next morning, the trappers awoke to clear blue skies, a dead calm, two feet of drifted snow and a temperature hovering around ten degrees above zero. Winter had finally come to the Bighorn country with a vengeance. But for the men, they were secure and happy in the knowledge that in their storage shed and drying in their cabin, they had taken 447 mostly Made Beaver and the trapping lying ahead of them along the Bighorn still looked great for the much valued web-footed rodent! And the men now eagerly awaited the beginning of their oncoming wolf trapping season in the foothills and mountains surrounding them.

However, the four trappers' desire was not immediately forthcoming. For the next 23 days, blizzard after blizzard rolled from beyond the land of the north wind, stormed over the Rocky Mountains and slammed across the northern plains with a vengeance! The only good thing that came out from isolating the trappers to their cabin and immediate winter woodpile was the fact that because of such blizzard conditions, their 'meat market' was always close at hand. The vast herds of buffalo found in the area because of the deep drifts of snow in the lower areas frequented the windblown meadow upon which the trappers' horses fed on a daily basis. When that occurred, it was an easy kill in order to replenish their meat supplies. Additionally, when the blizzards howled like a nest of 'banshees', the buffalo moved into the grove of aspen timber in order to get out from the hellish winds, chilling temperatures and blowing and drifting snows. When that occurred and if low on their meat supplies, the trappers only had to stagger over to the immediate area of their horse corral and kill a near at hand buffalo and supper was soon 'served'!

But by doing that, an ugly problem quickly reared its savage head. The local wolves, many of them starving in light of the terrible winter storms, took to feasting on the recently killed and left behind buffalo carcasses near the horse corral and it soon became evident therein lay a dangerous problem! Wolves were not fussy if they ate buffalo or horse meat, and the trappers quickly found their buffalo hunting days in the grove of aspens were over if they wished to ride on a horse back to Fort Henry come summertime…

Finally, the winter's spate of savage blizzards quieted down and the men saddled up their riding horses and two packhorses and rode out into the heavily timbered country to their north and west in order to begin their wolf trapping season. There on the much wind-swept ridges and rolling hills heavily visited by the struggling buffalo, the men picked out a close at hand animal and killed it. After stripping out the backstraps, the men opened up the buffalo carcass and cleverly lay several toothed Newhouse #14 wolf traps in and around the gut pile and carcass. This they did hoping for a wolf too damn hungry to worry about some of the man smells associated with the carcass and forgetting its natural instincts of caution, 'discovered' the wrong end of a wolf trap! This buffalo killing and wolf trap setting routine the trappers religiously followed and soon the trappers' evenings were spent under the faint light from their candles and fireplace de-fatting and placing on split-log boards the unfortunate wolves' beautiful pelts so they would dry. Soon come late spring, the trappers had amassed 54 beautiful and valuable wolf pelts either stored in their storage shed or still drying inside their cabin!

Emerging in a hurry one morning to attend to an urgent call of nature, Muskrat yelled over at Clem who was in the process of making breakfast saying, "Clem, make a good breakfast. We need to ride clear over to Wolf Mountain and check those last eight wolf traps, pull them and call our wolf trapping for the spring over until the next coming winter wolf trapping season." Then Muskrat ran for the horse corral and realizing he could not make it, had to stop out in front of 'God and everybody' quickly drop his buckskins and 'squirt' out the previous evening's supper of beans laced with red pepper flakes and the rich rice 'delight' Clem had made in one of the Dutch ovens in their cabin's fireplace loaded with rice, brown sugar, several cups of run, several pounds of raisins and a liberal sprinkling of cinnamon! Then come breakfast, the rest of the trappers, aware of Muskrat's hasty cabin exit earlier, got to 'tar and feather him' with embarrassing laughter when everyone noticed that the black-billed magpies had spotted Muskrat's early morning 'delight' and were now helping themselves to Clem's once digested, rice special... And to make matters worse, Muskrat's 'bad dump' day was soon heading for the "Crapper", BIG TIME!

Riding out later that morning after breakfast, the trappers led by Muskrat headed for the last of their previously set wolf traps. That they did with intentions of this being the last wolf sets put out because of the fast approaching spring's warmer weather which would be taking the wolf pelts out from their prime. For the next hour, the men rode out across the country and as they did, managed to ride their horses around vast herds of buffalo, elk, antelope and several smaller herds of bighorn sheep. (Author's Note: Bighorn sheep were originally a prairie grassland species. However, due to overhunting by the Indians and later the white man for its excellent eating and supple hide once tanned, that species of big game was driven from the prairies into the mountains where under careful management they remain and flourish to this day in a number of western states.) The weather that morning was pleasant, warming and the sky cloudless, as the men rode the remaining few miles over to their last buffalo carcass with the surrounding wolf traps.

Finally the buffalo carcass with the remaining wolf traps surrounding it hove into the trappers' view. Letting out a loud "WHOOP!" of joy being this was their last wolf set for the season, Muskrat had his horse break out into a gallop as he raced for the much picked-over buffalo carcass and in the process, scaring off a number of happily feeding black-billed magpies from the carcass. The rest of the trappers, not seeing any wolves in their traps just continued riding forward laughing over Muskrat's happy antics.

Riding up to the buffalo's much picked-over carcass and careful to avoid the areas in which the trappers had set their wolf traps previously, Muskrat bailed off his horse, turned around facing the rest of his oncoming trapper friends and let out another "WHOOP!" of joy over the end of wolf trapping and of course, for being the first to race over to and arrive at the much chewed-upon buffalo's carcass. Then the still oncoming trappers saw Muskrat all of a sudden make the funniest- looking, all 'scrunched-up' face like he smelled something smelling as badly as had his 'magpie special' he had left over by the horse corral back at their camp...

"URRRGHHH—URRRGHHHH!" roared a just-awakened grizzly bear sleeping off a heavy meal of buffalo and lying unseen directly behind the huge buffalo's carcass! Instantly, Muskrat's horse broke for the safety of the distant camp's horse corral upon seeing a very savage and half-starved grizzly bear fresh from hibernation, frothing at its mouth and storming over the top of the carcass! Now standing dumbfounded just a few feet away from the charging terror stood a surprised and scared witless Muskrat over the absolute danger he had just disturbed sleeping in its day bed! Having no time to raise his rifle and shoot due to the bear being just a few feet away and realizing the futility of trying to kill such a savage beast from feet away, Muskrat dropped his rifle and sprinted for the nearby grove of aspens lying all around the buffalo's carcass!

Meanwhile, the still oncoming trappers, upon seeing the savage charge from the previously sleeping and now extremely pissed-off grizzly bear roaring out from behind the buffalo's carcass, jerked their now frightened horses away from the scene and galloped off a short distance away from the close at hand danger! When they did and without thinking, they had left Muskrat to his own resources as to how he was going to handle the situation dealing with a half-starved bear fresh out from hibernation and extremely pissed-off over being all of a sudden awakened by the voice of a nearby human…

Meanwhile 'back at the ranch', Muskrat was running for his life as he sprinted for a nearby grove of aspens into which he could run and maybe scale a tree and get away from the furious bear's charge, since he knew that adult grizzly bears could not climb trees because of their very long claws. Hearing the coughing and growling bear right behind him, Muskrat sprinted for a tall aspen tree hoping to get there before the bear overtook his madly fleeing carcass and made a meal of him! Reaching the aspen mere seconds ahead of the bear, Muskrat lunged for its lower branches, slammed into its trunk and found he was scrambling up the tree faster than a squirrel could climb! However, he was not fast enough… Just as Muskrat reached the topmost part of the nearest aspen, he felt a violent paw slap across his 'last part over the fence' that was unfortunately hanging down within reach at that very moment in time of his long-clawed attacker!

"YEOOW!" SCREAMED MUSKRAT, as the long-clawed grizzly bear, just an instant behind and below him as he scrambled up the lifesaving aspen, standing on his hind legs reached up and paw slapped him across his madly fleeing hind end! When the bear slapped Muskrat across his hind end, he tore out the rear end of his buckskins and left four 2"-deep gashes from its long claws clear across his bottom! When the bear had slapped Muskrat across his bottom, the impact of the bear's paw swipe damned near knocked him from his perch in the aspen. But in the terror of the moment and the nearness of death, Muskrat found he had the strength and iron grip to stay on his perch in the aspen, madly bleeding and badly damaged bottom or not!

BOOM — BOOM — BOOM! went the simultaneous sounds of three rifles firing at the great bear, as it madly tore off great slabs of white bark from the lower reaches of the aspen tree in its frustration over losing the chance to kill what had just disturbed its sleeping off a heavy meal of buffalo! The very first heavy meat meal the starving bear had eaten since it had emerged from its winter long hibernation. (Author's Note: Members of the bear family during hibernation lose around one-third of their body weight while sleeping, waiting for the arrival of spring. Suffice to say, when they emerge from such a long 'sleep', they are in a starving condition and extremely ill-tempered until they have eaten sufficient quantities of food.) Suffice to say, the straight-shooting fellow trappers, now recovered from their very near death experience when they had ridden up to the buffalo's carcass only to be surprised by the Frontier's most dangerous predator, managed to place three killing shots into the grizzly bear's neck and head. However, in the great bear's last moments of life, its teeth still tore at the offending aspen that had frustrated the animal's efforts at catching and killing what had surprised and disturbed it from its day bed after feasting on its first 'meat' meal in months...

Somewhat later after the three men had finally gotten Muskrat's hind end to basically stop bleeding by wrapping part of his buckskin shirt around his badly damaged bottom, the rest of the men surveyed the scene around the buffalo's carcass. There they discovered that two of their wolf traps previously placed around the buffalo's carcass had held wolves. That they knew because there were still wolves' feet in the traps and fur, blood and snot all around the trap site. As for the two wolves originally held in the traps, they had been killed and eaten by the starving bear down to their bony feet! Then Buck Snort got an idea to commemorate the occasion of Muskrat being too slow on the uptake. Walking back to the grizzly bear's carcass, Buck Snort removed his tomahawk from his belt sash and chopped off the feet of the great bear. Those were stuffed into a pannier of a very nervous packhorse smelling the nearness of the bear and then the four men made ready to head back to their campsite with their somewhat 'wounded' compatriot.

Shortly thereafter, the trappers pulled their valuable wolf traps after Muskrat had 'mounted' one of the packhorses because his horse had run off during the initial attack and rode back to their campsite. However as they did, they followed Muskrat's horse's tracks in the snow in order to make sure they recovered the valuable horse. However, as for Muskrat, he 'rode' all the way back by standing up with one foot in each pannier carried by the packhorse. That he did so as not to place his badly damaged, very tender and still bleeding damaged bottom onto a saddle in order to circumvent the pain such a jiggling ride would place against the damaged hind end as the horse 'rocked' and bounced along.

Finally back at their campsite, the trappers dismounted and helped a now very exhausted Muskrat after having 'ridden' all that way standing up in a pair of panniers! There Wind Horse and Clem helped Muskrat into their cabin as Buck Snort re-fired up their outside fire and placed a large kettle on the hanging rods over the fire in order to get its water boiling. As he did, Wind Horse and Clem helped Muskrat undress from the waist down and lay on his belly over the top of their eating table inside their cabin. Then Wind Horse built a fire inside their fireplace in preparation for the 'Frontier Doctoring' soon to come... However, knowing what was to come and it would be nothing short of very painful, Clem opened up one of their kegs of rum and saw to it that his friend Muskrat began drinking deeply from the several offered cups of the 100 proof liquid anticipating the embarrassing 'discomfort' that was soon in coming...

Finally Buck Snort's kettle of water previously placed over the outside firepit was steaming away in the cool of the afternoon. With that, Buck Snort lifted it from the hanging rods, walked over to their cabin and walked inside. By now, Muskrat, waiting for the 'Doctoring' water to boil had gulped down four cups of rum and was in fine fettle. Then Buck Snort, the one who had been given the chore as a very young man back on his farm before it had burned down, the job of repairing cat, dog, horse and cattle bodily injuries because of his deftness with a needle and thread, 'drew the short straw'! Preparing himself for the unpleasant but necessary work that was soon to come regarding his badly injured friend Muskrat, Buck Snort drew a 'rum ration' as well...

Making sure Clem and Wind Horse were gently holding Muskrat face down, a man who was now softly singing church songs to himself he was so deeply into his 'rum cups', Buck Snort began doing what he had to do. First he used some of the hot water he had boiled over the outdoor fire and began carefully washing off Muskrat's bloodied backside. That took some doing because a lot of blood had coagulated and dried all over his rump. That meant he had to rub and scrub vigorously in order to remove all of the caked blood, which inadvertently caused even more blood to flow! When he did and then the warm water was applied to the badly damaged tissue, Muskrat humped up and made a loud groan as the damaged tissue was once again highly irritated! But Wind Horse and Clem gently held him down so he could not move. And now, Muskrat had gone from singing softly old church songs he had learned as a young man to drunken loud cussing everyone over what they were doing to him and his badly damaged 'last part over the fence'!

Finally getting all the dried, coagulated and caked blood removed, Buck Snort had to take his razor sharp sheath knife and dry shave all the hair off Muskrat's backside so he could completely close up the slashes in the wounded area without any rump hair getting into the closures and causing infections! When Buck Snort did the 'Barber of Seville' part of the operation, that of course jiggled and opened and closed the badly ripped tissue to the point Muskrat was now drunkenly advising he was going to kill anyone who further 'messed' with his backside… Clem and Wind Horse made sure that did not happen but they now knew if they were to let the muscular Muskrat go so he could get up off the table upon which he now lay, even for a second, there would be a first class fight in the offing! Then Buck Snort took some of their valuable rum and poured it liberally into the savagely ripped and open tissue... When he did, Muskrat went from softly singing Methodist church songs to loudly swearing like a drunken sailor, then to howling like a timber wolf with his 'man parts' caught in one of the trappers Newhouse #14 wolf traps, over the pain he was NOW feeling coming from the area of his backside!

By now, Buck Snort was sweating profusely over what he was doing to his dear friend like a traveling circuit 'preacher at election time'! Then Buck Snort wiped off the excess rum from the open tears in the flesh and deeply rubbed in some of their bag balm to aid in the healing process. With that application of the thick mixture into the open wounds, that action had Muskrat almost coming up off the kitchen table had not Clem and Wind Horse been holding him down with the weight of their two upper torsos lying directly over the back of their now highly agitated 'patient'. By then, both Clem and Wind Horse were also sweating at having to hold down the muscular, 6'-5" tall, 260-pound Muskrat, who was by then going to kill everyone within reach if he ever got up off the 'operating table'. And that included any of the nearby herds of buffalo watching on and laughing at what was happening up at the trappers' cabin...

Then it was time to get down to the 'brass tacks' of the most painful part of the 'Frontier surgery'! Buck Snort removed one of their leather sewing awls and a roll of the twine from a nearby shelf. Items that the trappers used to tie the beaver trap chain's "O" ring to an anchor pole, or lash the fresh beaver pelts to the willow hooping limbs. Taking the large leather awl, Buck Snort laid its point into the very edge of the fireplace's fire coals so it could heat up. When it glowed 'red', he removed the handle holding the needle from the coals and laid it down on the table until it had cooled. Then he threaded one end of the twine from a spool into the eye of the leather needle and cut off a length that he figured would be needed to sew up the entire first slash of the bear claw-ripped tissue across Muskrat's behind.

By now, Wind Horse and Clem were looking at Buck Snort like a 'robin in the spring would look at a nearby worm'… "Are you sure you know how to do this?" asked Muskrat's close friend Clem, in a high-pitched voice showing extreme emotion over the part he was being forced to play in the rather 'delicate' 'Frontier Doctoring' taking place on his closest of friends…

"Sure do," said Buck Snort, as he used the sleeve of his buckskin shirt to wipe the sweat from his brow. "Been doing this on every horse on my old farm and every udder-ripped milk cow since I was nine."

Then with those 'medical qualifications' and work-hardened hands, Buck Snort grabbed the first bear-slashed piece of 'meat' on Muskrat's hind end, squeezed the two pieces of hind end meat together and jabbed the coarse leather needle through the two sides of the ripped tissue!

"YEEEE—HO-WOOO!" SCREAMED MUSKRAT and then he passed out!

Twenty minutes later, a heavily sweating Buck Snort had finished sewing up all four bear claw slashed and ripped parts of Muskrat's hind end. "There," said Buck Snort with a sign of relief, "his hind end will now be just as smooth as a baby's bottom or as 'soft as a schoolmarm's thigh' once it heals," he said with the sound of satisfaction in his 'glad to be all done' emotion-filled sounding voice...

For the next two weeks, Muskrat slept on his stomach come evenings. He also never rode a horse and stood instead of sitting when the men gathered around their cooking fire while eating breakfast or supper. However, true to Buck Snort's prediction, as he rubbed bag balm and even some bear grease into the damaged hind end tissue when they ran low on the bag balm on a daily basis, the wound was healing just as smoothly as a 'baby's hind end or that of a schoolmarm's thigh'. But when Buck Snort applied the bag balm on a daily basis, a highly embarrassed Muskrat still threatened every time application time rolled around that he was, "Still going to kill everyone involved in his 'Frontier Doctoring' and the 'black-hearted horse' they rode in on as well!"

Thirteen days later came another fateful

day, namely 'the day of the thick twine stitch removal' from Muskrat's beautifully healing up bottom! Once again, the 'removing one's mind from the operation at hand Frontier style of pain reliever', namely after liberally imbibed cups of rum by the aggrieved party, the delicate operation began. Once again, Clem and Wind Horse, expecting a violent physical reaction to removing the stitches from the now healed tissue, forcefully held Muskrat belly down on the table in their cabin. Then "Dr. Buck Snort" upon seeing his patient forcefully restrained by Wind Horse and Clem, took his sheath knife and began cutting the twine stitches where they had been knotted across Muskrat's bottom. Then with another look forward of the 'operating table' to make sure the patient was completely restrained, Dr. Buck Snort applied more bag balm over the impacted area to soften the painful removal and then without warning, began yanking out the offending stitches instead of slowly pulling them...

"YEEEE – HOOO-WOOOW!" yelped Muskrat every time the stitches 'held' solidly in the healing tissue and had to be yanked extra hard so they could be extracted! Upon completion of that successful operation, Dr. Buck Snort wiped off the fresh blood running down the flanks of Muskrat from the holes the stitches left after being removed and once again applied liberal amounts of bag balm around the now again irritated tissue. "I am still going to kill you, Buck Snort," said Muskrat as he was let up from off the table and standing there, looked over his shoulder at his damaged rear end. Then reaching down and rattling his tanned deerskin bag of the grizzly bear's claws that had caused all of his backside agony, said with a big smile, "But at least I fared better than did the one originally wearing these beauties…" Then pulling up his buckskin pants, Muskrat said after looking at all of his friends standing there looking on with still worried looks over the giant of a man's reaction to having his damaged hind end re-visited, "I only hope I can return this kind of favor to each and every one of you fellas someday," then he laughed out of relief as did his much relieved friends…

Once again while waiting for the winter's ice to go out in the Bighorn's beaver waters, the trappers made ready for their spring beaver trapping season. In so doing, bullets were cast, powder horns refilled with fresh powder, 'possibles' bags filled with needed equipment, beaver traps smoked to rid them of the man smell, rifles and pistols torn down, lead and black powder fouling removed, parts checked and then reassembled. Then the best of the trappers with a whetstone, namely Clem, set the edges to every knife and tomahawk carried by the men. Additionally, all the riding and packing gear's leather was checked, re-sewn or replaced as needed in expectation for the summer trip back to Fort Henry, the eventual sale of the men's furs and then the selection of the men's provisions for the coming year afield.

Then come the first evening several days later that Muskrat found he could now gently sit on his sitting log by the outdoor firepit and eat his supper after having all of the stitches removed from his damaged bottom, his fellow trappers had a surprise for him. After putting away a heavy supper of beans, biscuits, buffalo and Clem's brand of 'trappers' coffee', Buck Snort arrived with one of their flat kegs (easier to carry on a packhorse) with four cups in hand. Then in celebration of having Muskrat back within the group of trappers and mostly healed up, the cups of rum flowed. Then Clem handed Muskrat a fairly large leather bag and told him to open it.

As Muskrat began opening up the mystery deerskin bag, he was told that it was a gift from all of his partners that he had not killed after suffering through all of the 'Frontier Doctoring'. There was laughter all around and then Muskrat finally opened up the deerskin bag and just sat there looking at its contents for the longest moment in time. Then he looked all around at his fellow trappers and as he did, he had tears in his eyes... Then catching himself, he quickly wiped his eyes with a sleeve from his buckskin shirt, reached in and withdrew a beautiful handmade grizzly bear necklace consisting of ten long claws, interspersed with red and blue glass beads! For the longest moment in time, he just looked at the spectacular necklace and then with a huge smile of gratitude, placed it around his neck. Then

Muskrat stood up so all the men could see how the spectacular necklace lay around his chest. With that gesture from his friends honoring a searing life's event, even more rum flowed that evening now abounding in much laughter and merriment. Then it was off to bed and when the men retired, they observed that Muskrat went to his sleeping furs and slept with his unusual gift still around his neck from his close friends. In fact from then on, seldom did Muskrat ever take off his 'grizzly bear claw good luck charm' necklace...

"Clem, make us up a good breakfast this morning. Buck Snort and I have decided that today we will start our spring beaver trapping season on the Bighorn," said Muskrat, as he hurried out from the cabin and trotted off to the aspen grove near the corral in order to take care of an urgent call of nature.

As he did, Clem noticed that when Muskrat ran, he could clearly hear his grizzly bear necklace clattering around his neck. Later after the men had finished a hearty breakfast of spitted buffalo, biscuits and coffee, they went to their storage shed and withdrew all 30 of their beaver traps. They also withdrew all of their anchor poles saved from the year before lying alongside the storage shed, spools of anchor twine like they had used on Muskrat's behind after the grizzly bear had 'dolled' him up, hammers, bottles of castor and several specialized, bevel only on one side, skinning knives. Knives that had been so altered by Fort Henry blacksmiths to reduce cutting through a beaver's pelt during the skinning process, which if 'holed' by regular bladed knives reduced its value. The trapping gear was loaded up into several panniers and then Buck Snort exited their cabin carrying their four, fully loaded reserve rifles that were to be carried in two of the horses' panniers 'just in case' they found the odds stacked against them during an Indian attack. Then shortly thereafter Wind Horse and Buck Snort exited the cabin carrying their extra breechclouts and buckskin leggings and loaded them into a pannier as well. Finally having cleaned up his cast iron cooking gear after breakfast, Clem joined in with the men saddling their riding and packhorses making them ready for their first day of spring beaver trapping on the Bighorn and some of its adjacent waterways.

Half an hour later, the four men streamed out from their campsite with Muskrat, healed-up bottom and all in the lead, followed by Buck Snort and Wind Horse leading the three packhorses, trailed by Clem acting as the caravan's rear guard. Muskrat led the men to where they had trapped and run their trap line the year before so they could look it over just in case they had missed some beaver. As the trappers had expected, they saw few beaver and most of the beaver dams in the old trap site were in a sad state of disrepair, signifying that the four trappers had pretty well caught all of the beaver in that old trapping location and it was time to move on.

Then Muskrat led the caravan to a spot where the men had finished running the end of their trap line in the late fall and made ready to begin their spring beaver trapping at that location. Then their plan was to begin trapping from that spot and working even further south from the mouth of the Bighorn where it entered into the Yellowstone. Following their normal routine, Muskrat took up a nearby position from where he could watch over the men doing the trapping and yet provide ample warning and provide immediate assistance in case danger reared its ugly head. As for Buck Snort and Wind Horse, they changed into their clothing worn during their trapping activities, grabbed up the gear necessary to set their first traps and headed out south along the Bighorn setting trap after trap. As for Clem, he watched over the trappers' riding and packhorses and supplied the traps, anchor poles and castor as needed.

By around noon, the men had set their 30 beaver traps figuring if they got overrun with their catches, they could once again reduce their trap number at that time. Then gathering together once again, they headed for a grove of nearby aspens in which they could dismount, rest, eat some jerky and maybe even catch some sleep until later in the afternoon when it came time to check their traps before heading back to their campsite. Several hours later the men left their resting place and with that, Wind Horse and Buck Snort once back on their trap line began checking it for any recently caught beaver.

The last six traps set at the end of their trap line had not caught any beaver but the next 14 traps in a row had a beaver in them! As Wind Horse and Buck Snort extracted the most recently caught beaver, Clem with his 'flying' knife kept ahead of the trappers in the skinning process. However, the last ten traps in their newly established trap line also held freshly caught beaver and those had been traps set close together. That being the case, it became necessary for all three of the men setting and checking the traps to pitch in with the skinning so that work would be done before nightfall. Twenty-four beaver later, Buck Snort had tiredly pulled the last ten of their 30 traps and with their day's catch in the panniers, four very tired trappers headed for their cabin. The new trap line had outproduced what the men had figured they would catch and as a result, it would be another long night and into the following morning de-fatting and hooping all 24 of their beaver 'Plus'! But first, the men stopped alongside several patches of willows and filled three of their panniers with fresh willow limbs suitable for hooping all of their newest catch of beaver, most of which were in the Made Beaver category or large in size, high dollar in value pelts.

Arriving back at their camp and after unloading all of their horses and letting them feed and water with the rest of their horses that had remained back in their corral when the trappers had left that morning, Wind Horse, Buck Snort and Muskrat headed into their cabin and began the laborious process of de-fatting and hooping 24 freshly caught beaver pelts. In the meantime, after hauling in several loads of firewood, Clem began his duties as camp cook in putting together an adequate supper for his hardworking partners in the cabin processing beaver pelts. After a supper of spitted buffalo meat, biscuits and coffee, Wind Horse, Buck Snort and Muskrat headed back into their cabin to finish the pelt processing. In the meantime, realizing the men needed a variety of food with their meals Clem set two pots filled with water holding rice in one and beans in the other so he could cook up extra food for his three hardworking partners. Finished with those duties, he too headed for the cabin and joined right in with the others in the de-fatting and hooping process, which carried the men into the wee morning hours before finishing.

Come daylight found Clem once again at his firepit cooking up buffalo, coffee and biscuits for his tired compatriots. Additionally, he drained the rice and bean pots, refilled them with fresh water and spices and set them to cooking on the hanging irons, so they would be ready for the supper meal with only a quick re-heating required. Then Clem brought in all of their horses who had been feeding all night in their nearby meadow, saddled those to be used for the day's activities checking their trap line, packed their three packhorses and put the remaining horses not used back into the corral for safekeeping.

Then the remaining three tired partners staggered out from the cabin after working all night on the pelts, took care of their calls of nature, washed up and headed for the firepit. There finished with the horses, Clem served his fellow trappers scalding hot cups of his brand of 'trappers' coffee' along with freshly baked biscuits smothered in honey and spitted buffalo meat. All four men then ate their meal in tired silence and then began gathering up their equipment for the day's activities. However, before the trappers left their campsite in order to check their new trap line, Clem pulled the cooked pots of beans and rice and set them off to one side on a cooling rock so they would be ready for supper with just a re-heat when the men returned.

For the next two weeks of beaver trapping, the men only ran 20 traps per day and many a day they found most of them filled with the highly territorial and inquisitive beaver. And come nightfall found all four men de-fatting and hooping the day's catch of beaver. Then as they continued moving their beaver trap line further and further south as they trapped out the previous trap lines' locations of beaver, they came to a large watered area just off the Bighorn River. Within that area of dense patches of willows and aspen, the men discovered numerous beaver colonies holding more beaver than they had ever seen before. That being the case, they further reduced the number of traps being used down to just 15, and many a trapping day found all 15 traps holding dead beaver! To the trappers' way of thinking, they had hit the 'Mother Lode of beaver trapping'! Unfortunately for the trappers and fortunately for the beaver, the furred rodent would soon be coming out of prime and the spring trapping season would soon cease!

One morning after the men realizing that their spring beaver trapping would soon be over because the beaver were beginning to show signs that they were coming out of prime, they increased their trap number back to 30 so they could harvest as many beaver as possible before they had to quit. One morning as Wind Horse 'leap-frogged' Buck Snort in his trap setting activities in a very dense and extensive patch of willows, he found a beaver slide area that showed over 100 fresh tracks of animal use! Grinning from ear to ear over his very active slide area 'find', he quickly set his trap next to the slide and then moved off into the deeper waters in order to set his anchor pole as he had done hundreds of times before. As he 'walked out' the trap chain, he approached a small, densely wooded island out in the middle of the huge beaver pond in which he was working. Near the island's shoreline he tightened the length of his trap chain and began noisily driving his anchor pole into the pond's bottom with his hammer so he could securely anchor his trap.

CRASH! Out from the island's dense cover erupted a cow moose with her ears laid back as she flat-out charged Wind Horse from her place of hiding from just a few feet away! Before Wind Horse could even move, "THUDDD!" went the cow moose's front hooves into his chest as she quickly lashed out at a dead run and hurled Wind Horse violently backwards in the direction from whence he had just come! "OOOFFFPH!" sounded Wind Horse, as the 900-pound animal struck him dead in his chest with both of her hooves! Landing on his back and unconscious from the impact of the vicious animal's attack, Wind Horse sank out of sight into the deeper water! When the cold waters closed over his face, that shock brought him back from being knocked unconscious. With that human instinct to avoid drowning whirling strongly in his senses, Wind Horse groggily attempted to stand up in the waist-deep waters. When he did, that just further inflamed the still close at hand moose's savage attack and once again she lashed out with her front hooves! And again, Wind Horse felt the heavy thudding impact from the moose's front hooves knocking him asunder! Then the moose savagely charged the trapper as he once again struggled to rise from the icy cold waters, only to find himself now being hoof-stomped into the muddy waters by the 900-pound and extremely irate animal!

Buck Snort, who after hearing all of the thrashing and crashing around in the dense willows ahead of where he had been setting a trap, stopped what he had been doing and moved forward to investigate as fast as he could walk along the muddy bottom. When he did, he saw his dear friend Wind Horse being 'hoof-stomped' into the mud by a highly pissed-off cow moose! Quickly drawing his pistol, Buck Snort hurriedly snapped off a shot at the heaving flanks of the close at hand moose in the process of stomping Wind Horse! The moose just swayed a bit as the heavy .52 caliber slug slammed into her side as she now tried head-smashing Wind Horse into the mud for the second time! Then since the shot had not been a killing one even though fired from just a few feet away, the cow moose whirled and with a 'bellow', lashed out with her front hooves at her new antagonist standing just a few feet away, Buck Snort!

WHUMP! went her front hooves into Buck Snort, who instantly found himself flying through the air and landing flat on his back in three feet of water! The next thing he remembered was having the moose's head slammed into his middle as she tried crushing him! Instinctively Buck Snort, even though hurting like a son-of-a-bitch, grabbed hold of the moose's ears and immediately found himself lifted from out of the water and given a violent head toss over the back of the moose! "SPLUUSH!" went Buck Snort as the muddy water now closed over his head once again and his now empty pistol went flying from his hand!

Clem, who after hearing the ruckus in the willows followed by the sound of a pistol being fired and hearing much bellowing from a cow moose, dropped his skinning knife and the beaver he had been skinning, grabbed his rifle from off his nearby horse and ran towards the thrashing and crashing going on in the willows! Busting through the willows, Clem bodily ran right into the bloody side of the now very much enraged cow moose as she tried head-butting Buck Snort into the muddy beaver pond bottom! Shoving his rifle barrel forward just as the cow moose realized she now had another 'target", whirled and when she did, she gave Clem a look at the world of wildlife 'devil incarnate'!

The look on the face of that moose almost gave Clem pause upon seeing it for the first time up so close and personal. The first thing he saw were the blood-red eyes of the moose looking hard at him, all the while blowing bloody and foaming snot from its mouth and nostrils from Buck Snort's earlier lung shot into the side of the animal with his pistol! The moose's mouth was agape in anger, pain and dripping blood, with its massive body now fully fueled with adrenalin!

Without hesitation and a calmness born of desperation, Clem extended his rifle barrel right into the cow moose's open mouth and pulled the trigger! **BOOM!** went his rifle, dropping the cow moose where she stood with a huge splash. And in so doing, she fell over DIRECTLY ON TOP OF BUCK SNORT, CRUSHING HIM UNDER HER GREAT WEIGHT!

Seeing what had just happened, Clem dropped his rifle into the water, reached down and grabbing the moose's front legs and with superhuman strength fueled with his own adrenalin, hefted the moose's front part of its body up off Buck Snort who came out of the water with a lunge! Blowing and snorting over almost having the life crushed out from him, Buck Snort out of the fear of being almost drowned and crushed at the same time, sprinted off a few feet from the action in panic. Then seeing that the moose was down but that Clem was standing there NOW looking at him with eyes twice their normal size and showing a huge amount of white around them as he looked past Buck Snort, realizing more danger of some sort was now near at hand, HE INSTANTLY FROZE!

Standing not ten feet away on the island from whence had charged the cow moose, now stood a sow grizzly on her hind feet! Standing alongside the mother bear stood two sub-adult 350-pound bears as well! Then Buck Snort seeing what Clem was looking at so close at hand felt his heart almost stop! Felt his heart almost stop when he realized he was standing in the water with no pistols that could fire since he had been immersed underwater and black powder does not fire when wet! And Clem after killing the moose with his rifle had dropped it into the water in order to heft the moose's body off his friend Buck Snort, and now he had no gun that could shoot as well! Then Buck Snort realized he was now so close to the sow grizzly who was standing and closely watching the moose killing incident from just eight feet away, that he could smell her breath as she "WOOOFED" and "WOOOFED" at what she was seeing!

THEN ALL HELL BROKE LOOSE ON THE ISLAND RIGHT NEXT TO THE THREE BEARS STANDING JUST FEET AWAY FROM THE MOOSE KILLING ACTION AND THE 'TRAPPER DOUSING'! **CRASH — CRASH!** UP JUMPED A CALF MOOSE FROM THE TALL GRASSES WHERE IT HAD BEEN HIDING RIGHT NEXT TO ONE OF THE SUB-ADULT GRIZZLY BEARS AND INSTANTLY THE CALF WAS IN THE WATER HEADING RIGHT FOR WHERE IT HAD LAST SEEN ITS MOTHER BEFORE SHE HAD BEEN SHOT! INSTANTLY RIGHT BEHIND AND AFTER THE FLEEING CALF CAME ONE SUB-ADULT BEAR GROWLING AND SNARLING EVERY LUNGING STEP OF THE WAY THROUGH THE WATER! WITH A LOUD BLEATING SOUND, THE CALF MOOSE DIED IN THE JAWS OF THE GRIZZLY BEAR

AND THEN EVEN MORE HELL BROKE LOOSE! THE OTHER SUB-ADULT BEAR, NOT TO BE OUTDONE, JUMPED INTO THE WATERS AND GRABBED THE CALF MOOSE BY ITS HIND END AND THE BATTLE FOR OWNERSHIP BEGAN, AS THE TWO 350-POUND GRIZZLY BEAR CUBS FOUGHT OVER WHO WAS GOING TO GET THE CALF FOR LUNCH! THIS THEY DID IN FRONT OF GOD AND EVERYBODY, INCLUDING TWO TOTALLY SURPRISED AND AMAZED CLOSE AT HAND AND SCARED ALL TO HELL TRAPPERS!

In the next instant, survival instincts took over and Buck Snort ran for the opposite shoreline in the pond, as did Clem after he had quickly retrieved his rifle from the muddy waters, and was running like a scared deer right behind Buck Snort. As the two men headed for the shoreline opposite where the bears were located, they saw a bedraggled Wind Horse slowly dragging his stomped body up out from the beaver pond. That they did just in time to see Muskrat come galloping up yelling and shouting at the bears in order to distract them from the three defenseless men emerging from the beaver pond's waters!

However, Muskrat's wild ride from his point of observation to aid his compatriots was for naught. The two bear cubs were still fighting over the now dead calf moose and the sow was busy dragging the calf's dead mother out from the beaver pond and up onto and then out of sight into the brush on the island. Soon the scene consisted of three soaked and bedraggled breathing-hard trappers standing alongside Muskrat. As for the three bears, they were now up on the island, out of sight and with lots of growling and snarling, in the process of fighting over who was going to get the next bite from the dead cow and calf moose… As for the trappers, the bears could have cared less. To their way of thinking, why eat a smelly and skinny trapper when they had a fresh 900-pound moose on 'the lunch table'…

By the time the damaged trappers had retired to their packhorses and retrieved their dry and ready to fire extra rifles, all was quiet on the nearby island except for the obvious sounds of three happy grizzly bears feeding on two moose. It was then that the men realized what had happened. Apparently when Wind Horse had attempted to set his beaver trap too close to the cow and her calf moose, the mother moose objected to the closeness of the human, especially with her young calf so close. That was when she had thundered into the pond and had kicked the 'jelly' out from Wind Horse, and when Buck Snort had decided to join in the battle, got the 'jelly' knocked off his 'peanut butter sandwich' as well! Then when Clem got involved, the 'hurrah' really got interesting. However, when the bears decided they would rather have a fat cow moose over a smelly and skinny trapper smelling of castor, it had been no contest as to their menu selections, THANKFULLY…

With a reloaded Clem and Wind Horse with their reserve rifles and watching, Buck Snort quietly slipped into the beaver pond 'of note' and retrieved their anchor pole and previously set beaver trap. Then the four trappers mounted up onto their horses and moved further away from the still happily feeding bears and after a brief rest to make sure they still 'had all of their body parts', continued setting the rest of their beaver traps. However, they were setting their beaver traps somewhat more slowly than earlier in the day due to a pile of hurt felt throughout their bodies. That they did because Wind Horse was black and blue from stem to stern, as was Buck Snort from discovering a moose's kick was no different than that coming from an angry mule with an attitude...

After the 'moose madness in the marsh', the trappers finished out the spring beaver trapping season without further incident. When that portion of the beaver trapping was all said and done, the four men had managed to trap another 413 high grade spring Made Beaver! With that number and the 447 beaver taken during the previous fall's beaver trapping season, the men had collected and bundled up a total of 860 mostly Made Beaver while trapping along the Bighorn and its many adjacent watered areas! Those pelts and the 54 wolf pelts taken during the winter wolf trapping season made for a great year. Like Muskrat had said months earlier, Indians always seemed to have a sixth sense when it came to big decisions, and Wind Horse's earlier suggestion the trappers move to the southwest to one river further along the Yellowstone had been a great suggestion.

Then as the trappers began making plans to travel to Fort Henry come summer in order to trade in their pelts, a big decision had to be made. That decision regarded whether they continued trapping in the coming seasons along the very productive Bighorn or move on and see what lay on the other side of the mountains. One evening after a supper of ironically spitted moose meat, the men decided they would remain in their old cabin and continue trapping along the Bighorn the coming year. They would just cache a lot of their goods and leftover provisions in some sandy and dry soil near their cabin, and that way they would have extra horses not carrying their leftover provisions but bundles of furs. Little did the men realize the irony of their decision and the future impact that would have not only on the closeness of Fort Henry, but being close location-wise to the coming introduction of the "Rendezvous" system of acquiring one's provisions and the selling of their furs. Like Muskrat had said, Indians usually make pretty damn good decisions when it comes to living and life, and Wind Horse had been right-on in his decision to move along the Yellowstone to just one river further west, namely the Bighorn...

One month later after caching many of their leftover provisions and a lot of their cooking and trapping implements, the trappers made their final preparations for heading back to the northeast and Fort Henry to trade and reprovision for the coming fall and spring beaver trapping seasons. Come the fateful day of departure for Fort Henry, little did the men realize that monumental change was coming that would have a powerful effect when it came to the future of the United States. Also, little did the men realize what long-lasting effects they and their kind were about to make when it came to exploring and eventually opening up the West, and the destruction of the cultures of many of the Indigenous Peoples as well as the demise of many of the continent's animal populations. Animal populations that because of widespread human settlement and expansion would be adversely impacted like those of the buffalo, and including those of the beaver which have never fully recovered their population number to this very day...

CHAPTER FIVE

FORT HENRY AND TROUBLE!

COME THE MORNING of departure, Buck Snort nailed the door to their cabin shut to keep the critters out since the group would be returning to the same area along the Bighorn come late summer. Then putting his tools back into their storage shed and since they had finished eating a big breakfast, the men mounted up and headed out for Fort Henry lying far to the northeast up where the Yellowstone met the mighty Missouri River. For the next six days of travel from daylight to dark, the men traveled without incident. The country was rich in buffalo herds and as the men traveled through, they had roasted buffalo, Dutch oven biscuits and coffee for every breakfast and supper and jerky for a noonday snack.

Come day seven of their travels, a brisk and

cold wind was blowing from out of the north-west. Finally with the arrival of numerous dark and forbidding scudding low hanging clouds forecasting summer thunderstorms and rain, the men headed into the dense brush and timber along the Yellowstone for the protection that would offer. Once there, they holed up for the night for the protection such dense vegetation offered during the coming wet series of summer thunderstorms. Drifting their long caravan of heavily loaded packhorses into the cover the densest timber provided, they stopped their travel early to avoid as much as possible the effects of the heavy oncoming rains, high winds and fierce lightning accompanying such moisture-laden events that were already occurring further to the northwest.

As Buck Snort, Muskrat and Wind Horse hurriedly unloaded their pack animals and stacked their packs around their campsite in a defensive arrangement in case unforeseen Indian troubles came their way, Clem gathered up dry firewood, made a fire and began preparing the men's supper of just coffee and Dutch oven biscuits. This he did because for the last four hours of travel, the men had run across numerous heavily used trails of Indians' unshod horses' hoofprints! Not wanting to cross trails with groups of superior numbers of Indians, the men headed into the covering brush and timber found along the Yellowstone and just figured they would 'kill two birds with one stone'. By 'running to ground in the timber' they could avoid the heavy summer rains soon to be upon them and avoid any unforeseen clashes with groups of possibly hostile Indians that were also traveling in country. The men knew the deadly Arikara did not come that far west, but they sure as hell were deep in the country heavily traveled by the murderous Gros Ventre and Blackfeet. Because of that, they dared not chance any battle with those groups because they usually traveled in superior numbers when deep in the country of the Crow where the trappers now had camped for the evening.

Finally having watered and picketed all of their horses in a dense cottonwood grove, the men responded to Clem's yell that supper was ready. The men, tired from a long day on the trail and having to tend to all of their horses and packs, just quietly ate what was set before them and did not complain. As they did, the wind from the northwest picked up and soon, big wet and cold raindrops were felt drifting through the canopy of leaves in their grove of cottonwood trees. With that, the men hurriedly finished their supper and then headed for their sleeping furs safely placed under large cottonwoods in order to stop most of the rain from reaching them and getting their sleeping gear all wet. That was further helped by having a buffalo skin placed over their sleeping furs in order to keep things drier during rainstorms as well.

As they did, Muskrat noticed that their horses were all looking up from the river bottom with interest watching or smelling something going on back up on the distant prairie. That was when he spotted a long line of warriors who had not discovered the presence of the trappers camped in the dense brush of the river bottom, heading to the southwest along the riverbank on their side of the river! Soon, the men had quickly recovered all of their extra weapons and had laid them alongside their sleeping furs just in case the Indians smelled the smoke from the men's dying campfire and came over to investigate. However, with the swirling winds, ominous lightning to the northwest and increasing rains coming down, the Indians appeared to be heading for another area and the men were safe for the evening. But even then, the men rested rather lightly that evening just in case more Indians came along and discovered their back trail of shod horses' hoofprints. Soon that worry subsided when heavy rains came from out of the northwest and any evidence of the trappers' horses' hoofprints were quickly washed out of sight and away forever.

The next morning found the trappers reloading all of their packhorses in a dense fog created by the previous evening's violent summer thunderstorm. After just a breakfast of coffee and jerky and ever mindful of all the physical evidence of Indian activity in their location, the trappers once again continued heading out along the Yellowstone to the northeast towards Fort Henry. However, this time Muskrat rode further ahead just on his riding horse as a scout for any signs of danger from marauding Indians while the rest of the men brought up the rear of their fur caravan. However, as the rest of the caravan followed Muskrat, they made sure they stayed right along the Yellowstone River's bank in case they had to duck out from sight of any oncoming Indians into the river bottoms. This they did even though knowing they were in the territory of the friendly Crow Indians, they could not take any chances of stumbling upon superior numbers of the white man-hating and deadly Blackfeet or the oftentimes far-ranging and even more murderous Gros Ventre.

Three days later, the four tired but now happy as well as relieved fur trappers arrived in view of Fort Henry. When they did, they were surprised to see so much human activity swirling around and within the fort. That plus the interior walls of the fort were bristling with lookouts all carrying their rifles as if expecting an Indian attack at any moment! Upon their arrival at the front gates, the four trappers were quickly hurried inside the fort's protective log palisades. When the men and their horses had been driven safely inside the fort's protective walls, they were met by a very happy to see them and much relieved over their safe arrival, Major Andrew Henry.

"What the hell is going on, Major?" asked

Muskrat, mindful of all the heavily armed activity ongoing within and around the fort's location.

"You men are damn lucky you got here safely. We figured we have already lost a number of other trappers coming to the fort like you men to attacks from the Blackfeet and those damn Arikara. In fact, ever since we have built this here fort where she now stands, we have been almost under constant attack both day and night by both of those tribes! It seems we have created a fur trade competition problem with those two Indian groups who do not want us competing with them for the fur trade they have going with other white trappers and Indian tribes," advised a tired-looking Major Henry.

"What the hell are you going to do? There is no way you all can live here under the constant threat of Indian attack, nor can you expect that all of your trappers will be able to make it inside your gates alive when they are bringing their furs to sell as well," said Buck Snort.

"Well, be glad you fellas arrived safely when you did. We are preparing to abandon this here fort forthwith and move it further to the southwest along the Yellowstone somewhere where we will be deeper in the country of the friendly Crow Indians and then rebuild. In fact, we should be ready to move any day now and we will do so in force so any Indians wishing to attack us had better think twice before doing such a foolish thing. That being said, we sure could use you four trappers and your guns when we up and move and your muscles and building skills when we rebuild the fort. What do you say?" asked Major Henry hopefully.

Two days later, Major Henry led his men out from the now abandoned Fort Henry located near the mouth of the Yellowstone where it emptied into the Missouri River and headed to the southwest along the Yellowstone River in a long and heavily armed caravan. Thirteen days later the long caravan of fur trappers and men from the old Fort Henry stopped where the mouth of the Bighorn River emptied into that of the Yellowstone. There near the same grounds where once stood Fort Manuel built in 1807 by Manuel Lisa, a St. Louis merchant and pioneer fur buyer, Major Henry decided to rebuild Fort Henry.

For the rest of that summer of 1823, 80 or so men from the old Fort Henry and Major Henry's company fur trappers rebuilt the new Fort Henry at the mouth of the Bighorn River. As they did, Buck Snort, Wind Horse, Muskrat and Clem worked alongside the fort's men in helping to rebuild the new fort. Then upon completion, the Major supplied the men all of their needed supplies for the following beaver trapping seasons from the new fort's supplies for helping in the rebuilding process that took most all of summer.

After the new Fort Henry had been completed, the Major set his company fur graders and sorters to work evaluating the four trappers' 1822-23 fall and spring catch of beaver and wolf furs. As it turned out still being under contract as company trappers, Buck Snort and company were again faced with only receiving half of the going price for their beaver. That meant that year beaver pelts were going for $6 and Buck Snort and company received only $3 for each of their like in kind 860 beaver *'Plus'*, and $45 each for their 54 dark-furred wolf pelts. The total amount the men received for their beaver pelts came to $2,580, and for their wolf pelts, $2,430, or a total of $5,010! After the Major had checked his sorters and graders' math and without any kind of comment, wrote out a Letter of Credit from the Ashley-Henry Fur Trade Company redeemable in St. Louis at the company's main fur house for $5,010! Then sprinkling some sand from his 'sand shaker' over his freshly inked signature made with a swan's quill pen, Major Henry shook off the sand meant to aid in drying the signature and handed the paper to Buck Snort. Never had Buck Snort seen such a large amount of money in his life, nor had Muskrat, Wind Horse and Clem as well…

After everyone had a chance to see what they had made off the sale of their furs and what they had earned in a single fur season as company trappers, the paper was handed back to Buck Snort. "Here you go, Buck Snort," said Muskrat handing the Letter of Credit over to his younger partner. "You are the best one with our money so you hold it until we all decide we have had enough of this walking around in cold water and that we have made enough for all of us to live comfortably somewhere in the civilized part of this here country. But until then, we are 'cutting a fat hog in the ass' with our trapping in and around the Bighorn and until that kind of success dries up, we need to keep doing what we are doing, 'come hell or high water' or no longer can stand Clem's terrible cooking." Upon hearing the last part of what Muskrat had to say, the rest of the men had a good-natured laugh at Clem's expense. Without a word and proud that all of the men trusted him with such a great amount of money if they ever made it back down to St. Louis, Buck Snort walked over to his riding horse and placed the Ashley-Henry Fur Trade Company Letter of Credit into his saddlebag for safekeeping.

Then Major Henry walked over to where the men stood in a group still somewhat dazed over the vast amount of money his trappers had earned saying, "Tonight, my house. All of you be there for supper, some good rum and maybe a cigar or two for not only being such good trappers but damn good help in getting this here new fort back up and running. Then tomorrow, I suggest you head for my warehouse and reprovision before it is all gone. I say that because we will then have to wait for the spring run-off so the water on the Yellowstone is deep enough for our supply keelboats to come upriver with new supplies."

For the rest of that day, the men let their horse herd graze in the grasslands near the fort while all four of them provided guard duty in order to prevent any theft of their valuable livestock. That evening the horses were brought back inside the walls of the fort and the men bunked down in the Clerks' bunkhouse. The next day after a breakfast of just biscuits and coffee, the men once again herded their horses out the fort's gate and into a nearby prairie. There the men lounged around while some slept as their horses put on the 'feed bag' in preparation for the trip south along the Bighorn and back to their cabin some miles distant from the new fort's location.

That evening as per the Major's invite, the men entered his home and were treated to a supper like they had not had for many months. As a centerpiece, roasted buffalo over an outside spit adorned a table set with a tablecloth, china and silverware. Red wine flowed as Major Henry's three Chinese cooks 'spread the table' with freshly baked homemade bread, home churned butter, chokecherry jam, baked trout freshly netted from the Yellowstone, new potatoes from the fort's garden, fresh onions, pickled beets, mustard greens with sauce and finally, all the apple cobbler the men could choke down on top of everything else they had 'wolfed-down'. Then the men adjourned to the porch and with the ever-present mosquitoes, smoked cigars and drank cups of rum until the men had 'foundered'...

The next morning found the men in the Major's supply warehouse with stomachs still full from the evening before and heads that seemed to be barely 'holding' onto their necks... With Clem in the lead, selections of flour, tins of dried yeast, dried apple slices, sacks of rice and beans, bags of green coffee beans, brown sugar and flat kegs of Fourth Proof rum were selected right off. Then all of the men got involved as different grades and tins of rifle and priming powder along with 100 pounds of pig lead were stacked off to one side. Then came more fire steels, beeswax candles, tins of bag balm, whetstones for knives, axes, files and shovels came next. Then the next hour was spent as the men tried on and stacked off to one side, new wide brimmed hats, capotes, gloves, socks, woolen pants, English-made shirts, moccasin-making leathers, awls, needles, spools of thread, spices missed during the first go around in selecting foodstuffs, and leather strapping for saddle and pack repairs. Since the Major was allowing the men to select whatever they needed for their next year trapping afield because of all of the work the four men had done in helping to rebuild the new fort, they made sure they had selected plenty of everything they could possibly need from the stocks of that which was available. Those selections did not include any extra rifles, tins of powder, horse pistols, rifle and pistol parts, building or cooking implements, because the men already had all of those items either in hand or back at their cache near their cabin on the Bighorn. But extra straight razors, combs, two mirrors, bath soap, shaving soap, a bottle of lilac water, and five carrots of tobacco were also selected.

Then while the men were making their final selections of needed provisions overlooked during their first selection 'go-around', trouble reared its ugly head from an unforeseen corner! Into the warehouse stomped four heavily bearded and burly-looking trappers who none of Buck Snort's group had even seen before. As it turned out, they were noisy, bossy with the Company Clerks and smelling strongly and acting accordingly of copious amounts of freshly consumed rum. Moments later after they had pushed their drunken way into that part of the warehouse where Buck Snort and his group were still putting together the final touches on their needed selections, the genesis of the four heavily bearded trappers loudly became apparent. From all of their loud 'bragging and blowing', it soon came to light that the new men were rogue Hudson's Bay men from Canada who had deserted that company for that of the Ashley-Henry Fur Trade Company. Soon those men became such a noisy pain in the ass that Buck Snort and crew hurriedly finished making those selections of goods

needed, had the Company Clerks record such selections and then began hauling their items from
the warehouse. That they did, followed by words
of derision from the Hudson's Bay men regarding the fact that Buck Snort's group had a "Damn
War Hoop" as an equal partner and part of their
contingent of fur trappers… Upon hearing those
rather unwelcome words, Wind Horse slowly
turned and looked hard at the mouthy men, then
turned and quietly walked off followed by more
hoots and hollers of derision. However, none of
those men had looked into Wind Horse's eyes
when they had such things to say. If they had,
they might have been a little more careful in their
choice of words. Had they done so, they may
have seen "Hell's A-Coming and He Was Riding
a Black Horse"…

Following their 'run-in' with the four mouthy
Hudson's Bay men in the warehouse, the men
took all of their horses over to the Major's
blacksmiths and had all of their old horseshoes
removed and new ones attached in preparation
for the coming trapping seasons afield, and that
included Wind Horse's solid 'BLACK' saddle
horse… While awaiting the re-shoeing of all of
their pack and saddle horses for the coming year,
Buck Snort's eyes fastened upon a beautiful and
what appeared to be a much spirited and distinc-
tively marked pinto horse in the fort's reserve
herd of horses for those newly arriving or old
company trappers in need of a horse.

Walking over to the fort's reserve horse herd wrangler who was standing nearby talking to one of the fort's blacksmiths, Buck Snort asked him to 'cut' the very interesting-looking pinto from the fort's horse herd and bring him over so he could take a closer look at what appeared to be a very much spirited animal. Upon closer examination and from information supplied by the fort's horse herd wrangler, the deserters from the Hudson's Bay Fur Company had brought the pinto in for sale and appeared to be very happy to get rid of him. The one and same four Hudson's Bay men who had caused Buck Snort some heartburn while over at one of the fort's warehouses when he and the rest of his company of men were selecting out the needed provisions for the coming trapping seasons. Hudson's Bay men who took offense to the fact that Buck Snort's crew of fur trappers had an Indian among them and counted him as an equal. 'Shaking' off the information regarding the horse's previous owners and their obvious lack of couth, Buck Snort, upon hearing those welcome words regarding the horse's availability, especially since his group of fur trappers had need and use for another good packhorse due to their successes as fur trappers and not having enough packhorses in their horse herd to carry all of their bundles of furs and any provisions at the same time, looked even more closely at the horse in question.

Standing off to one side so he could look more

closely at the horse's overall body confirmation, Buck Snort all of a sudden came to a funny
realization. The damn unusual horse, the one
with an almost hidden quality of some sort of
excellence, was looking at him as closely as Buck
Snort was looking at the horse! That realization
caught Buck Snort so far off guard that he found
himself taking a second closer look at the much
spirited and uniquely gifted animal to see what
the hell was catching his eye and causing him to
look even more deeply into the purchase of just
another horse, or was it…?

About then Buck Snort felt a hand on his elbow
and that surprised him so much since he was so
much into trying to see what was causing him to
look so uniquely and closely at the big pinto, that
he 'jumped like a bug on a hot rock'!

"HEY, didn't mean to cause you to jump like
that but are you seeing in that animal what I am
seeing?" asked the old horse wrangler. Then before Buck Snort could respond to the wrangler's
unusual question, he continued on talking as he
kept a close examining eye on the animal now
standing stock-still as if it were some sort of a
stone statue. "Are you seeing something special
in that animal, because I sure as hell am. Near
as I can figure it, that animal came from some
Indian's horse herd since he arrived here unshod
and then he somehow ended up in the hands
of those four mouthy men who deserted the
Hudson's Bay Fur Company. Then when those

four trappers arrived here, they sold that there horse to the fort as if he were carrying some sort of a bad talisman, evil spirit or something."

"Yeah, I am seeing something special about that horse as well but just can't put my finger on it. To my way of thinking, that damn horse is almost part human the way he is acting and looking back at me the same way that I am looking at him. Damn if I can put my finger on it but there is something almost magical or surreal about that horse," continued Buck Snort, as he continued looking at the steed standing stock-still in front of him looking at Buck Snort as if sizing him up as well… "Damn, I wish I knew what I was seeing and feeling but I damn sure can't. Hell, I have been around horses, mules and oxen all of my life but never saw anything like I am seeing in this one," he slowly said. Then turning, Buck Snort with a grin said, "How much for this here pinto?"

"Well, the Major saw in this horse that same unique spirit that you and I are seeing. Like us, he could not put his finger on what he was seeing or feeling but after a time, called him a "War Horse" of some sort like a commanding officer would find underneath him when heavy in battle… The Major told me not to sell him for less than $100," said the wrangler…

Without taking his eyes off the magnificent pinto standing stock-still in front of him, Buck Snort said, "I will take him and settle up with the Major when we are finished selecting all of our supplies." However when he uttered those words, he saw that damn pinto finally blink for the very first time since the two of them had met... "Please see to it that he is reshod and that his teeth are floated if need be. I or someone from my party will be around to pick him up and add him to our herd afore we leave. In the meantime, make sure no one else tries to buy him because that is the horse, special qualities and all, that I personally want," said Buck Snort still intently examining the animal. However when he uttered the words accepting the horse for their herd, he would have sworn from the look the horse had given him, he understood that Buck Snort had just purchased him, AND THE DAMN HORSE APPROVED OF THE SALE, ESPECIALLY AS IT CONCERNED WHO WAS DOING THE PURCHASING... Two days later, for better or worse, the big pinto was picked up and added to Buck Snort's herd of packhorses... When that sale was finalized, the old horse wrangler could have sworn that horse was happy with its new owners, especially the one who had initially purchased him...

CHAPTER SIX

TROUBLE COMES IN "THREES" ON THE BIG-HORN AND FRONTIER JUSTICE IS SERVED!

FOUR DAYS LATER after leaving the new Fort Henry, Buck Snort and company arrived back at their former campsite and found it as they had left it. After removing the nails holding their front door shut to keep the critters out, the men unloaded those provisions needing to be kept inside their cabin for safekeeping and to keep the weather off their newly purchased provisions. Those remaining non-perishable provisions were then stored in their adjacent storage shed. Following those activities, their livestock was unpacked, unsaddled and let out to feed in their nearby meadow where the men could keep an eye on them. Following that, the men spent the rest of their day digging up their earlier cache located behind their cabin, removed their gear and provisions from the cache site and put those items back inside their cabin, the storage shed and around their outdoor cooking fire for use as needed.

The following day found all four of the men cutting, hauling, splitting and stacking their winter's wood supply next to their cabin so they wouldn't have to tote it so far come the deeper snowdrifts of winter. Then after a day of rest from all of the hard work cutting and hauling wood, the men spent a day hunting buffalo in which six barren cows from a nearby herd were killed. The rest of that day was spent in butchering out those animals before they spoiled and hauling their best cuts of meat up to their cabin, some of which was placed on their meat poles so the meat could cool out and glaze. However, the majority of the meat was quickly cut into thin strips as the men then began their smoking fires and racked that meat so it would soon be made into jerky for the many months when they were afield and living on short rations. Once all of the meat had been properly smoked and made into jerky, that meat was placed into tanned deerskin bags and hung from the walls and ceiling beams of their cabin to keep the rodents and bugs at bay. Then the men's beaver and wolf traps were hung over the smoking racks, smoked to remove the man smells and then left hanging in the storage shed for future use come the fall, winter and spring trapping seasons. One day, realizing the fall beaver trapping season was fast approaching, Buck Snort had all of the men bring him their rifles and pistols. Then he disassembled all of them, cleaned out the lead and black powder fouling, oiled and then reassembled them so they would be ready for whatever came their way, good, bad or ugly. In the meantime, Wind Horse and Muskrat cast a small mountain of lead balls from their lead pigs so the men would have plenty of the 'business end' for their weapons. Then all of the men cleaned out their 'possibles' bags and resupplied them with greased wadding, fire steels, lead balls, flints and jerky. Lastly, the men refilled all of their powder horns with fresh priming, rifle and pistol powders. Now they were ready for what the Frontier could 'throw' at them and it wasn't long 'before that pitch was in the wind'…

Come the last days of September and with the approach of colder weather, the men began feeling the urge to take a look at the beaver waters where they hoped to begin running their trap line during the fall trapping season. Those urges were 'brought to a head' when Buck Snort exited their cabin one morning only to see his breath and see that the evening before had brought a heavy morning's frost.

"Hey, Clem, best fix up a good breakfast this morning because I will bet that when Muskrat leaves the cabin this morning, he will be more than ready to go and see what we can trap," said

Buck Snort, as he headed for the area used by the men to take care of their calls of nature.

Clem bent over adjusting his bowl of biscuit mix placing it closer to their outdoor fire, so the extra warmth could help the yeast rise in the dough and just waved his hand in understanding. Then he grabbed a long-bladed butcher knife and headed for the men's nearby meat pole in order to cut some additional buffalo steaks from one of the quarters hanging on the camp's meat pole in the morning's cool. Moments later back at the fire with four large buffalo steaks in hand, he headed for his work table near the fire. There he trimmed the bird poop off the red meat just removed from the meat pole and removed just a small amount of the excess fat covering the meat after removing its coating of bird poop as well. Following that, the steaks were skewered next to the fire, coffee grounds were added to the coffee pot hanging over the fire on hanging irons and then somewhat later after the yeast had caused the dough to rise sufficiently, began placing biscuit-sized lumps of dough into the two Dutch ovens so they could begin the baking process.

Right after breakfast, the four men began saddling their riding horses and packing all of the needed trapping gear into the panniers on the packhorses. Half an hour later, the men streamed out from their campsite with Muskrat in the lead, followed by Buck Snort and Wind Horse trailing their three packhorses and lastly, Clem brought up the rear of the caravan with his sharp eyes always on the lookout for trouble and in case his even sharper shooting skills would be required.

One hour later found Buck Snort and Wind Horse in the water setting beaver traps, followed by Clem assisting with needed materials associated with beaver trapping. As for Muskrat, he sat off to one side on his horse some 40 yards distant on a higher rise watching over his three friends running the trap line. As was the usual routine, Buck Snort and Wind Horse initially on their first day of trapping set out 30 of their beaver traps in the beaver-rich waters, just to make sure. Then if they got 'overrun' with their beaver catches and subsequent pelting duties, they would reduce the number of traps utilized accordingly on a daily basis. That way, they would not have to be up all night just de-fatting and hooping such a heavy load of fresh beaver pelts brought in with the use of and catching ability of having so many traps in the water.

Once again, the trappers found themselves 'knee deep' in the furry rodents at every turn in the Bighorn's watered areas chosen for the start of their fall beaver trapping season! As the men rested in a grove of cottonwoods at the end of their first day of trap setting, Muskrat said, "Appears to me we may have gone overboard once again in setting out all 30 of our traps. Time will tell as we run a check this afternoon on what we just set but in the meantime, I say we go and fill a couple of panniers with fresh willow cuttings so we will be ready for whatever we manage to catch today and need to hoop tonight."

No further words were necessary as the men realizing the wisdom of Muskrat's words, mounted up and headed for a large patch of willows growing alongside a series of adjacent beaver ponds. About an hour later after carefully cutting two panniers full of robust willow limbs, the men paused for some jerky and then re-mounted as they headed for the top end of their trap line just set. 'Sure as God made beaver good eating', the first eleven traps held a large in size, Made Beaver! Then trap number twelve did not hold any beaver but did hold a large and highly pissed-off as well as valuable river otter, which was dispatched with a head strike from a nearby stick so as not to damage its fur. Then the next six traps held beaver before an empty but sprung trap was checked. By the end of the day, the men had managed to trap 23 beaver and an adult river otter in their 30 traps in the beaver-rich waters they had chosen to trap that first morning of the fall beaver trapping season...

During the next three days, the men managed to trap 71 beaver and the one river otter in their 30 traps before they reduced their number of beaver traps run on a daily basis. Also, by day three of staying up most of their nights de-fatting and hooping all of their catches, had pretty much exhausted the men. Following those hectic days with 30 traps, the men reduced their trap line to just 15 traps and even then were averaging at least ten beaver per day of trapping in the chosen beaver-rich areas.

Finally swinging into a routine that still allowed the men to get some rest after all the de-fatting and hooping work required, off the trappers went to check their line of 15 traps one bitter cold November morning. Swinging into their normal routine, Muskrat, after taking the high ground, threw his right leg over his saddle so he would be comfortable in such a sitting position and began watching over his partners as they began running their trap line. The next thing he knew he was being waved in by the three men running their trap line. Realizing something was wrong, Muskrat quickly rode down to his partners and as he rode up, he could see looks of concern spread across all the men's faces!

"Muskrat, someone is running our trap line and is removing our beaver from the traps, and then stealing our valuable traps! And to make matters worse, whoever it is walks like an Indian but is not an Indian as near as I can tell from his moccasin prints," said Buck Snort.

Then Wind Horse quietly said, "Whoever is stealing our traps and beaver walks like a heavy-footed white man and not like an Indian who walks on just the sides of his moccasins!"

For the next hour the men ran the rest of their trap line only to find that all of their traps had been discovered, tended and then removed! Then Wind Horse said, "For the last several days, I have had the feeling that we were being watched. I have not said anything because I was not sure but just had that feeling. Now I know why, after seeing that someone had been watching and when they realized we were not around and watching our trap line, slipped in and stole our traps. I still have that feeling that we are being watched and suggest that we ride back to our campsite, get the 15 traps we left back in our storage shed, bring them out all in plain view and without a lot of looking around, set those traps just like we are going to continue trapping anyway. Then we make like we are leaving, ride out from the area and then quietly double back to see who is so bold that they think we will not react to their damn thievery."

Then Buck Snort said, "I support what Wind Horse just said. However, to make this ruse work because whoever did this is bound to be woods-wise and clever, we must make it look like we are not dumb. Then if we just carry on like nothing out of the ordinary has happened or that we figure some lone Indian chance discovered our trap line and is raiding it, whoever it is may take our 'bait'. So let us get some more traps and make like we are just stubbornly going to carry on. Muskrat, you ride back and get the rest of our traps and 'make a big show' of bringing them back here. In the meantime, we will stay here looking like we are going to carry on shortly by looking for more beaver slides. That way that should 'suck in' those who did this and then later we can spring our trap and 'can take care of business'…"

So as the remaining three trappers made a big show of looking like they were confused and dumbfounded over what had happened, were still looking for the rest of their traps as well as new beaver slides and marking them with a stick, Muskrat returned to their campsite. An hour later he returned and as he rode up to the three men, he held up several traps as if showing the men they could now carry on in spite of their lost traps… Then as if making up for lost time, the men returned to their trap setting without a whole lot of looking around like they were look-ing for whoever took their traps in the first place. Then a trip to a nearby willow patch was made to cut some more willows just like they normally did and then back to their campsite they rode like nothing was out of the ordinary.

Riding back to their camp, the four trappers dismounted and unsaddled all of their stock and let them out into the meadow to feed just like they ordinarily did in case someone was watch-ing their actions. Then the trappers adjourned to their cabin and built a smoky fire in their fireplace like they were there for the duration. Giving the appearance they were there for the night and giving their time spent in the cabin to around an hour, the men then streamed out from their cabin. They quickly rounded up their saddle horses and then streamed back through the edges of timber to where they could look back onto the area of their trap line in order to see what was happening if anything and yet not be detected.

However when they did, Wind Horse had discovered a number of shod horse tracks in the timber leading away from the four trappers' cabin, out through the timber and to a place where horses had stood obviously looking over the four trappers' trap line from a place of hiding. There four unidentified trap thieves had obviously watched Buck Snort and company running their trap line in the beaver-rich area of ponds and waterways adjacent the Bighorn River. Then to hide the trap thieves' activity after Buck Snort and company had left the area, only two of their horses had been led out from hiding over to the trap line where the dead beaver and stolen traps were then loaded into a pannier on a packhorse. Then three unidentified men's tracks appeared to lead from the trap line overlook at the edge of the timber back into the deep timber where they mounted up and had ridden back north along the Bighorn still hidden at the edge of the timber. There they met the fourth of their number trailing a packhorse loaded with the stolen traps and dead beaver. From there, all four men rode far to the north once again to an unknown destination.

Carefully working their way through the covering timber, Buck Snort and company eventually arrived at the location where they could overlook the new area where they had just set their remaining 15 beaver traps and yet could remain hidden in the timber. When they arrived, they discovered the trap thieves' horses tied off in the timber out of sight! Dismounting, tying off their horses as well and then slowly working their way through the timber closer to its edges so they could see and hear better, Buck Snort and company observed four heavily bearded individuals 'running' their just set trap line together for a change, removing several dead beaver from those traps and loading the dead beaver and traps into a single horse's pannier! It was then that Wind Horse recognized two of the men, namely deserters from the Hudson's Bay Fur Company, who had derogatorily commented back at Major Henry's supply warehouse about the fact that Buck Snort's group of trappers had in their group a "War Hoop", meaning the presence of Wind Horse! With that realization of who the four trap thieves were, namely the Hudson's Bay Fur Company men, Wind Horse now knew for sure that "Hell Was A-Coming and He Was Riding a Black Horse..." It was at that same moment in time that Buck Snort, Muskrat and Clem also realized that "Hell Was A-Coming and He Was Riding a Black Horse", if the metallic clicking sounds of their four rifles being readied to 'full cock' meant anything to the casual listening ear...

Laughing and chortling among themselves and heard clear back to where Buck Snort and company were observing from their close at hand hidden position, the four Hudson's Bay Fur Company men hurriedly located all of the newly set beaver traps by looking for the very distinctive dried wooden anchor poles sticking up out of the marsh. Upon their discovery, they were jerked out from the pond's muddy bottom and then the trap's chain was followed back to each individual trap. There they snapped the empty traps and tossed them into a pannier on one side of their packhorse and the anchor poles and any dead beaver into the pannier on the other side. Finally locating and springing the last of the new 15 traps recently set, the four men broke for the timber still hiding their riding horses, all the while trailing their single packhorse. Running right up to the very edge of the timber laughing all the way in self-congratulatory style, the men simultaneously let out a yell of joy over their successful trap stealing and life destroying activity of the four Buck Snort trappers that they had trailed all the way back to their cabin months earlier after they had left Fort Henry. Apparently doing so after observing Buck Snort's trappers back at the fort successfully selling such a large number of valuable Made Beaver and then figuring if they followed them to their beaver trapping waters they could in turn, steal them blind. And by stealing all of those trappers' traps, put them out of business and then take over their excellent beaver producing waters for themselves after the trappers with no traps had abandoned their trap site... Four Hudson's Bay Men who had set up their campsite several miles away and had all along intended on destroying Buck Snort's company of trappers and driving them out from the beaver-rich area so they could have it all for themselves, were now about to 'reap the whirlwind'...

THWACK! went a speeding round .52 caliber soft lead ball explosively into the forehead of the Hudson's Bay Fur Company man who had caustically remarked back at Fort Henry about a "War Hoop" being in Buck Snort's company of trappers, meaning Wind Horse... A speeding lead ball fired by sharpshooting Wind Horse, which upon impact blew the entire top half of the 'mouth's' head into a bright red fog of his life's essence... From the explosion of the man's head, it was obvious "Hell Had Come Riding a Black Horse" and Wind Horse did in fact ride a "Black Horse"...

In the dense white cloud of black powder smoke spewing from the edge of trees from four rifles, a second speeding .52 caliber lead ball emerged from the smoke and smashed into the nose of the other derisive speaking Hudson's Bay Fur Company man regarding his mouthy derogatory statement regarding the presence of a "War Hoop"! That speeding round ball of soft lead exploded that man's eight-pound head heavy with blood vessels, gray matter and bone chips into such a fine spray that even the black ants found in the killing field the next day had trouble finding enough of that head shot man in which to make a meal... Once again, "Hell Had Come" from Buck Snort's business end of his rifle and had put an end to an individual who had such an appropriate and violent end coming his way...

The third .52 caliber lead ball fired that morning at one of the trap thieves by Muskrat was just a little off dead center. That lead ball struck the man in his 'Adam's apple', severed his neck-flesh and spine, dropping his head onto the earth behind him with a surprised look over what had just happened still on his heavily bearded face...

By now, the fourth trap stealing trapper realized he and his compatriots had walked into a deadly ambush! With such a realization quickly burned into his brain, he turned as if to flee and took a .52 caliber ball directly into his left ear! Suffice to say, the resultant explosion of that man's head also provided little in the way of remaining food value to the black ants found in the area the next day as well...

Then after each man had quickly reloaded his rifle in case any curious Indians arrived at the sounds of the shooting scene of death and destruction, the men walked out and retrieved the four dead men's knives, tomahawks, rifles, powder horns, 'possibles' bags and pistols. Then mounting their own horses and trailing the four dead men's horses, Buck Snort and company began backtracking the trap stealers' earlier horse tracks coming down from the north of the 'killing field'. In so doing, they left the remains of the four trap thieves where they fell for the wolves and grizzly bears to discover and enjoy... Two hours later of more backtracking, Buck Snort and company arrived at the trap stealers' cabin tucked away in a draw some four miles away from Buck Snort's cabin. There after looking all around to make sure they were safe from any kind of a like in kind ambush like they had just pulled on the Hudson's Bay men, Buck Snort and company removed all the remainder of the trap stealers' horses from their corral, packed them with all of the dead men's year's worth of provisions and the furs they had caught on their own or had stolen from Buck Snort and company, burned their cabin and headed back to their own campsite.

Upon their arrival at their own campsite, Buck Snort and company unloaded the four dead men's year's worth of provisions and placed those goods that were perishable or needed to be kept dry like black powder, into their cabin for safekeeping. All other cooking implements, traps, leather gear and the like was then placed into their now chock-full storage shed for safekeeping. Then the dead men's four riding horses and eight packhorses were hobbled and let out into the nearby pasture along with the rest of the trappers' horses, so they could get 'acquainted' with each other and familiar with their new pasture so they would not run off when not hobbled later on. Following that spate of activity since the men had decided to just relax after completing their 'day's work', Clem fired up his outdoor cooking pit and set about making a celebratory supper for his crew to remember.

Into two Dutch ovens went rice and beans so they could begin soaking along with a bag of dried apple slices to soak as well in another kettle. Then over to their meat pole and with a little help from Wind Horse, Clem removed an entire backstrap from one of the cow buffalo quarters hanging in the wind. Once cleaned up, trimmed of all the dried bird poop routinely found on exposed meat hanging from the meat pole and cut into chunks and placed in another Dutch oven with a 'load' of red pepper flakes, salt, dried onion flakes and some flour for thickening, that 'Dutch' was hung over a low fire to slow cook. Then into a mess of biscuit and cobbler dough went several measures of dried raisins and set off to one side of the fire to rise.

In the meantime, Buck Snort and Muskrat disassembled all of the dead men's pistols and rifles, removed the lead and black powder fouling and then after oiling, reassembled them so they would be ready for any subsequent action where they might be needed. As the weapons were being cleaned and reassembled, Wind Horse using several different levels of coarseness of whetstones, put an edge onto each of the dead men's sheath knives and tomahawks for later use as well.

Come suppertime, found the four trappers gathered around their outside fire with a keg of rum appropriated from the four dead men who would have no further use for it and made it 'lighter in weight'. The day had started off rather badly for Buck Snort and company but had ended even worse for the four Hudson's Bay men causing the problem. Now Buck Snort and company figured they would end their day in celebration because their earlier problem was no more and all of them were in 'fine fettle' and getting 'finer'... Then Clem outdid himself in the 'cooking department' by serving the men a bean and rice dish, buffalo stew with red pepper flakes, biscuits, coffee and upon completion of those foodstuffs, the men gorged themselves on an apple cobbler, heavily mixed with brown sugar, cinnamon and a dash of rum for a 'kicker'. It was amazing just how well all of those trappers slept that evening after killing four of their own kind...

In order to make up for lost beaver trapping time, the trappers changed their normal operating procedures. Instead of just running only 15 of their traps, they increased that number to 30 realizing the winter freeze-up was almost upon them which would close down their fall beaver trapping season. For the next 17 days the trappers kept an eye on the weather and ran a trap line of 30 traps. Then when freeze-up came, they were more than ready to call it quits come the end of their fall beaver trapping efforts. However, in pushing themselves right to the brink of exhaustion during their fall beaver trapping efforts, they now had 513 trapped and bundled beaver *'Plus'* to show for such Herculean efforts!

Come freeze-up, Buck Snort called it right in removing all of their beaver traps just two days before a "Blue Norther" roared down out from the northwest and froze all 'free' waters stone solid to a depth of four inches! Then for the two days following that damn cold weather event, the men stayed mostly in their cabin, played cards and got in a lot of sleep to make up for the many long days right up to freeze-up de-fatting and hooping such a huge number of freshly caught beaver pelts.

Following that, for the next two days a cold wind blew out from the northwest portending another snowy weather event was on its way. In fact, by day two of such high winds and extremely cold weather, the temperatures dropped to below zero and stayed there, and many times the wind blew so hard that one night the cabin shook so violently the men had a hard time sleeping.

However by day three, the sun dawned weakly, the temperature rose above zero and the men were dying to get outside in order to care for their livestock, replace their depleted woodpile and maybe go on a buffalo hunt and acquire some fresh meat. Putting on his cold weather gear, Buck Snort walked out the door of their cabin that first morning of good weather, stretched his arms AND THEN NOTICED THAT THE GATE TO THEIR CORRAL HAD SWUNG WIDE OPEN AND THERE WAS NOT A HORSE IN SIGHT! IN FACT, A QUICK EYE SWEEP OF THEIR MEADOW FIGURING THEIR HORSES SOMEHOW HAD SOMEHOW ESCAPED INTO THEIR MAIN FEEDING AREA WAS MET WITH SEEING NOTHING BUT A SNOW-SWEPT MEADOW... WHATEVER HAD HAPPENED, THEY WERE NOW MISSING THEIR HORSE HERD OF FOUR RIDING AND TEN PACKHORSES, AS WELL AS THE FOUR RIDING AND EIGHT PACKHORSES ONE TIME BELONGING TO THE FOUR TRAP STEALING HUDSON'S BAY MEN!

Yelling at the top of his voice for the rest of the men to get up and then quickly pissing in their front yard (why he had gotten up so early in the first place), Buck Snort ran over to the horses' corral. A quick look around in the windblown layer of snow showed a large number of moccasin prints left behind! Now really yelling at the top of his voice and seeing a number of moccasin tracks heading up to their storage shed, Buck Snort ran in that direction to take a look as well. There upon his arrival, he discovered that the door to their storage shed was wide open and a number of their packsaddles were missing as were most of their bundles of fur! Additionally, their valuable six kegs of rum and the eight kegs of rum they had taken from the four dead trappers were missing as well!

Then it dawned on Buck Snort that the Indians who had taken all of their valuable livestock had done so during the night when the howling winds had covered all the noises they would have made in rustling such a large herd of livestock and stealing all of their furs and kegs of rum! By now, the rest of the trappers, most only half-dressed, were tumbling out the door of their cabin in response to Buck Snort's yelling. With what they saw in the total absence of all of their horses, it didn't take long for worried looks to fly across everyone's faces! Here it was the dead of winter and all four of the trappers were afoot and without any horses in which to successfully pursue the horse thieves! To the trappers' way of thinking, without those horses, it being winter time and they being deep in hostile Indian country, they were 'dead men walking'…

Realizing the very 'life or death' predicament they all now found themselves facing, the four trappers without a word being spoken between them broke and ran for their cabin! Once inside, there was frantic activity in dressing into their best cold weather gear, stepping into their heavier winter moccasins, jamming everything needed for a prolonged fight into their 'possibles' bags, refilling all of their powder horns, loading up several bags of jerky, and making sure everyone now carried a damn good rifle and two reliable pistols apiece! From the number of moccasin prints in the snow around the corral and storage shed, there had to be at least ten horse thieves, maybe even more! Without it being said, in the back of everyone's mind, whatever happened if the horse thieves were run down, some of the trappers may not be coming back because of the odds they would more than likely be facing. So out the door of their cabin the four grim-faced men trotted as they lined out hot on the trail of the fleeing horses and their captors.

With Wind Horse in the lead since he was the group's best tracker, the trappers quickly broke into the 'tried and true' gait any Frontier man instituted when facing such dire circumstances and needed to cover great amounts of ground fast. That trappers' gait under such circumstances meant the men trotted for 100 yards and then walked for 50. Then that regimen was repeated time and time again until the ground that needed covering was covered. Surprisingly, trappers utilizing such a regimen in pursuit or just to cover great distances in the shortest period of time could cover many miles in a day without tiring badly.

For the rest of that day, the four trappers pursued their horse thieves without rest and come nightfall, they found themselves sheltering under a dense thicket of western juniper. Sleep was hard to come by because of the intense cold and just eating snow to replace the water they lost from their body's exertions under such strenuous pursuit, but the men huddled together and by daylight the next morning they were once again hot on the trail of the stolen horses. However, as they began their second day of tracking and trying to watch the trail ahead for any signs of ambush at the same time, Wind Horse noticed something. When they had started their pursuit of the stolen horses, their animals' hoofprints were far apart showing the trackers that the horse herd was being pushed hard in order to outdistance any chance of pursuit. Now Wind Horse noticed the hoofprints of the horses were closer together and not being pushed as hard, as if thinking any form of pursuit was now out of the question. With that thinking in mind, the thieves could relax somewhat and not push their valuable horseflesh so hard being it was the dead of winter, grazing times were restricted and they had to be running on 'short rations' as well.

Once again come nightfall that second day of pursuit, found the trappers still hot on the trail but once again facing a cold freezing night out on the trail without the warmth from a fire. The entire time the men had been heading almost due north and were now deep into the very center of the land of the dreaded Blackfeet Indians. That did not set well with the trappers but like had been thought earlier, they were 'dead men walking' anyway without their horses... While huddling together for the warmth their bodies generated, Buck Snort leaned over to tighten his winter moccasins. When he did and took in a deep breath of air upon straightening back up, HE FROZE!

For the longest moment in time he just took in several deep breaths of the cold night air as if smelling for something. Taking another deep breath in the darkness, Buck Snort heard Wind Horse whisper, "Are you smelling what I am, My Brother?"

"I smell pinewood smoke like that coming from a campfire!" said Buck Snort quietly.

"I smell it as well! It is very faint but I am sure I smell the smoke from a pinewood campfire," said Wind Horse, with the sound of excitement rising up in his voice over what might be coming if in fact they did indeed smell wood smoke from a nearby campfire out there in the middle of nowhere!

Upon hearing such conversation, all the previously tired but now highly energized trappers were deeply drawing in deep draughts of the cold night air as if 'looking' for the smell of 'hope' in the air as well. Soon all of the men were acknowledging that they could also faintly smell pinewood smoke! The trappers' next move in the darkness was almost automatic. Every man re-checked the priming pan on their rifles and pistols to make sure they had not lost any powder in the jogging run throughout the day, making sure the weapons were more than ready to 'go' if called upon...

With that, the men fanned out in a line abreast position and began slowly walking through the timber in the snow in the direction their noses were leading them. Walking off the ridge they had previously occupied and down into a deep valley, the men finally saw the faint flickering light from two campfires far below! Another hour of sneaking through the timber finally found the four trappers watching the events occurring down below around two campfires from their place of hiding up on the hillside. From their positions, they were able to count 13 Indians moving around in much animation all brought on by the numerous cups of rum they had previously imbibed! Additionally, there were four other Indians lying around the campfires obviously passed out from too much celebrating the earlier successful raid involving the trappers' stolen horse herd, kegs of rum and valuable bundles of beaver pelts.

Being that the trappers were outnumbered and not wanting to chance any deaths among their little group in a firefight with that many Indians, the men decided they would wait out the drinking party being held below where the trappers were hidden. Then when 'demon rum' had taken its intended effect upon the Indians and the odds were more favorable because of too much drink passing over the thieves' lips, then and only then would the trappers strike. For the next hour, the men once again shivered in the snowy darkness while the Indians below danced and had a great time. Indians not realizing "Hell Was A-Coming" and soon a number of the rum-induced celebrants would be joining their own 'Cloud People' in the Indians' 'Upper World'!

Finally, when for the most part the party of Indians celebrating below had adjourned to their blankets in order to sleep off a good drunk, they left six Indians awake to provide guard duty and to keep the campfires blazing away. Finally after another hour of waiting quietly on the hillside, the four trappers made peace in their each and own way with their God of choice. Then with a last look among themselves, they began sneaking slowly down towards the light of the two camp-fires and the remaining now-dozing six Indians sitting next to the fires trying to keep warm and enjoy their rum-induced world...

Once again in a line abreast after previously setting out their battle plan of attack, the four trappers slowly stalked right up to the six Indians dozing by their campfires. Once behind each sleeping Indian and looking over at each other for the 'go' command, Muskrat nodded and swung his tomahawk all in the same motion! In a quick flurry of violence, the four trappers' tomahawks found the six heads of the dozing Indians sitting by the two fires and with soft sounding thumps, sent those six Indians up to their own Cloud People! Then quickly dropping their bloodied tomahawks and whirling around in order to face all the sleeping Indians cuddled up in their sleeping furs off to one side, the four trappers jointly cocked their rifles and once again with a nod from Muskrat, Buck Snort yelled out, "HEY!"

For what seemed to be an eternity, not one rum-impaired Indian moved from his sleeping blanket. Then almost simultaneously, the strange yell heard just seconds earlier finally managed to register through the eleven 'rum-soaked' sleeping 'mounds' and then all hell broke loose! Instantly and in different speeds of movement incumbent upon how much rum had been swilled earlier by each individual, the 'sleepers' arose from their blankets. When they did, they did so only to hear a crescendo of explosions, see white billowing clouds of black powder smoke enveloping them to a man, all 'graced' with speeding lead balls of death fired from the four trappers' rifles! Fired rifles that were then quickly dropped, followed by the trappers' eight pistols being drawn and fired from their shooters into those Indians still groggily standing from less than 15 feet away with their buck and ball…

Later that night, the four trappers, after imbibing several cups from their now-retrieved stolen kegs of rum, slept soundly and warmly wrapped up in the dead Indians' blankets next to the first warmth from the first campfires they had enjoyed in two days. The next morning, the trappers feasted on the remains of a calf elk the Indians had killed the day before for camp meat and once again, enjoyed several cups of rum... for medicinal purposes, of course...

The rest of that morning after breakfast, the trappers loaded up all of their packhorses, then mounting their own riding steeds, herded the entire number of horses, including those 17 belonging to the Indians and headed for their campsite. The men left the dead Indians where they fell for the wolves and any grizzly bears not in hibernation, and burned all of the Indians' blankets. The men burned all of the Indians' blankets because when all of them had awakened the next day after killing off their owners, discovered to a man they were now heavily infested with biting lice! So much that all of the trappers scratched all the way back to their campsite!

Arriving back at their campsite two days later, the men unpacked all of their pack and riding horses and let them into their meadow in order to feed. As for those horses belonging to the Indians, they were hobbled and then let out into the wind-swept meadow to feed as well with the rest of the livestock. Then more than ever mindful of the louse infestation they now harbored and under instructions from Muskrat who had suffered through such infestations earlier in his life and not wanting to spread the biting bugs into their cabin, he had Clem build up a large outdoor fire and set several kettles of water on the hanging rods over the flames. Then shivering like a pack of dogs 'passing peach pits', Muskrat had everyone undress in the winter weather and toss all of their clothing into the fire in order to kill the lice and any eggs they may have lain therein!

Following that, once the water was hot, each man was instructed to take out his sheath knife and using some of their soap, lather up their entire bodies and shave off all of the hair on their bodies, including that on their heads! This, instructed Muskrat, would allow their bodies to be pretty much cleansed of any louse or egg infestations and 'living quarters' in which future lice could survive. Somewhat later, Clem, Wind Horse, Muskrat and Buck Snort were looking at each other's naked and shaved bodies in the winter's cold air, like 'buffalo bumped owls'! Especially since each trapper had to help shave one another's bottom where they could not reach and genital areas! And when it came to the group shaving of the genital areas, the air was full of cautionary instructions when one another's sharp sheath knives were applied... Then Muskrat took one of the kettles of hot water, partially filled it with ashes from their firepit, mixed it up into a pasty-thick 'goo' and began thickly painting his whole body with the warm and gooey paste! By now, the rest of his group figured Muskrat had gone mad! Especially when a gray-coated Muskrat except for his two weird-looking eyeholes, ordered everyone else to do the same. When no one moved over those orders Muskrat said, "If you want the lice to get into our cabin and begin living there and on our bodies, don't do what I am doing. But the ash mixture with its chemical properties smeared on my body will kill off any remaining lice and their eggs. This is the only way I know how to do so as taught to me by my Beloved Mother to kill all of the lice off."

Moments later, the remaining three men were coating themselves with the gooey ash and water mixture from head to toe because they had enough of the incessant itching they had just undergone for the last two days while riding back to their campsite! Then as everyone walked around like the 'gray men' they were, Muskrat had Clem draw some more kettles of water from where he had broken the ice in their nearby creek and heat the same. Later once the water had been heated, Muskrat had the men wash off in their creek in the cold water then run over to their campfire and wash up with the warm water and soap. Then when they were rinsed off, Muskrat let everyone and their shivering hairless bodies into their cabin. There Clem built a fire in their fireplace, heated up some coffee water as the men dressed, using their second set of reserve clothing and winter moccasins so they could warm up. Then it was back to their piles of English-made clothing that were still usable like shirts, socks and the like, which were cast into a large pot and boiled to kill the remaining lice and their eggs. Aside from all of the initial grumbling from the now bald-headed men, the incessant itching from the skin parasites picked up from sleeping in the dead Indians' blankets was never a problem ever again...

For the next two days, except for cooking water and bringing in more wood, the trappers seldom left their cabin. There they fashioned new winter clothing from their reserve supplies and tore down the eleven rifles and four pistols taken from the dead Indians, cleaned them from the previous lead and powder fouling they individually carried, oiled and then reassembled them so they would be ready for action if called upon to do so in the coming days. However with the reserve of rifles and pistols already in the trappers' care, the thought was come the next time they were selling their beaver skins, they would sell the extra Indian weaponry as well.

Finished with their 'cabin duties', the men headed up into the surrounding forest, cut additional rail timbers, horse-dragged them down in the snow to their corral site and expanded their corral in order to make room for all of the Indians' horses. Because the ground was frozen, there were no postholes dug and the corral was just extended using the sides of nearby aspens onto which to nail the extra railing needed to expand the corral's size. Once the expanded horse corral had been finished, the trappers loaded up two panniers with their wolf traps and associated wolf trapping gear. The following morning with Muskrat in the lead and Wind Horse and Buck Snort each trailing two packhorses, followed by sharp-eyed and sharpshooting Clem, the men headed off on their first wolf trapping trip of the winter season.

However, another change had been made in light of the fact the trappers had killed off 17 Indians, all determined by Muskrat to be Blackfeet, whom all figured would soon have a party of their own kind coming down and looking for them. With that thought in mind, the trappers had made a change in their normal routine in that they were now better armed if challenged by superior numbers of Blackfeet. One of the packhorses trailed by Buck Snort carried two panniers. And those two panniers now carried 15 fully loaded rifles that had been taken from the Indians just killed and from the four Hudson's Bay trap stealing men. With that kind of reserve weaponry along with what each of the trappers personally carried, if given just a fair chance against superior numbers of Indians, they figured they could give a good and deadly accounting of themselves.

Following their old tried and true method of trapping wolves, the men located several groups of buffalo and killed four old bulls which because of their larger body size would make better trap bait. Then since wolves routinely followed buffalo herds hoping to kill off the old and infirm, the trappers opened up the animals and spread their insides out onto the ground around each dead animal's carcass to increase the welcome smell of death in the area. Which when done would attract the winter-hungry wolves even more easily to the carcasses and trap sites. Then two wolf traps were set around each buffalo kill site and hoping a wolf's hunger would override his caution upon approaching the buffalo's carcass, thereby causing it to step into a trap. With that, the men left the area. However, from the four old bull buffalo killed and used as bait sites, their backstraps had been removed and now rested in one of the horse's panniers for the next couple of suppers once the men were back at their cabin.

For the next two weeks the four trappers ran their wolf trap lines and were catching from two to five beautifully furred wolves every time they ran those trap lines. Then one morning, they got surprised. While running their last set of wolf traps at the end of their trap line, all of a sudden about 30 Indians rode out from the timber on both sides of the trappers and quickly surrounded them! Realizing they had been caught out in the open, the trappers quickly dismounted and using their horses as shields, formed into a clump of horses and heavily armed and determined men ready to extract the highest price for their lives once the shooting started…

As the trappers awaited their fate being so heavily outnumbered and determined to make the Indians pay and pay dearly if they attacked, all of a sudden one lone Indian rode his horse forward from all the rest of those surrounding the four trappers and continued slow-walking his horse forward towards the determined to give their all if attacked, trappers. Stopping his horse a few yards away from the trappers standing behind their horses, the Indian just sat there on his horse for a few moments looking at the trapped men. All of a sudden, that Indian dismounted and standing there facing the trappers, slowly raised his right hand and arm in the universal Plains Indians' sign of greeting!

"Well, I'll be damned!" said Muskrat, who knew sign language learned from his earlier days as a trapper out on the prairies. Handing his horse's reins to Buck Snort, Muskrat stepped out from behind the clump of trappers' horses and raised his right hand in 'greeting' as well. With that showing of friendship on the part of the trappers, the lone Indian began walking towards the group of trappers. Walking up to Muskrat and in perfect English the noble-looking Indian, obviously one of rank within the tribe, said to Muskrat, "Welcome to our land, killers of the hated Blackfeet!"

Stunned over hearing such words, Muskrat replied, "You speak English?"

"Yes, I speak the language of the white man very well. I learned as a boy when the "Black Robes" (Franciscans) came to my "Lodge Grass" village and lived with my people the "Crow" for over a year. My name is "Black Wolf" and I see that the white man trappers are trapping the 'little people of my namesake'."

Still in shock over the Indian speaking English, Muskrat hesitated for a moment not knowing quite what to say in the trappers' defense of trapping Black Wolf's 'namesake people', namely the gray wolves. Then he extended his hand saying, "My people call me "Muskrat". Behind me stand my friends "Buck Snort", an Indian named "Wind Horse" and a man whose name is just "Clem"."

"My people tracked you all the way from what we call 'Buffalo Valley", where we discovered 17 of the much-eaten-upon bodies by the animals, Blackfeet. Blackfeet we had been chasing ever since they attacked one of our smaller wintering bands of people, killed all of the warriors, took their horses, women and children and then with their prisoners, some of them returned to their country in the land of the Blackfeet "From Beyond the North Wind". We found where you and your kind ambushed all 17 of those remaining Blackfeet, who stayed in my country killing, raping and stealing the children of those of my kind they caught not looking. We followed your old tracks to here to see who had done such a good deed. How did you do that, white man, with only four of you against the 17 Blackfeet?" asked Black Wolf.

"Black Wolf, there is nothing to tell. Those Blackfeet stole all of our horses one night so we tracked them down on foot and killed them for being very bad Indians," said Muskrat as he looked Black Wolf coldly in his eyes…

"You are very brave, white man, or very foolish to have attacked so many fierce Blackfeet with so few warriors on your side. Or maybe it is that The Great Spirit looked favorably upon you and yours," said Black Wolf quietly, but impressed over what the trappers had accomplished in killing 17 of the sworn enemy of the Crow Nation.

"Black Wolf, we are just a short ways from our cabin. It is cold and my men are hungry. If you and your men are cold and hungry too, what say we kill a buffalo and you and your men follow us to our cabin where we can cook up the buffalo, make some biscuits, coffee and share this food around a warm campfire as friends," said Muskrat.

For the longest time Black Wolf just looked at Muskrat trying to figure the crazy white man out. A crazy white man who had attacked a larger number of fierce Blackfeet killing all of them, and now had just invited 30 of his warriors, people he did not know, to their cabin for something to eat and drink. Then Black Wolf said, "We have already been to your cabin earlier this morning and you have no meat hanging from your meat pole. My men will kill a buffalo and bring the meat to your cabin. Then you and my kind can sit down and share a meal in peace between our two peoples."

With those words, Black Wolf whirled, mounted his horse and returned to his warriors. After a short conversation with his warriors, Black Wolf turned in his saddle, waved 'Good-bye' and then the Indians disappeared in the direction of the trappers' cabin. Turning, Muskrat returned to his group of now much relieved and surprised trappers saying, "Clem, we will shortly have all of those Indians for breakfast at our cabin. We need to hurry up and return so we can get a fire going, get some coffee boiling away and every oven you have baking biscuits. The Indian I talked to is named Black Wolf and he is a Crow, who are mostly friendly to the white man. They have been tracking us ever since our fight with the 17 drunken Blackfeet. They apparently were after them for killing a number of their people. When they found the bodies of the Blackfeet, they saw our tracks and began backtracking us to see who had done such a killing and them a favor. Their trackers led them to where they found us this morning. As such, I invited them to come to our cabin in peace and have some breakfast. Black Wolf agreed and he and his men are going off to kill a buffalo and bring the meat to our camp to be cooked since they saw that our meat pole was empty. So if we don't want to disappoint our new friends and guests, we best make haste for our cabin and begin making preparations for a crowd of hungry Indians. And being they are 30 or so in number and we are only four, I sure as hell don't want to disappoint them if they are coming for fresh biscuits, buffalo and coffee."

Racing back to their campsite, once dismounted and after corralling the horses, everyone pitched in making ready for the Indian guests yet to come. In so doing, Clem got his campfire going while Wind Horse and Buck Snort went to their storage shed and brought forth the three Dutch ovens they had gathered up after the trappers had killed off the Hudson's Bay men and then raided their cabin for their supplies. Those heavy cast iron kettles were soon at the fireside and being prepared for use by Clem to be used in conjunction with their own three Dutch ovens. Then Wind Horse returned to the storage shed and brought forth a sack of flour and a tin of yeast so Clem could work his 'biscuit magic'. In the meantime, Muskrat brought forth all of their cups, extra plates and second two-gallon coffee pot so with their own regularly used coffee pot, they could boil up four gallons of the brew at a time. Then as Buck Snort cut more wood for the cooking to come, Clem went into the storage shed and brought forth a sack of brown sugar cones. This he did because he figured the Indians soon to come would prefer their coffee sweet instead of as strong as an 'angry mule's kick' like he usually made for his men. Soon the two coffee pots were boiling, the Dutch ovens were heating up and the biscuit dough was rising inside of the trappers' cabin alongside the fire in their fireplace, so the yeast would have time to cause the dough to rise and be ready for the baking to come.

About then a thundering herd of horses and mounted Indians rounded the finger of trees below the cabin site and rode up to the trappers' cabin. Four of the Indian horsemen offloaded slabs of fresh buffalo meat into the arms of Clem and Wind Horse and then the Indians dismounted and quickly gathered around the firepit upon smelling the fresh aroma of coffee boiling away. Soon many eager hands were outstretched holding cups and bowls used as cups, so they could drink the 'devil's brew' that Clem was serving just as fast as he could pour and add some brown sugar.

Since Clem was busy serving his brand of 'trappers' coffee' with the added brown sugar, Wind Horse cut up the buffalo meat and spitted it on metal stakes over the campfire. Then Buck Snort and Clem formed biscuit-sized lumps of dough and placed them into the plethora of Dutch ovens around the firepit, set them over the coal beds and then covered the flanged lids with heaps of coals shoveled on top. Soon the air around the crowded campfire smelled of sour body odor from the Indians who had been in the saddle for the last week without a chance to bathe, the great aroma of boiling coffee, the cooking smell of roasting buffalo meat fat dripping into the flames, and the delicate smell of Dutch oven biscuits by the score. It finally got so crowded around the firepits by hungry Indians, Clem had to shoo them off so he could continue working his magic around the fires in order to feed such a bunch of damn hungry men...

As Clem lifted the flanged Dutch oven lids covered with hot coals with a hay hook exposing golden brown biscuits, he soon had numbers of Indians surrounding every 'Dutch' whose lid he lifted wanting biscuits. Soon because of the demand, with Wind Horse forming the biscuit dough and placing the dough balls into the bottom of the Dutch ovens, Clem was soon serving the much-sought after golden brown biscuits about every three minutes to numbers of greedy outstretched hands, hot biscuits or not! Then Buck Snort and Muskrat began serving slices of spitted buffalo meat and just as fast as they cut the meat off the spits, many eager hands were shoved forward with a knife on the end of it wanting a slice of meat on their plate or thrust in between slices of biscuits so a biscuit and buffalo meat sandwich could be had, or just eaten off the end of a sheath knife... Thus went the trappers' morning as an entire 20-pound sack of flour was emptied making biscuits, all the buffalo meat eaten and six gallons of hot coffee served! Additionally, a five-pound sack of brown sugar cones was consumed in the Indians' coffee as sweetener as well! Finally what seemed like a never-ending outstretching of hands and plates finally stopped, and now with much belching and happy talk around the firepit, Black Wolf's Indians had finally eaten their fill.

It was then that Black Wolf rose from a sitting log along the edge of the firepit and after a respectful hushed silence had fallen among all of his men and the hard at work trappers filling in as cooks said, "Today we from the mighty Crow Nation have met and eaten with our new white man trapper friends. As me and my warriors have seen, the trappers are great warriors and have killed many Blackfeet who are our enemies. So I say to our new friends, welcome to the lands of the Lodge Grass Band of Crow Indians. Let it be known to all that the four trappers that we have eaten with this day are our friends and will be so forever as long as the grass is green and the buffalo cover our land." Having said his say, Black Wolf walked over to each trapper and shook his hand in friendship. Then without further ado, the Indians still having a distance to go to get back to their band and winter encampment, mounted up and with a wave of his hand, Black Wolf and his warriors rode across the meadow and out of sight as they headed south along the Bighorn River to their winter campsite.

(Author's Note: Black Wolf's original campsite location many years later in 1876, was near what was to become a dark and bloody final resting ground to over 250 soldiers and Indian scouts from the Seventh Cavalry, who were swept away by over 1,000 fighting Sioux, Northern Cheyenne and Northern Arapaho warriors defending their culture, a way of life, their land, women and children. A number of Black Wolf's kin acting as scouts for General Custer would also die along-side their fellow compatriots from the Seventh Cavalry in that great and historical battle, which was the actual beginning of the end of a Native American culture that had existed for over 1,500 years in the United States...)

For the next two months of winter, Buck Snort and his group of trappers ranged far and wide in their wolf trapping quest. In fact, several times the group of trappers ranged further south than they ever did trapping wolves. When they did, after setting out their wolf traps, they would return back to their cabin riding along the Bighorn River checking out the new beaver trapping areas. Areas that were still frozen over but the trappers could at least see what the possible opportunities were available once the ice went out and the spring beaver trapping season was upon them.

It was during one of those long distance trips setting out their wolf traps that Wind Horse found himself one morning intently watching their back trail. On one of those occasions when he was closely examining their back trail, he caught Buck Snort's attention. With that, Buck Snort rode over to his friend who was sitting on his horse and quietly watching their back trail.

"What is bothering you, My Friend?" asked Buck Snort as he rode up.

"I don't know but my instincts are telling me we are being watched," replied Wind Horse as he continued watching their back trail.

While Clem and Muskrat were in the process of setting their last in a series of wolf traps, Buck Snort and Wind Horse closely examined the back country they had just traveled. However, after a while of doing so, they both relented and rode over to give Clem a hand in setting their last wolf trap. Finally finished with the concealing of the last wolf trap, the men mounted up and headed for the Bighorn River once again so on the way back to their campsite they could look over the potential trapping opportunities for beaver come the spring trapping season. Several hours later the tired and now cold men rode their horses into their campsite, removed their saddles and turned them loose with the rest of their horses so they could feed in their nearby wind-swept meadow. Then the men walked over to the creek in their area near the corrals and once again broke up the winter's thick ice so there would be some open water so the horses could water upon their return to the corrals later in the day.

Then each man gathered in an armload of wood and took it into their cabin so they would have wood for their fireplace. Shortly thereafter with the fireplace 'roaring' away, the cabin warmed and the men removed a lot of their heavier winter clothing as the cabin heated up. Later as Clem put the finishing touches to the men's supper, Buck Snort and Wind Horse dressed once again into their heavier winter clothing, grabbed up their rifles and headed out on foot into their meadow to round up and bring their horses in for the night. After herding their rather large horse herd by the creek's open water so they could drink, the horses were then corralled and the gate tied shut and bolted with their chain and bolt. However, as Buck Snort and Wind Horse walked back to their cabin, Wind Horse once again paused and looked down across their meadow in the evening's fading light as if looking for something. Seeing nothing, he just shook his head as if trying to shake off a nagging feeling, walked into their warm cabin behind Buck Snort and closed the heavy log front door.

Finishing a great meal of rice and beans, Dutch oven biscuits and coffee, the men retired to the work space at the rear of their cabin and tended to finishing up the dressing of the last wolf pelts caught several days earlier. As they did, Clem set about cleaning up after supper and 'dressing' all of his cast iron so it would be ready for the next meal. Then he too headed for the back of their cabin where the rest of the men were seated upon their log chairs working and dressing out their freshly caught wolf pelts and 'boarded' them so they would dry. And when Clem did, he smiled as he arrived in the back of the cabin where the pelting work was done. There hanging on or stacked alongside the walls were 61 already dried or drying wolf pelts, most of which were the more valuable darker colored ones!

Later into the evening, Buck Snort, after eating such a big supper, felt the urge to empty out his system of the previous day's supper. Knowing he would not be outside long taking care of his urgent call of nature, he just slipped on a capote, grabbed up his rifle and hustled out the front door of the cabin before he had a 'wreck'! Trotting around behind their cabin where he had a sitting log upon which to sit when having one of his bowel movements, Buck Snort did not dither along on his urgent mission. Dropping his buckskins, he turned and sat down on his frozen sitting log and began taking care of business which involved expelling lots of loud and very smelly gas along with a substantial amount of solids!

As he did, he could not help but remember his time back at the orphanage when he had been poisoned with rat poison by the three meaner and older boys who were leaving the facility the next day. Three older boys who out of spite had slipped rat poison into the orphanage's oatmeal and in so doing, Buck Snort's later ingestion of the poisoned food had badly damaged his digestive system. Damaged his digestive system so badly that frequently in his later life he had bad gas problems, especially if eating beans, rice or anything made from wheat, like Clem's biscuits!

As Buck Snort sat there on his sitting log out back of their cabin passing great amounts of gas along with his bowel movements, he failed to hear the arrival of three horses quietly approaching in the snow and stopping at the front of his cabin. However, shortly thereafter he did hear a lot of loud noises and shouting coming from inside his cabin after hearing the front door slam shut over and above the loud gaseous noises he was making ridding his system of his previous night's supper! At first he thought maybe when he was scraping a wolf hide preparing it for being 'boarded' he had left some of his badly smelling gas behind before he left to 'take care of business'. And if he did, it had just been discovered by one of his compatriots much to that person's chagrin! Then Buck Snort began to quietly laugh to himself if he had in fact left his 'calling card' behind and someone had inadvertently 'fallen prey' to its bad smell. That thought in mind, he began laughing once again over someone's grief, knowing he would catch hell when he returned to the group.

However, the shouting that he had heard earlier after hearing the front door to their cabin slammed open had not diminished and he then realized that something was badly wrong and strangely out of place in the cabin! Then Buck Snort heard Wind Horse shouting really loudly and knowing his friend, realized that he was doing so in order to provide some sort of a warning to him as he sat outside in the cold on his sitting log 'taking care of business'!

Squeezing out the last of his 'business', Buck Snort jerked up his buckskins, grabbed his rifle lying along his side propped up on his sitting log, cocked back the hammer and then began sneaking around the side of their cabin as he headed for the front door. Quietly walking around the side of the cabin, Buck Snort was surprised to see three unknown riding horses tied off on their hitching rail! As he did, he could now hear crashing of things inside the cabin and then finally the realization set in that the three riders from the horses tied off in front of the cabin represented danger to himself and his compatriots!

Seeing that the front door was slightly ajar leaving an opening for him to look through and see inside, Buck Snort moved slightly forward and in so doing, could see his three friends standing at the back of their cabin with their hands raised above their heads! However, because the opening was so slight, he could not see the identity of who was causing his friends to surrender. Using the end of his rifle barrel to just move the heavy log door open ever so slightly, Buck Snort could now see the backs of three burly, heavily bearded and buckskin-dressed men holding rifles on his three friends. That was when he could also see the looks on the faces of his three friends changing from concern to one of hope upon seeing what Buck Snort was quietly doing. And in so doing, all three of his friends were now not looking at their three assailants but obviously looking right at him through the now slightly opened log doorway…

When that slight eye movement and change in the demeanor of his three friends shifted from one of terror to that of hope, those 'changes in looks' were also observed by the three burly men holding his friends at bay with their rifles! THAT WAS WHEN ALL HELL BROKE LOOSE! QUICKLY SHOVING THE LOG DOOR OPEN WITH THE END OF HIS RIFLE BARREL, BUCK SNORT FOUND HIMSELF LOOKING AT CURTIS, DARRELL AND HARRY! THE SAME THREE OLDER BOYS AND BULLIES AT THE ORPHANAGE WHO HAD EARLY ON BEATEN HIM SEVERAL TIMES OVER AND HAD REPEATEDLY RAPED HIM BEFORE WIND HORSE HAD ARRIVED AND JOINED FORCES WITH HIM AS A FIGHTING PARTNER! THE SAME THREE MEN WHO HAD PUT THE RAT POISON INTO THE FOOD AT THE ORPHANAGE AND BEFORE THEY HAD LEFT, THREATENED HIM WITH DEATH IF THEY EVER SAW HIM AGAIN AFTER BUCK

SNORT HAD FINALLY MANAGED TO BEST THE THREE MEN IN A FIGHT WITH THE HELP OF WIND HORSE!

BOOM! WENT BUCK SNORT'S RIFLE AND FROM JUST FOUR FEET AWAY, SHOT THE FACE CLEAR OFF OF CURTIS JUST AS HE HAD RECOGNIZED WHO WAS AT THE DOOR AND WAS IN THE PROCESS OF RAISING HIS RIFLE TO SHOOT BUCK SNORT! WHEN BUCK SNORT SHOT, HIS CLOUD OF WHITE BLACK POWDER SMOKE ENVELOPED THE THREE MEN HOLDING CLEM, WIND HORSE AND MUSKRAT AT BAY. WITH BUCK SNORT'S SHOT, CURTIS'S BODY FLEW OFF TO ONE SIDE FROM THE IMPACT OF THE HEAVY .52 CALIBER LEAD BALL FIRED FROM SUCH A SHORT DISTANCE AWAY! THE NEXT THING HARRY AND DARRELL SAW EMERGING FROM THE WHITE BLACK POWDER CLOUD OF SMOKE ENVELOPING THEM WAS A WILD-EYED BUCK SNORT WITH HIS SHEATH KNIFE UPRAISED! BEFORE ANYONE COULD EVEN BLINK, ITS LONG BLADE HAD BEEN PLUNGED INTO THE RIGHT EYE OF HARRY TO THE HILT, SENDING BOTH MEN CRASHING TO THE FLOOR IN THE HUMAN IMPACT OF THE ATTACK! DARRELL, FINALLY RECOVERING HIS SENSES FROM ALL THE FURY SURROUNDING HIM, SWUNG HIS RIFLE BARREL TOWARDS BUCK SNORT AS HE ROSE UP OFF THE BODY

OF HARRY WITH HIS KNIFE IN HAND!
"THUMP-THUMP-THUMP!" WENT THE SOFT
SOUNDS OF THREE TOMAHAWKS THROWN
SIMULTANEOUSLY BY WIND HORSE, CLEM
AND MUSKRAT, WHICH SLAMMED INTO
THE BACK OF DARRELL'S HEAD, NECK
AND BETWEEN HIS SHOULDER BLADES
BEFORE HE COULD GET OFF HIS KILLING
SHOT INTENDED FOR BUCK SNORT! IN AN
INSTANT, DARRELL DROPPED HIS RIFLE
AND INSTINCTIVELY AND AS A REFLEX,
GRABBED THE BACK OF HIS HEAD WITH
BOTH OF HIS HANDS AS IF TRYING TO
REMOVE THE OFFENDING TOMAHAWK.
HE DIED BEFORE HE HIT THE FLOOR OF
THE CABIN, MAKING A SOFT "CRUMPLING"
SOUND...

In an instant, Clem, Muskrat and Wind Horse
grabbed up their nearby rifles in case there were
more deadly surprises waiting just outside their
open doorway! But there was no need for the
danger had now passed and in all three cases, the
just moments before assailants were finding their
lifeblood draining away from their bodies as they
lay sprawled out across the cabin floor! Then
in a fit of disgust and inhuman strength clearly
remembering his brutal rapes at the hands of the
three bullies back at the orphanage as a younger
man, Buck Snort picked up the bodies of Curtis,
Harry and Darrell and individually body-tossed
them out from the cabin and into the front yard

almost hitting the men's three horses. Quietly, Clem, Muskrat and Wind Horse walked outside, pulled their tomahawks from Darrell's body and wiped the blood off their blades on the dead man's shirt so the steel in their blades would not corrode or rust...

The next day after breakfast, Buck Snort and Wind Horse tied ropes around the necks of the three dead men, dragged their bodies down to the Bighorn River and tossed them out onto the river's ice. There they were left for the critters of the skies and land to enjoy. Then come spring-time, whatever was left of those three would have drifted into the river's depths and remained there forever. Wind Horse and Buck Snort never mentioned the three men again except years later when in a different place and time, made sure their old friend Cliff Fulton, the orphanage's blacksmith, knew of the three bullies' demise...

Suspecting the three dead men had to have a camp somewhere nearby out where Wind Horse's instincts had stirred from within and near their latest wolf trap line, the four trappers set out backtracking the three dead men's horses' hoofprints. A day later of riding southward along the Bighorn River, they discovered the three dead men's camp and cabin. There they discovered eight very hungry and thirsty horses in a corral which were immediately let out to feed and wa-ter. Then somewhat later after those horses had put on the 'feed bag' and watered somewhat, they were packed with the three dead men's supplies, provisions and 263 fall trapped beaver pelts. Then the four trappers realizing they now had 263 beaver pelts from the three dead men and an additional 316 they had acquired earlier from the dead Hudson's Bay men, they had no further need to winter trap wolves for the money that would have generated. Realizing the extra wealth they had acquired in beaver pelts alone, the four trappers pulled all of their wolf traps and trapped those animals no more that winter since they had already trapped and pelted out 61 of those beautiful animals for later sale at the new Fort Henry.

In short, with the spring beaver trapping season facing the men and the bounty that would bring, they were already rich men… Especially so when they considered the previous Letter of Credit from the Ashley-Henry Fur Trade Company that Buck Snort possessed in his saddlebag from the previous year's 1822-23 beaver and wolf trapping sales. Then if one considered the huge horse herd they now possessed and could sell to Major Henry back at the new Fort Henry, the men were well on their way to being able to purchase land back in Missouri and enjoy life to the fullest whenever they so desired. However, it was very apparent that the men were still interested in continuing their trapping efforts in the years to come so they could see more of the unexplored West… There was no two ways about it, the love of adventure and even danger became so natural and ingrained into the heart and soul of every Mountain Man that it led numerous times to the continued exploring of all aspects of the wilderness and for many, kept them there forever... The rest of that winter's months were spent in caring for their extensive horse herd, hunting buffalo for food, repairing pack and saddle gear, casting bullets and planning for the coming spring beaver trapping season which would soon be upon them. However, during one of their evenings when their work was done as was their supper and the men were sitting around in their cabin drinking a cup of rum, Muskrat all of a sudden got 'quiet as a mouse pissin' on a ball of cotton'... Finally when the other three men noticed how quiet and introspective the normally talkative Muskrat had gotten, they began looking at him for an explanation. Realizing his fellow trappers were looking at him with questions in their eyes, he said, "I just realized trouble came to all of us in 'threes' this trapping season here on the Bighorn. I am beginning to feel that is a bad luck omen as are the increasing number of trappers flooding into this area from Fort Henry at the start of every spring trapping season. I am wondering and just saying, maybe we four ought to move on and leave this area to all of those coming down from Fort Henry in ever increasing numbers and find ourselves another place less crowded. I say that because it seems with us, with people come trouble. As I said, just saying, trouble coming at us in 'threes' is not a good sign and all of us need to pay closer attention in the future to whenever Wind Horse and his Indian heritage has an inclination that something is wrong. The many years of his Native American history coursing through his veins has to account for something..."

Stepping out from their cabin one spring morning with rifle in hand, Buck Snort stopped and breathed in deeply the morning's cool air. Then looking skyward, he checked for what the skies were 'telling' him regarding the day's weather. Looking back down, found he was looking at Muskrat sitting by their outside campfire looking intently back at him...

"What do you think?" asked Muskrat. "Do we trappers start today or wait another few days before we begin our spring beaver trapping?"

"My itching hide tells me it is time to head south on the Bighorn and see if we can catch a beaver or two before someone else traps them all out," said Buck Snort with a smile over being 'caught' sensing his surroundings. Then he walked over to the grove of male aspens budding out their catkins every way from Sunday and took care of a call of nature. (Author's Note: Male aspens bud out their catkins in the spring of the year before their female counterparts.) Then Buck Snort headed over to their shaving trees, washed up, shaved and combed his hair. Then placing his straight razor back on his shaving stump along with his comb, Buck Snort walked over to their outside campfire where Clem handed him a cup of hot coffee guaranteed to open even the sleepiest set of eyes.

"I agree," said Muskrat as he blew on his hot cup of coffee and then took a sip. "I think all of the ice is out and with that, the beaver will be in their prime for a few more weeks before they begin losing their heavier winter coats."

About then Wind Horse arrived at the fire after taking care of a call of nature and washing up over by their creek. "When are we going to start our spring beaver trapping?" he asked, unaware of the earlier conversation between Buck Snort and Muskrat about starting their spring beaver trapping season.

Muskrat and Buck Snort just smiled, realizing their spring beaver trapping would start that very day. Clem, overhearing all of his partners' conversations just smiled and shook his head as well. As the camp's cook as well as the main beaver skinner, de-fatting and hooping partner, his days were now going to get longer, a lot longer...

Later that morning right after breakfast, found the men loading up four of their packhorses' panniers with extra rifles, traps, hand axes, bottles of castor, twine and a number of their dried wooden anchor poles. Then their saddle horses were curried down and saddled, as Buck Snort returned to the men's cabin and retrieved a tanned deerskin bag full of jerky for the men to have for their lunch. Leaving their camp in their usual caravan arrangement, the men rode out to the Bighorn and then turned south.

Riding past the end of the previous year's trap line because they had trapped out all of the beaver in and along that area of the Bighorn, the men continued riding even further south to a new beaver trapping territory. Then all of a sudden, the men discovered that the Bighorn River split and a smaller river ran further to the southeast. Muskrat and Buck Snort sat side by side on their horses discussing this new portion of the old Bighorn and what to do, when Wind Horse trailing his two packhorses rode up alongside the two men saying, "Best we cross the Bighorn and follow and trap along this river running to the southeast. Since it is smaller than the Bighorn but comes from it, let us call this smaller river the "Little Bighorn". And since from where I am sitting on my horse I can already see much sign of beaver, I say we go that way and start trapping along that waterway. That way maybe we can get away from all the new trappers coming down from Fort Henry."

Then Muskrat said, "At the end of last winter when we were discussing that trouble came to us in 'threes' last year, I also suggested that we listen more to what Wind Horse has to say about his inclinations. After all, he has that Indian blood coursing through his veins and his people have been surviving here a lot longer than any of us white men. So with that in mind, I say we go where Wind Horse suggests. And I like the name he has for our newest beaver trapping adventure, so I say it's onto the Little Bighorn for whatever riches or failures 'she' decides to share with the four of us."

Moments later, the trappers found a shallow ford where they could safely cross the Bighorn River and did so. They then proceeded along the river running slightly to the southeast that they had now named the Little Bighorn. About a quarter-mile below the junction where the Little Bighorn River entered the Bighorn, the trappers stopped riding and sat there on their horses looking over a large watered area adjacent the river in amazement over all the fresh signs therein of beaver living in the area! That entire area was dotted with conical beaver houses, ponds were stitched across in many places with typical mud and stick beaver dams, as all along the banks there was much evidence showing numerous signs of fresh beaver slides and trees being girdled or in the process of being cut down by the numerous beaver living there. Moments later found Buck Snort and Wind Horse dressing into their beaver trapping clothing, grabbing traps, anchor poles and hand axes, and setting out to locate the best spots in which to set out their beaver traps into their newest spring beaver trap line.

For the rest of that morning with Clem assisting the two trappers, the men laid out all 30 of their beaver traps full well knowing that at some point in time they would have to reduce their number because of the beaver's extensive number in the area. Once the trap setting work was done, typically the men headed for a grove of cottonwoods and dismounted so their horses could feed as the men rested. By early afternoon, the men had once again mounted up and rode back along their newest trap line checking to see if they had caught any beaver. Any beaver caught were skinned, the traps reset and the men proceeded on until they had checked their entire trap line. Then it was back to their cabin with their first day's catch, the 18 beaver pelts were de-fatted, hooped and stacked along the cabin's walls so they could dry. Thus became the trappers' daily routine along the Little Bighorn until the beaver went out from prime and then the men's traps were pulled.

That first evening after the last trap had been pulled and the remaining pelts had been de-fatted and hooped, the tired men gathered for a celebratory supper of spitted buffalo (the men's favorite), beans, biscuits, coffee and using the last of their dried apple slices previously soaked in water so they would re-hydrate, a Clem-special Dutch oven cobbler. After such a supper, the men and the local mosquitoes enjoyed several cups of rum and smoked their pipes in celebration of another successful beaver trapping season as they sat on their sitting logs around the campfire. However, heavy in the air besides the ever-present clouds of mosquitoes and pipe smoke were the men's conversations regarding moving on to newer beaver trapping grounds come the fall beaver trapping season.

As it turned out, the end of their spring beaver trapping line was now on the Little Bighorn and approximately 13 miles away from their current cabin site. By the men's third cup of rum, they had decided they would move their campsite away from their current homesite and move over to the Little Bighorn so they could be closer to their work. There they would establish a new cabin near their newest trap line and away from the increasing number of trappers moving down from Fort Henry who were also trapping along the Bighorn River and now its many adjacent waterways. That, plus the spring beaver trapping season on the Little Bighorn had already produced another 303 beaver 'Plus', most of which were Made Beaver (adult in size), and there had been no sign of diminishing number of beaver the further south the trappers ran their newest trap line!

For the next three weeks, the four trappers were 'neck deep' in work preparing for their annual summer trip to Fort Henry in order to sell their furs, extra horses, implements acquired from the Hudson's Bay and three 'orphanage' men's camps, along with all the extra firearms acquired from the Indians and trappers alike and not needed. Buffalo and deer were hunted for camp meat and the making of jerky, as well as more tanned deerskins to cover the fur bundles, extra bullets were cast, new packsaddles were constructed from leather supplies to accommodate all of the beaver 'Plus', and packsaddle leather goods from the other dead trappers were repaired for use as well. Additionally and importantly, new hobbles were made from tanned deer hides in order to better control their large horse herd come nightfall and keep them from wandering off while on the trail. Lastly Buck Snort and Wind Horse disassembled all of the men's personal rifles and pistols, removed their lead and black powder fouling, oiled the moving parts with bear oil and then reassembled them for use on the coming difficult trip to be made to Fort Henry.

Come the day of departure from the Bighorn campsite, the men were up way before dawn because of all the 'horse packing' that needed doing. Several days earlier, the men had already assembled all of the packs and filled all of their panniers for the trip ahead to Fort Henry. Now on the day of departure, the men had to load all of the packs and panniers onto their packhorses. Then as Clem prepared a late and last breakfast at their campsite, Muskrat, Wind Horse and Buck Snort began loading all of their packs upon their packhorses. Somewhat later after breakfast had been had by all, the last packhorse had been loaded by around noon!

Making sure all of their mares were roped and trailed together, so the other younger horses and new horses to the herd would follow and with Muskrat in the lead followed by the rest of the group trailing horses as well, the men made quite a picture. In the group of four men, they were controlling and herding their own 14 riding and packhorses, the 17 horses taken from the fight with the 'horse-thief' Indians, the eleven riding and packhorses acquired from the three 'orphanage' men, and the twelve riding and packhorses taken from the Hudson's Bay men! Needless to say, trailing and riding 54 horses took some doing and a whole lot of luck that a number of them weren't killed and eaten by bears, run off by Indians or just plain wandered off by themselves when the harried herders were not looking or paying attention!

However, four days later four very tired and harried trappers rode into sight of Fort Henry near the mouth of the Bighorn. What a welcome sight that proved to be after four long, wild and wooly days on the trail with 54 horses and only four herders! When they rode up to the fort's front gate, Muskrat and company were met by a very surprised and happy to see the safe return of his old friends, Major Henry. However, truth be known, Major Henry was especially happy to see such a large herd of valuable horses arriving even more so. Horses were always in short supply with his trappers and fellow Indian traders because of losses to lightning strikes, grizzly bear attacks, theft from other Indians, horse wrecks, injury, snake bite and freezing to death during the harsh winter months! Standing there looking on in disbelief as the large herd of heavily packed and loose horses were driven by him and into the confines of the fort, Major Henry just shook his head in wonder! Major Henry could also not believe the number of bundles of beaver furs he was seeing going by on a number of the fully loaded packhorses as well...

Once the entire herd of milling horses was securely inside the confines of the fort and under control, Major Henry walked over to the four tired-looking trappers saying, "I can't wait to hear this story as to how you four men came into so many bundles of furs and such a number of horses. I suggest all of you plan on having supper with me and my Company Clerks this evening, and over a number of cups of my Fourth Proof rum, I want to hear this story in every detail."

Dismounting, the four trappers shook the Major's hand and before he could ask any further questions, Buck Snort said, "Major, if our asses drag any lower, we are apt to lose the rear ends from our buckskins! What say you have your graders and sorters get to work right away on our furs before all of us stretch out on this here very ground and sleep for the next two days..."

Within moments and under several barked-out commands, the Major had several of his men drag out some chairs for the trappers to sit upon and rest their weary bones. Then he had his entire contingent of graders and sorters unpacking all of the trappers' packhorses and begin tearing down the bundles so the furs could be sorted out and graded. Five hours later, the Major's Clerks had counted and graded out 1,395 beaver 'Plus' at $4/pelt whose company trapper value came to $5,580, or a small fortune in that day and age. Additionally, Buck Snort and company's 61 beautiful dark-colored wolf skins garnered a total value of $2,745. Two days later after the blacksmiths had examined the 42 horses the trappers were willing to sell, they determined they were to be valued at $3,150. Lastly, 40 St. Louis-style beaver traps had been taken from the cabins of the Hudson's Bay men and from the three 'orphanage' men, and for those the Major paid $280. When the Major finally settled up with Buck Snort and company, he issued a Letter of Credit good at the Ashley-Henry Fur Trade Company warehouse back in St. Louis for the princely sum of $11,755! When Buck Snort, Wind Horse, Clem and Muskrat 'took a gander' at that figure inked out onto their Letter of Credit, not a sound was heard from any of them... None of the men had ever seen so much money in one place or in any place for that matter! After each man had handled the Letter of Credit in awe, it was once again handed back to Buck Snort, who promptly walked over to his horse and placed it with his other Letter of Credit from the previous year's trappings into his saddlebag. But little did the men realize that "Banker Buck Snort" was not through 'wheeling and dealing' with the Major and for that they would have to wait for suppertime...

That evening, Buck Snort and company arrived at the Major's big house located inside the fort's walls after they had set up their own camp in a nearby grove of cottonwoods outside the fort's walls. There the four rough-looking Mountain Men were seated at a long wooden table covered with a linen tablecloth. Placed in front of all of the men were dishes from China and real silverware eating utensils. By now, all four of the rough-cut men were looking at each other in disbelief over such a magnificent-looking table setting! Then the three Chinese cooks began bringing in trays of food running from roasted buffalo backstrap, grilled onions, fried potatoes, loaves of home-made bread fresh from the Major's iron cook stoves, bowls of wild grape and chokecherry jams and jellies, cooked turnips with real churned butter, baked beans with chunks of pork fat, and all the elderberry pie the men could hold! All of those supper treats were later washed down with numerous cups of the Major's high grade and expensive Fourth Proof rum...

Then as the men sat back in their chairs from their feast and began smoking the Major's cigars, he asked the men saying, "Alright, I have held off on all my questions regarding how you came into that huge horse herd and all of those bundles of beaver furs for the entire supper. Now it is all of you men's turns to tell me how you came by so many furs, all of those shod and unshod horses and lived to tell about it."

For the next hour the tall tales of what had happened and how the men came by so many furs and horses spilled out into the 'light of day' on the front porch of the Major's home. The look on the Major's face said it all. Utter disbelief registered on the Major's face throughout all of the storytelling and then his questions just 'flew' once the storytelling was done.

As it was, the Major remembered the Hudson's Bay men as rogues from their own company in Canada and their rough manners and bearing. He also remembered the three 'orphanage' men fur trappers as strange and ominous. But overall, he was glad to see his old friends and most of all, very happy to get all of their furs and a chance to buy all of their extra and most valuable horses, which he in turn intended to sell to his less fortunate company trappers and to the friendly Indians who came to trade at the fort that summer as well.

It was then that Buck Snort, the 'penny-wise' kid who had worked hard all of his life and saved everything that he had made for a 'rainy day', looked Major Henry in the eyes saying, "Major, we would like to thank you for the great meal.

None of us have had such a meal in many a year and tonight was a special treat. Now I think I may have a treat for you as well. The two groups of white men we had to fatally deal with and that mess of horse-stealing Indians we tangled with as well, left a lot of supplies behind when the black powder smoke had finally cleared away. We saved most all of those supplies and aware of how hard it is to get provisions and associated living implements out here in the wilderness, we have a deal for you. After those groups tried doing the four of us in and were not successful, we came by what goods they left behind fair and square. So now, we four are the proud owners of over a dozen extra riding saddles and 15 packsaddles. Additionally, we have over 20 various rifles and pistols we took off their bodies that we have no need for, as well as a number of cooking implements, axes, shovels, hammers, St. Louis-style beaver traps and the like. If you would like, we would love to offer those items to you for purchase and use with your company trappers, Free Trappers and the friendly Indians that you trade with. In return, we would like to procure in a straight-across trade with you for all of those goods, all of our coming year's supplies and provisions at no cost to us. If you feel that is a square deal after looking over the quality and number of goods we have for release, then we will have a deal that would be satisfactory to both parties."

Upon hearing those words, Major Henry said, "Buck Snort, as short of supplies as we always are, you're damn right I am interested. Let us get together tomorrow and if any of what you have is in good usable condition, we will have a deal! Now my friends, we still have a lot of this Fourth Proof rum that no one has drunk up, so I suggest we get with it because tomorrow will come early and we still have a lot to get done."

The following day, Major Henry and one of his Company Clerks reviewed all of the extra firearms, riding and packing gear, cooking implements, beaver traps, knives, and axes, and declared those items more than acceptable under the terms and conditions Buck Snort had outlined during the previous evening's supper. Not wanting to waste any time, Buck Snort and company retreated to the Major's warehouse and began selecting the goods and provisions they felt they would need at their planned new campsite to be located somewhere along the Little Bighorn River. However, no selections were made before taking stock of all the goods and provisions they still had and those they had gathered unto themselves from the dead Indians, and 'three orphanage' and four Hudson's Bay men in earlier battles.

Those assessments made as to provisions on hand, the four men forged ahead on their own in the Major's warehouse like a 'mess of ants to sugar'. Supplies of black powder, lead pigs, cleaning tools and spare rifle and pistol parts were added first and foremost to their pile of selected supplies. Then supplies of flour, beans, rice, tins of yeast, jugs of honey, jugs of bear oil for the Dutch ovens' use when making biscuits, sacks of coffee beans, sugar cones, cinnamon, several bags of salt, black pepper, white pepper, hard candy, dried apple slices, dried raisins and red pepper flakes rounded out the food items, since they still had many such like in kind items acquired from the year's previous battles with the two groups of renegade white fur trappers.

However, ragged and badly worn clothing currently on hand being worn by the trappers was another matter. Since the Frontier was rough on the men's clothing, every man took the time to try on for proper fit woolen shirts, woolen pants, gloves, wide brimmed hats, capotes, winter moccasin-making materials, twelve pair of socks, and new breechclouts and buckskins to be worn when setting beaver traps.

Then remembering they would be building another cabin and set of corrals, kegs of spikes and nails headed up the list of needs, along with whetstones for axes, shovels, tomahawks and knives, a new saw, logging chains, files and heavier hammers. Then passing bins of 'transport items', new bridles, new saddle blankets, panniers, curry brushes, supplies of repair leather, and a keg of horseshoes in case their stock threw a shoe while out on the Frontier went into their getting bigger by the minute selection pile. Since the men still had a number of cast iron frying pans, bean pots, Dutch ovens, hanging irons, meat spits and cooking implements, they passed on adding anything heavier to their lists of cooking needs.

Lastly the men added the smaller necessaries such as a dozen fire steels (easily lost), beeswax candles, tins of bag balm to treat injuries to man and beast, sewing needles, spools of thread, leather awls, rolls of gray cloth to repair ripped, torn or worn out clothing, rolls of different grades of tanned leather to make saddle or packsaddle repairs on the trail, shaving soap, regular soap, straight razors, Indian-tanned deerskins for beaver bundle covers, and of course, eight 'carrots' of tobacco, twelve clay pipes (easily broken), and eight flat kegs of Fourth Proof rum (easier to pack than round kegs)…

The next day, the men took all of their riding and pack animals over to the blacksmith shops and had all of their horses' horseshoes removed and replaced. Then confronting the Major later in the day with a list of their provision selections and for the work performed by his blacksmiths, the Major called the trade between Buck Snort and himself sound and shook hands on the prearranged 'trade transaction'. The supply deal sealed with the Major's approval, the men spent the next day packing all of their items into panniers and packsaddles and took everything back to their campsite under the cottonwoods and stowed them under several buffalo skins to keep out the summer rains.

Then the men spent the following month hunting for their daily camp meat supplies and visiting with a large number of their returning fur trapping friends as they entered the fort's grounds to sell their furs and resupply for the coming trapping seasons as well. Many an evening was spent celebrating the fact that they had not 'gone under' and toasting a cup of rum to those memories of friends who had... The rest of the time was spent having get-togethers with the Indian ladies, having shooting contests, seeing who was the fastest runner in camp, holding horse races, cook-offs and just general good and all around hell-raising by all of the members of the trapping community glad to be safely among those of their own kind once again even if it was just for a short while...

CHAPTER SEVEN

TRAPPING ON THE "LITTLE BIGHORN", "BALL LIGHTNING", HELPING A FRIEND

BY THE END OF JUNE 1824, Buck Snort and company were just about all celebrated out at the fort with all of their friends and fellow trappers. However, the Fourth of July was just around the corner and a big birthday celebration was in the planning stages by Major Henry for all of his trappers and the friendly Indians on-site. With that kind of celebration in the offing, the decision was made to stay for that 'hurrah'. Then because they still had to find a new campsite on the Little Bighorn, build a new cabin, construct a set of horse corrals and then get ready for the fall beaver trapping season, they would up and leave shortly after that 'United States Birthday Celebration'.

The day before the big Fourth of July celebration, nets were set in the Yellowstone to catch some of its big trout for the feast to come, buffalo hunting parties went forth to procure six cow buffalo to be roasted, elk hunting parties went forth to kill at least four elk, and the several hundred Crow Indians present around the fort trading in their furs made ready to dress in their finest for the white man's celebration and big feast as well.

The **BOOMING** sound of the fort's cannon firing right at daylight on the Fourth of July signaled the start of the day's festivities and in return and recognition of the day's importance, much firing of rifles and pistols throughout the campsite by trappers and Indians alike were heard constantly throughout the day. The rest of that day saw festivities like never seen before on that part of the Frontier. Trappers, especially those known as Free Trappers, ones who answered to no one except 'God' and themselves, paraded around dressed in their finest beaded buckskins as did a number of other better-off trappers. Many of the trappers' horses were also 'dressed' in their finest for the occasion beginning with the firing of the fort's cannon and continuing throughout the day in a celebratory whirlwind of drinking, fighting, horse races, shooting contests, wrestling matches, whoring around with the 'looser' Indian ladies willing to trade 'favors' for the white man's goods, and even more drinking!

Then come the afternoon just outside the fort's gate, a huge firepit had been built the night before and was in the process of cooking a number of whole buffalo and elk for the occasion and the big feed for the several hundred trappers along with the Indians and their families. Additionally, the Major had trotted out ten kegs of his finest Fourth Proof rum and within minutes, long lines of happy trappers and Indians festooned the area with much excitement around each keg! Once the elk and buffalo had been roasted to mostly done, long lines of hungry men, big meat eaters one and all, lined up for their share of the meat. When they did, the Major's three Chinese cooks trotted out armloads of freshly made homemade bread which was then sliced and placed on several tables near numerous tubs of freshly churned butter made from the fort's milk cows for the men to enjoy. Additionally, there were huge pots of beans and rice mixtures for the hungry crowd as well. Soon, the crowd, tipsy from all of the free-flowing rum, got louder and louder as the celebrating, drinking and feasting progressed. The happy birthday celebration lingered on until late at night when all of the meat, bread, beans and drink had been largely consumed. Then as the festive crowd diminished into the night's darkness, a pack of nearby wolves set to howling and thus supremely ended the young country's Frontier celebration of another 'birthday'…

Four days later, led by Muskrat and trailed by Buck Snort, Wind Horse and Clem, the four trappers headed south along the Bighorn River en route the Little Bighorn River further to the south and their new home. As it turned out, they were trailed by Black Wolf's entire band of Crow Indians. A band of horseflesh and humanity showcased by women, children and noisy dogs of every make and kind surrounded by a dust cloud-raising horse herd and numerous stern-looking Crow warriors riding on the edges of the stream of peoples providing protection, as they headed south back to their main summer campsite on the Lodge Grass. For the next three days, the trappers and their friends traveled and supped together come evening times and sat around several campfires talking into the cool night air.

When Black Wolf and his band of people finally arrived at their campsite on the Lodge Grass on the Little Bighorn River, he rode over to the trappers as his band dispersed to their individual winter campsites. When Black Wolf rode up to where the trappers were sitting on their horses, he was accompanied by another young man. Upon his arrival, Black Wolf proudly introduced all of the trappers to his teenage son named "White Buffalo", who had been sick days earlier. When Black Wolf introduced his son, all the trappers could see he was more than proud of his young son. One who had been named after the extremely rare and considered sacred by the Crow Indians, white buffalo. When he did, the trappers could also see in White Buffalo's eyes how proud of his father and great Crow chief he was as well. The trappers then advised Black Wolf they were heading further south along the Little Bighorn looking for a place to build their new cabin near good beaver trapping water.

Black Wolf then told the men of a place of many beaver and moose just a short distance further south near some wooded foothills where the Little Bighorn turned and went to the southwest. There he advised was a place all along the river where many beaver lived where the foothills ran right alongside the river. The trappers thanked Black Wolf for the advice and directions and then made sure he once again understood that he and his people were always more than welcome at the trappers' new cabin. They also advised Black Wolf that if he was to bring his young son for a visit, they would have Clem make one of his white man's favorite apple cobblers in his honor. Those words pleased Black Wolf and he advised that someday he and his son would come and visit and looked forward to the food the white men trappers called 'apple cobbler'. With those words, Black Wolf and White Buffalo gave a wave of their hands and returned to their people's winter campsite. Watching them ride off, Wind Horse had a strong feeling the trappers, Black Wolf and White Buffalo would meet again someday, and it would not be under the best of circumstances...

With that, the trappers once again turned and

headed to the south along the Little Bighorn. By late afternoon of travel, the trappers arrived where the Little Bighorn turned and flowed to the southwest. When it did, they could see the wooded foothills looming on the western side of the river as had been described by Black Wolf. There the men found a shallow ford and crossed over to the foothills side of the river without incident. Now traveling to the southwest alongside the river, the men rode up to a large grove of cottonwood trees, bifurcated by a small stream with a nearby meadow deep in grasses. There Muskrat stopped and as the rest of the men rode forward in order to be alongside so they could look as well, they began discussing the area with a new homesite in mind. All along the river up to that point were many beaver ponds, beaver houses and a great number of their typical mud and stick dams. Additionally as Black Wolf had advised, there were cottonwoods along the river showing signs of beaver cutting activity as did the nearby groves of aspens and numerous stands of willows adjacent the many waterways.

As the men quietly continued surveying the area, Wind Horse said, "Looks like home to me. Best we get our packhorses unloaded and set up our camp before it gets too dark." Upon hearing those words from his Indian friend, Muskrat just grinned over his Native American's friend innate perception of what the other members of his party of white men were feeling...

About an hour later, the men had dismounted, unloaded all of their packhorses and arranged their packs in a defensive circle around their designated sleeping area, even though they were in the territory of the friendly Crow Indians and then built a fire. As Clem began unloading several of the packs holding the cooking implements and provisions, the rest of the men brought in enough firewood for several days of fire and then hobbled and herded their hardworking horses and sent them out to water and graze. Come nightfall, found all of the trappers' horses still hobbled and tied off on a nearby picket line run from tree to tree through some of the cottonwoods. The care of their livestock and the caution the trappers exhibited were based on their years of experience over the fact that the Blackfeet and Gros Ventre Indians frequently roamed far and wide 'scavenging the countryside' for horses and the like. And anyone living in their area of depredations was not long for the world if they let their guards down even for a minute. Then after a quick supper of just biscuits and coffee, the tired men adjourned to their sleeping furs near the horses' picket line and aside from the hordes of mosquitoes found thereabout, slept soundly under their heavy buffalo robes.

The next morning, the men were awakened by Clem clanking his pots and pans around his newly established cooking fire area. But the smell of hot coffee hung heavy in the air and soon the men were up and at it. First the horses were let out to graze and then the men washed up in the small creek running through the cottonwoods. After another meal of just coffee and Dutch oven biscuits made with raisins and lots of brown sugar, slopped with honey from one of their jugs of the sweetener, the men walked about within their grove of cottonwoods looking for a suitable cabin site.

Finding a flat piece of ground with good drainage high above any anticipated spring runoff from the Little Bighorn, the men marked off a 25' by 25' section of ground. Then Wind Horse and Buck Snort removed several shovels and an ax from their packs and began clearing out the chosen cabin site down to the mineral soil. In the meantime, Clem and Muskrat grabbed up their rifles and an hour later were back in camp with a very fat cow elk. Shortly thereafter, the elk had been hung from a cottonwood limb, skinned out and left to cool and glaze in the shade of the grove of trees for the men's meals to come.

Shortly thereafter, the ringing sounds of axes and a single buck saw could be heard in a grove of nearby pine trees along with the occasional crashing sounds of falling trees hitting the ground. For the next five days, the four trappers fell and bucked up the fallen pine trees into the correct lengths for the men's new cabin. Ten days of hard labor hauling down with their horses the pre-cut logs bucked to size, setting their cabin's stone foundation, raising the walls and constructing a roof, followed with the basic completion of their cabin by nightfall on the eleventh day! Once again their supper consisted of the last of the cow elk, Dutch oven biscuits, beans and Clem's brand of 'trappers' coffee'. Later on their sitting logs while sitting around the firepit, the tired but relieved men broke out several cups of their rum and their clay pipes. Into those clay pipes was stuffed some of the great smelling James River smoking tobacco and for once, the men put the mosquitoes on the run versus the other way around. However, those mosquitoes from the surrounding beaver waters got 'even' once the men put away their pipes for the evening and retired to their sleeping furs under the leaves of the cottonwood trees...

On day twelve the men rested after killing a cow buffalo from a small nearby herd, quartered the beast and hung those quarters from several newly made meat poles so they could cool out and glaze. Then the next day as Clem went to work making one of his big suppers of beans, biscuits, coffee and a rice, raisin and brown sugar dish, the other three men cut out the front door and windows to their cabin and with split logs, framed the same. Then as Buck Snort began constructing chairs and a table for use inside the cabin with the advent of inclement weather, Wind Horse and Muskrat built the heavy log front door and hung the same on thick bull buffalo leather straps. Then they made window frames for holding the eventual tanned deerskin coverings, so a little light could be let in through the thinly shaved skins with most of the cold and rain being kept out. Following those labors, a log floor was cut and laid over the dirt and wooden pegs were made and placed into previously drilled holes in the log walls and ceiling beams for hanging sacks of provisions up off the floor to avoid spoilage from rot or bug infestations. Lastly, the four men cut an opening in the northern wall of the cabin and using mud and rocks from their creek, constructed their fireplace adorned with hanging rods and flat warming stones adjacent the fireplace opening. As for building a small storage shed to hold their extra gear, the men declined to do so as they had at their earlier cabin on the Bighorn River. With a cabin that was 25' wide and 25' feet long, the men figured they had enough space in their current cabin to accommodate all of their gear, provisions and bundles of furs to come, so a storage shed was not necessary. That way they figured such items would be immune from theft as long as they were near at hand. Following that, the trappers moved all of their gear, packs, panniers, provisions and sleeping gear inside their newly constructed cabin, so they would be safer from theft by any wandering Indians or ruin from inclement weather soakings from any summer torrential rains that happened to come their way with a modicum of summer frequency, as the men were discovering.

Then for the next week, it was back onto the

heavily timbered hillside with horses and logging chain in tow. There their winter wood
supply was cut from dead lightning-struck or
bug-ridden trees and hauled down the hillside
by horse teams and placed near their cabin for
use as a winter wood supply when the winter
snows deepened. Lastly, smaller pine timbers
were cut and hauled down into the cottonwood
grove to be used as fence rails around their new
corral site. There those timbers were spiked into
the sides of the living cottonwood trees, from tree
to tree, using those cottonwoods as anchor posts,
until the men had constructed what they called a
'living corral'! While much of the corral building
was ongoing, Clem had cut even smaller trees
and constructed a series of smoking racks right
next to their cabin so that would help in keeping
the bears away when the buffalo jerky-making
process to come was in full swing.

Tired of mostly biscuits and coffee for many
of their meals, the men decided it was time to
fill their meat poles with quarters of buffalo and
load the newly built meat racks with fresh meat
strips so the jerky-making process could begin.
The following morning with all of their packhorses in tow carrying panniers and packs, the
men headed down to the Little Bighorn River,
crossed a set of shallows and headed out onto
the surrounding prairie looking for just the right
small herd of buffalo from which to kill several
fat cows for the men's meat poles and smoking

racks. Making sure the men stayed downwind from the numerous herds of buffalo and when riding out in the open, lying across their saddles so it looked just like a number of wild horses trooping by, the men continued their stalking.

Riding across the prairie and trailing their packhorses, Buck Snort kept nervously looking skyward. Ever since they had left their cabin, what he was seeing quickly building far to the northwest had made him a little uneasy. Ugly rolling blue-black looking storm clouds seemed to be building far to the north but the weather where they were that morning was beautiful, calm and unusually warm. There was no wind, the air was 'soft' with moisture hanging heavy in the air and the morning's temperature had been balmy. So with those factors present, the normally weather-wise Buck Snort, happily along with the rest of the men, sallied forth out onto the prairies on a very welcome and enjoyable buffalo hunt for their daily meat supplies.

About an hour later, Buck Snort, Clem and Wind Horse had sneaked to within 30 yards of a quietly feeding herd of buffalo and in a matter of seconds and with three quick shots from their rifles, had three fat cow buffalo down. Then the butchering work began because buffalo once down, spoiled very quickly due to their size and summer heat unless the meat was rapidly removed and cooled out. So like 'red ants on a disturbed ant mound', the trappers with their knives, axes and whetstones were all over their 'kills' butchering out the rather large animals and strapping the great slabs of meat or quarters onto their packsaddles or into the panniers for transport back to the men's cabin.

As the sweat rolled off the hard at work men dressing and butchering out the three downed cows, Buck Snort all of a sudden realized they were no longer working out in the hot sun. A dark shadow had raced out across the prairies by oncoming clouds blotting out the sun from the northwest as the men, totally occupied in the butchering-out process, had failed to notice the oncoming weather change. Seeing the dark shadows now racing out across the prairies, Buck Snort, covered with buffalo blood, snot and bodily juices from the butchering process, glanced skyward and then did a double take! The earlier ugly blue-black storm clouds far to the northwest were now rolling up and down low across the prairies, sometimes only yards from the ground, with a vengeance! It was then that Buck Snort and the rest of the men finally noticed the wind from out of the northwest had picked up, the temperature was quickly sliding downward and the air was no longer feeling 'soft' but now heavy with the feeling of oncoming moisture. Additionally, the faraway rumblings heard earlier were not those from disturbed buffalo herds moving across the prairies as earlier thought, but that coming from the Heavens signaling a monster summer thunderstorm was heading towards the trappers! And the ominous rumblings were that of thunder generated by severe bolts of lightning now arcing across the skies and over the prairie upon which they stood! By now, the men had quit their 'cutting and gutting' when it came to the three dead cows and were anxiously scanning the skies realizing it was never safe to be standing up out on the prairie during one of its classic 'Hell in the Heavens' summer thunderstorms rolling across the land!

By now, Buck Snort had sheathed his knife and was in the process of wiping his bloody hands off on the front of his buckskins as he continued looking skyward in concern. It was then that he saw a huge bolt of lightning reaching down to the ground a mile or so back towards their cabin and in an instant, sent a plume of smoke skyward where a lone cottonwood had once stood! "Best we get the hell out of here and try and find some low ground before we end up like that cottonwood," said Buck Snort, as he headed for his now very nervous riding horse standing nearby who was seeing and feeling the drastic weather change coming his way as well…

By now, the winds had picked up to such force that the grasses of the prairie were all lying down almost flat to the ground! That was soon followed by very large and cold raindrops hitting the dry prairie soils, making small explosive puffs in the dry, buffalo hoof-pounded dirt portending more was to follow. By now, the men had mounted up and trailing their pack animals were racing for a nearby draw where they could dismount and be below the prairie ground level to avoid any lightning strikes. Then as more and more thunder constantly 'clapped' through the air and the smell of ozone acridly permeated their surroundings, the now noticeably darkened skies were constantly being backlit with bright flashes of deadly lightning. By now the wind was blowing about 40 miles per hour, the large cold raindrops were flying horizontally above the ground and there was so much static electricity in the air that the hair on the men's heads and arms was standing straight up! Additionally, the manes and tails of the horses stood up in the static-filled air as well! By now, the 'claps' of thunder were coming so close in occurrence and from almost overhead of the now huddled in a gully trappers, that each and every thunderclap was hurting the men's ears because of the concussive pressure changes in the air... Additionally, there were so many constant flashes of lightning in the air that the darkness that had earlier overtaken the prairie had changed into almost constant flashes of 'bright white flashes of daylight'!

Then new sounds of terror began filling the airwaves! This new sound was not as sharp sounding as were the overhead thunderclaps but more of an earth-shaking thundering noise. Then the men realized, **STAMPEDE!**

ALL THE NEARBY BUFFALO HERDS WERE NOW MADLY STAMPEDING ACROSS THE PRAIRIES BECAUSE OF THE TERROR NOW RAINING DOWN FROM THE SKIES IN THE FORMS OF BOLTS OF LIGHTNING AND THE TREMENDOUS THUNDERCLAPS THAT WERE NOW ALMOST CONSTANT IN THEIR PRESENTATION! SOON THE 'GROUND-THUNDERING' SOUNDS WERE COMING THE WAY OF THE TRAPPERS! REALIZING WHAT WAS HAPPENING, THE FOUR TRAPPERS GRABBED UP THEIR RIFLES AND HOLDING THEIR BARRELS DOWNWARD SO THE METAL IN THEIR RIFLES DID NOT ATTRACT THE ALMOST CONSTANT BOLTS OF LIGHTNING RACING AROUND THE SKIES, THE MEN ANXIOUSLY WAITED. THEY DID NOT HAVE TO WAIT LONG, FOR SOON CAME A 'HEAVING BROWN CARPET' OF TERRORIZED BUFFALO COMING THEIR WAY! REALIZING THEY WERE SOON TO BE NOTHING MORE THAN JELLIFIED FLESH ONCE SEVERAL THOUSAND BUFFALO STAMPEDED IN TERROR OVER THE TOP OF THE HUDDLED MEN, THEY BEGAN SHOOTING THE LEAD BUFFALO IN THE HERD COMING THEIR WAY! THEN THEY GRABBED THEIR RESERVE RIFLES FROM A PANNIER AND KILLED SEVERAL MORE LEADERS OF THE ONCOMING HERD. HOWEVER, THEIR KILLING A

FEW LEADERS OF SEVERAL THOUSAND TERRORIZED AND STAMPEDING BUFFALO COMING THEIR WAY DID LITTLE GOOD. QUICKLY RELOADING THOSE RIFLES IN A DRIVING RAIN WITH ALMOST CONSTANT LIGHTNING STRIKES ALL AROUND THEM, THE MEN DESPERATELY HURRIED, FULL WELL KNOWING THEY WOULD SOON BE DEAD MEN UNLESS THEY COULD KILL MORE LEADERS IN THE ONCOMING STAMPEDING HERD AND TURN THEM AWAY FROM THEIR PRESENT COURSE OF TRAVEL!

THEN THE MEN FROZE IN AMAZEMENT AND THEN TERROR OVER WHAT THEY WERE NOW SEEING! THERE WAS SO MUCH STATIC ELECTRICITY IN THE AIR FROM THE CLOSE AT HAND LIGHTNING STRIKES THAT THE ONCOMING HERD OF STAMPEDING BUFFALO GLOWED WITH A BLUE EFFERVESCENCE! NOT THE WHOLE ANIMAL BUT ALL OF THEIR HORNS! SEEING SUCH AN EERIE SIGHT, THE MEN FROZE AS THE CRAZY NOW WITH FEAR CHARGING BUFFALO ALL WITH GLOWING BLUE HORNS AND SHOWING THE WHITES OF THEIR EYES, ROUNDED THE HILLSIDE AND CAME DIRECTLY AT THE MEN NOW TRAPPED IN THEIR GULLY!

BOOM! WENT A HUGE BOLT OF LIGHTNING RIGHT INTO THE CENTER OF THE HERD OF STAMPEDING BUFFALO AND

WHEN IT DID, IT BLEW AT LEAST 20 DEAD ANIMALS HIGH INTO THE AIR! THEN TERROR OF TERRORS OCCURRED! OUT FROM THAT HUGE LIGHTNING STRIKE RIGHT INTO THE CENTER OF THE HERD OF STAMPEDING BUFFALO EMERGED A GIANT BALL OF WOBBLING LIGHT! THEN THAT GIANT BALL OF LIGHT THAT WAS ABOUT THREE FEET ACROSS, RACED OVER THE BACKS OF NUMEROUS BUFFALO KILLING THEM IN THEIR TRACKS! AS THAT BOLT OF "BALL LIGHTNING" RACED OVER THE BACKS OF THE STAMPEDING BUFFALO KILLING THEM IN THEIR TRACKS, IT TURNED THE HERD NOW THOROUGHLY TERRORIZED OVER WHAT WAS HAPPENING AND IN SO DOING, SENT THEM AWAY FROM THE TRAPPED TRAPPERS STILL STANDING IN THE SMALL SWALE IN THE PRAIRIE AWAITING THEIR FATE... FINALLY THE ORB OF BALL LIGHTNING DISAPPEARED, WEAVING AND BOUNCING ITS WAY OUT ACROSS THE PRAIRIE LEAVING SMOKING GRASSES IN ITS WAKE. THANKFULLY, ITS TIMELY APPEARANCE INTO THE HERD OF BUFFALO MANAGED TO TURN THE HERD AND SEND IT THUNDERING ON ITS WAY AWAY FROM THE SURE DEATH OF THE TRAPPERS AND THEIR HORSES...

FOR THE NEXT HALF-HOUR, THE HEAVENS WERE RENT WITH CLAPS OF

THUNDER, TORRENTIAL DOWNPOURS AND STREAKS OF LIGHTNING RUNNING EVERY WHICH WAY ACROSS THE SKIES AND ONTO THE LAND! IN FACT, SO MUCH RAIN FELL THAT THE TRAPPERS SOON FOUND THEMSELVES AND THEIR HORSES IN KNEE-DEEP WATERS NOW RUNNING THROUGH THEIR LITTLE GULLY INTO WHICH THEY HAD FLED SEEKING SHELTER EARLIER IN THE STORM... THEN AS THE CENTER OF THE STORM RACED ITS WAY ACROSS THE PRAIRIES TO THE SOUTHEAST, THE TRAPPERS COULD HEAR MORE BUFFALO RUMBLINGS UNDER THE CENTER OF THE STORM AS THE TERRORIZED ANIMALS TRIED OUTRUNNING THE DEADLY ELECTRICAL VIOLENCE FALLING UPON THEM FROM THE SKY.

Then other than a strong cold wind coming from out of the northwest, residual rains and the fading sounds of distant thunder and bright flashes of faraway lightning strikes, the violence from the skies was all over... (Author's Note: "Ball lightning", the type just observed by the terrified trappers, is a very rare and barely understood phenomenon. The Author while working illegal airborne coyote shooters from his stakeout position just west of the Town of Devils Lake in North Dakota as a Special Agent for the U.S. Fish and Wildlife Service, was caught out in the open in just such a violent summer thunderstorm as pitifully described in the preceding paragraph. Lying down in a gully with my faithful Labrador retriever named Shadow, to avoid being struck by lightning, I rode out just such a violent weather event in 1975! During that violent summer thunderstorm, in terror as well as excitement over what I was experiencing firsthand, I watched such a weather event swirl overhead and on one occasion observed just such a "ball lightning" phenomenon. There was a huge flash and tremendous clap of thunder as a bolt of lightning struck a clump of wild plum bushes not 100 yards from where we were sprawled out in a low spot in the ground to avoid just such a strike from a bolt of lightning ourselves.

When that huge bolt of lightning struck the plum bushes, out from that ground strike bounced a bluish-white ball of light about the size of a basketball! That ball of light without making a sound zipped across the prairie for about 40 yards, all the while maybe 15-20" above the grasses! Then in the next instant, it went out and disappeared! After that storm had safely passed as had the threat of lightning, dog and I got up soaked to the skin and walked over to where I had seen that ball of light traveling across the tops of the prairie grasses until it had disappeared. When we did, we discovered a burned streak across the prairie grasses for the distance I had seen that bolt of "ball lightning" travel until it disappeared. I can clearly remember the smell of wet burned grasses in that area as I examined the area with keen interest. To this day I have never again seen such a rare event, even though I have been caught in a number of violent summer thunderstorms out on the prairie as well as in some of the Rocky Mountain states. What a wonderful life's experience to have seen such a rare event that even today, science has a hard time explaining or replicating such a phenomenon even under the best of laboratory conditions.)

Still fearful over being struck by lightning from the fast moving and violent storm, the trappers waited for a long while before moving out from their low spot on the prairie and mounting up onto their horses. However, when they did, they rode over to the numerous piles of dead buffalo killed by lightning for a 'look-see'. When they did, the trappers first became aware of the intense smell of burned hair, burn marks on the animals' bodies and in all cases, the extended intestines exploded out the anuses of the dead buffalo!

The trappers did not feel right in butchering out any of the lightning-struck buffalo fearful of spoilage, so they went back to the buffalo they had killed just before the storm arrived and finished butchering out all three of those animals. Then without delay, the men rode back to their campsite and hung parts of the buffalo onto their meat poles to cool out and form a glaze on the meat. They then took the rest of the buffalo meat, cut it into thin strips and hung it over the meat smoking racks until they just groaned with all of the weight of the fresh meat. With that, Clem started a low heat smoking fire so the meat would start to dry out. That he did by using intense smoke generated by using old and some-what rotten cottonwood for the heavy smoke it routinely produced in order to help in keeping the flies and yellow jackets from eating and lay-ing eggs on the fresh meat. Then as the rest of the men curried down their horses and hobbled them so they could be turned loose to water and graze, Clem went to work on his supper prepara-tions just as if nothing out of the ordinary had happened during that rather unusual day…

That night after supper and several cups of rum and a smoke, all the men headed to their sleeping furs inside the cabin except for Clem and Wind Horse. Those two were responsible for keeping a low heat/high smoke fire going under the meat smoking racks and for keeping any nearby bears away from getting into the valuable meat stocks and helping themselves. However in the middle of the night, Clem got Buck Snort and Muskrat up so they could do their part in tending to the smoking fires as Wind Horse and Clem then got some sleep.

Come daylight, Buck Snort got Clem up so he could begin making breakfast, while Muskrat and Buck Snort then went to the creek, washed up and shaved. Then those two brought in their horses from the meadow where they had fed all night, removed their hobbles and placed them back into their corral for safekeeping. With that, Muskrat and Buck Snort dragged out all of their beaver and wolf traps and hung them from the smoking racks to rid them of their man smells now that the meat racks were lighter since the meat had 'smoked down' and dried out considerably from its original moisture-heavy weight. Then as Wind Horse cast a mound of balls for the men's pistols and rifles, Buck Snort tore down all of the men's personal rifles and their reserve rifles, checked their parts especially the springs, removed the lead and black powder fouling, oiled them and then reassembled all of the weapons so they would be ready for whatever came their way at a later date. By now, breakfast was more than ready so the men feasted on their favorite, namely Dutch oven biscuits slathered in honey, spitted buffalo meat done medium well and Clem's eye-opening brand of powerfully strong coffee.

One day later the meat on the smoking racks had been made into jerky, placed into tanned deerskin bags traded for at the fort during their annual celebration which had been tanned by Indians, and hung from the wooden pegs in their cabin for later use while out on the trail. Finally caught up with most of the work that needed doing around the cabin site before the fall beaver trapping season started in late September when the beaver were beginning to come into their prime, the men mounted up and rode out to have a look at their new beaver trapping country and the opportunities it presented. And as the men rode forth, they were hoping that Black Wolf had been correct about the plethora of beaver to be found in the area they now occupied, as he had previously reported and they had initially observed.

As it turned out, the men hadn't ridden a mile along the Little Bighorn in and around the numerous beaver ponds and swampy areas when all of a sudden, **CRASH-CRASH-CRASH-WHOOM!** Out from a dense patch of willows just ridden alongside, Buck Snort had his riding horse slammed into by a very surprised and now trying to escape moose from the close at hand perceived danger of nearby smelly trappers and their horses! When the surprised cow moose stormed blindly through the dense brush in the marsh and then slammed right into the side of Buck Snort's horse, he was knocked asunder and fell into the marsh on the far side of his horse with a loud **KER-PLUSH!** Unfortunately, Buck Snort's horse, broadsided by a panicked 1,100-pound moose, was knocked fully sideways and then fell into the marsh as well! That marsh's deep mud was all that saved Buck Snort from injury because when his knocked-all-to-hell horse fell on top of him, that animal's weight just drove him into the mud, allowing him to avoid further or lethal injury...

Then as Buck Snort pulled himself free and then lunged up out from the mud of the marsh and from under his horse, covered with 10,000 years of 'goose crap and tule roots', blowing and gagging in surprise, he heard **BOOM—POW!** Clearing the mud from his eyes, he just had time to lunge out of the way from a now fatally shot cow moose falling his way! However, Buck Snort was not so lucky when a fully grown calf moose, panicked like its mother, took off running through the dense willows right behind its fleeing mother, ran into Wind Horse's accurate pistol shot and died in stride! When the calf moose died in full stride, its 400-pound body plowed through the willows and hammered right into a surprised Buck Snort just as he cleared the marsh's mud and 10,000 years of 'goose crap and tule roots' from his eyes, nose and face after his horse wreck!

WHOMP! slammed the just head shot calf moose right into a stunned Buck Snort, knocking him back down once again into the muddy marsh waters and into more 'goose poop and tule roots'! When Buck Snort finally came out from the marsh that second time right after being knocked silly by a dead and flying sideways calf moose, he was bleeding from the nose, had an eye that would soon turn black, a badly split lip and was missing a lower front tooth! Within moments the marsh's madness with a moose finally untangled itself, with one sore-as-a-boil riding horse which had been broadsided by a 'flying' dead moose and a muddy and bloody Buck Snort smelling badly of 10,000 years of 'goose crap and tule roots' after being immersed into the marsh's 'soup' several times by horse and moose alike! And if that was not enough of an indignity to suffer, the calf moose had let loose a world of moose poop after being head shot, and Buck Snort was once again the recipient of being underneath just such an 'offering' when that young moose had fallen onto him as well... Suffering that last indignity of the day, Buck Snort's horse was too injured to ride home, so that trapper had to walk back to their campsite smelling of marsh mud, goose poop, rotten tule roots and moose crap! That he happily did because when Buck Snort's horse had fallen on him, it had badly mashed his ribs and tore the muscles in one shoulder so badly that he was in no mood or condition to ride a bone-jarring horse all the way back to their distant camp. The only nice thing that happened that day was that Buck Snort did not have to stand knee-deep in the marsh's waters and help gut out and butcher the cow and calf moose. Especially since he was in the process of hobbling home with a gimpy horse, a rifle and set of pistols covered with mud and unable to fire, and a body strongly smelling of 10,000 years of 'goose poop, moose dump and tule roots'...

That afternoon when the rest of the men rode

back into camp with the moose quarters and rib sections on their packhorses, there sat a cleaned-up and better-smelling after having just washed up in their creek, Buck Snort on his sitting log by a blazing campfire in his last pair of clean buckskins. That Buck Snort did with the help of a third cup of rum in hand and surprisingly not feeling too much pain from his horse-crunched ribs or shoulder. And that night during supper, Buck Snort got to eat the hell out of a mess of excellent tasting spitted moose meat from the same damn animal that had 'roared' out from the marsh and 'hammered' him and his horse into the marsh's mud... Lastly, since he and his horse were all stove up, Buck Snort got to 'duck' a lot of the work around camp until the rest of the men finally saw through his 'injuries' charade and made him partake in the daily labors just like the rest of the men had to do and shoulder his share of the load.

A week later after the 'moose madness in the marsh', found all of the men once again riding the marsh's fringes examining the potential beaver trapping opportunities soon to be upon them. Finally deciding to begin trapping right next to their new campsite and working their way south as they trapped out the beaver along the smaller Little Bighorn River and its adjacent marshes, the men were more than ready for the start of the fall beaver trapping season. However, it was finally decided to wait just a bit longer in order to make sure the animals to be trapped were in their prime.

Thirteen days later, the four trappers streamed out from their new campsite more than ready to begin their fall beaver trapping season. As usual, Muskrat took the lead followed by Buck Snort and Wind Horse trailing their usual three pack-horses all carrying loaded panniers full of needed trapping gear and extra firepower in case they got jumped by hostile Indians. Last in that fur caravan rode Clem on a horse carrying an extra rifle in a scabbard, two additional pistols in holsters aside his saddle and carrying his own rifle and another set of pistols in his sash. Clem was armed in such a way because the men were in new Indian Territory and during their several days of 'riding the marshes' checking the beaver sign, had ridden across numerous unshod pony tracks from many bands of Indians moving through the terrain. With that in mind and mindful that they had observed numerous trails of Indian ponies and in each case had been outnumbered, they provided for their defense accordingly in case they were attacked. And unless surprised themselves, Indians routinely attacked the tail ends of a fur trappers' caravan, based on stories from other surviving trappers because of the usual chaos it caused those being attacked from the rear. That being the historical case, Clem, the old buffalo hunter, was more than armed and quietly ready for the occurrence of just such an event...

Up until late in November, Buck Snort and Wind Horse performed the group's trapping duties with Clem acting as the on-site trappers' assistant and the sharp-eyed and damn accurate shooter Muskrat performing guard duties from a short distance away. As expected, their Little Bighorn River and its adjacent waters proved to be the beaver-rich waters all the men had expected and more. Soon the men were once again only running 15 of their 30 traps because of such numerous daily catches of the furry rodents and the many long hours required after the catch in the skinning, de-fatting and hooping duties required to properly process the fresh pelts. After just about a 30-day session of trapping from late in September until the third week in November, the men had trapped and hooped 252 beaver and most of those were Made Beaver or adult in size beaver! And they still had until freeze-up before they had to pull their traps and switch over to the trapping of the many wolves found in the country preying on the numerous deer, elk and buffalo found locally. Realizing because of the weather in the northern latitude in which they were trapping and the early onrushing end of their fall beaver trapping season, the men finally increased their trap number to 25. They just figured they would tough it out and catch as many beaver as they could up until the end and then rest up after freeze-up. So out went the extra traps and with those increased catches, the men just worked into the early mornings of each day processing their pelts and in so doing, just made more use of their extra rum supplies and chewing tobacco to offset the sleep they were losing.

Stepping out from their cabin early one morning, Buck Snort could feel the sharp oncoming seasonal cold on his cheeks and in the tingling ends of his fingers. Then looking over at Clem hard at work around their outdoor fire making breakfast he said, "Clem, make an extra batch of those damn good biscuits this morning. I feel it may be a long day afore the four of us are done for the day."

As Buck Snort mouthed those words, Wind Horse exited the cabin and looking skyward said, "Today will be a long and cold one if those clouds stacked up to our northwest mean anything." Then as he looked closer at the scudding gray clouds in the skies to their northwest, he felt a shudder go through his body. AND FOR SOME REASON, THAT SHUDDER RUNNING THROUGH HIS BODY WASN'T BECAUSE OF THAT MORNING'S COLD... Then Wind Horse shook off that feeling of foreboding because he had to take care of an urgent call of nature and RIGHT NOW!

Later that morning as the icy cold November waters of the marsh closed around the two trappers' 'man parts' as they moved into the marsh to begin their daily trapping activities, they both gave out loud exclamations of shock and discomfort. Then all they could hear was Clem laughing loudly over Wind Horse and Buck Snort's shouts of extreme icy cold water discomfort! However, cold water or not, the fall beaver trapping season was fast coming to a close and the two men doing all of the trapping just toughed it out as they went through their normal trapping activities. Moving faster than normal due to the icy cold waters and the men's fast-numbing feet and legs, trap after trap was either tended or set as the work dictated. Meanwhile, as the day's cold catches were streaming in and back to Clem, he now found his fingers beginning to 'ice up' as well, as he skinned each dead and stone-cold beaver handed to him by the trap-setters. Soon 19 beaver pelts graced the men's panniers as Buck Snort and Wind Horse continued setting the remaining number of traps in their inventory just as fast as their numbing feet, legs and hands would allow in the icy waters. Finally their work was done and the men just figured because the waters were so cold, they would just head for home with their heavy catch of the day and get an early start on the de-fatting and hooping required. Then when those chores were finished, maybe then they could get a decent night's sleep for a change.

All of a sudden, the men heard a rattle of shots being rapidly fired in anger near a finger of trees not 100 yards distant from where they were dressing back into their warmer clothing!

That was also when they saw Muskrat racing his horse for the small clump of men getting dressed by the marsh. Seconds later, Muskrat drew up his horse next to the trappers in the process of now hurriedly getting dressed in his just-created cloud of flying dirt clods and dust.

"OVER BY THAT FINGER OF TREES TO OUR WEST IS WHERE THAT SHOOTING IS TAKING PLACE! I JUST SAW TWO INDIANS RACE INTO THOSE TREES ON THEIR HORSES BEING CLOSELY FOLLOWED BY ABOUT A DOZEN OTHER INDIANS FIRING ON THOSE TWO FLEEING INDIANS! I SWEAR, THE TWO INDIANS FLEEING THE OTHERS SHOOTING AT THEM HAD TO BE OUR FRIENDS BLACK WOLF AND WHITE BUFFALO FROM THE LOOKS OF THE MATCHED PINTOS THOSE TWO MEN NORMALLY RIDE! THAT BEING THE CASE, WE NEED TO GET OVER THERE AND GIVE THEM A HAND BECAUSE IF WE DON'T, THEY WILL SOON BE DEAD BEING SO OUTNUMBERED!" bellowed out Muskrat, all out of breath and in a hyper-state of excitement over what he knew might soon be coming next in the lives of the four trappers in the way of destiny.

Moments later as Clem, Buck Snort and Wind Horse finished hurriedly dressing into warmer clothing, Muskrat kept watch just in case any of the Indians chasing the two fleeing Indians saw the trappers and came their way with 'blood in

their eyes' as well. Finally clothed and still hearing a lot of shooting, Muskrat leaned down from
his horse saying, "If we can get to that clump of
trees over yonder, we can then sneak right up
into that bunch of Indians chasing what looks
like our friends and shoot the hell out of them
before they even realize we were in country!"

Moments later, the trappers were 'horsed' and
quickly picking their way through the marsh and
using its dense brush fields as cover, making their
way towards the clump of trees Muskrat figured
if they could reach without detection, they could
ambush and 'back-shoot' the larger group of
Indians before any of the trappers were injured.
Finally reaching the covering clump of trees and
upon hearing the battle raging on just ahead of
them in the dense pine forest, the men quickly
dismounted and tied off their horses. Then the
men ran over to the packhorse carrying all of
their extra rifles and jerked them out from the
panniers in which they had been carried. In just
a moment's time, aware if the two lone Indians
were their badly outnumbered friends, they had
best hurry before they were all killed, so the men
made sure all of the reserve rifles were cocked
and ready to fire. Then with each trapper carrying two rifles and two pistols in their sashes,
the four trappers began stealthily quick-walking
toward the sounds of intense shooting and the
clouds of white black powder smoke now hanging heavy in the air in the timber from whence

most of the firing was originating from a high number of shooters.

Then quickly spreading out in a line abreast and stalking in behind the dozen or so Indians shooting heavily into the stand of timber where the two Indians being pursued earlier were now firing back from, the trappers quietly flitted from tree to tree in their deadly stalk! That they did until they were very close to the unaware Indian attackers to their front. By then all of the return fire from the two trapped Indians had ceased. That was not a good omen to the trappers' way of thinking under the urgency of the moment, because it meant they were either dead, severely wounded or out of powder and lead and were now really in harm's way! However as was later determined, in all actuality the two trapped Indians had observed the trappers sneaking up behind their attackers and had ceased shooting at those attackers out of fear of hitting one of their trapper friends coming to rescue them from the bad situation they found themselves in...

About then, the trappers found themselves sneaking through the tied-off Indian attackers' horses whose owners were still to their front firing heavily at the two trapped Indians, unaware of the danger sneaking upon them. Silently sneaking their way through the Indian attackers' horses, the four trappers kept moving forward until they were directly behind the attackers but still hidden by the dense stand of timber surrounding them! Buck Snort, through hand signals, made sure all of the trappers were safely hidden behind their own individual pine tree for their protection. Then each trapper quickly stacked his reserve rifle against the tree they were hiding behind for quick retrieval and then taking their personal rifles, took deadly aim at one of the Indian attackers directly ahead of them who were so close one could almost reach out and touch them with the end of their rifle barrels...

"NOW!" shouted Buck Snort upon seeing that everyone was ready, after he had selected a large fat Indian directly to his front, centered his blade sight in the middle of the man's back, then squeezed his trigger and saw his target grab his back and instantly disappear in the white cloud of black powder smoke from Buck Snort's fired rifle rolling his way and enveloping him! Now it was especially smoky to the front of all the trappers since they had all fired in unison and in so doing, enveloping all of the Indian attackers to their front in clouds of white black powder smoke! THEN THE CRAP REALLY HIT THE FAN! AFTER BACK-SHOOTING FOUR INDIAN ATTACKERS TO THEIR FRONT, HERE INSTANTLY CAME RUNNING ALL OF THE REMAINING SURVIVORS AFTER THE INITIAL FUSILLADE FIRED BY THE TRAPPERS WITH THEIR PERSONAL RIFLES IN HAND. AS THE ATTACKING INDIANS SCRAMBLED AND BOLTED IN PANIC FOR THEIR HORSES,

THEY DID SO RIGHT THROUGH THE ENVELOPING CLOUD OF WHITE BLACK POWDER SMOKE! WHEN THE INDIAN SURVIVORS BURST THROUGH THAT CLOUD OF SMOKE MAKING A RUN FOR WHAT THEY CONSIDERED WAS THE SAFETY OF THEIR PREVIOUSLY TIED-OFF HORSES, FOUR MORE DIED AFTER BEING SHOT WITH THE TRAPPERS' QUICKLY RETRIEVED RESERVE RIFLES! THOSE FOUR INDIAN ATTACKERS ALL DIED WITHIN FEET OF THE END OF THE TRAPPERS' GUN BARRELS! AND WHEN THOSE FOUR INDIANS WERE SHOT FROM SUCH CLOSE RANGES WITH SUCH A HEAVY LEAD BALL, ALL FOUR BODIES WERE LITERALLY EXPLODED BACKWARDS INTO THE REMAINING INDIANS FLEEING AND COMING TOWARDS THE TRAPPERS! THEN WITHIN SECONDS, EIGHT MORE INDIAN ATTACKERS DIED AS THEY TRIED MADLY 'BULLING' THEIR WAY THROUGH THE LINE OF TRAPPERS TOWARDS THE SAFETY OF THEIR TIED-OFF HORSES, NOW IN TOTAL PANIC, AS THE TRAPPERS JOINTLY FIRED THEIR TWO PISTOLS EACH LOADED WITH BUCK AND BALL AT THE CLOSE AT HAND FLEEING TARGETS! THE LAST TWO SURVIVORS OF THE ATTACKING INDIANS NOT SHOT BECAUSE THE TRAPPERS WERE NOW HOLDING EMPTY WEAPONS, DIED UNDER THE RAZOR-SHARP BLADES OF

THREE HASTILY THROWN TOMAHAWKS BY BUCK SNORT, MUSKRAT AND WIND HORSE, AS THEY TRIED RUNNING BY THE TRAPPERS IN TERROR TO THEIR TIED-OFF HORSES...

Then quiet reigned as clouds of white black powder smoke slowly dissipated through the dense stands of timber as the trappers hurriedly reloaded all of their firearms just in case. Moments later after seeing all the 'danger was done', Chief Black Wolf and his son White Buffalo arose from behind the downed pine log they had been using as cover during the firefight and just stood there quietly until the trappers had quickly reloaded all of their firearms. Quickly reloading all of their firearms after any kind of a battle was the 'First Rule' of any Mountain Man who wanted to see the next sunrise... Then observing the trappers looking intently at the two of them in obvious recognition after the extremes of emotion from all of the killings had partially subsided, Chief Black Wolf and White Buffalo walked a little further back into the timber and retrieved their two signature pinto riding horses hidden out from harm's way.

Then Chief Black Wolf and his son walked out from their location in the deep timber and moved over to where the four trappers now quietly stood. Raising his right hand and arm in the universal sign of peace and recognition, Chief Black Wolf said, "My son and I were coming over to visit our friends the trappers this morning when we ran into this Gros Ventre war party. We are fortunate that we ran into the timber and took our defensive stand before they could run us down with their horses out on the open plains and kill us. Then we were even more fortunate that our trapper friends were out trapping, heard all of the shooting and came over to see what it was all about. It was a good thing that you came when you did. We were about to be overrun when you four ambushed and managed to kill all of our attackers before they killed us, being that members of the Crow Nation are historical enemies of those from the Gros Ventre Nation."

Buck Snort and Muskrat then both shook the hand of Chief Black Wolf and that of his son. That was followed with just a quiet nod of their heads in recognition of their two friends' survival because the trappers were still 'coming down' from the killing emotions they still felt inside. Then for the next few moments, the trappers and their two friends quietly collected up all of the knives, rifles, pistols and tomahawks from the 18 dead Gros Ventre. That done, the trappers walked back to their tied-off horses with their arms full of weapons and placed them into an empty pannier for later trading at Fort Henry. As that was being done, Chief Black Wolf and White Buffalo saw to it that all of the dead Gros Ventre would wander forever in the 'Lower World' because they were now missing some of their body parts... After the trappers had gathered up the Gros Ventre's 18 riding horses and led them over to where they had tied off their own riding and packhorses, there they quietly waited still coming down from their emotional 'high' from all the killing. The trappers waited until Chief Black Wolf and White Buffalo had scalped all of the dead Gros Ventre and had also removed the dead Indians' trigger fingers! That the two Crow warriors did in the belief that now that their enemies were missing body parts, they would wander forever in the 'Lower World' because of not being complete of body. As such, they could not join their kin the 'Cloud People' in the 'Upper World'. Nor could they if they even found their scalps, kill any of the Crow people who scalped them because they also lacked the trigger fingers to do so...

Following those acts practiced by many of the sects of Plains Indians, the trappers and their two Crow Indian friends rode back down to the beaver ponds and there all of the men washed the blood from their hands as well as their clothing from the blood being blown back upon the trappers' bodies from such close-in killing and lastly washed off their tomahawks. The trappers trailing all of the Gros Ventre's 18 horses and their two Crow friends who were lucky to have survived such an ordeal, then headed for the trappers' campsite having had enough excitement for the day...

Upon their arrival, Clem immediately went

over to their outdoor firepit, stoked the fire's coals and soon had a roaring fire in the making. Then on went the always present coffee pot and soon the air around the camp smelled aromatically of coffee boiling away. In the meantime, the trappers checked out the 18 recently captured horses. There they discovered that nine of those horses were shod, indicating that the now dead Gros Ventre had previously run a number of white man trappers 'to ground', killed them and had taken their shod horses. As for the remaining nine Indian horses, they all were unshod. Realizing the value of their new horse herd, the trappers made sure all of the unfamiliar horses were hobbled before they were turned out into the trappers' meadow so they could feed and water alongside the trappers' horse herd. That action also allowed for the Gros Ventre's horses to become familiar with their new surroundings as well as getting acquainted with the trappers' horses as well.

Following that key bit of work with the horses, Buck Snort, Wind Horse and Muskrat removed their single buck saw and axes from their cabin and headed out onto the hillside to begin cutting some more railing timbers for the needed corral expansion. As they did, Clem visited with Chief Black Wolf and White Buffalo as he commenced showing them how he made up one of his special dishes in honor of the trappers' guests. Two hours later the extra corral rails had been cut and hauled down to the old corral site so it could be expanded in size in order to accommodate their 18 new horses. In the meantime, that time frame had also allowed for the time needed for Clem's bread dough to rise for the baking to come. About then Clem yelled for the three trappers to wash up and come on over to his firepit. When they did, after the hard work and being emotionally drained from the morning's 'deadly activities', all of the men were treated to one of Clem's special dishes, namely Dutch oven apple cobbler. That was precisely why Chief Black Wolf and White Buffalo had come to visit the trappers in the first place and instead, had gotten into a life and death battle with the Gros Ventre war party. After finishing the entire 16-quart apple cobbler made from dried and now soaked apple slices, the chief proclaimed their misadventure with the Gros Ventre had been entirely worth it...

A week later, the beaver waters froze over but not before the trappers had pulled their traps in the nick of time. But before they had pulled their traps, they had added another 111 'Plus' to their horde of 252 fall beaver trapped in 1824! Then in preparation for the wolf trapping that was yet to come, the men partook of a buffalo hunt, bagging four heavy with winter fat, cow buffalo. Soon their smoking fires were creating clouds of smoke as smoking racks heavy with buffalo meat began being made into jerky. Four days later, tanned deerskin bags traded from the Indians at the fort hung from the cabin's rafters and pegs in the walls, heavily loaded with the sweet smelling Mountain Man staple, namely buffalo jerky. Then the men smoked all of their wolf traps to get rid of the man smell, cast more rifle and pistol balls, refilled all of their powder horns with fresh powder and one week later, left their camp on their first wolf trapping venture of the season.

Once again as they had in previous winter wolf trapping seasons, the men selected several small herds of buffalo in the area, killed one, opened it up and spread out its entrails so the smell of death would permeate the area. Then several Newhouse #14 toothed wolf traps were cleverly concealed in the offal and then the trappers moved on to another small herd of buffalo several miles away and repeated the process five more times until their twelve wolf traps had all been cleverly set. Following that, each day thereafter the men tended their traps, removed the dead wolves or killed those remaining alive in the traps, skinned, de-fatted and 'boarded' the fresh pelts so they would properly dry. For the next two months the trappers stayed very busy with their wolf trapping sessions until around the second week of February.

Then all hell broke loose weather-wise and soon howling snowstorms, daily sub-zero temperatures and deep snowdrifts finally forced the trappers to call off their wolf trapping ventures because of the increasing dangers and difficulties found when one ventured forth under such deep snow and adverse weather conditions. Then the weather turned even worse and in fact, one of the worst winters on record befell the land. So much snow fell that the men had trouble just getting around even in their area of their campsite. Finally the men made 'bear-paw' snowshoes so they could get about when it came to allowing their horse herd out daily to feed and guard them against attacks by hungry wolves.

Finally the spring weather became so bad that even the buffalo crowded into the timbered area around the trappers' cabin, eating the bark off the cottonwood and aspen trees because finding enough grasses to maintain life and limb became so difficult. Then the starving wolves became an even bigger problem. Following the starving buffalo herds, found the wolves soon in and around the trappers' horses kept in their corral! Finally in order to protect their horses from the hungry wolves, the men had to guard the horses around the clock during the daytime and nighttime hours. At night found two of the trappers tending a roaring fire near the horse corral just to keep the hungry wolves at bay and the buffalo from breaking down the corral rails and crowding in with the trappers' horses out of fright from the incessant wolf attacks. Then during the daylight hours, two of the trappers on their 'bear-paw' snowshoes had to stay with the feeding horse herd in order to allow them to graze on the wind-swept slopes and keep the hungry wolves at bay as well. However, not all of that was bad. Between the normal wolf trapping season and during the depths of winter and all of the wolves that were shot trying to get at the horses, the trappers either trapped or shot and killed 98 wolves during that 1825 winter and spring season! The most wolves they had ever taken! And of those wolves either trapped with leg-hold traps or shot, all were prime specimens except one. And that one had been partially chewed up in a fight by another wolf while caught in a trap.

Finally the harsh weather turned for the better and soon vestiges of the spring of 1825 began showing itself. And the grasses of spring could not have come at a better time when their blades began poking up through the cold soil. All of the trappers' horses were gaunt and showing many of their ribs due to the harsh and long winter with little to eat. However, with the new grasses, the horses began 'waxing fat' and soon were recovered enough for the men to ride and pack them on a daily basis. But the better condition of the trappers' horses brought little solace to the men! First of all, one did not fare well when riding behind horses which had recently fed on new and rich grass shoots! In short, the more than grievous methane smells being emitted by the horses when in caravan from eating such rich nourishment equaled those coming from Buck Snort during his times of stress as a

result of his earlier rat poisoning at the orphanage, and the smells his intestines could generate...   Additionally, several times during the
spring of 1825 when the weather allowed, the
men rode around their beaver trapping waters
checking things out and in so doing, were highly
discouraged at what they were seeing! Few live
beaver were found swimming in waters normally associated with high numbers of the valuable
furbearing rodents! Those found swimming in
the shallower waters of the Little Bighorn were
discovered to be in extremely poor body shape
or obviously starving! It then became apparent
to the trappers that the harsh winter months just
experienced had destroyed for the most part the
beaver number because of starvation all along
the Little Bighorn and its adjacent lack of cover
in the shallower river! No matter how hard the
men looked for good beaver sign or how far they
traveled along those waterways, the beaver for
the most part were absent or severely reduced in
number because of the previous harsh and long
winter conditions. And any beaver subsequently
test-trapped were in such poor body condition
that their pelts were essentially worthless, as was
their meat for eating because of the lack of fat in
the tissue.

Finally one day after an exhausting ride south
along the Little Bighorn and finding more of the
same when it came to scarce numbers of beaver
due to the killer winter just experienced, the men

held a 'council of war' that evening upon their return to camp. While Clem prepared supper of rangy buffalo meat, Dutch oven biscuits, beans and coffee, the men realized if they were to survive on the Frontier as Mountain Men fur trappers, they were going to have to move on to even newer and better beaver trapping grounds. When that decision was finally acknowledged, little did the trappers realize at the time that General Ashley and Major Henry had already decided the 'fate' of their company trappers and keepers of Fort Henry as well as its future, currently located at the mouth of the Bighorn River in the year of our Lord, 1825...

Two weeks later, Buck Snort and company stopped at Chief Black Wolf's Lodge Grass campsite. There they spent several days and shared a buffalo hunt with their friends, Chief Black Wolf and his son White Buffalo. While there, Clem made the chief's favorite white man's food, namely his great tasting Dutch oven apple cobbler loaded with brown sugar and cinnamon every evening for the chief and his family. Then letting Chief Black Wolf know they would be seeing him later on in the summer at Fort Henry during the annual fur sales and reprovisioning celebrations, the trappers bid their Crow Indian friends 'Goodbye', turned their pack string north and headed for Fort Henry. Little did any of the men realize this would be their last trip to historic Fort Henry to sell their furs and procure provisions for the coming fall of 1825 and the 1826 spring beaver trapping season...

CHAPTER EIGHT

TRAPPING ON THE "LITTLE BIGHORN", "BALL LIGHTNING", HELPING A FRIEND

Several days later after leaving Chief Black Wolf's Crow Indian Lodge Grass campsite, Buck Snort and company rode into view of Fort Henry with their fur caravan and their 18 extra horses taken from the Gros Ventre in an earlier battle. Riding up to the main gate of the fort, the men were greeted by Major Henry and a number of his company men designated to operate the business of trade, hunt buffalo for the men of the fort to eat and provide protection against Indian attack. But as they did, Buck Snort and company also noticed that the fort was as active as a disturbed beehive!

When questioned as to why so much activity, Major Henry just shook his head saying, "You Gents best dismount and follow me to my house inside the fort. Since you have been afield all of this time, you have not been made aware of what is happening. So I need to make you aware of what has happened, and 'in the wind' is 'a new day and a new way' of doing business in all of our futures as Mountain Men fur trappers."

Giving each other in his party a number of questioning looks, Buck Snort and company followed Major Henry through the gates into the fort and were once again surprised at seeing all of the activity swirling around them indicating that a major and significant move was in the offing. Dismounting, tying off their horses and then following the Major inside the cool of his home inside the walls of the fort soon found the men seated around his supper table with a cup of rum in hand and lots of questions spelled intently clear across all of their faces.

"Here is what is happening," said Major Henry. "General Ashley has ordered that Fort Henry be abandoned and the Ashley-Henry Fur Trade Company is moving on to 'a new way and a new day' of conducting our fur trade business! The General has decided that the 1,000-plus mile trip up the Missouri River by keelboat is just too difficult, expensive and dangerous. Following that, one also has the long and many times shallow haul up the Yellowstone River as well, just to get to this fort. It also seems every time we pull our keelboats upriver past the Arikara Indian Villages, some of which are located right on the Missouri River, we end up in a deadly battle royal with those villages. So far, every time that happens we lose a number of good men and even a boat or two with all of our expensive supplies going to the bottom of the river or they are captured, looted and then the Indians burn our boats to the waterline. Therefore, General Ashley has sent word upriver to us by a couple of Taos Free Trappers who were trading their furs at St. Louis, that the fort is to be abandoned and from now on he is going to initiate a new way of conducting our fur trade business! He is initiating what he is calling a "Rendezvous System", whereby he takes the trappers' supplies to a central location somewhere near the Rocky Mountains where all the beaver trapping is going on, instead of making everyone travel to a stationary fort located out of the way. A stationary fort that we are finding is always susceptible to being attacked by the Arikara, Blackfeet or some other tribe that is hostile to us white men fur trappers not wanting us trapping or hunting on their lands. Therefore, all the activity you are seeing going on around us is to abandon this fort to the elements and local Indians immediately and head south into Mexico Territory, where General Ashley has arranged to meet all of the rest of our company and Free Trappers at a previously designated site amenable for all come early this summer. It seems General Ashley, when visiting with the Taos Trappers who brought their furs all the way from the Taos area to St. Louis to sell for a better price, got the idea of a Rendezvous System of supply taking place in the beaver trapping areas instead of a stationary fort located off the beaten path. According to the two Taos trappers he just sent to Fort Henry, they are to lead us southward to where General Ashley and the rest of his company will meet us later this summer in order to provide us our year's provisions and purchase our furs. Then General Ashley will return to St. Louis to sell those furs just purchased and begin purchasing new supplies needed for the next year's Rendezvous, whose location will be determined by the trappers at this summer's first Rendezvous. There he will meet us in the heart of the beaver trapping country having come all the way from St. Louis via pack train with a large number of men carrying the supplies all of you men will need for the coming year. And in order to do that, he will be accompanied by several other Taos Free Trappers who have a Mexican license to trap beaver in the area in which we will be going to south of Fort Henry. Also, General Ashley will be led by a Free Trapper named Johnson Gardner who has trapped in this new area in the Mexican Territory where we will be heading just as soon as we can get packed up and can get the hell out of here. No two ways about it, it will do us all good to be out from 'under' the moccasins of the Blackfeet and Gros Ventre. Once on this first pre-selected Rendezvous site location identified by those Taos trappers who are trapping and familiar with that neck of the woods, General Ashley will purchase all of your furs and see to it that all of you are provisioned for the coming year as Mountain Men trappers for his company, as well as all the Free Trappers and those friendly Indian tribes looking to sell their furs and 'provision up'."

Then Major Henry ever the gracious host, re-poured the amazed over what they were hearing men's cups full from his expensive Fourth Proof rum supplies and then continued saying, "General Ashley has arranged for these Taos Free Trappers familiar with the new area in which we will be heading to lead us there once we leave this fort in a few days. They will guide us to where General Ashley will meet all of us and any others trapping in that area who wish to trade with him sometime in June near as we can figure. As I have been told by those recently arriving Taos Free Trappers, we will be heading for a place deep in the Territory of Mexico to our south but where beaver, muskrat, wolves, buffalo and river otter abound. We will be heading for a Rendezvous location at a place called Henry's Fork of the Green River which is supposedly between the confluence of Burnt Fork and Birch Creek, wherever the hell that is! We best hope no hostile Indians ambush us and kill our Taos Free Trapper guides because if they do, there sure as hell will be a mess of us wandering around in this here Mexico Territory somewhere to our south until hell freezes over or the good Lord decides to take the lot of us into his fold," said the Major with an easy laugh. Then the Major seeing the four company trappers had once again finished all of the rum he had poured for each of them earlier, saw to it that their cups were once again filled to the brim for the third time since sitting down at his table and learning of their coming fate and new type of future for the years ahead. Like the Major had said earlier, "A new way and a new day…"

Then with a big grin of realization the Major said lightheartedly, "Now, the way you four guzzled down my expensive Fourth Proof rum, I suspect you have been out of rum for some time. If that is the case, I suggest that you fellas load up on some of the rum that I still have left in my warehouse before we up and pack it away for the rather lengthy trip I am told we are facing. But I wouldn't wait too long because as I have said, I just have a little left and when it is gone it is gone. And since we will not be purchasing any furs until General Ashley arrives at this Rendezvous site, you can pick up any rum supplies on credit until you can sell your last year's and this spring's beaver and wolf pelts to the General when he arrives."

After some more talk on the preparations being made for the move in a few days, the men adjourned to their horses and heeding the Major's advice, headed for one of the fort's warehouses being that they were just about out of rum. There Buck Snort and company made arrangements to purchase eight flat kegs of rum from the fort's ever-dwindling and being quickly packed away remaining stores. That they did as he had suggested, that they could settle up with the Major once they arrived at the Rendezvous site and sold their furs, as well as the extra horses gathered up in the earlier shootout with the 18 Gros Ventre who had attacked Chief Black Wolf and his son back on the Little Bighorn.

(Author's Note: It was a good thing that Buck Snort and company purchased those eight flat kegs of rum at Fort Henry when they did. Firstly, flat wooden kegs were easier to pack onto packsaddles than were the usual rounded, larger and heavier-sized kegs. Secondly, General Ashley in his industry and excitement upon arranging for supplies for his first 'new way' of doing business under his proposed new Rendezvous System of the fledgling American fur trade, had forgotten to purchase in St. Louis and include in his supplies any whiskey or rum! That was a severe oversight on the General's part and from that Rendezvous until the end of the fur trade system in the field years later when most of the beaver had been extirpated from the Rocky Mountains, and civilized mankind had switched his likes from wearing beaver hats to those made from the silk of a worm smuggled out from China, that critical supply item of whiskey or rum was never again EVER overlooked…)

One week later found a long string of riders and fully loaded pack strings leaving the abandoned Fort Henry, heading south along the Bighorn River and traveling just past Crow Chief Black Wolf's Lodge Grass encampment. There they turned slightly to the southwest as General Ashley's Taos Free Trappers familiar with the area led the way from what was at that time in history, the lands of the fledgling and expanding United States. And from there, they went into what was then the Territory of Mexico, which later became the State of Wyoming. Twenty-four days after leaving old Fort Henry behind, a tired string of mostly company men trappers and fort workers streamed into what was called by other trappers in the area, the Green River Valley. Once there the men turned and headed for the confluences of Burnt Fork and Birch Creek on the Henry's Fork of the Green River.

At that destination, the trappers scattered closely about setting up their individual campsites, gathered in firewood and staked out their horses so they could graze and water. As for the Major's men from the old Fort Henry, they too staked out their horses after unpacking all of their pack animals. That they did as they set about all of the remaining supplies brought from the old fort under the shade of a grove of cottonwood trees. Then those mounds of supplies were covered with buffalo hides to prevent them from being wetted during any commonly occurring summer thunderstorms frequenting the area. Next, a group of ten men and their packhorses designated as 'group hunters' left the new campsite and went buffalo hunting. Four hours later those ten men returned leading their heavily loaded packhorses carrying panniers full of bloody and still dripping buffalo meat for all of the men's suppers. Prior to their arrival with the fresh buffalo meat, another group of men organized by the Major had dug out a large firepit area, hauled in numerous armloads of firewood and had a fire going in order to produce lots of coals for the soon to be prepared and baked in a number of the ubiquitous Dutch ovens the trappers' old standby of biscuits. Then with the designated camp cooks spitting chunks of fresh buffalo meat over the coals of the campfire and with the smell of coffee mingling with that of spitted buffalo meat, the campsite began taking on a homey atmosphere. A homey atmosphere coupled with the joyous talking and laughing of men happy to be at the first fur trade Rendezvous site in a location which was later to become 'America' and no longer the Territory of Mexico.

In the meantime, General Ashley with approximately 25 men herding along numerous heavily loaded packhorses and guided by Taos Free Trapper Johnson Gardner who was familiar with how to get to the Green River Valley many hundreds of miles distant, had left St. Louis several months earlier. General Ashley and his pack string traveled up along the banks of the Missouri River until they arrived at the North Platte, then Gardner turned Ashley, his men and their pack string of trappers and headed them inland. Subsequent travels and many long days later had taken the company of men and packhorses alongside Independence Rock by the Sweetwater River and past that waterway's famed rapids named "The Devils Gate". Then the historic gathering of men and packhorses from the first Rendezvous System of what eventually came to be named the American Fur Trade, crossed over the Continental Divide through the lowest pass in the Rocky Mountains, namely the historic South Pass. The group then descended along the Big Sandy River past numerous groups of Indians watching on and fearful of attacking such a large body of men heading into the Green River Valley near modern-day Daniel, Wyoming.

As luck would have it, General Ashley's column of fur trappers and packhorses crossed paths with famous "Man of the Mountains" and well-known Mountain Man, Etienne Provost. Etienne Provost, a French-Canadian and Taos Free Trapper and trader, was recognized by his peers as one of the most skilled of fur trappers, traders and explorers in the American Southwest. As such, Provost after meeting Ashley's men and being familiar with the immediate area selected for the first of the Rendezvous sites, guided them to the location of what was to become the first

American Rendezvous at Henry's Fork near Birch Creek in the summer of 1825.

Arriving during the last of June after a 78-day trip from St. Louis, General Ashley, being the astute businessman that he was, held off all trading until he was assured that most trappers in country or heading his way carrying their valuable loads of peltries, had arrived. Then on July the first, General Ashley opened up the business of purchasing furs and the selling of provisions to all in attendance. As it turned out, approximately 140 fur trappers and friendly Indians had arrived and were in attendance at this, the first of the numerous subsequent fur trade Rendezvous.

Those trappers gathered for this first Rendezvous were composed of 29 deserters from the Canadian Hudson's Bay Fur Company who felt they were being shortchanged and overcharged by their own company, and tired of such treatment 'jumped ship' so to speak to Ashley's outfit. Additionally, there were 13 men from Etienne Provost's group of trappers, seven men accompanying Jedediah Smith, already famed American fur trapper and explorer, 25 men and herders from General Ashley's company, 30 men under Major Henry from the abandoned Fort Henry, 25-30 men associated with another fur trader whose last name was Weber, coupled with a loose assortment of Free Trappers and a fairly large gathering of friendly Indians from all over the area. Because the General had such a great distance to travel back to St. Louis from the Green River Valley when his business was finished and fearful of being caught by the coming harsh winter weather found in the Rocky Mountains, the business of purchasing furs and the selling of the coming year's provisions at this first Rendezvous held in 1825 only lasted one day and then it was over! Future Rendezvous were represented with much more drinking, hell raising, celebration, singing, dancing, shooting contests, spitted oxen and buffalo suppers, and the like! Additionally future Rendezvous lasted many times from one to two summer months or until the trappers had spent all of their hard-earned money, had run out of drink or both.

And as a matter of course and business because of the distance traveled to and from the Rendezvous sites, dangers encountered and expenses incurred, General Ashley was charging 700-1,000% more for items at that first Rendezvous than an individual might pay if purchasing that same item in St. Louis! This overcharging for items at all of the following Rendezvous became a standard practice by traders once afield, and soon became known sarcastically among the Mountain Men and not happily anticipated as "Mountain Prices".

Realizing the shortness of the self-imposed time period in which to trade in their furs and purchase what was needed for the coming year before the next Rendezvous could be held, there understandably was a great deal of pushing and shoving once the business at hand began among the trappers and General Ashley's core of company traders... When it finally came time for Buck Snort and company to trade in their furs, all four trappers made sure they watched General Ashley's graders and sorters 'like a hawk would watch a nearby meadow mouse' for any under-grading chicanery! That they did because being original company trappers, they were only being paid a price of $3 per pound for each Made Beaver (adult and large in size pelt), whereas Free Trappers were being paid $5 per pound for those same weight peltries! And since Buck Snort and company (Muskrat refused to deal with facts and figures because he was illiterate) had only trapped 363 mostly Made Beaver the fall before and none during the spring trapping season because most beaver in their area had died out due to the winter's extremely harsh living conditions, the trappers only received $1,050 for their beaver pelts! However, their 98 mostly adult and dark-colored wolf skins garnered an additional $4,410. As for their livestock sales, the trappers sold nine of their 18 horses captured during the deadly battle with the Gros Ventre for an additional $900. They decided to keep the remaining best horses for themselves in case they had horses injured or stolen. Lastly, the trappers sold all of the tomahawks, sheath knives in beautifully beaded sheaths, and all 18 of the Gros Ventre's flintlock rifles to the Ashley-Henry Fur Trade Company for another $330! Those last items were quickly gobbled up by trappers with lesser or possessing poorer quality basic equipment or those who were after the fancy beaded items in which to wear and strut around in. In the end, Buck Snort was handed an Ashley-Henry Fur Trade Company credit slip amounting to $6,690!

With credit slip in hand, Buck Snort, Wind Horse, Clem and Muskrat followed the stream of other trappers over to where General Ashley's traders were assembled. There they were using buffalo skins laid out on the ground as 'makeshift tables' and some hastily assembled log tables, holding a worldly assortment of everything a fur trapper needed for the coming year in the form of tins, bags, barrels, kegs, wooden boxes, sacks, piles and heaps of bladed instruments of all kinds and sorts. Additionally, there were the newest types and models of stacked rifles and mounds of summer and winter clothing! Amidst all sorts of swearing, pushing, shoving, grumbled threats, jostling and hasty grabbing, a number of sweating, smelly, gruff, rough and dressed from head to foot in sweat and grease-stained 'pine smoke' smelly buckskins, the trappers fumbled and fought over those goods that were available.

Having scouted out the area holding all of the available provisions earlier before they had a chance to sell their furs and horses, Buck Snort and company had decided which trapper of their group would be responsible for acquiring that coming year's particularly needed supplies, so all of them would not be ganged up at the same pile of goods selecting one and the same items. By skillfully splitting up their group of trappers and each member being singularly responsible for the separate much-needed items, within two hours of hustle, bustle and selection, Buck Snort and company had managed to select every needed item and amount considered necessary for the coming trapping seasons. That they did by availing themselves of every selection opportunity contrary to many other groups of trappers who went away empty-handed during their one-day provisioning opportunity after trying to make their selections as a group. Once the men had selected what they needed in the way of provisions, they settled up with General Ashley to the tune of $1,543.50. Since they had an Ashley-Henry Fur Trade Company credit slip good for $6,690 in goods, the men had more than enough money to cover the cost of the goods they had just selected. When all was said and done, General Ashley provided a Letter of Credit redeemable back in St. Louis at the company's main fur house and place of business or another such Rendezvous to Buck Snort for $5,146.50. That valuable Letter of Credit was then promptly placed in his saddlebag along with his previous Letters of Credit amounting to several thousands of dollars... Letters of Credit which the group of men hoped to redeem in the future when they decided to give up fur trapping, head back to Missouri, buy some land and settle down in quiet and peace. That was if the 'Grace of the Frontier' was bestowed upon each and every one of them afore they all became grizzly bear scat ripening out in the prairie sun...

And since General Ashley had also failed to bring along any blacksmiths to meet the Rendezvous trappers' needs, Buck Snort, thinking ahead, 'filled the bill'. Buck Snort as a young man had learned the trade of a farrier under the orphanage's blacksmith Cliff Fulton's direction. As such, he skillfully managed to gather up a number of new assorted horse and mule shoes out from a supply barrel for all of their riding and packhorses, with extras to spare in case their friends needed some. And since both he and Wind Horse had served under the same blacksmith in learning the trade of being farriers, for the next whole week all they did was remove old shoes, trim and re-shoe fellow trappers' horses needing new 'footwear' who lacked the farrier and blacksmithing experience. And since those two men possessed a skill and the needed farrier tools that other trappers with sore-footed horses lacked, the two men made a pretty penny off those less fortunate whose horses needed new footwear and had not planned accordingly in the provisions acquisition and purchasing 'hurried-up' one-day process allowed by General Ashley.

But hidden in among the providing of a much-needed and extremely valued service to a number of fellow trappers' horses, much valued information regarding new untapped beaver trapping locations was obtained by Wind Horse and Buck Snort from helped trappers regarding the rugged country they now found themselves in since the Fort Henry trapping area had now been abandoned. Then come each evening around the firepit and with their suppers 'under belt', the men discussed what they had learned regarding new beaver trapping grounds information in the unfamiliar country they now occupied. Information gathered from those more experienced trappers waiting to have their pack and riding steeds re-shoed for the coming fall and spring trapping seasons.

As such, it was decided among the men that they would remain in the Rocky Mountains instead of moving out onto the prairie's numerous watered areas, because every trapper they had worked with while shoeing their horses had advised that new and rugged mountain chain had beaver galore in just about every waterway. That was especially so in what were called the Wind River Mountains lying to the northeast of where the first Rendezvous was currently being held.

One evening after a supper of beans, Dutch oven biscuits and a raisin and rice cobbler, the men eager to be afoot and on their horses once again, decided they were 'burning daylight'.

Decided they were 'burning daylight' in that they had to find a good location in which to build a cabin and horse corral away from other beaver trappers in a new location that was heavily populated with beaver. They had also decided that to do so, they had to leave ahead of a number of other more experienced trappers in order to stake out their claim in good beaver trapping country before the others left the Rendezvous and arrived on the same site in the field. And since a goodly number of the over 100 or so trappers still at the Rendezvous site showed little inclination to leave since they were still deep into celebrating with others of their own kind, Buck Snort and company decided to 'strike while the iron was hot'.

The next morning right after a rather hearty breakfast of buffalo, biscuits and coffee, found Buck Snort and Muskrat quietly leading a number of heavily loaded packhorses followed by Wind Horse and Clem doing the same. Waving their 'Good-byes' with hands and head nods to a number of their friends as they passed by, the men turned towards the Green River and followed along that waterway as they headed to the northeast. Headed to the northeast because as had often been reported, that area was a land of beaver-rich waters located in the Wind River Mountains by those friends and other fellow Mountain Men who had their riding and pack animals previously shoed by Wind Horse and Buck Snort.

For the next two days and 40 miles of hard travel in and among the many timbered slopes and valleys, the four trappers and their heavily loaded packhorses labored from daylight until dark. On day three of their travels as the men headed along the Green River towards a very distinct and massive mountain (named Whiskey Mountain by latter-day settlers), the men marveled over what they were seeing. There they discovered pine, fir and spruce timber that reached to the heavens 'skirted' throughout by vigorously flowing streams holding many flashing 'silver darts' of finned inhabitants. Herds of elk and mule deer abounded at every turn in the trail. So did bighorn sheep, black bear, mountain goats on the craggy rims, as well as 'explosions of coveys' of greater sage grouse flushed on the sagebrush flats. And as a constant, quiet singles or doubles of blue grouse were discovered along the numerous animal trails as Buck Snort's caravan of trappers quietly wound their way through the magnificent stands of timber! Additionally, numerous grizzly bear were surprised feeding on large animal carcasses like buffalo or roaming on the rocky hillsides rolling off rocks of a size that would have tried the strength of a large man to move. This the great bear did, as they dug for a meal of the tasty yellow-bellied marmots in their burrows under the rocks, or 'Whistle Pigs' as the trappers called them because of their sharp calls uttered upon seeing white humankind for the first time in their lives passing by their burrows on the many talus slopes.

Camping for the evening on a sandy spit along the Green River on that third evening, the men unloaded all of their horses, hobbled them to prevent easy theft by Indians and let them graze on the tall and high energy grasses found in abundance growing along the waterway. Doing as they always did when it came to their safety traveling in a new land occupied by the 'Sons of the Prairies and Mountains', the men surrounded their campsite and sleeping area with their heavily loaded packs and saddles as cover in case they were ambushed by hostile Indians or investigated by a curious grizzly bear smelling the men's supper cooking and ambling into their campsite to 'help himself to the great smelling grits'. The next morning after taking a cold bath in the nearby Green River and shaving, the men brought in their still feeding livestock from the river bottom and began the hard work of packing all of their packhorses and saddling their riding horses for the day's travel as Clem prepared breakfast. Breakfast that morning consisted of only jerky, as well as a small mountain of biscuits and coffee as the men relaxed around their campfire and enjoyed as they always did, Clem's light, fluffy and always welcome Dutch oven offerings. Then as the sun's rays peeked over the mountains and began warming the air in the river valley occupied by the trappers, the men using the day's beginning as their 'time piece' mounted up. Shortly thereafter, they began riding once more towards what appeared to be an opening in the mountain range at the base of the towering mountain the men now found themselves riding alongside, with the Green River acting like a 'sparkling blue ribbon' leading the way into the land of what they hoped would be their new home.

About an hour later, all of a sudden Buck Snort and Muskrat stopped their horses at the edge of a large meadow, raised their hands into the air as a sign to stop and then pointed to their noses as if alerting Clem and Wind Horse to an unusual and suspicious smell! Then alerted to something else unusual, Buck Snort pointed to a tall fir tree previously hit by lightning that was currently holding an active osprey nest. An active osprey nest as was evidenced by a pair of nervous birds, letting the whole world know of an unusual and disturbing event that was ongoing close to the base of a tall tree they were using as a nest site! Sitting there on their horses and nervously fingering their flintlock rifles lying across their laps as the active and very upset parent ospreys continued letting the world know they were unhappy with the happenings below their nest site, the men's eyes kept sweeping the timber for any signs of danger. However as they did, all of the men could now very plainly scent the smell of recently burned pinewood and badly burned meat of some kind! Taking in deep draughts of air through their noses and watching the active pair of ospreys out from the corner of their eyes, the men soon discovered the direction from whence came the 'telltale' mystery smell and unusual situation that had the nesting birds all riled up.

Continuing cautiously along the Green River as it meandered through the large meadow the trappers now found themselves riding through, they rounded a finger of pine and fir trees 'stabbing their way' into the meadow. It was then that the men spotted a newly built log cabin with its recently bark-stripped logs gleaming in the rays of the late morning sun nestled in the timber. Drawing up their horses at the edge of the timber and osprey meadow, the men now quietly sat there on their horses surprised over finding the area already occupied by other trappers. As they did, Buck Snort chanced looking down at the ground of the open area leading up to the cabin. There on the ground, he discovered that they had just ridden onto a trail of freshly appearing shod and unshod horse tracks leading down from the cabin, turning and heading up the valley along the Green River to the northeast towards an unknown destination.

Sensing the possibility of danger with all of the obvious tracks from a large number Indians' unshod horses and what they potentially represented, Buck Snort 'hissed' and then pointed towards the fresh tracks with the end of his rifle barrel being held in his right hand. When he did and the numerous unshod horse hooves' 'information' registered with the men, they began nervously fingering their rifles in case they would be urgently needed, as their Frontier-experienced eyes now quickly swept the area looking for any telltale signs of danger! Then seeing no obvious near at hand dangers but still hearing the numerous unusual-sounding disturbed calls from the osprey parents and seeing their nervous flying about, the trappers out of curiosity began slowly backtracking the mystery trail of mixed horse tracks leading away from the trappers' cabin.

As the men cautiously rode their horses towards the trappers' cabin and its nearby horse corral, they soon observed what had initially attracted the men's noses to a now very shocking and grisly scene. A scene whose previous grisly activity could have easily led to what had the nearby nesting ospreys so upset! There 'in front of God and everybody' tied to several corral posts appeared to be the remains of the bodies of four men! Bodies which were charred black as coal after being tied to corral posts and extensively tortured from all outward appearing signs of the missing external members of their hands and faces and then with fire, brutally executed!

As small wisps of smoke and steam still lazily curled upward over the men's obviously still warm and charred remains, the four quietly 'horsed' and shocked trappers held their rifles in hand at the 'ready' as they sat 'high in their saddles' so they could see better around them! That they did as their eyes continued collectively sweeping the area for any signs of danger of what was ultimately to become named the "Osprey Nest Camp" by the trappers. The four men continued 'holding' at the 'ready' just in case any lingering signs of Indians with bad intentions were still in country. Said suspected culprits doing all of the killing and burning of the four trappers based on all of the typically Indian unshod horses' tracks leading into and out from the location of the trappers' cabin and horse corral. Then together but still in high alert, the four men slowly rode right up into the main campsite's grisly area... As they did, they became aware of all of the four burned trappers' provisions and cooking implements strewn about the front grounds of the nearby cabin! Strewn about were provisions and clothing that had been obviously removed from the cabin, deemed worthless to the raiding Indians' way of thinking and subsequently discarded about in the yard area in abandon between the cabin and a still-smoldering grilling and outside firepit cooking area. Even further evidence in the minds of Buck Snort and his company of trappers regarding the killing culprits' identities, as they looked over the characteristic degree and signs of the dead trappers' initial surprise. Surprise over being ambushed by a large number of Indians, captured before they could really fight back to any degree, then subsequently tied to corral posts. Then from all the looks of missing fingers and sliced off ears and noses scattered about on the ground around the charred bodies, that form of torture came before being brutally burned alive! Because of a large number of black-billed magpies, crows and ravens sitting in the nearby trees waiting for the bodies to cool so they could feast on the remains, wisps of steam still curling skyward from the bodies and the osprey parents still flying around in a highly agitated state near their nest tree, made it plain the killings had recently occurred and that the killers were still nearby in country...

Dismounting in disgust in front of the cabin over what he was seeing as the rest of the trappers remained horsed and vigilant in case further danger suddenly reared its ugly head, Buck Snort slowly approached the cabin with rifle in hand and a tight feeling in his chest. Then after a slight pause at the open front doorway and a look back to make sure all the rest of the men remained on high alert, Buck Snort cautiously stepped through the opening and peered inside into the darkened cabin's interior. The cabin's interior had been looted from all appearances of disarray and what had not been apparently needed or desired by the Indian attackers, had been tossed asunder.

Then Buck Snort heard what sounded like a child's whimpering coming from the back portion of the cabin, which from all appearances had been the location of the unfortunate trappers' sleeping area. Not really sure what was making the 'whimpering sounds' but suspecting the worst, Buck Snort with rifle raised and ready to fire, slowly walked toward the sounds of something sounding like a living thing in intense pain. Rounding an overturned table and peering behind it, Buck Snort found a large, about 70-pound hairy dog whose breed he recognized from his days in the orphanage as that of being an Airedale terrier. The dog was weakly standing in the middle of one of the dead trappers' sleeping areas as if defending the bed site and protruding from its left hip was a deeply lodged Indian's arrow! An arrow appearing not shot to kill by its attacker but cruelly 'placed' in order to intentionally painfully wound an animal obviously trying to defend its white master! There lying at the dog's feet was the horribly mutilated body of what appeared to be what was left of a fifth trapper! Then to Buck Snort's abject disgust, it became obvious as to what had happened and why that trapper had not been tortured and burned alive like all the others found outside!

As he walked over to the dead trapper lying on his sleeping furs, Buck Snort could see that the man had recently been in a terrible and violent losing grizzly bear confrontation! As evidence, both of the trapper's badly compound-fractured legs and terrible blue-black looking long rips and tears in his legs and upper body flesh bore mute testimony as to the violence of the earlier confrontation between bear and man! About then, the intense and almost liquid-like heavy smell of the beginning stages of putrefaction hit Buck Snort's nostrils! An odor of the lingering stages of death that was so horribly intense that its airborne denseness of smell could almost be tasted by the tongue, bearing mute testimony as to just one of the stages of suffering the injured trapper must have endured before his impending demise... The man, as a result of not only his terrible physically painful injuries but the massive infusions of fetid grizzly bear saliva injected while being torn asunder, had become so infected that instead of the Indians burning him alive as they had the other trappers in his party, had just been shot full of 13 arrows as he lay there fever-ravaged in his sleeping furs!

Then it appeared that the man's loyal dog had tried to protect the badly crippled man and some Indian had intentionally shot the dog in its hip not intending to kill the large animal but just to seriously wound it and let it die a horrible lingering death as his master had been undergoing... Realizing what he was seeing, smelling and the misery it was generating inside the body of the loyal animal standing over its deceased master, Buck Snort could feel the killing rage and anger for those who had done such a cruel thing rising inside him by leaps and bounds! So much so that if he ever caught anyone doing such a cruel thing in the future to any living thing, he would personally see to it that such a human being would die just as violently at the hands of the trapper looking on at the scene lying before him just as sure 'as there was a living God'!

That was when the badly wounded dog, no longer able to stand and defend its dead master because of its own loss of blood and raging infection in the wound, let out another whimper and then pitifully fell over on its side! Without thinking about maybe being bitten by the badly injured dog, Buck Snort quickly laid down his rifle, scooped up the badly injured dog and gently carried it out through the open doorway of the dead trapper's cabin in his arms with tears of anger welling up in his eyes... With that, Buck Snort laid the injured dog gently down under a well-shaded spruce tree on a previously discarded buffalo robe so it could watch what the trappers would be doing, and then the trappers went to work around the camp.

That afternoon among the other work needed doing, the charred bodies of the trappers from the corral posts were removed as was the dead man from inside the cabin. Those five trappers were then buried out behind their newly built cabin in a single grave close together as the friends they had been in life. Then because the oily sweet smell of putrefying human flesh inside the cabin was so still so pungent from the stench of the injured trapper with the broken legs and rotting body parts, the men just opened up its deer hide windows and log front door in order to let the strong smell of death evaporate and drift away with time. Later that afternoon, Buck Snort and company had supper around the dead trappers' old firepit and as Clem was cooking their food, the other three men cleaned up the campsite from all of the scattered-about previous owners' provisions and implements. Those that were found usable to the trappers' way of thinking were placed back inside the cabin. Those items that were spoiled, soiled or destroyed beyond repair and were of no further use were cast into the fire at the outside firepit and burned up after the men's supper was done.

Then with plenty of remaining daylight, Buck Snort, Wind Horse and Muskrat unloaded all of their own packhorses, hobbled them along with their unsaddled riding horses and let them out to pasture and water in the nearby meadow under several sets of watchful eyes just in case... But because the cabin still smelled so strongly of 'death', the men set up their sleeping furs under the canopy of some aspen trees next to the original trappers' corral and as a precaution against any subsequent Indian attack, surrounded their sleeping furs and blankets with those stacks of saddles and packs. As Buck Snort and company continued setting up their campsite for a 'stay' that was still undetermined with their rifles close

at hand in case the original Indian attackers returned, their silence over the barbarity of what
they had experienced earlier in the day among
themselves was 'deafening'... That was when
Clem, realizing the day's intensity of events
required some 'soothing of the savage beast'
among his own kind, broke out a keg of their
rum purchased back at the old Fort Henry, and
soon each man lounged around their campfire in
the gathering darkness in clouds of the always-
present mosquitoes but still a 'deafening' silence
of their own mortality hung heavy in the night's
air...

For the longest time that evening, the only
sounds heard were those coming from a crackling campfire, the incessant hum of mosquitoes
and the howls of celebration of a jack rabbit kill
by a nearby pair of coyotes. Finally Buck Snort
broke the intense silence surrounding the trappers saying, "I realize this may not be the time in
light of what all of us have experienced in some
measure here today, but here is what I have been
mulling over. All the way into this beautiful
country we have seen nothing but tremendous
numbers of big game and beaver. We have seen
no other trappers in this area other than those
killed by the Indians in this camp, and here we sit
drinking our rum right next to a well-built cabin
and a set of horse corrals that would more than
satisfy all of our needs were we to take it over
as ours and live here. The corral, except for the

few burned posts that held the other trappers' bodies can easily be replaced and is more than adequate for our needs and the size of our horse herd. That being said, if we were to stay here, we would not need to build another homesite for the fall and spring beaver trapping seasons. The firepit has been well-placed and with the small stream passing near the corral, we would have all the clean water we would need in order to live in this place if we choose to do so. From what else we saw coming into this area, the herds of buffalo were not great in size but would be more than adequate for all of our meat, tallow, sinew and hide needs, as would be the numbers of elk and deer we saw moving through the area. Then since the trappers at the Rendezvous voted to have next year's Rendezvous in roughly the same area as was this year's, that would mean we would only have a short trip back to where we would need to go for next trapping season's provisions as well as a place in which to sell our furs. That is if we choose to take this place as ours and live here. So as I see it and unless all of you have a problem, I say we take this entire camp and make it our home for the coming fall and spring beaver trapping seasons. And if our beaver trapping successes found in this area along the Green amount to what I think they will and continue to be from all of the sign we have seen riding into this area, we maybe can live here next year as well."

Then Buck Snort paused in what more he had to say as Clem delivered another hot batch of his Dutch oven biscuits to all of the men sitting around the campfire. Shortly thereafter as a treat for all of the men's bad case of the 'sweet tooth', Clem brought around a jug of honey that had been placed near the edge of the firepit so it could warm up, so his 'doughy delights' could be slathered with warm honey. Once his biscuits had been slathered in honey like one would do a mess of pancakes, Buck Snort began once again with, "The way I see it the four of us have two major issues facing us. First, I suggest that come the 1826 Rendezvous, we four confront General Ashley and Major Henry and advise them that we have met the terms of our earlier company contract and henceforth, we wish to declare ourselves as 'Free Trappers'! That way in the future we would be paid top dollar for all of our furs instead of the lower prices paid to company trappers for those same quality and size of furs. Bottom line, we have been more than fair to the General and now it is time for 'the shoe to be worn on the other foot'."

Looking around and seeing that he still had the rest of his group's rapt attention, Buck Snort continued with what was seriously sticking in his 'craw' and needing saying and considering. "Those killing sons-a-bitches who did in these five trappers at this here campsite for no other apparent reason other than they were white men fur trappers, must be dealt with! By that, I mean we need to hunt down and kill every one of those Indian bastards responsible for killing the trappers from this campsite or at some point in time we may end up just as those five poor bastards we just came upon today! And with that in mind, I don't really fancy being captured, tortured and then burned to a crisp! With that outcome in mind, if we stay here and do nothing about those killers, those killing sons-a-bitches may damn well return and if they do and catch us looking the other way, we will end up shot all to hell or burned to a crisp at the stake like those four 'crispy critters' we just buried out behind this here cabin today."

Then running down on what he had to say since his friends had said nothing ever since he had taken 'front stage' and was carrying on like he had been, Buck Snort stopped talking. Then he found himself looking hard at all of his fellow trappers and 'family' for some sort of sign over what he had just espoused and mentally searching for what they might be thinking. Since not a single word had any of his friends uttered since he had begun, Buck Snort gathered up the fringe on his 'buckskins' and continued by saying, "Alright, I think it has been decided. Since none of you have uttered a damn word since I began speaking about our future here in this area as Free Trappers, I will continue. I read from all your silence over what I have been saying that all of you are in unison over the points I have raised. And since these five dead trappers have no further use for this here 'hell-for-stout' cabin just built and set of corrals or the damn good-looking beaver trapping waters all along this hellish good-looking stretch of waters along the Green River, I declare they are now ours for the taking!

Now comes the dangerous part of my proposals. I say we need to hunt these trapper-killing Indian bastards down and like the Good Book says, 'we do unto them as they have done unto our own kind'… And I say we start such a deadly 'cold-tracking' chore tomorrow at daylight afore their murderous trail gets any colder. Because if we don't, their trail will get so cold that we can no longer successfully cold-track the bastards down who did this and do unto them that which we need to do in order to set things right according to what the Good Book says we ought to do!"

Seeing that Buck Snort had about 'run down', Muskrat spoke up saying, "If Buck Snort has it in his 'craw' to kill those who killed these trappers, then I say we had best move all of our provisions and goods inside this here cabin first afore some summer thunderstorm comes along and wets down all of our valuables. That or some damn 'griz' comes waddling along and eats what he wants and scatters all the rest that he doesn't 'cotton' to all over hell and creation. And since I don't 'cotton' to eating moldy provisions or sleeping in piles of fresh bear scat, like Buck Snort, I say either we get 'cracking' and get down to the dirty business of killing, or we move on to better pastures and hope our luck is better than these five we laid into the ground this date."

Then before anyone else could address Muskrat's 'provision concerns' issue, Clem spoke up saying, "What about this damn 'arrow-shot' and crippled-up ole dog? He is in no condition to travel and we damn sure can't just leave him here all by himself to up and wither away. And surely none of us wants to just up and kill this poor ole damn dog either, especially after all he has gone through in losing his master and getting the hell shot out of him. I think if he were to heal up right and proper-like, he would be a good one to watch over all of us so we would not suffer as did his master once he gets used to the four of us. I am just saying..."

For the longest moment in time, no one said anything about Clem's concerns overriding that of Muskrat's issues regarding summer thunderstorms wetting down all of their provisions, packs and the like, or a grizzly bear eating and crapping all over the provisions left out in the open. Then Buck Snort 'took the bit in his mouth' once again saying, "We aren't going to leave that dog here at the cabin all by hisself. I plan on removing that arrow from his hip later this evening, slapping some bag balm into his hip wound and then just leaving it open so it can drain and heal up all by itself. As for taking him along, he is just going to have to ride in a pannier full of grass because it ain't Christian to leave him or our horses for that matter, to up and fend for each other in this harsh country while we are on the hunt for those killers of the trappers. Those horses are in no way acquainted enough with this pasture surrounding this campsite as it 'belonging to them' and there is no way we can just leave them in the corral. If we did, they just might starve if we were unable to get back to them in time to let them out before they all died from lack of eats or thirst! Especially if it takes us a number of days to run down our trappers' killers and render unto them what they have coming according to the Good Book. So with that in mind, this dog goes along with me and our valuable horses will do so as well, if I have my 'druthers'. With that in mind, we can leave our belongings in this here cabin until we return. Let us just hope a 'griz' doesn't come along looking for a meal and a warm and sheltered place to take a 'dump' and then decides to call this here cabin his new home afore we can return from our manhunt." With Buck Snort's final words, the campsite grew quiet and then the men began making ready for the rest of the work that needed doing that evening before they called it a day.

Later true to his word and with their provisions issue resolved after they were stored inside their new cabin still strongly smelling of 'death', a pot of warm water was placed alongside the badly wounded dog. Then Buck Snort, after feeding the dog some of Clem's leftover biscuits smeared liberally in venison grease left over in a three-legged frying pan to help whet the sick animal's appetite, made ready his previously heated and now cooled sheath knife. Buck Snort then very carefully, so the dog would hopefully understand he was there to help, began gently lancing the badly pus-laden tissue surrounding the arrow wound to lessen the pressure and rid the animal of his source point of pain and infection. Then with a degree of hesitation and some trepidation because of the large size of the dog and his more than ample set of teeth, Buck Snort carefully removed the badly bent steel-tipped arrow point from the living musculature with the tip of his knife blade. Remarkably throughout this entire procedure, the dog just intently watched Buck Snort like 'he' understood what was going on and did not try biting the man working over his painfully infected hip wound... Soon the wound had been cleaned out with warm water, generously bathed with bag balm and then the wound was left open so it would heal. However by morning, the dog had licked his hip wound clean of the bag balm and leftover pus and appeared to be somewhat stronger and more alert. That was especially so after having something more to eat, the majority of the pocket of pus removed from the wound, and had gotten a fairly good night's sleep. The next day the dog was still unable to stand on his own other than just weakly, but he could stand! Then being fed all the venison and leftover biscuits he could hold the following morning and that was a gutful, the dog was carried over and gently loaded into a partially grass-filled pannier where he lay there, just high enough inside so he could comfortably see out and watch what was going on around him as he was packed along with the rest of the trappers' valuable riding and pack string.

Then with Wind Horse in the lead of the pack string because he was the group's best tracker when it came to 'cold-tracking' old trails and had the added value of having "lynx eyes", especially when it came to seeing what needed to be seen, a common trait found among many an Indian warrior, the men with a quiet and killing determination ventured forth. But as they did and because of the number of Indians they figured they would ultimately be facing if they were able to catch up to and be able to run to ground those killers of the Osprey Nest Camp's five previous trapper owners, the trappers fairly bristled with what they considered would be their much-needed and readily available firepower.

Carrying all of their personal and the group's spare weaponry, each trapper's horse carried spare .52 caliber flintlock rifles in a scabbard on each side of their saddles! Then each trapper sported his own personal flintlock rifle laid across his lap for quick retrieval as well as a brace of pistols in their belt sashes! Additionally, each man carried a tomahawk in his back belt, knew how to use it and possessed a fixed look upon his face that clearly reflected the deadly moment in time they would soon be facing if successful in their pursuit of the trappers' killers from the Osprey Nest Camp! All of the men also realized that if that group of trapper-killing Indians was not successfully pursued and 'run to ground', they could someday once again return to the Osprey Nest Camp, catch Buck Snort and company not looking and many of that group of trappers would die a horrible death, if not all of them! The reality of that understanding and the intense looks borne on all of the men's faces reflected the 'dedication to that Frontier moment in time' they now faced. A moment in time in which the Osprey Nest Camp's trappers 'now on the hunt' could kill just as violently as was necessary in order to make sure they were the ones who saw the next sunrise and their 'targets of this deadly adventure' ultimately came to see nothing but eternal darkness...

For the next two long days, Wind Horse led the men on an almost due easterly track as he followed the getting-fresher by the hour, sets of shod dead trappers' horses and the large attacking party's unshod horses' tracks leading from the Osprey Nest Camp and heading upriver. Additionally, the Indians' herd of horses now being followed from the Osprey Nest Camp appeared to be trailing a loaded travois. A loaded travois leaving deep drag marks in the soil, which really made tracking the Indian group by Wind Horse much easier.

Little did Buck Snort and company realize that the travois being pulled by the Indian group now being followed carried a young and very valuable wounded warrior named "Red Hawk" from the earlier Osprey Nest Camp battle between the Northern Arapaho Indians and the five now dead original trappers. A young Indian warrior who just happened to be their chief's now badly injured son. A young warrior who was ambushed during the battle by a trapper just emerging from an outhouse and upon seeing the armed Indian warrior sneaking by so close at hand and getting ready to attack his camp, that he attacked in self-defense! In so doing, the trapper's tomahawk cut so deeply across a surprised Red Hawk's shoulder blades that the deep cut rendered it very difficult for the warrior to use either of his arms or be able to forcefully protect himself! Fortunately, another attacking Indian also sneaking close by and upon seeing the ambush killed the attacking trapper before he could render a second and killing blow to Red Hawk! However, the trapper's initial tomahawk strike was so damaging to Red Hawk's shoulder muscles that the attacking Indians after the battle were forced to construct a travois so Red Hawk could be carried home. That they did since it was now very painful for the young warrior to use either of his arms in mounting a horse or ride long distances holding the horse's reins because his shoulder muscles had been so badly damaged!

Come the evening of the third day of deadly slow but steady pursuit, found Buck Snort and company entering a small beaver-rich valley nestled in among a number of heavily forested mountain chains. Upon that fateful entry, the trappers' God of choice smiled down upon 'his own' and as it turned out, The Great Spirit did not smile down upon those of 'his own' at that same moment in time... Entering the valley and upon smelling the strong smell of burning pinewood from somewhere ahead, Wind Horse held his group of tired but now emotionally charged men back out of view in a deep stand of timber. That he did as he alone moved carefully forward on foot as he began scouting out the area from whence emanated the mystery wood smoke smell. Mystery pinewood smoke smells hopefully being generated by those deadly Osprey Nest Camp trapper-killers dragging a travois that Buck Snort and company had been carefully pursuing for the last three days...

Finally, after an additional hour of extremely careful stalking on foot into the area emanating the telltale stronger pinewood smoke smells and now that very distinct smell of charred human flesh, Wind Horse came upon 13 Indians still celebrating around a campfire their recent killing of the two new trappers they had ambushed a day earlier! Two trappers who had been caught in the act of preparing their suppers and when suddenly confronted by 13 cleverly stalking Indians with evil in their hearts, had paid the ultimate price for their lack of preparedness while happily living as fur trappers out on the Frontier…

There around that trappers' campfire now drunkenly danced the trapper-killing Indians around two vestiges of what had been just a day earlier, the bodies of those latest two trappers! Trappers who were now nothing more than charred vestiges tied to corral posts of what God had created and the Indians had put asunder… An Indian war party of late from another fur trappers' campsite now called the Osprey Nest Camp also located along the Green River, who three days earlier had burned four other trappers alive as well… Those latest trappers' burned black bodies 'headed' by gleaming white skulls, flesh burned free, bore mute testimony to the dangers found on the Frontier if one was not 'smiled upon'… Then as the Indians drank down the last of those recently killed trappers' rum supply and feasted on the remains of a dead elk hanging from those trappers' meat pole, found Wind Horse quietly slipping away back into the oncoming darkness.

About an hour later found him returning to his group of pursuing trappers with a look in his eyes that coldly spoke to those surrounding him of his innermost feelings over what was next to come... Gathering together the deadly quiet group of trappers around him Wind Horse said, "There are 13 Indian warriors celebrating the successful surprising and killing of two new trappers in the clearing next to what was those trappers' new cabin. Like those five trappers we found at our Osprey Nest Camp earlier, these latest two trappers appeared to have been tortured after being captured and then cruelly burned alive at the stake as well! As for the Indians, they are celebrating by drinking from a keg of those two trappers' rum supply and cooking up great slabs of elk meat taken from a previously killed elk hanging from the trappers' meat pole as well. They have also been in the process of looting the two dead men's cabin and lean-to and seem to be getting drunker by the moment. I suggest we let them continue drinking and eating and when they turn in for the evening for a night of drink-infused sleep that is when I suggest we attack. That way our chances of seeing the next sunrise, outnumbered as we will be, is much better than it now is with the four of us against the 13 of them."

The intense deadly cold stares coming back from the trappers after Wind Horse had briefed the men in the moonlight said it all... Well, that and the cold night's air was also 'cluttered' up with a rather foul smell emanating from one of their own which was normal when danger was close at hand, hence Buck Snort's namesake... For the last three days they had ridden hard after those who had mercilessly killed the five trappers back at what Buck Snort and company were now calling the Osprey Nest Camp. In so doing, the pursuing trappers had lived with their personal thoughts and feelings every horse's step along the trail as they passed through beautiful but they knew damn well, could be very dangerous country. Now they were at a place in time when the reality of the moment and the possible likelihood of their own demise was at their very doorstep. But not a man wavered in his determination over what was to come and what he must do, realizing 'but for the grace of God go I, especially if I am just one step slower than that of my enemy...'

Later with the deepness of night and following the advice of Wind Horse, found the four trappers carrying all of their weapons because of the number of fierce warriors they were about to face in what could be a violent and deadly battle! That they did as the four of them slinked through the eerie moonlight illuminated stands of timber as they headed directly towards the 'dancing' light of a huge campfire burning just a few more yards further away in the timber! However, when the four trappers cautiously sneaked up to the edge of that fire's light, they were surprised to discover all of the reported Northern Arapaho

Indians standing around their fire eating spitted elk meat, loudly talking and enjoying themselves... And surprisingly, not one Indian appeared to be under the influence of the two dead trappers' rum! From all appearances, the small supply of rum the two dead trappers had on hand had apparently been quickly consumed by the large number of Indians present and rapidly assimilated into their bodies. It now appeared that Buck Snort and company would be facing 13 soon to be aroused warriors, who were more than ready to do battle once the 'deadly dance of death' began! And once again, the four trappers knew that Buck Snort and his riled-up guts were close by if the lessened air quality was any indicator as to why he had been given his name by Wind Horse in his earlier years after being initially poisoned back at the orphanage... A poisoning that had somehow managed to affect his lower intestines when the high emotion of danger was close at hand, causing Buck Snort to discharge clouds of odiferous gasses which were readily apparent to the casual nose residing in the area. Fortunately for the group of Indians about to meet their Maker, they just figured the rank smell was present because one of their own had burned his piece of elk meat...

Seeing and now sensing the outstanding physical and well-being emotional condition of the enemies soon to be faced, Buck Snort had his company of men quietly fade back into the darkness of the timber and night from whence they had just come. This they did until they were out of sight and sound of their now realized more than deadly enemies. There after a quiet but hurried conversation back in the timber, the men turned to their 'possibles' bags carried on their persons, retrieved their bullet worms and ram-rods, and quietly removed their single lead balls from their loaded rifles and pistols. Then all of the men's rifles and pistols were reloaded with the ever-deadly load combination, especially in close quarters, of increased powder charges and buck and ball! This they did figuring that if they filled the air with enough deadly buck and ball projectiles at such close quarters as was now anticipated, any aims that were a little off would not matter. Especially with the air being satu-rated with deadly flying chunks of lead in almost every quarter imaginable upon which they had been aimed! Following that hail of death soon to come, any confused living beings left stand-ing would then be facing four maddened trap-pers with their deadly tomahawks at extremely close quarters! And no matter how one looked at those deadly swinging bladed weapons, when that moment in time came, men would die vio-lent deaths that night...

Then the four trappers once again slinked their way through the darkened timber towards the dancing light being emitted from the Indians' nearby campfire. As they quietly arranged their positions once again in hiding so that each man had a clear field of fire so such firing would be the most effective at such close-in ranges and once ready, Buck Snort held up his left hand as a 'shooting' signal for when they should begin. Then slowly increasing the numbers of his fingers raised, as he kept his eyes on the 13 Indian men feasting and loudly visiting unaware of the close at hand dangers at the edges of firelight around their firepit, his fingers went to 'three' being held up as the command to fire was then silently reached!

THE DARKNESS IN THE TIMBER AT THE EDGE OF THE FIRELIGHT SUDDENLY EXPLODED INTO ALMOST THE LIGHT OF DAY AS THE FOUR TRAPPERS RAPIDLY FIRED THEIR PERSONAL RIFLES INTO THE MASS OF UNSUSPECTING INDIANS, DROPPED THOSE WEAPONS, GRABBED THEIR EXTRA RIFLES LAID CLOSELY AT HAND ALONGSIDE THE SIDE OF A TREE AND QUICKLY DISCHARGED THOSE INTO THE DENSE AND NOW CONFUSED GROUP OF INDIAN MEN STAGGERING AROUND THE CAMPFIRE IN PANICKED WOUNDED OR DYING CONCERT! WITH THOSE EXPLOSIONS TEETH FLEW FROM MEN'S JAWS, EYES WERE BLOWN FROM EYE SOCKETS AND CHUNKS OF FLESH FLEW FROM FACES, CHESTS AND ARMS BECAUSE OF THE DEADLY HAIL OF BUCK AND BALL BEING FIRED FROM SUCH

CLOSE RANGES UNDER HEAVY POWDER CHARGES!   ALL THE RAPID SHOOTING WAS ACCOMPANIED WITH SCREAMS OF PAIN, PANIC, TERROR AND SURPRISE ON THE PARTS OF THE INDIANS! THEN OUT FROM THE STILL DENSE AND ROLLING WHITE CLOUDS OF BLACK POWDER SMOKE EMERGED FIVE SLIGHTLY WOUNDED AND STILL FULL OF FIGHT INDIANS RUNNING AT THEIR SHOOTERS! THAT WAS WHEN THE COLLECTIVE FIRING OF EIGHT PISTOLS LOADED WITH BUCK AND BALL INTO THE FIVE CLOSE AT HAND MEN MADE THEM INTO HYDROSTATICALLY FLYING AND EXPLODING GLOBS OF DYING FLESH, SNOT AND CHUNKS OF SHATTERED BONE!

THEN OUT INTO THE LIGHT OF THE CAMPFIRE AND RESIDUAL CLOUDS OF WHITE BLACK POWDER SMOKE FROM ALL OF THE RAPIDLY FIRED WEAPONS "FLEW" FOUR TRAPPERS WITH TOMAHAWKS UPRAISED! THIS THEY DID MOVING WITH A FURY BORNE OF DESPERATION, FEAR, HIGH EMOTION OF THE MOMENT AND A DEDICATION TO THAT DEADLY PLACE IN TIME THAT SPOKE TO THE VIOLENCE OF LIFE AND EVEN SOMETIMES DEATH FOUND OUT ON THE FRONTIER... MOMENTS LATER, 13 NORTHERN ARAPAHO INDIANS' SKULLS HAD BEEN VICIOUSLY SMASHED TIME AND TIME AGAIN BY THE BLADES OF

THE TRAPPERS' TOMAHAWKS, STILLING THOSE FEW REMAINING EVIL BEATING HEARTS! THUS ENDED THE DEADLY 'BUCK AND BALL BATTLE' AT THE TWO DEAD NEW TRAPPERS' CAMP!

ALL OF A SUDDEN, A 14TH INDIAN OVERLOOKED EARLIER BY WIND HORSE, ONE WHO HAD BEEN AWAY FROM THE OTHERS TAKING CARE OF A CALL OF NATURE WHEN WIND HORSE HAD SURVEILLED THE ORIGINAL GROUP OF INDIANS, EXPLODED ONTO THE SCENE OF DEATH RIGHT NEXT TO BUCK SNORT'S SIDE WITH TOMAHAWK UPRAISED AND READY TO STRIKE A KILLING BLOW!

"UURRRRR!" CAME A TERRIFYING GUTTURAL-SOUNDING NOISE FROM OUT OF THE DARKNESS AS THE DOG SPED OUT FROM THE TIMBER, AFTER LEAVING HIS PANNIER UPON SEEING THE MAN WHO HAD HELPED HIM EARLIER LEAVING WITH THE OTHERS. AND IN SO DOING, DID SO SENSING THE URGENCY OF THE MOMENT AMONG THE MEN LEAVING. LEAVING HIS PANNIER AND QUIETLY TRAILING THE FOUR TRAPPERS IN THEIR MISSION OF DEATH, THE DOG JUST FOLLOWED IN THE DARKNESS NOT SURE WHAT TO DO OR WHAT WAS COMING NEXT. HOWEVER, SENSING THE URGENCY OF THE MOMENT EMANATING FROM THE SOUR ODOR OF

DEATH COMING FROM THE EMOTIONAL
SWEAT RISING FROM THE FOUR SNEAKING
TRAPPERS CAUSED THE DOG TO GO INTO
HIGH PRIMAL ALERT!

THEN THE DOG ALL OF A SUDDEN
OBSERVED HIS FRIEND BUCK SNORT
IN IMMINENT DANGER BY THE VERY
SAME INDIAN HE RECOGNIZED AS THE
ONE SHOOTING AN ARROW PAINFULLY
INTO HIS BODY BACK AT THE TRAPPERS'
CABIN DAYS EARLIER WHEN HE TRIED
PROTECTING HIS ORIGINAL GRIZZLY
BEAR-WOUNDED OWNER... WITH THAT
RECOGNITION, THE DOG LUNGED FROM
OUT OF THE DARKNESS AND WENT
AIRBORNE DIRECTLY FOR THE FACE OF
THE INDIAN WHO WAS ATTACKING A
SURPRISED AND UNPREPARED BUCK SNORT
FROM BEHIND. **"URRRGH!"** GROWLED THE
DOG AS HIS FANGS TORE INTO THE FACE
OF BUCK SNORT'S ATTACKER NAMED
"WAR EAGLE", TEARING OFF GREAT
CHUNKS OF THE MAN'S FACE AS THE
INDIAN JUST ATTACKED SCREAMED OUT
IN PAIN AND TERROR! THEN STILL NOT
FULLY RECOVERED FROM HIS EARLIER
HIP INJURY FROM THAT INDIAN'S ARROW
AND THE FOLLOWING INFECTION, THE
WEAKENED DOG COLLAPSED ON TOP OF
THE INDIAN JUST ATTACKED WITH THE
MAN'S FACE STILL FIRMLY LOCKED IN HIS

VISE-LIKE JAWS! THAT WAS WHEN A NOW QUICKLY RECOVERED BUCK SNORT FROM THE UNEXPECTED INDIAN'S ATTACK FROM OUT OF THE DARKNESS, FATALLY APPLIED HIS TOMAHAWK BLADE... THEN SECONDS LATER, THE EXHAUSTED AND STILL VERY MUCH WEAKENED DOG WAS PICKED UP FROM OFF THE INDIAN AFTER HAVING HIS JAWS PRIED OPEN FROM THE DEAD INDIAN'S FACE AND TENDERLY CARRIED FROM THE SCENE OF BATTLE BY A STILL EMOTIONALLY CHARGED BUCK SNORT. TO BUCK SNORT'S WAY OF THINKING, HE HAD MORE THAN JUST FOUND A "NEW PARTNER", AND HIS NEW PARTNER "HAD MORE THAN JUST FOUND HIM"...

Other than a three-note call of a disturbed great horned owl now fleeing through the darkened timber away from the rapidly firing rifles, pistols and primal human noises, only the crackling sounds from the 14 dead Indians' fire and heavy emotional breathing from the four trappers greeted the men's ears. Well, that and the almost audible sounds of the men's still rapidly beating hearts and the almost uncontrollable and emotional primal urges on the part of all the trappers to urinate!

Then the four trappers, all unhurt because of their hugely successful surprise and aggressive mode of attack, as well as accurate shooting of buck and ball into 13 massed Indians at a very close range, plus the savage and surprise attack by their 'new partner' saving Buck Snort's life, walked into each other's arms! 'Walked' into each other's arms out of the deep respect for each other and the lives they shared and had been allowed to continue sharing through their first and highly successful, 'Buck and Ball Battle' against hugely overwhelming odds…

******

BOOM – BOOM – BOOM – BOOM! went quick explosions of rifle and pistol shots being fired within the two dead trappers' nearby campsite awakening a badly injured Northern Arapaho Indian warrior named Red Hawk who had been left to rest in the dead trappers' cabin. Left to rest after he had been badly injured in the three days' earlier attack on the five unsuspecting trappers back at what had been recently named the Osprey Nest Camp. Surprised over hearing numerous shots being fired within the campsite and the screaming and shouting of dying men obviously locked in a deadly battle, the Indian lying on the two dead trappers' furs with a badly inflamed tomahawk shoulder wound stirred. At first because his mind was so feverish, the wounded Indian dismissed the sounds of rapid shooting as just another pain-induced nightmare streaming across his inflamed brain. Finally his native survival instincts kicked in and now deeply concerned, he forced himself up from the pus-stained dead trappers' sleeping furs and crawled over to the cabin's open doorway. A doorway that had been purposely left open to keep the cabin cool and air out the horrible smell of a badly wounded and now infected and smelling badly, Red Hawk!

Just as he crawled to the door's opening, Red Hawk observed a ragged and hairy-looking white man's dog of huge proportions attacking one of the fellow members of his war party in the light of that group's huge bonfire! Red Hawk then observed in the fire's dancing light, a white fur trapper immediately recovering from that Indian's surprise assault against him because of a dog's savage facial attack upon the Indian attacker. When he did, the surprised white trapper with a swipe of his tomahawk smashed open the skull of Red Hawk's fellow war party member and brother, killing him in a huge splash of red in the fire's light! Now more than awakening to such deadly violence and upon hearing a number of men screaming and moaning in fear and pain, the badly wounded Red Hawk just rubbed his feverish film-coated eyes in disbelief! Seconds later as his eyes somewhat cleared, he realized he was seeing and experiencing a deadly struggle for life in real time between his people and the white men fur trappers! A struggle that was not going in the right way for the Northern Arapaho...

Then Red Hawk saw three more heavily armed fur trappers emerging from the darkness surrounding the Indians' campfire with bodies now strewn about in great numbers. As they did, those three men walked over and embraced the trapper who had just killed his BROTHER WITH A VICIOUS SWIPE OF A TOMAHAWK! Then the wounded and suffering Indian saw the white fur trapper who had just killed his brother with his tomahawk, carefully lift a large dog from off the body of his now dead family member and fellow warrior and carried that trapper's lifesaving animal off into the darkness…

Realizing through a 'fog'-clouded mind that he would be the next to die upon discovery by the four attacking fur trappers, Red Hawk, brother to War Eagle who had just been killed by Buck Snort's tomahawk, began crawling dizzily away from the two dead trappers' cabin towards the dead trappers' nearby horse corral in the darkness. There after his fourth try at getting a bridle into the mouth of one of the two dead trappers' horses, Red Hawk was finally successful. Then as the four trappers around his brother's campfire began collecting up all of the now dead Indians' weapons and making sure all of them had been killed in the hail of buck and ball and tomahawks, Red Hawk was able to quietly crawl away from the recent deadly scene of battle. That Red Hawk did with his horse's bridle reins firmly clutched in his teeth as he crawled off leading the animal quietly away from the scene of death to avoid discovery and his own death.

Making sure he had crawled far enough away

from the recent slaughter of his brother, two cousins and fellow warriors in order to avoid discovery and his own death, Red Hawk, between vomiting and stopping when his head 'swam' forming halos at the edges of his eyes from the raging fevers in his body, finally slid into a small gully. Rolling to the bottom of the gully, he finally lay still in a nearby fast-flowing creek in the bottom of the gully in utter exhaustion. By so doing he was finally able to escape certain death at the hands of the four killing trappers back at camp by now being out of sight and mind. Out of sight and mind from the four trappers who were now in the urgent process around the campfire of reloading all of their rifles and pistols in case there were other unseen Indians still lurking in the brush to deal with, like the one who had sprung from surprise upon Buck Snort and had almost killed him...

Soon Red Hawk's exhaustion turned into a deep sleep as his fever continued raging throughout his stilled body now lying partially submerged in the fast-flowing creek's waters. A lifesaving creek that was fortunately flowing over and cooling his feverish body as it brought his body temperature back in line to those levels of the living. Come the following morning, Red Hawk discovered that he was far enough away from the previous evening's scene of death and because of lying in the cooling waters of the creek into which he had fallen, his temperature had broken and

374 | Terry Grosz

he could now move around more normally. As it just so happened, when Red Hawk had fallen into the creek, he had landed in a miraculous position. Being partially submerged in the creek's fast-moving and cooling waters, Red Hawk's position in the creek allowed the cooling waters to fast-flow over and around his inflamed wounds on his shoulder blades all night long! As a result of lying in such a position, his open wounds were constantly washed through and through and his inflammation temperature in the tissue-damaged area was vastly reduced.

Feeling better come the dawn, Red Hawk found a downed pine tree in the creek bottom and with the reins from his stolen horse still firmly clasped in his teeth, crawled up onto the rotting log. From there using its height, he was able to weakly mount his horse and begin slowly riding away from his family and friends' scenes of death with several things burned into his mind. First, he was going to survive so he could someday return and personally kill every one of those four trappers for what they had done the evening before to his flesh and blood. But one thing was for sure, those four trappers doing the killing of his friends and family had to be living close by. And in order to make sure he killed those responsible for his family and fellow warriors' deaths, he would kill every trapper in the Green River drainage area of the most recent battle when he returned after healing up, just to make sure he killed all of them that had been involved! Lastly, Red Hawk would remember the face of the trapper who had killed his brother with a vicious swipe of his tomahawk! That was a face he would someday happily watch the life drain from his eyes in the most gruesome form of death that he could bring upon his brother and cousins' killers once he had laid his hands upon all of them and his brother's killer in particular...

Then making sure one of the reins was firmly tied around his right wrist in case he got dizzy from the slight fever that he still carried in his body and fell off his horse, he would still have his horse 'in hand'. Then slumping exhaustedly over the shoulders of his horse, Red Hawk turned its travel to the north and hopefully back towards his band of Northern Arapaho with a 'fire' in his heart and belly that was not of that caused by the 'fever' still raging throughout his body! Somewhat later, he turned his horse into the Green River at a shallow ford and began riding upstream in the shallow waters in order to have his horse's tracks washed away by the river's currents. That he cleverly did, so if followed by the four trappers looking for him once they discovered he had been there and escaped, in order to make sure he could not return at a later date with another war party and kill off those who had just killed off those of his own kind.

******

Come the following morning after the 'Buck and Ball Battle' with the Northern Arapaho Indians now positively identified by the physical evidence of their horse and travois trail leading directly from the Osprey Nest Camp to the current site as the identity of the Indians doing all the killing of the five trappers, Buck Snort and company were finally satisfied. That concern of identity finally settled, found Clem, Wind Horse and Muskrat tending to another gruesome chore. That chore, one of dragging the Indian dead off a short piece from the two dead trappers' cabin, scene of the recent 'Buck and Ball Battle' and dumping them into a small gully. Then when all of the Indian dead had been so placed, a number of logs and limbs and armloads of brush were gathered up and tossed over their bodies. Following that effort, a fire was lit and the three trappers watched over and continually fed that funeral pyre until the Indians' bodies were burned beyond recognition.

Then the trappers adjourned to the cabin near where the deadly 'Buck and Ball Battle' had occurred the evening before. There Buck Snort's trappers gathered up and using the two dead trappers' provisions and cooking implements found scattered around at the scene, began cooking up a much-needed and hearty breakfast of elk meat, biscuits, beans and coffee. That they did while Buck Snort continued caring for his still weakened but recovering 'new partner', named

"Dog". A new partner who had saved his life the night before and now Buck Snort was going to save the dog's life in turn or damn sure know the reason why he had failed in that endeavor... And if there was a given in Buck Snort's life, it was that he never abandoned his friends, two- or four-legged.

For the next two days, Buck Snort and company quietly remained around the two dead trappers' camp, collecting together all of the dead men's implements, furs, horses and provisions that they could use in preparation for their long trip back to their new cabin and later while making a living on their own new trapping grounds along the Green. As they did, a pleasant surprise came with the discovery of 169 bundled beaver pelts caught by the two dead trappers during their previous fall trapping season stacked up in the inside of the back of their cabin. As a result of that timely discovery, those excellent and valuable pelts became the property of Buck Snort and company! Additionally, they were also now the owners of 14 rifles once belonging to the dead Northern Arapaho Indians as well as 5 pistols. Firearms which could be sold at the upcoming 1826 Rendezvous to other less well-off trappers or local friendly Indians attending the Rendezvous 'shindig' as well.

Finally come the day of departure from the 'Buck and Ball Battle' site, with Dog once again riding in his straw-filled pannier, the men begin lining out all of the groups of horses for their return trip to their already-built new Osprey Nest Camp and corrals. Muskrat was assigned to trail their own horse herd and Clem those eight horses once belonging to the two trappers just killed at the recent 'Buck and Ball Battle' site. Wind Horse and Buck Snort then drew the duties of trailing the 15 horses recovered after the battle previously belonging to the Northern Arapaho Indians who no longer had any use for them...

Organizing and lining out each group's horse strings in preparation for the trip back to their new cabin on the Green River, SAW BUCK SNORT ALL OF A SUDDEN FREEZE! NOT BELIEVING WHAT HE WAS SEEING, BUCK SNORT QUICKLY STOOD UP IN HIS STIRRUPS SO HE COULD SEE BETTER AND BEGAN COUNTING THE HORSES IN THE INDIANS' HORSE HERD. SURE AS THERE WAS A HELL FOR ALL NON-BELIEVERS, THERE WERE 15 HORSES ALL LINED OUT AND READY TO TRAIL THAT BELONGED TO THE INDIANS HE AND THE THREE OTHER FUR TRAPPERS HAD SURPRISED AROUND THEIR CAMPFIRE AND KILLED EARLIER! THEN AS BUCK SNORT SLOWLY LET HIMSELF BACK DOWN INTO HIS SADDLE, HE REALIZED THEY HAD ONLY DRAGGED OFF 14 INDIANS TO BE BURNED... Seeing Buck Snort freeze after recognizing a problem with the Indians' horse herd, Wind Horse spun around in his saddle and figuring out why his friend had frozen in place when looking back at the Indians' horse herd, stood up in his stirrups and counted the number of horses being trailed as well. Then Buck Snort found himself staring hard into Wind Horse's now-narrowed eyes over his worrisome and potentially deadly discovery. Eyes that were looking back at him with the look of 'realization' spelled clear across his face as well!

"CLEM, MUSKRAT!" shouted Buck Snort. Moments later all four trappers were gathered into a clump of horseflesh and concerned humanity. "I counted 15 Indian horses but we only dragged 14 Indian bodies over to that gully and burned them! Based on the number of those Indian riding horses, we are missing one Indian who for some reason apparently escaped our buck and ball surprise! And all of you know what that means if he survives, returns to his band and brings forth another killing bunch of them sons-a-bitches. If that happens, you can bet the next time he will be looking specifically for the four of us! And if that happens and it will, we all are more than likely going to pay the ultimate price," said Buck Snort with a grim look of realization crossing his face...

For the next few long and worrisome moments, Clem and Muskrat stood up in their stirrups and counted the number of Indian horses in disbelief over Buck Snort's possible life-changing discovery as well. Moments later, all of the fur trappers'

horses had been returned to the two dead trappers' corral or were tied to the corral railing as
the four men with Wind Horse in the lead, began
quickly scouting around the campsite looking
for clues as to what had happened to that 15th
Indian. Soon Wind Horse had picked up the
culprit's trail and within moments, the four men
streamed out from the dead trappers' campsite
hot on the trail of a single shod horse heading
away from the camp leaving an obvious cold trail.
However, after an hour's ride on the trail of that
single shod trappers' horse leading away from
the two dead trappers' campsite, the four men
found themselves quietly sitting in their saddles
along the Green River shaking their heads in disbelief. There the single shod horse's hoofprints
led across a sandbar and into the Green River at a
set of shallows and even after four more hours of
exhaustive riding and careful examination along
the Green looking for where that horse may have
exited the water, those horse's tracks were never
seen again... Plain and simple that single Indian
had escaped his pursuers and disappeared into
nothingness. As the four men rode back towards
the two dead trappers' 'Buck and Ball Battle'
campsite in quiet defeat, they all carried in the
backs of their minds what might possibly happen
in the future. Especially if that escapee gathered
up another war party and those Indians returned
with blood in their eyes looking for the four trappers who had killed off everyone in the first war

party at the recent 'Buck and Ball Battle' site... Later that afternoon, the four trappers returned to the 'Buck and Ball Battle' campsite and spent a rather restless night knowing that one Indian had escaped and what that would mean if and when he returned... The next morning found the four trappers on the trail further west along the Green leading back to their Osprey Nest Camp, previous home to the captured and burned alive four original trappers. Three days later the four tired men and their strings of horses streamed back into their new campsite and home for the fall and spring beaver trapping season as well as that of the coming wolf trapping season.

As Clem began making supper preparations like nothing out of the ordinary had just occurred after the men's arrival back at their campsite, the rest of the crew grabbed their saws and axes and walked up onto a nearby hillside. There they began cutting more timbers from a stand of second-growth pine trees so they could enlarge their horse corral in order to accommodate their increased in size herd of other trappers' and Indians' valuable horses. While that was being done, Clem kept a careful watch over the now happily feeding and watering horse herd in their nearby meadow as well as tending to his supper chores.

But there was a bright spot in camp that evening regardless of the overriding foreboding still 'dogging' the men over the escape of one of the

Indians from the war party during the recent 'Buck and Ball Battle'. During the last day of their return travel to Buck Snort and company's new Osprey Nest Camp, Dog had left his ride in the pannier and now trotted alongside that of Buck Snort's horse like he belonged there all along. That Dog did in such a manner that all of the men realized Buck Snort and Dog were now one and the same when it came to being new Frontier partners and woe to anyone who 'seriously messed' with either of the 'new partners'…

CHAPTER NINE

TRAPPING THE GREEN RIVER, FELLOW
TRAPPERS, THE RETURN OF "RED HAWK"

NOT KNOWING WHAT TO EXPECT in return from the lone Indian who had escaped during the evening of the 'Buck and Ball Battle', Buck Snort and company remained vigilant for the next month back at their Osprey Nest Camp fearing some form of retaliation from the escaped Indian's band. Then as time wore on, like typical humans, Buck Snort and company relaxed over what they feared might be coming in having to face the deadly unknowns regarding the arrival of a war party. A war party being led by the lone escapee from the 'Buck and Ball Battle', now healed up and with revenge in his heart over the unknown trappers for the tribal and personal family losses he had suffered in that deadly battle.

Being human and as expected of an American fur trapper on the demanding Frontier, other more pressing issues reared their heads on a daily basis requiring the men's attention. Other more pressing issues such as procuring their winter's supply of wood, putting up a supply of jerky for the lean winter months when out on the trail trapping wolves, casting up a mound of balls for their rifles and pistols, disassembling all of their rifles and pistols one or two at a time, removing the lead and black powder fouling and then reassembling that much-needed weaponry, smoking their beaver and wolf traps to remove the man smells, and the increased care needed for their now much-larger horse herd. Then if those duties were not enough, the trappers found themselves facing the almost weekly and very important hunting trips procuring fresh meat supplies of elk, mule deer and the occasional Rocky Mountain bighorn sheep for the 'meat happy' trappers' daily meals.

Toward the end of September with the beginning arrival of the cooling fall weather patterns and the beaver finally beginning to come into their prime, Buck Snort and company, along with their ever-faithful dog named Dog, ventured forth numerous times examining the beaver trapping grounds. That they did, all the while ascertaining the potential fall trapping opportunities along the Green and its numerous adjacent waterways. What they discovered by the end of September in the way of beaver trapping opportunities quickly 'warmed the cockles of their hearts'! There were extensive signs of beaver in most every waterway they explored, as had been reported by their trapper friends back at the 1825 Rendezvous who had previously experienced trapping portions of the Green. The conical-shaped beaver houses abounded in most ponded areas and the furry rodents were observed swimming in their waterways, as well as out and about repairing or tending to their numerous 'stick and mud' beaver dams stitched across the waterscapes throughout! Additionally, there were many younger beaver observed swimming interspersed throughout the areas which indicated to the experienced eyes of the trappers that a balanced and healthy population of the furbearer abounded in the area. There were no two ways about it, the four Buck Snort trappers were soon to have their work cut out for them in the coming long days ahead when it came to running their trap lines and processing their valuable catches. All of which was based upon what the men were seeing in the number of beaver throughout the area and the signs of everyday activity those furry rodents had left behind repairing their dams and houses as well as new bankside willow and tree cutting activities...

With a fully healed-up dog now used to leading the way, out from the men's campsite one morning streamed the four trappers to begin their fall beaver trapping season of 1825 with their confidence, gusto and expectations running high. Trailing Dog was Buck Snort followed by Muskrat and Wind Horse leading a total of three packhorses, with Clem bringing up the rear of their caravan. However, in light of the ever-present possibility of problems from various Indian tribes on the warpath with the American white men fur trappers, all three of their packhorses now carried the trappers' extra fully loaded long guns in their panniers not carrying trapping gear. Those panniers they found themselves carrying just in case the men found themselves facing superior numbers of hostile Indians while routinely working out on the beaver trapping grounds, or facing another war party slaughtering white trappers led by the lone Indian revenge-seeking escapee from the 'Buck and Ball Battle' from some months earlier...

As was typically the beaver trapping regimen, Buck Snort and Wind Horse selected the areas to be trapped based on the number of freshly used beaver slides or other fresh signs of that animal's activities. Clem in turn, acted as the two trappers' support person on the trapping sites and the group's main and highly efficient skinner. Lastly, Muskrat, the group's ever faithful lone guard and sentry against danger emanating from 'man or beast', took to any nearby high ground so he could watch over the trapping team from the best vantage point and in so doing, provide the highest degree of protection to his 'family' of fellow trappers.

As in years past, the expert beaver trappers 'running' their usual complement of 30 beaver traps to start the season, soon found themselves quickly overwhelmed by their daily catches of anywhere from 15 to a high of 23, mostly Made Beaver (adults) being trapped per day! As quickly became the case, after spending a number of long nights and into a number of early morning hours de-fatting and hooping a large number of beaver pelts so they could dry, the men were running short on sleep. That being the case, as done in past years, the men reduced their trap-set number from setting 30 traps per day down to just 15 a day so their catches would be reduced and their hours of needed sleep increased per evening.

(Author's Note: Historically speaking, most individual beaver trappers only ran from six to eight traps daily. That was because until around 1835, there were so many beaver to be caught out on the Frontier just as Lewis and Clark had pronounced upon their return from their great cross-country expedition, that catching a beaver for every trap set by experienced trappers was in most cases, not an issue but a given. Then in addition to all other work needing to be accomplished, de-fatting and hooping any more than six to eight beaver pelts daily became quite a chore unless the party of trappers was quite large. Then in those cases involving larger parties of trappers, trappers could be designated to remain behind in camp and just tend to the processing of beaver and other animal pelts, thereby freeing up field trapping teams. Hence, most well-experienced individual beaver trappers only ran from six to eight traps daily. However, the larger the group of trappers, the more traps that could be run.)

Additionally, that reduction in trap number allowed the men more time on a daily basis to 'raid' the area's numerous willow patches in their quest to find and cut green, right-sized branches for hooping of pelts in which to begin the drying process. But with the 'catching' being so productive and predictable, the four men soon discovered their time running from that of weekly hunting trips, woodcutting, bundling previously processed beaver pelts (into 60 or so pelts per bundle, running about 90 pounds to a pack which was ideal for packing on their packhorses), watching over their valuable horse herd to keep the local Indians, other white man trapper scoundrels and always hungry grizzly bear populations at bay, ended up using almost every hour of daylight in their busy days when their trapping season and subsequent 'catching' was in full swing!

Finally by the latter part of November, Buck Snort and company had trapped, processed and bundled up an astonishing number of 363 beaver pelts! Truly, trapping that portion of the Green River had been an excellent choice made by the four trappers when it came to successfully making their fortunes and being able to purchase new provisions during the upcoming Rendezvous. Additionally, there had been an extra bonus in their selection of their current campsite's location immediately adjacent the Green River besides that of finding a ready-made cabin and set of horse corrals. Once there on-site, the group discovered that they had a constant grizzly bear problem in their section of the country with the great bears hunting constantly along the nearby Green River for beaver and larger animals coming to the river to drink. As they did and upon smelling the nearness of the corralled horses as another food source, the bears routinely made attempts to raid the horse corral. That was when an added and unexpected bonus 'reared its head', especially come the early stages of winter before the bears went into their annual hibernation. True, they had lost three horses to the hungry bear's depredations before the bear problem had been sufficiently addressed with a number of well-placed rifle bullets. But in the process, the four trappers had also killed 14 such deadly predators and now had amassed a like number of beautiful and much valued by the fur buyers come Rendezvous time, prime tanned bear pelts! Collateral with that bear bonanza was the unforeseen bonus of the 169 Made Beaver pelts Buck Snort and company had collected back at the two trappers' cabin after the 'Buck and Ball Battle'. A battle that would ultimately bring on additional unforeseen consequences as well as an arsenal of rifles, pistols and horses retrieved after the battle from the dead Indians and trappers which would be sold later at the upcoming 1826 Rendezvous.

"Hello the camp!" was a shout heard coming from the nearby Green River one morning, when the complement of four Buck Snort trappers was quietly enjoying their breakfast prior to commencing their daily beaver trapping activities.

Those four Buck Snort trappers eating their breakfast before leaving for that day's trapping activities, upon unexpectedly hearing the sound of unfamiliar human voices coming from the nearby river, quickly found themselves scrambling for their close at hand rifles! Moments later the four heavily armed and now alert Buck Snort trappers observed four unknown trappers and their pack animals coming up from the Green River and heading towards their cabin.

Soon Muskrat, Wind Horse, Clem and Buck Snort were to make the acquaintances of new fur trappers to the area, namely one Jack Jones, Billy Bob Randel, "Griz" Peterson and Alvin Jaconetti. However as the newcomers swung down easily from their saddles and introductions and acquaintances were made all around, everyone from that group took notice of the rather unusual fact that one of the men having breakfast owned a rather large, mean and ugly-looking dog. Within moments however, it soon became apparent as to which of the men owned the dog when each of the four newly arriving men shook Buck Snort's hand. When those handshakes were being offered and accepted, that rather large dog stood right by the man named Buck Snort at his side as if to make sure everything being done was cordial and not dangerous to that dog's master and that dog's way of thinking…

As the four new trappers with heavily bearded smiles all around quickly introduced themselves one by one to Wind Horse, Buck Snort, Clem and Muskrat, it was apparent they were friendly. As was the Frontier tradition in those days, such 'glad to make your acquaintance' looks were followed by a Mountain Man's typically firm handshake letting the recipient know 'there was a real man on the other end of that handshake'…

Then one of the new trappers identified as Jack Jones and apparent leader of the new group of men said, "We couldn't help but smell your elk meat cooking away on a spit, the wondrous smell of hot coffee on such a cool morning and the glorious smells of Dutch oven biscuits being baked as well. As such, we were a-hoping there was some left for four hungry strangers in which to partake, if you gents were to be so kind and as good Christian men were to make such a neighborly offer on a beautiful day."

Clem, ever the friendly one no matter just how 'strange' a stranger was, said, "The coffee is hot, let me fetch some more cups and then I can begin fixing you chaps right up with some eats." With that, off he went to their nearby cabin to 'fetch' some more coffee cups, as Buck Snort spitted some extra elk meat on their cooking rods and soon those "Sons of the Frontier" were visiting among themselves like it 'was old home week'. That the Buck Snort 'strangers' did because it was always a treat in meeting someone else on the Frontier and having new folks around with which to 'chew the fat'. Plus strangers many times brought news from the outside world, so new faces in a trappers' camp were generally most always welcome unless they were hostile, 'Sons of the Prairies' sorts...

Soon the reason for the strange trappers' surprise visit became clear. As the conversations progressed, it quickly became clear that the four strangers were looking for new beaver trapping sites because they had trapped out their old trapping grounds on the lower Green. Then while moving up the Green looking for 'new trappings', they had discovered working evidence of Buck Snort and company's beaver trapping activities. Not wanting to 'poach' on those unknown trappers' grounds or get shot in the process for 'trying', Jones and company rode on ahead looking for the homesite location of the unknown trappers. As they did, they followed that newly discovered trappers' sets of shod horses' tracks as an aid in locating the current area's trappers' campsite. Then once there and talking, see if the country was big enough for all of them in which to trap beaver.

After more discussions regarding the fact that Buck Snort and company wanted to trap even further upriver themselves, it was finally decided that Jones and his company of trappers would move at least five miles further east on the Green and then begin trapping ever eastward from that area upriver once they started trapping themselves. That way, they figured there would be beaver trapping a-plenty for both groups of men and that was decided as a viable and fair working relationship. Plus, it was always nice to have neighbors for the extra protections that could offer sometimes just as long as there was plenty of the furry rodents' number 'to go around'... Shortly after breakfast and more 'conflab' taking place, the two groups of men separated company. Jones and his group of Mountain Men continued on upriver further to the east for at least for another five miles and advised that upon finding a good location, that was where they would build a new cabin and have it ready in which to live come the fast approaching winter months. Then come the spring beaver trapping season of 1826, they would do their trapping further east from their cabin and that would leave all the country between their new cabin and Buck Snort's current trapping grounds for his contingent of trappers in which to trap.

Then as Jones and company were mounting their horses and making ready to leave, Buck Snort got an idea. Hailing Jones back who had just started to ride off, Buck Snort advised Jones and his men of their earlier battle in the area that Jones and company were thinking of locating. Without fanfare, Buck Snort quietly made Jones's trappers aware of that previous battle's outcome and the fact that the two burned alive trappers in that area of battle Jones and company were thinking of relocating into, had left a brand new but smaller in size cabin and set of horse corrals already completed. Upon hearing those welcome words relative to the possibility of an available but small completed cabin and set of horse corrals, Jones's eyes fairly lit up! Especially since it was getting late in the year and having to build a new cabin and set of corrals would just set them back time-wise in all the other activities they needed to complete before the winter snows arrived.

Somewhat later after hearing Buck Snort's entire story about the much-needed killing of the Northern Arapaho war party, Jones and company headed out with full bellies and directions to the two dead trappers' cabin and horse corrals. That they did with high hopes that with a little extra building work, they could occupy a campsite that was almost ready for the four of them and in the heart of what appeared to be good beaver trapping country according to what they had observed while riding into the area and from what they had heard from their recent breakfast-supplying new 'neighbors'...

As for Buck Snort and company, later that morning after Jones and company had departed, they headed out and began checking their previously set traps and kept setting new ones where they had left off on their trap line from the day before. Two weeks later Buck Snort and company pulled those traps because of what appeared to be oncoming adverse weather building up from out of the northwest from whence most of their big storms came howling down upon them come winter. Several days later just as sure as grasshoppers were good to eat when roasted, winter arrived, the trapping waters froze over and the great fall beaver trapping season of 1825 on the Green for all intents and purposes, was over. With those activities finished for the year, the trappers' beaver traps were pulled and put into storage. Then their wolf traps were brought out from storage, smoked to reduce the man smell and set out along the horse corral to air out and be ready for packing once the men began that new phase of animal trapping.

Later that evening as the men sat around their cabin's fireplace smoking their pipes and drinking a cup of rum after the wolf traps had been 'smoked' and set aside for later use, Buck Snort came up with an idea. Full of himself, along with a wonderful supper fixed by Clem under his sash and followed by several cups of rum, he proposed a very unique idea to the rest of the men. And since they were still several weeks out from beginning their wolf trapping season when the wolves were finally in their prime and the grizzly bears had gone into hibernation thereby reducing the chances of dangerous conflicts with the great bears, the men generously agreed to Buck Snort's 'neighborly' suggestion. Then it was off to their sleeping furs since the next few days promised to be hard and long ones once up at Jones's new upriver 'Buck and Ball Battle' trappers' campsite if all went according to plan and the 'creeks didn't get any higher'…

"Hello the camp!" bellowed out Buck Snort, as he and company rode into Jack Jones's new campsite trailing a number of loaded packhorses at the site of the earlier deadly 'Buck and Ball Battle' along the Green River as surprise visitors. "There had better be more of that good smelling elk meat for my men to eat if you men want some extra help from my lads enlarging your new cabin so the four of you have a decent place to call home," Buck Snort exclaimed in a 'smiling' tone and tenor-sounding voice as he and his men rode into camp, acknowledged by Jones's men's welcoming waves of their hands.

Somewhat later, the men were eagerly eating breakfast together and visiting as work plans were made for the next few days. And for the next 14 days, the nearby green pine and Douglas fir timber fell to the sounds of two single buck saws and several axes in action. Then the eight fur trappers and new friends worked together scraping the bark off the just-felled logs and enlarged a cabin for Jones and his group of men to occupy before the 'deep' of winter along the Green set in with all of its fierceness and yet northern snowy beauty. Following that stint of time, Jones and company now had a newly enlarged home and set of horse corrals. Conversely, Buck Snort and company had new and friendly neighbors and fellow Mountain Men five miles or so located up-river on the Green from their Osprey Nest Camp!

However, the groups of men did not separate before Clem and fellow trapper and designated camp cook for Jones's crew of trappers, Alvin Jaconetti, brought forth a celebratory supper one evening of spitted elk backstrap, a pot of heavily spiced rice and beans, Dutch oven biscuits loaded throughout with plumped-up raisins and caramelized brown sugar, coffee and a huge apple cobbler baked in a 16-quart, third Dutch oven… Suffice to say when several cups of rum were added to the men's menu later that evening, a happy group of celebratory diners and neighbors they did make… However shortly thereafter found all of the tired 'lumberjacks' heading for their sleeping furs and a good night's sleep without worrying about another day's hard work building a cabin and set of corrals.

The next morning right after breakfast, both groups of men parted ways so they could begin making their preparations for the start of each other's winter wolf trapping activities along the many ridges and heavily timbered mountain chains in the area. Several days later while waiting back at their own camp for the first snows of the season to arrive, Buck Snort's crew of Mountain Men made the most of their time by gathering in a more than ample supply of winter's wood, coupled with several successful elk hunting trips along with the much-needed elk jerky-making activities.

Then when the first winter snowstorm of the season 'boiled' from out of the northwest and confined the men to the immediate area around their cabin, the men spent that time patching up their heavy winter clothing. Additionally, Buck Snort and Wind Horse brought forth their supplies of heavy wool blankets purchased earlier at the first Rendezvous and began making form-fitting capotes for each of the men to be worn during the worst of the cold weather. As they did that, Muskrat and Clem saw to it that their 'possibles' bags were cleaned out and restocked with fresh horns of powder, a one-pound tin of new powder for each bag, additional flints, fire steels, extra balls, greased wadding, jerky, and buffalo fur gloves to be used during the worst of the winter days they would soon be facing while out setting and tending their wolf traps.

The following day after those first snowstorms of the season had moved off eastward and the day turned out cold and clear, found Dog and the men heading out into the surrounding hills and mountains looking and listening for any signs of wolf pack activity. A short distance from the men's cabin soon found them killing a six-point bull elk and butchering out his backstraps and a ham, which were then placed into a packhorse's pannier for the men's evening supper. Then Clem opened up the belly of the elk to spread the smell of death around the area so hungry wolves would be more than attracted to that location because of that 'smell of death'. That was then followed with the clever setting of a number of their toothed wolf traps around the elk's carcass, hoping any approaching wolf's hunger would offset his usual caution and lead him into the jaws of the deadly Newhouse toothed leg-hold traps. Later that same afternoon, the men had scouted out several other likely wolf trapping locations and had baited those locations as well with fresh whole carcass elk and mule deer kills and collateral rings of wolf traps. Following those 'baiting' actions, the trappers found themselves heading for their cabin as the chill night air rolled down upon them from the now deeply snow-covered higher mountain ranges and timbered slopes surrounding them. The winter of 1825 was now upon the Frontier with a vengeance...

Later as Clem prepared the men's supper inside the cabin's fireplace, the remaining three trappers let the rest of their horses not used that day out from the corral so they could feed and water. However, that was done under their watchful eyes in case any horse-hungry Indians wandered by or a late in hibernating, or deadly "Winter Bear" as they were called, decided to stop by and 'look in' on the feeding horses for a late winter snack or some extra riding stock.

(Author's Note: A so-called "Winter Bear" in that day and age as known by the 'old timers' was usually a grizzly bear that had been unable to pack on enough fat to make it through its months' long period of hibernation. Since the bear could not make it through the long months of hibernation, many times found such an animal wandering through part of the winter months attempting to pack on enough 'groceries' so it could safely go into hibernation and survive the long period of not eating as it slept. Historical records are replete with men and women on the Frontier crossing swords with such bears and most often when doing so, coming out on the losing end of life! A winter bear had such a reputation for savagery being in such a starved condition, that it killed mercilessly and devoured everything of food value in sight. In short, a winter bear brought terror to any of those living out on the Frontier not prepared for such a confrontation by such a wild beast, and many who confronted such a savage animal usually ended up out on the prairies or in the mountains later as a cooling-out bear scat!)

Then it was back to the trappers' warm cabin for a cup of rum and some of Clem's special Dutch oven thick stew of rice, beans, red pepper flakes, rice and chunks of fresh elk backstrap meat. And such a feast was always accompanied with Dutch oven biscuits and Clem's style of coffee that could stand a horseshoe up in a coffee cup and it would not fall over... Then under the light from their numerous beeswax candles scattered about their cabin and from that of the fireplace, the men quietly ate their supper, smoked a pipeful of tobacco after they had finished their suppers and then adjourned to the warmth of their sleeping furs and buffalo robes. It was there that Buck Snort had the added luxury of sleeping with his warm-bodied partner Dog, lying close at hand alongside the trapper. A four-legged partner that now never left his side alongside his horse, by the indoor fireplace or upon his buffalo robe sleeping furs inside the cabin come nightfall. To Dog's way of thinking, he had lost one partner to a number of Indians' arrows and he wasn't about to lose another, especially one human who had so lovingly cared for him, a rather ratty-looking 'rag' dog, no matter when or where the circumstances...

Thus became the trappers' daily regimen adjacent the Green and its mountain ranges for the next two winter months, broken up only by more cutting of wood, watching over their valuable feeding horses, breaking the ice so the horses could water, tending their wolf traps, resetting those traps in new areas, de-fatting and stretching of wolf hides, as well as the even more important chore of casting rifle bullets from the trappers' ever-present supply of lead pigs. However one fine December morning, the men's woodcutting detail was interrupted when Jones's group of Mountain Men rode into Buck Snort's campsite announced by a welcoming shout, while leading a long string of packhorses.

A quick get-together of the men soon produced a stream of horseflesh and humanity leaving Buck Snort's campsite on a group elk hunting trip seeking a 'mountain' of fresh meat needed by both camps of trappers. Jones and company had traveled all that way to Buck Snort's campsite because Buck Snort's area had the best historical elk wintering grounds and also the best hunting going because of the density of such animals found on those wintering grounds. Additionally, Clem was the better cook found between the two trappers' camps… And by hunting with such a large gathering of trappers, there was safety in numbers of the sharpshooting Mountain Men in case any groups of objecting Indians were also found out hunting for their needed meat supplies and happened upon the scene. By late afternoon, the men from the two campsites had 18 cow elk down, all gutted and butchered out, taking only the more tender hindquarters and finer back-strap cuts of meat. With both camps of men now trailing heavily loaded packhorses with excellent tasting meat, they then headed for Buck Snort's nearby Osprey Nest Camp. That they did seeking the warmth and comfort its roomy cabin and larger fireplace offered. Somewhat later as the sun began setting and the dropping temperature and collateral snot freezing beneath one's nose and in the men's beards became the word of the day as a result of the intense cold, it was time for supper and maybe a cup or two of rum. However, seeking such shelter and such was put on hold until other chores were completed.

Camp cooks Clem and Alvin Jaconetti began putting together a Mountain Man-sized supper to celebrate the men's successful hunt, which just so happened to be on Christmas Day, as the other six trappers hung all of the rest of the elk meat in such a manner from the camp's meat poles so it could quickly cool out and glaze. And when the men hung such tremendous amounts of meat from the camp's meat poles, the campsite's resident Northern chickadees, gray jays and pigmy nuthatches all celebrated Christmas Day as well by descending upon the steaming and inviting elk carcasses and helping themselves to the scattered about on those carcasses, rich globs of fat. Following that, all of the men's horses were set loose with their hobbles to feed in the nearby meadow while the rest of the men either cut more firewood, broke a nearby stream's ice so the horses could water or watched over the men's large horse herds as they fed to make sure they were not molested by man or beast. Later after the horses had been herded back into the

404 | TERRY GROSZ

corral for the night, the men adjourned to Buck Snort's cabin and there the men celebrated in fine style their Christmas Day supper with roasted elk backstraps, Dutch oven biscuits slathered in honey from several jugs purchased months earlier at the Rendezvous, bean and rice stew heavily flecked with red pepper flakes (to aid the men in having bowel movements because of their usual and almost exclusive heavy meat diets), coffee and a raisin and rice compote loaded with brown sugar shavings to satisfy each man's sweet tooth.

Later as the men relaxed in the warm cabin and told stories about their experiences and growing up on the Frontier, they continued with the celebration of the Christ Child's birth by smoking their clay pipes full of rich tasting James River smoking tobacco along with a number of cups of rum enjoyed long into the following morning's hours. Finally the men spread out on the cabin's wooden floors and under the warmth of their buffalo robes, slept away the night and far into the following morning with thoughts of Clem's promise of his special style of Dutch oven apple cobbler loaded with raisins, brown sugar and cinnamon as part of his breakfast meal instead of that of "sugar plums dancing in the men's heads"...

******

Red Hawk, now fully recovered from his serious shoulder wounds received from a trapper's tomahawk strike in a months' earlier battle along the Green River at the Osprey Nest Camp, quietly sat on his horse clothed in his heavy winter buffalo robe garb. That he did along with six equally warmly dressed for the winter's elements fellow warriors from his father's, "Chief Iron Eagle", band of Northern Arapaho Indians. Sitting there quietly in his saddle, Red Hawk through misted-up eyes due to the evening's bitter cold, could hardly believe his good fortune. Here, after a number of months of healing up from grievous shoulder wounds back at his father's tipi where he had been tended to by his mother and sisters, now found himself once again back in the field ready for battle. Back in the field in a location where a major event in his earlier life had occurred that had damned near killed him. An event that had later cost the life of a brother, several cousins and fellow warriors at the hands of avenging trappers in a subsequent deadly battle at another trappers' cabin days later... It was here at this same now quiet-looking campsite he and his braves were now overlooking, where Red Hawk had suffered that vicious tomahawk chop across his shoulder blades that cut clear to the bone the musculature of both of his shoulder blades! Shoulder blades that were sliced so deeply it had almost cost him his life because of his loss of blood and a later raging infection!

Now healed up, he was quietly looking at the same scene of a lone trappers' cabin with smoke curling lazily up from its chimney through cold-squinted eyes as the darkness of night was settling in deeply across the land. The same cabin now full of eight of the much-hated white men fur trappers that he and his men had crossed trails with earlier in the day. Eight trappers who had been out elk hunting on a winter elk feeding ground, who had not seen Red Hawk's men and did not know they were now being stalked with deadly intent! Stalked by the one Indian escapee after the 'Buck and Ball Battle', one who had escaped the killing and had now returned with a wicked and killing revenge in his heart over what had happened earlier to him and the rest of his people!

It was just then that the rest of that battle's ugly memories came flooding through Red Hawk's being as did his almost palpable bitter taste of hatred for all white men found or occupying his ancestral lands! But those strong thoughts of bitter hatred were not allowed to cloud his memory this time as they had in the earlier battle, as to why he was there and what he must now do to avenge his brother, cousins and fellow warriors from the earlier deadly fight.

Shaking the family losses and killing thoughts of personal revenge from his memory banks, Red Hawk brought his 'being' back to where he was and where it needed to be… Sitting there on his horse in the evening's bitter cold, Red Hawk was aware that his small group of six equally dedicated warriors was outnumbered by the eight trappers. Eight trappers who were unknowing of the danger close at hand that they would soon be facing, were for the moment safe within the confines of the thick log walls of the cabin he was now quietly surveying. Not wanting to chance losing another cousin who was currently with him on this revenge-seeking trip and his other close friends to the normally straight-shooting trappers, especially like those safely holed up in the cabin, Red Hawk came up with another plan of attack which could ultimately be just as deadly to the enemy at hand. Sitting there in the winter's cold silence, all of a sudden a knowing and deadly smile of realization slowly crossed his face.

Yes! he thought. *He and his warriors would steal all of the trappers' horses in the dark of night when the men were sleeping and escape with them! In so doing, being that it was the dead of winter, the trappers would then be on foot without their horses and would more than likely quickly perish in the winter's icy cold weather, ambushed by other Indians or in the jaws of hungry predators such as wolves. Yes, that is what he would do instead of trying to somehow ambush the trappers who were safely behind the cabin's protective thick log walls or out in the open in a deadly field of fire. Yes, he would steal all of their horses and let the winter's cold, others of his kin or the always savage and hungry packs of wolves found in the area kill the trappers off, he thought with a deadly cold-looking and calculating smile. A smile that was 'well-heeled' with devious and enjoyable thoughts of revenge! Yes, he thought, death by freezing to death or in the jaws of a vicious predator was preferable to that of a quick end by a bullet or the strike from a tomahawk from either him or his six men!*

Enduring the now freezing cold, Red Hawk and his men quietly sat on the saddles of their horses until all lights and signs of activity such as loud talking or laughter had disappeared or died down inside the trappers' cabin. However, Red Hawk, battle-tested beyond his years, kept his men at bay for another hour just to make sure the trappers in the cabin were very deep in their warm food and rum-induced sleep. That he also did because after seeing a large dog accompanying the elk hunting trappers earlier in the day, wanted to make sure the dog was sleeping deeply as well when he and his men decided to strike. Otherwise, his men's subsequent activities might awaken the dog, which would give the alarm and ruin any chance he might have in effecting the full impact of his revenge against the much-hated white fur trappers…

Upon the anointed hour to strike when he figured the trappers and dog were in their deepest sleep, Red Hawk's six men quietly rode over to the trappers' corral holding their large herd of valuable horses. Quietly dismounting, Red Hawk had four of his men walk over and position themselves in front of the cabin's door with their rifles at the ready just in case someone inside came forth upon hearing any suspicious noises coming from the horse corral. As all of that activity was ongoing, Dog in his 'doggy world' had chosen that moment in time to be 'chasing slow rabbits' in his 'dream world' and heard nothing suspicious sounding going on outside. Well, that and all of the deep snoring from eight trappers inside the cabin covered up many of the normally heard sounds of night…

Then upon his silent arrival at the corral gate holding back a large number of horses now all curiously watching over what was going on around them in the moon's soft light, Red Hawk saw something that caused him to freeze! There at the corral's gate as if by design, stood his old "Buffalo Horse", one that had been stolen from him earlier in life! A highly intelligent horse, which instantly in the soft moonlight saw and smelled his old master and began quietly 'nickering and whickering' his recognition call instantly! With that, Red Hawk bailed off the horse he was riding and ran over to the corral. There he quickly opened up the gate and letting it swing out of the way, moved silently but determinedly in the moonlight towards the herd of now nervously milling horses over to his ever-faithful but previously stolen, Buffalo Horse. A very devoted and loving pinto horse he had figured he would never see again after it had been stolen from in front of his tipi a year earlier! Then wrapping his arms joyously around the horse's neck, the two of them stood together in the moonlight in a state of happiness that is only found between a man and his favorite horse… And when that moment occurred, what happened to the eight trappers still sleeping inside their cabin was of no consequence to an extremely happy Red Hawk over being surprise-reunited with his favorite pinto horse!

(Author's Note: One of the most prized possessions an Indian could own in buffalo country in those historic days of the Frontier and era of great herds of buffalo was what was commonly called by a number of names by the Plains Indians, a "Buffalo Horse". Hunting buffalo was dangerous because of the buffalo's innate cantankerous mindset and athletic ability to very quickly turn when running at full speed and gore a closely pursuing buffalo hunter's horse! When such a killing move was made by the oftentimes frantic buffalo trying to avoid its pursuer, the horse and its rider would be bodily lifted up off its feet and with a buffalo's tremendously strong neck and shoulder muscles, be head-tossed up, over and underneath the hundreds of thundering hooves from other nearby fleeing buffalo! When that happened, sometimes the Indian rider was tossed upon the backs of the stampeding buffalo and soon fell off and under those animals' hooves, or fell off his horse and under the hundreds of pounding hooves. Either way, the death of the horse and its Indian rider was the same, namely being turned into "buffalo-jelly" under hundreds of powerful and thundering hooves… However, a rare number of Indians' horses possessed an almost sixth sense when chasing buffalo during a hunt. A very rare and valuable horse with an innate sixth sense as to when the buffalo being pursued was going to turn without warning and attempt to gore the pursuing horse and thereby unhorse its rider as well. When a pursued buffalo suddenly and unannounced began making his oftentimes deadly quick move against that rare horse with a deeply developed sixth sense of survival, that horse without being so instructed by its rider, would already be moving out of the way, thereby saving itself and its rider from harm. There were many documented cases throughout the rich North American history of Plains Indians whenever an Indian became the owner of such an almost magically gifted horse, in order to prevent theft by Indians from other hostile tribes, he would stable such a valuable horse inside his earthen home or shelter such as those types of homes occupied by Indians, many of whom lived among the Missouri or Knife River Indian River Villages in the current-day State of North Dakota or elsewhere in buffalo country. In so doing, such protective actions prevented such a grievous loss of a rare horse by theft from Indians from other tribes.)

As the rest of Red Hawk's men standing in front of the cabin or his young cousin over at the corral quickly realized what a special moment was happening in the soft moonlight between the man and his very specially gifted horse, they let their leader have his discovery and rare moment in time with his just-recovered horse. Let Red Hawk have his special moment of discovery and manifest itself in true Native American Indian style. Especially with an animal that had over time let his People truly become one with the animal and land from which they had been 'released' once the Spanish and their mode of travel had arrived in the New World. It was as if The Great Spirit had again let man become one once again with his Buffalo Horse in a special moment in time that was for all time, as long as the thundering herds of buffalo graced the rich prairie soils... The excited shaking of the horse's body in the hands of his old master said it all once their two hearts through fate had become intertwined once again... As fate would have it, Red Hawk's particular Buffalo Horse had been stolen from Red Hawk's Northern Arapaho summer campsite a summer before by a Lakota Indian. That Indian had later been killed by some Hudson's Bay Fur Company men and the horse captured. In turn, the horse had been sold by the four Hudson's Bay Fur Company deserters to Major Henry at the old Fort Henry before it was abandoned. That trapper after purchase from Major Henry, had the Buffalo Horse reshod and unknowing of the horse's innate value, just incorporated that animal into his pack string. Months later, that same trapper was one of the two trappers killed by the Northern Arapaho in the later 'Buck and Ball Battle' along the Green River... After that deadly battle, Buck Snort and his company of trappers had come into ownership of that animal, hence that gifted horse being once again unknowingly in and among their horses in the trappers' corral... *A horse whose travels and traditions were yet to be fully realized until finally circuitously united with Buck Snort for eternity...*

******

Moments later all of the trappers' horses streamed quietly out from the corral in the freshly fallen snow and were soon lost in the quiet of the winter's cold and moonlight as they were herded eastward along the Green River Valley. Come daylight two hard days and nights later, Red Hawk and his six warriors tiredly slipped into the just-discovered Jones's encampment further upriver along the Green. There after a cautious approach, they found it deserted and covered with a blanket of freshly fallen snow, as was that of the surrounding countryside signifying the long absence of the cabin's white men owners who were now at the Osprey Nest Camp elk hunting. Seeing the camp had been deserted since before the last snowfall and realizing that his men were cold and hungry after their two all day and night rides in the saddle after stealing all of Buck Snort's camp's horses, Red Hawk had his warriors light down from their exhausted horses and stretch their tired and cold limbs. That he did after they had allowed the horses to feed for about two hours and then chased all of the stolen horses into the deserted trappers' camp's corral for safekeeping and had shut its gate. Then still cautious as to why the trappers' camp was deserted, Red Hawk and his warriors cautiously approached the front door and then moved inside only to find the cabin was cold and empty of its owners. Then with his hand, Red Hawk checked the ashes in the fireplace only to find them stone cold as was its stone area surrounding the hearth. Red Hawk then walked over to the sleeping area in the cabin and felt the sleeping furs for any sign of warmth from a trapper recently sleeping under such covers and found them cold as well.

Realizing the trappers had abandoned their cabin for some reason days earlier and didn't appear to be anywhere nearby, not realizing they were the same trappers he and his men had just set afoot back at Buck Snort's cabin several days earlier, Red Hawk and his small war party relaxed. Then being 'bone-cold' from their two all-night rides on cold riding horses, one during a violent snowstorm, built a roaring fire in the fireplace so they could warm up. Then as the fire began warming up the inside of the trappers' cabin as well as the Indians who were now inhabiting its living space, the men started relaxing. Then as hunger overtook the now warming men, they began looking around inside the cabin and outside for any sign of food. Then remembering the snow-covered part of an elk hanging outside from a meat pole, the Indians made short work of that animal's better frozen cuts with a nearby ax and soon meat was sizzling over the fire in the fireplace.

Later that morning after sending out several of his warriors to check their back trail and finding no one or nothing trailing them, they returned to Red Hawk with the good news. Receiving the news that the intense winter's cold, the snow-covered ground from the recent snowstorm and the distance from the trappers' cabin where they had stolen all of those men's horses had deterred any foot pursuit, Red Hawk just grinned over the good news. Good news, especially in light of the fact that another snowstorm had begun moving into the area from the northwest and more 'trail-erasing' snow was now starting to heavily fall…

Smiling over his little band's being looked upon with grace by The Great Spirit, Red Hawk decided his men could now safely stay another night in the comfort of the trappers' cabin so they could rest up and then immediately leave once the new snowstorm had left the area. That decision to stay another night was further supported when one of Red Hawk's men discovered a partial wooden flat keg of rum stored in the rear of the trappers' cabin in among the other supplies... That night, Red Hawk's men celebrated the fact that they were to feast on white man supplied roasted elk meat, sleep in a warm white man's cabin and in their own beds instead of out on the cold trail and lastly, have a supply of the white man's 'firewater' and elk meat to make their evening stay even more comfortable.

However, Red Hawk, son of the great Northern Arapaho Chief Iron Eagle, was no fool. He again just before dark and at the leading edge of an ominous-looking, black-clouded arriving snowstorm from out of the northwest, sent two of his best warriors out into the worsening elements to check their horses in the corral to make sure everything was alright with their stock. Following that, the two men were to walk back a ways once again on their now snow-covered back trail checking to see if by chance the group of trappers who had all of their horses stolen earlier were on the trail of the Indian horse thieves or if they perchance had perished in the last snowstorm or had been killed and eaten by wolves since all of them were still on foot. Shortly thereafter, those two men returned to the trappers' cabin soaked to the skin from the now heavily falling wet snows with a report that their back trail was still clear and that no pursuing trappers were in sight. Additionally, "Spotted Tail", leader of the group assigned to watch their back trail, reported that the snows from the newest snowstorm were falling at such a heavy rate that any tracks left previously by the band of fleeing Northern Arapaho would soon be lost to the ages and forthcoming wind-driven deepening heavy wet snows.

That evening, Red Hawk and his men slept soundly and warmly under the roof of a solidly built trappers' cabin, sound in the knowledge that a blanket of freshly falling snow was covering all of their previously made tracks. They too like the Christ Child of the white man's current Christmas season, had found shelter at a warm "Inn" of sorts and instead of being celebrated by "Wise Men" with incense and scented woods, celebrated with the white man's freshly roasted elk meat and the last of the trappers' precious rum... The next morning a cautious Red Hawk once again sent two of his best warriors out to check on their horses to make sure they were still there and hadn't been taken by other Indians. Additionally, they were to walk back and check on their party's cold back trail to see if they had been followed by the trappers whose horses their war party had stolen several days earlier and ascertain if they were soon about to be discovered by those 'horseless' trappers, all the while holed up in another trappers' cabin in order to ride out the worst of the most recent snowstorm.

By then the heavily falling snows had quit and the sky was deep blue in color without a cloud in it. The air was crisp and off in a distance, the Indians could hear wolves noisily trailing some unfortunate critter on the way to becoming their breakfast somewhere down along the trail. About an hour later the two men sent out earlier returned with the word that their back trail was still clear, that the wolves had caught whatever they were after and could be heard off in the distance fighting over who was going to get to eat what, and that they themselves after walking back on their back trail a long distance were now hungry and cold as well...

******

As luck would have it, Buck Snort and Jones's contingents of trappers had loaded up with all the jerky they could carry the following morning when they discovered all of their valuable livestock had been taken by a small number of Indians! Leaving the Osprey Nest Camp immediately after making arrangements for foot pursuit, the 'tough as horseshoe nails' trappers hit the trail of shod and unshod horse tracks, snowstorm or not and thus began their foot pursuit around the clock if necessary. That they did realizing that if the horse-thieving Indians ever made it back to the protection of their winter encampment, the trappers would be wildly outnumbered by that camp's occupants, could not win that battle and without their horseflesh under them, would soon be 'dead men walking'... So for the next almost two days, the trappers with Wind Horse way out in front acting as their scout never quit chasing their stolen horse herd! Fueled with their supplies of jerky and eating snow for moisture, the trappers relentlessly pursued the horse thieves with only black thoughts being present in their hearts regardless of the fact that this was the Christmas season... By late afternoon on their second 24-hour day of pursuit and after being caught in two different snowstorms, the trappers got a break. As the group of trappers plowed their way through the recent heavy snows, they all of a sudden saw Wind Horse trotting back towards them. Realizing something important was happening, the men collectively took cover and waited for the scout of their party to join them. Once reunited and after he had gotten back his 'wind' from his long run, Wind Horse advised the group that he had just observed two unknown Indians following their back trail as if looking for something or SOMEONE! Taking cover, Wind Horse observed the two Indians examining their still-evident back trail horse hoofprint indentations in the snows as if looking for any sign of pursuit by the trappers who just had their livestock stolen. Seeing no evidence of white men pursuing them, the Indians had turned around and backtracked their own trail. Waiting until the Indians had disappeared from sight, Wind Horse slowly followed their tracks and in so doing, discovered that the suspicious Indians were holed up in Jones's new cabin as if waiting out the latest oncoming snowstorm. He also observed a corral clear full of the stolen horses once belonging to the aggrieved trappers! Not wanting to give himself away or the fact that pursuit was so close at hand, Wind Horse waited until darkness had started setting in and then to avoid discovery, took off on a different trail and headed back to alert the following trappers that they had finally successfully run to ground the horse thieves at Jones's cabin.

Hours later, Wind Horse stumbled upon his pursuing trappers and once advised of what he had just observed and it being late at night, the trappers moved off into the nearby deep timber and built several fires. After several hours around the warming fires, the trappers moved out with Jones in the lead because he was most familiar with his cabin's physical surroundings and knew the best way to attack the Indians holed up inside. Once the trappers were on-site of Jones's cabin several hours later, the men laid out their battle plan for the morning's coming attack and then headed for their chosen places of concealment as outlined and set out by Jones. Finally in the cold and the last of the ongoing snowstorm's remains snowing upon them, the trappers quietly waited out the oncoming morning and their individual fates... Come the first vestiges of daylight, the almost frozen and still-hidden trappers found their heart rates increasing and welcomed the increase in body temperature that accompanied their readiness. That readiness increased even further when the aggrieved trappers could hear a number of men stirring and making noises inside Jones's cabin as they arose for their day's endeavors and soon they could see smoke arising from the cabin's chimney as the men cooked breakfast...

******

After another hearty breakfast of roasted elk meat, Red Hawk and his warriors happily began looting the trappers' cabin, taking what they wanted and stacking those provisions off to one side inside the cabin for later collection and transport back to their band's main winter encampment. Then after dressing for the cold and snow that awaited them along the trail, they picked up their previously selected supplies and headed for the door. As they did, a happy group of Northern Arapaho warriors they did make with full bellies of roasted elk meat, as they began exiting the cabin with their armloads of looted provisions. With those provisions in hand, they headed for the corral so they could load, mount up and head for their winter encampment with all of their stolen trappers' horses and the packs on their packhorses full of valuable white man's provisions to be proudly shared with other less fortunate members of their band. Especially with those women and children of their tribe who had no men to care for them. No men to care for them having been lost in battle or dead because of horse wrecks, grizzly bear attacks, or other like deadly 'ill winds'.

Exiting through the front door and walking out across the open space in front of the trappers' cabin with his arms full of looted provisions and followed by the rest of his men doing the same thing, Red Hawk happily breathed in deeply of the morning's crisp mountain air. As the victorious horse-stealing Indians streamed away from the cabin and headed for the corral, Red Hawk was suddenly surprised to see the form of a buckskin-clad Mountain Man rising up from behind a nearby pile of snow-covered logs used by the trappers for their winter wood supply. A determined- looking Mountain Man covered with a light coating of the previous night's freshly falling snows, SHOULDERING A RIFLE! About then, Red Hawk saw a bright flash at the end of the Mountain Man's rifle barrel just as a caliber .52 lead ball struck him squarely in the face! Six more **BOOMING** sounds followed a micro-second later, as all of those lead balls struck their surprised Indian targets walking out in the open unawares, in front of the cabin carrying armloads of stolen provisions!

Ironically all seven of those Northern Arapaho Indian raiders died within feet of where their earlier brethren from the same band of Chief Iron Eagle's men had died when ambushed at night by Buck Snort's trappers months earlier! Killed Chief Iron Eagle's entire war party earlier after they had killed the two original trappers who had built the very same cabin that Red Hawk and his warriors had just slept in the previous night while comfortably 'riding' out a recent snowstorm… The very same smaller cabin Buck Snort's men had helped Jones's group of trappers enlarge just weeks earlier so it could more easily accommodate Jones's larger group of fur trappers. And as fate had also provided, a warm sleeping area for seven Northern Arapaho Indians hellbent on stealing a number of nearby trappers' valuable and life-sustaining horses in the hopes once those trappers were afoot in the dead of winter, they would soon die from exposure from all of the elements. With the violent 'cracking' sounds of such shooting 'splitting' the quiet winter morning's air like 'thunderclaps', a large flock of nearby black-billed magpies roosting in the leafless aspens noisily fled the scene of death and destruction aimed not at themselves but at seven other 'predators'…

Good morning, you horse stealing son-of-a-bitch and Merry Christmas several days late, said Buck Snort to himself, as he reached into his 'possibles' bag so he could retrieve what he needed in order to reload his rifle…

As he continued walking over towards Red Hawk's body twitching its last earthly movements and staining the freshly fallen snows bright red where he lay after being explosively head shot, Buck Snort continued casually reloading his rifle as his eyes continually scanned the area for any other signs of danger. As he did,

Buck Snort, surrounded by a foul odor as was his characteristic physiological reaction to violence hence his namesake over being poisoned earlier in life, did not realize he had just ironically finally 'downed' the lone Indian escapee from an earlier battle on this exact spot with another bunch of Northern Arapaho Indians... Northern Arapaho Indians that this same badly wounded escapee had been leading months earlier, bringing a reign of terror to the Green River area trappers to an end. That this same badly wounded from a tomahawk 'blow' escapee had cleverly done by riding his subsequent stolen trapper's horse into the swiftly flowing Green River in order to hide its tracks... Nor did he realize that fate would intervene again, having Buck Snort killing the father, a great Northern Arapaho Indian chief who would soon be on his own revenge-seeking mission some months later to kill the trapper who had just shot his last living son in the face... Nor at that stage of the game as a Mountain Man plying his trade on the Frontier, would it have made any difference how Buck Snort felt regarding completing the chain of deadly events he had just ignited with the killing of Red Hawk...

However, that day's victory events would ring hollow some months later over the discovery and keeping of a uniquely marked rifle by Alvin Jaconetti three days after the 'Christmas Ambush Battle' just culminated! And the events that followed after its discovery by one with a wicked and evil heart hellbent on the destruction of those white men holding such a uniquely marked rifle...

Walking through the killing field where Red Hawk and the rest of the Northern Arapaho Indian war party had just been felled, Alvin upon looking down at the body of Red Hawk, quickly stopped and did a double take. There lying alongside the body of Red Hawk was a beautifully marked Indian Trade rifle of .52 caliber.

Picking up Red Hawk's ornately decorated rifle with all means and designs of brass tacks on the stock and forearm, "Will you 'lookee' here!" said Alvin in surprise. "Look at this fine-looking rifle I just found lying alongside this here Indian Buck Snort just shot hell out of," he loudly exclaimed in the remaining emotions of the killing moments that had just previously occurred...

"Let me see what the hell you found," said Griz Peterson, reaching for the rifle so he could take a closer look at what had Alvin all excited like a 'bug on a hot rock'.

"No, I want to keep this one," said Alvin, as he pulled the ornately decorated rifle closer to his person.

"Come on," said Griz. "I think I know what you have if my memory does not fail me from my experiences dealing with some of the Plains Indians early on in my life as a trapper while living out on the prairies way east of here."

With that, Alvin slowly handed the gaily 'tack-decorated' rifle over to Griz, and by now the rest of the men had gathered around the old trapper looking on in amazement at Alvin's find of Red Hawk's ornately decorated rifle. After quietly looking the rifle over closely from 'stem to stern', Griz said, "Yep, it is just like I remembered and suspected. First of all, this here rifle is one of them damn rifles that those Hudson's Bay people are handing out to 'special' Indians working and supporting them against us 'beaver-trapping' Americans. Let's see if I remembered what another trapper I worked with out on the Northern Prairies taught me about what all of you are looking at. This 'tack work' is called "Togia" by the Northern Cheyenne Indians. If I recollect correctly, it means to talk or write the strong language of a "Wakan", who is a holy man, by using "Oowa" or some kinds of marks like these here tacks scattered all over this here Indian rifle's forearm and on both sides of its stock. Buck Snort, I would say you killed some sort of an important Indian of some kind, like maybe a chief or high ranking member of a band or something. The placement and arrangement of these here brass tacks instead of plain old iron ones is also important. See here, most of the tacks are placed on the right side of this here rifle. By their special placement on mostly the right hand side means the owner of this here rifle was someone really important. See here, look at these here symbols made with them tacks which look like crosses. This large one here of a cross means our dead man belonged to a warrior society and this here smaller one means the holder of this here rifle was a leader or the head of some sort of a special society. Then look here on the other side of the rifle is some sort of a special society mark like really good fighters or some of the bravest ones in the tribe. HOLY COW, LOOK AT THIS TACK SYMBOL! I HAVE SEEN ONE OF THESE SYMBOLS BEFORE ON A RIFLE TAKEN FROM A DEAD INDIAN WE GOT INTO A SHOOTOUT WITH YEARS AGO OUT ON THE NORTHERN PLAINS. THIS HERE SYMBOL FROM TACKS ON THE LEFT SIDE OF THE STOCK SAYS THIS HERE MAN OR AT LEAST WHOEVER OWNED THIS HERE RIFLE AT SOME TIME OR OTHER WAS A CHIEF! DAMN, BUCK SNORT, YOU SHOT SOME KIND OF A CHIEF OR REALLY IMPORTANT PERSON! MAN, I HOPE THE REST OF HIS KIND DOES NOT COME LOOKING FOR HIM AND FINDS US WITH THIS RIFLE AND HAS A LOAD OF BLOOD IN HIS EYES OUT TO KILL WHOEVER KILLED THIS SPECIAL KIND OF A CHAP!" quietly said Griz reverently, as if saying out loud what he had just discovered would bring down the wrath from some sort of Indian God or the like... Then pausing and looking over at Buck Snort with a kind of wild look in his eyes, Griz said, "That symbol represents that the holder of this rifle is what the Indians call a "Thunder Being"! Damn, Man, I hope these chaps don't come looking for the guy who shot the owner of this here rifle with blood in their eyes because if they do, we are all going to be in a tub of shit clear to our eyes and then some."

With those words, Griz slowly handed the ornately decorated rifle back to Alvin like it was almost too hot to hold or something. He then carefully wiped off his hands on his grease-covered and soiled buckskins like that would help if anyone came looking for the killer of the owner of the much-decorated Indian Trade Rifle. And in so doing, would now overlook Griz because he had cleaned his hands off on his badly soiled and sour body odor-'flavored' shirt and pants, making him now hard to find after having handled the special rifle... As for the rest of the group, the enthusiasm over discovering such a specially marked rifle had somewhat rubbed off, as they continued looking all around the nearby treeline as if expecting more Indians to come popping out from the timber shooting away at the fur-clad Mountain Men with 'blood in their eyes'... However, with the drifting away of the white clouds of black powder smoke also went any further danger that day.

Later that day after disposing of the seven Northern Arapaho Indians' bodies so the ever-present and hungry wolves could make short work of them, Buck Snort and Jones's companies of fellow trappers returned all of the looted provisions now collected up from the snowfield back to the trappers' cabin. Then as Alvin and Clem prepared Dutch oven biscuits, coffee and spitted elk meat for the men's supper, the rest of the trappers began the process of removing their wet outer clothing since buckskin did not retain hardly any bodily warmth of the wearer when wet. Wet clothing previously received after an all-night march under cover of a driving snowstorm so the men would be ready to do battle with the Northern Arapaho come daylight at what they had hoped would be at Jones's cabin. The Jones's cabin being the only one in the area where the Mountain Men figured the Indian horse thieves had 'holed' up because of the foul weather. And in actuality, the place the revenge-seeking Red Hawk and the rest of his Northern Arapaho warriors had 'chosen' from whence to begin their trip into the Upper World of the Happy Hunting Grounds in order to join the rest of their ancestors, the Cloud People…

After the hungry trappers had eaten everything that Clem and Alvin had prepared for them for their supper that evening after the one-sided 'Christmas Ambush Battle', as the trappers now had named the deadly action, the last of their wet clothing was removed and hung on the wooden pegs throughout the cabin so those garments could also dry out as well. Then stacking a number of bundles, bags and sacks of provisions against the inside of the cabin's front door to prevent any surprise Indian attack during the night from being able to get inside the cabin, the battle and weather-exhausted men laid out everywhere on the wooden floor that they could find space in the cabin so they could sleep and then slept like 'the baby Jesus' did for the next twelve hours... *Yes, it had been a very merry Christmas*, thought Buck Snort, as he drifted off to sleep accompanied by the sounds of seven exhausted Mountain Men soundly sleeping and the more than welcome body warmth from Dog lying by his side, his newest partner in what would prove out to be more than a savage land. Especially if one did not have a good 'chaw' of sweet-tasting tobacco between his 'cheek and gum', a trusty rifle in hand, possessing the eyes of a golden eagle and the attitude of an angry wolverine...

The following morning, the trappers removed all the provisions and sacks of flour, coffee and rice they had stacked against the inside of the front door of the cabin to prevent any kind of a surprise Indian attack the night before and headed out to take care of their individual calls of nature. As they did, Buck Snort grabbed up his rifle as he always did and headed for the front door as well so he could 'clean out' the previous night's rich supper. However as he did, he heard a shout from Muskrat and Clem who were in the process of separating out all of the trappers' horses into their individual camp's horse strings for return to their rightful owners and corrals.

Running to the front door suspecting the possibility of an Indian attack, Buck Snort was greeted with a view of the backside of his uniquely marked pinto horse purchased back at Fort Henry fleeing towards the north on what appeared to be 'wings of wind'. A very unique horse which was almost human in his actions as observed earlier by Buck Snort, which had been sold to the fort's horse wrangler by the four Hudson's Bay Fur Company deserters. Because they were a horse shy of what they really needed in their own packhorse herd, Buck Snort had 'crossed trails' with the uniquely marked pinto. A unique pinto horse in more ways than one as Buck Snort was soon to discover. One in which the more he looked the horse over for any obvious signs of physical flaws, that strange horse appeared to be doing the same to him when observing Buck Snort... In fact, the more Buck Snort now more than casually examined the pinto horse as a possible purchase, the more it appeared to be sizing Buck Snort up and down just as critically as well. Further discussions with the fort's old horse wrangler who had grown up with horses the same as had Buck Snort and really knew his 'horseflesh', had advised that the horse in question appeared to be a very special horse. In fact, those very special traits observed that day by Buck Snort and the old horse wrangler were possibly those described somewhat reverently by many of the Plains Indians as that of a Buffalo Horse.

Now he was gone as the fur trappers watched the mysterious pinto horse disappearing into the timber on the north side of the Green. Watching that horse disappearing into the timber with such speed and sense of purpose, Buck Snort suspected the horse was heading back to the remembered location of its original band of Indians or home as that horse knew it. Watching that special horse disappear, Buck Snort felt a feeling of loss for what reason he knew not why. He had really wanted to get to know that horse better, perhaps even taking it as his main riding horse because of its special appearing properties and unique levels of intelligence it had routinely exhibited when it had been worked around the men. And for some reason, Buck Snort felt a unique sense of loss in what could have been a very special kindred relationship between himself and an animal that was just as interested in him as he was in it… It was then that Buck Snort noticed that Dog had quietly walked up and was standing alongside his right leg looking off in the direction that the pinto horse had disappeared. Seeing and sensing Dog's interest in the direction the horse had disappeared, Buck Snort began wondering more about what could have been more than just a special relationship between a man, Dog and their pinto horse…

Then a shout from Clem advised the rest of the men that breakfast was ready and if they didn't come and get it, it would be thrown out for the critters to eat. That wasn't even a choice as the ever-hungry Mountain Men streamed for the front door of the cabin and what goodies awaited them behind the walls of the cabin. Pausing at the front door of the cabin and looking one more time in the direction the pinto horse had escaped, Buck Snort thought, *I wonder what could have come from that relationship had I just given it a chance?* Then the overpowering smells of biscuits and cooking elk meat overrode those thoughts and Buck Snort broke and headed for the indoor fireplace and the location from whence all the good smells were coming…

By the time their wolf trapping season was over and spring beaver trapping season began on the Green, the men were more than ready for the change. However, they had done very well wolf trapping in their catching, stretching and bundling an even 90 prime wolf skins! *However, those wolf skin numbers were fine in and of themselves, but there was still that pinto horse thing always in the back of Buck Snort's mind and maybe what could have come from that...*

******

Northern Arapaho Chief Iron Eagle snuggled down even further into his buffalo robe and grizzly bear throw-overs as he lay there in his tipi smelling a pot of venison and cornmeal cooking away that was heavily laced with great smelling dried wild onions that his wife "Little Fawn" and daughters had picked and dried the previous fall. Then Iron Eagle heard the rustling of a buckskin skirt falling to the floor of his darkened tipi and moments later felt the warmness of his naked wife's lithe figure settling in alongside him. Forgetting the venison and cornmeal cooking away over their small fire, he gathered up his wife in his strong arms and made sure she knew he would love her forever and a day…

Somewhat later, Iron Eagle sat alongside his wife and together the two of them quietly ate their breakfast together so as not to awaken his two sleeping daughters. About then he heard the sounds of three horses reining up in front of his tipi and then a hushed voice requesting his presence outside. Rising and throwing his grizzly bear robe over his massive shoulders, he strode outside into the cold winter morning's air only to have a frown form on his normally stoic face in an instant. There sitting on their two horses were two of his best warriors. In the hands of one of those warriors were the reins of a large in size pinto horse, the favorite riding and Buffalo Horse of one of his sons! A son who had led a war party far to the south to kill the white man trappers and rid them from the country of his ancestors and in revenge for killing a brother and two cousins, kill those trappers who were responsible for those deaths… The meaning of his young son's favorite horse in the hands of his warriors, a horse that was never far from his son's hands without the presence of that individual, was stone-cold obvious…

Walking over to the horse, he laid his hands upon the horse's head, petted it and looked into the horse's pale blue eyes as if they would tell him something of his son's whereabouts. The chief found that the horse's eyes were lifeless in their essence. It was obvious to the chief that those eyes had previously seen much great sadness! Turning to his warrior sub-chiefs named "Scarred Wolf" and "Big Buffalo", Chief Iron Eagle said, "With the 'Moon of the New Leaves', I will lead a war party to the lands far to our south. The lands the white man is crawling all over in his efforts to catch the 'Little People Who Eat the Trees'. Until then, no one is to know of the return of this horse without it carrying my son Red Hawk, other than the two of you. Take this horse over to my brother "Charlie Left Hand's" band and have him keep him there in his horse herd so no others, especially my wife, learns of its presence back at our band's horse herd. Let my brother know that no one is to ride this horse because it is a "Death Horse", and will be trailed down to the lands trapped by the white man and left under a burial scaffold if we find what is left of the body of my son. If not, we will leave this horse's body on a ridge top so my dead son can see him and they can then be reunited in the Upper Land of our ancestors, the Cloud People. Now go and speak no more about this thing because if you do, Red Hawk will just wander the 'In Between Lands' and his heart will never rest. Now go and return with ten of your best warriors during the 'Moon of the New Leaves' to my tipi, and then we all will ride south and avenge my son so he can rest with his own kind and alongside that of his favorite Buffalo Horse." With that and an impassive face, Chief Iron Eagle returned to his tipi with a heavy heart and the realization that both of his sons now resided with the Cloud People.

******

With Dog in the lead, Buck Snort and company streamed out from their Osprey Nest Camp and headed eastward along the Green until they arrived at the location where they wished to begin their spring beaver trapping season. Trapping as they usually did, they once again discovered running only 15 of their 30 traps was more than sufficient to begin filling up their cabin with large numbers of freshly hooped and drying beaver pelts, especially when sleep became an issue because of the long hours of work in the evenings de-fatting and hooping the skins. That problem became even greater because of all of the larger Made Beaver pelts needing to be de-fatted and hooped. In short, processing 60-70 pound beaver took a lot of time...

As was the four trappers' usual trap setting procedure, Wind Horse and Buck Snort scouted out the trapping area for evidence of good beaver activity such as fresh slides and set their traps. Clem on the other hand, saw to it that Wind Horse and Buck Snort were supplied with whatever they needed and when a dead beaver was retrieved from one of the traps, set about immediately and expertly skinning out the catch. Lastly, Muskrat saw to it that the overall area being trapped by his friends was devoid of any dangers, such as a protective cow moose watching out for her calf, extremely aggressive grizzly bears with or without their young of the year fresh out from hibernation, or Indian trappers out on the prod looking for the hated white man trespassers in areas in which they conducted their own beaver trapping. (Author's Note: Most animal trapping was historically done by American Indians doing about 90% of the total amount of trapping done in the United States, especially in the West during the fur trapping heydays! The Indians did so as trappers because they were able to easily trap animals of lesser importance because of their everyday occurrence in large numbers and in turn, traded their pelts and hides in for many of the white man's oftentimes scarce trade items which were considered of significant importance such as cooking implements, firearms and the like. This was especially so during any given year during the heyday of the West's Mountain Man fur trappers, where only about 1,000 white men were afield doing their trapping and of that number, about 25% disappeared every year due to accidents, horse wrecks, grizzly bear attacks, drownings, starvation, snake bites, all manner of death suffered at the hands of Indians, freezing to death, being killed by competing Hudson's Bay Fur Company trappers along the Canadian boundary, and the like.)

Buck Snort and company followed their usual routine after setting out their traps, of resting in a grove of nearby aspen or cottonwood trees eating jerky and discussing the morning's events as they watched their back trail and the end of their newest trap line. Then come early afternoon, the previously set trap line was checked to see if any beaver had already been trapped and if so, those carcasses were once again removed, skinned on the spot, the trap reset and then the group traveled to the next trap until the entire trap checking procedure was repeated. Then on the way back to their campsite after setting and/or running their trap line, the men visited the larger patches of green willows, selected, cut and filled several panniers full of green willow branches to be used after the fleshing out and de-fatting process had been completed for the much-needed hooping and drying to come. Thus became Buck Snort's company of trappers' daily routine after including the breakfast and supper events along with the wood gathering, horse care and weekly hunting trips to augment their fresh meat supplies. However, as the men worked their trap line and performed their other necessary duties, their minds were not far from thinking about the upcoming summer Rendezvous soon to be held at a place named Malachite's Big Hole in a place previously identified as Cache or Willow Valley. There they could once again sell their beaver 'Plus', wolf skins, any extra horses gathered up from their battles with the Northern Arapaho, as well as all of the firearms taken from the dead Indians during such battles. *Little did the four trappers realize that before the spring beaver trapping season was over, they would have much more for sale and in so doing, make their fortunes almost 'in one fell swoop' as Mountain Men fur trappers...*

******

Warrior sub-chiefs Big Buffalo and Scarred Wolf led the big pinto horse last ridden by Northern Arapaho Indian Chief Iron Eagle's last son Red Hawk, over to a tall and stern-looking Indian seated upon his horse at his encampment site. Once there, Northern Arapaho Indian warrior sub-chief "Elk" took the reins of what he and others considered a Death Horse. Then turning in his saddle, Elk beckoned to another seven Indians quietly sitting on their horses off to one side of the Indians' horse herd and with that, ten Northern Arapaho Indian warriors of the highest fighting abilities when it came to warfare, combat and survival, somberly rode over to Northern Arapaho Indian Chief Iron Eagle's tipi located about one mile away.

Chief Iron Eagle was seated by his small fire inside his tipi burning sacred sage leaves and using his right hand, whisked the sacred sage leaf smoke away from the fire and over his seated form as he chanted out a sacred string of prayers to guarantee him success in what he was about to do. Then looking over, he saw his wife Little Fawn was now awake and intently watching her husband with her large and dark eyes as he continued performing his sacred ritual with the smoking sage leaves and age-old prayers designed to bring luck and favor upon the one talking to The Great Spirit.

In a flash, remembering her husband was leaving that morning on a long trip, Little Fawn hustled her small body out from under the warm buffalo robe she had been sleeping under just moments earlier. Within moments she began making her husband his much-loved breakfast of warmed cornmeal mush laced with chunks of venison along with his special favorite, namely wild onions dug from out of the ground on rocky hillsides, dried and later cooked in a pottery pot by using only fire-heated stones to cook the meal. About 40 minutes later she had just served her husband his third helping of his favorite morning dish, when she heard horses approaching their tipi from off in a distance and numerous barking dogs from his band heralding the approach of strangers as well.

Upon hearing a number of horses quietly coming his way, Chief Iron Eagle quickly finished the last of his venison and cornmeal mush, arose and then exited his tipi without saying a word to Little Fawn. He remembered how hard she had taken it when she found out about the loss of her first son. Not wanting to 'stoke those old fires of remembrance', he said nothing of his mission for the next few weeks other than he was riding south into the lands of the white man and just quietly exited the tipi. Standing outside his tipi in the morning's early light, Chief Iron Eagle breathed in deep draughts of mountain air as he saw a small group of ten serious-looking and heavily armed and mounted riders coming his way. Then upon hearing the rustling of the newly forming aspen leaves in the aspen grove where his tipi was located, he smiled. It was now the 'Moon of the New Leaves', or the time he had chosen to form a small war party, ride south to the river the white man called the "Green", attempt to locate the four trappers living along the river who had killed his two sons, several cousins and a number of other tribal members on previous raids from his band, and kill them all! It was then that the evil thought of how he was going to do just that flooded across the chief's mind in a flash! Then he smiled, since he had no idea of where those four fur trappers lived along the Green, what they looked like or what role they had in the deaths of his two sons, he had come up with a plan that guaranteed him success in his mission of revenge for the loss of his sons. Then Chief Iron Eagle heard the aspen leaves rustling in the soft morning breezes behind him once again and took that as a good omen from

The Great Spirit on how he planned on exacting revenge against the hated white man American fur trappers. Once again he smiled broadly as his more than deadly plan flooded across the recesses of his mind. He was going to keep his plans for revenge simple. His eleven-member raiding party would raid up and down the river called the Green by the American fur trappers during the spring beaver trapping season when every American trapper would be hard at work. Then he would simply surprise, attack and kill every trapper they encountered! Following those killings, he planned on leaving every trappers' burned body along the river on stakes or in the trappers' camps as warnings to every other trapper wishing to trap in his ancestral grounds of what awaited him! With those staked-out and burned bodies as evidence, he hoped any trappers left in the country realized they must flee the area or suffer the same consequences. If those warnings did not work and the much-hated white man trappers continued flooding into the grounds of his ancestors, then he would team up with his brother Charlie Left Hand, and bring down their 100 or so warriors from both of their bands and leave nothing but scorched earth and dead fur trappers up and down the Green for miles on both sides of the river in order for the fur trappers to get the message, leave and go somewhere else! As those thoughts of vengeful death slowly faded from his mind, he once again heard the aspen leaves moving quietly behind him as a good omen for what he planned to do...

About then as the Indian horsemen quietly rode up to where Chief Iron Eagle stood, they reined up and sat quietly in their saddles out of the great respect they held for the old chief. That was when all of the men were surprised by Chief Iron Eagle's next move. Walking over to the big pinto horse, the horse his son Red Hawk had last ridden, his son's favorite Buffalo Horse and the one now called The Death Horse by tribal members, Chief Iron Eagle just stood stock-still closely looking the large horse over. Typical of the large and seemingly 'smart as a whip' pinto, he seemed to be looking the old chief over just as closely as he was being examined as well...

Then to the surprise of everyone assembled around the old chief's tipi that morning, he reached up and looped his right arm around the big pinto's neck! When he did, there was a collective gasp heard above the sounds of rustling aspen leaves nearby from the ten other men who had also come to know and fear the big pinto because of the recently given name as "The Death Horse"! A name that when given culturally to a horse by the Northern Arapaho People, meant whoever rode that horse thereafter was a man marked for a violent death... Then as the chief forced the bridle into The Death Horse's mouth, the rest of the Northern Arapaho war party just looked at each other in surprise, as a touch of fear rippled among the lot of Indians sitting there on their horses! That action by the chief was then followed with 'much spirit' when he briskly brushed off the large animal's back with gusto! Then a saddle blanket was removed from a nearby chokecherry bush where it had been left to dry, smoothed out with his hand, laid upon the pinto's broad back and then quickly followed by the old chief's saddle! Soon, the actions around the so-named "Spirit Horse" as he had been called by Red Hawk when he was alive and The Death Horse by those now sitting on their horses around the big and powerful pinto, had everyone's rapt attention! The warriors all understood the meaning of naming a horse a 'Death Horse' and its dark implications to anyone who rode such an animal. All of those riders realizing the importance of what was now symbolically occurring before their eyes, just looked upon Chief Iron Eagle with 'frozen looks' of disbelief, shock and now, a new kind of respect for what he was doing in the face of the spirits...

Then having saddled and cinched down The Death Horse, Chief Iron Eagle 'snapped' a quick look over at the other members of his war party sitting quietly on their horses, looking as if they had been turned into stone! When he did and in such a rapid manner with the turn of his head, it caused every man of the group to snap back their heads in surprise! It was as if the looks Chief Iron Eagle had just given his men might evilly reach out and touch each and every one of them based on what he was doing with The Death Horse! Then Chief Iron Eagle seeing the reaction he had just caused among his tough as a hickory stick warriors, threw back his shoulders laughing out loud, surprising and making the men nervous all at the same time once again!

It was then that Chief Iron Eagle quietly said, "My medicine is very strong this morning in the 'Moon of the New Leaves'. All of you need not be afraid. I have been in communication with the spirits and bathed myself in the smoke from the sacred burning sage leaves. I will ride this horse of death and in so doing, will use it to avenge the death of my sons or die trying. But my heart is strong and good and my need to avenge the loss of my sons and the other members of his war party killed by the white man fur trappers has been blessed by The Great Spirit!" With those strong sounding words, the old chief waved over to the aspen grove in which he had pitched his tipi and when he did and as if on command, The Great Spirit seemed to once again move the leaves in the aspen grove in support. However, when the trees rustled their leaves that time, no one heard or felt any kind of a wind that needed to do so... But for the most part, that fact of windless rustling of aspen leaves was lost on the group of warriors now truly amped-up over the coming adventure soon facing all of them.

"Therefore, sub-chiefs Elk, Big Buffalo and

Scarred Wolf and the rest of you men, know that you will be riding with The Great Spirit on this trip and before it is all said and done, we all shall return home victorious and will have avenged not only my two sons but your friends and fellow warriors as well. When we return, we will be greeted as great warriors and songs of praises will be sung around our many campfires when we venture forth in many other such missions of joy and fulfillment," said Chief Iron Eagle with a wave of his right hand towards the Heavens as if gesturing for The Great Spirit to smile down upon his riders. With that, Chief Iron Eagle swung easily up into the saddle of initially his son's and now his big, wise and 'spirit-powerful' pinto horse. Moments later the group of now excited warriors had ridden out of sight to the south. Ridden towards a river called the Green by the much-hated white man fur trappers and towards fulfillment of a mission blessed by The Great Spirit as was acknowledged by the rustling of the aspen leaves caused by the wave of the chief's hand when no wind or breeze was blowing...

However, unbeknownst to the others, Chief Iron Eagle some weeks earlier had met with his chief Medicine Man and asked for his and The Great Spirit's blessings on this, his forthcoming trip. A trip where he and a number of other warriors were to ride into the territory of the white man fur trapper, look for the ones responsible for the death of his sons War Eagle and Red Hawk and a number of other Northern Arapaho warriors and kill all of them to avenge their tribe's losses. Then they were to steal the trappers' valuable horses and beaver furs and then return to his band's main spring camp. There upon their return to share the spoils of the trip with other less fortunate band members. By so doing, they could clear from the lands of their ancestors the much-hated American white men fur trappers and thereby allow their ancestors' spirits to finally rest in peace… However, Chief Iron Eagle also had other ideas on what to do with some of the white man's supplies they would take from the American trappers trapping up and down the Green. He had made up his mind that most of the beaver pelts taken from the American trappers would be sold to their Canadian brothers for newer rifles, more powder, lead and whiskey from that of the Hudson's Bay Fur Company's warehouses. Then in turn, those supplies would be distributed among many of his younger weaponless men. That would be done so when they rode south once again into battle, realizing the white man was like the hordes of grasshoppers on the prairie, they would be better able to kill more of the American fur trappers with such newer and more modern weapons. That the Medicine Man had later guaranteed after a cleansing ceremony in a sweat lodge and much burning of the leaves from the sacred big sage bush.

However in warnings from his dreams when asking for success and protections, the Medicine Man had warned Chief Iron Eagle that two days prior to going forth on the trip to the Green, neither he nor his men were to eat any kind of food made with the help of the white man's metal like cooking pots or game taken with a white man's firearm. Accordingly the Medicine Man had advised that those protections provided for in his dreams, held for all members of the war party having come directly from The Great Spirit. According to the Medicine Man, those protections received in his dreams only extended to those of the war party who only ate from or with implements supplied by Mother Earth like stone knives or pottery, or taken with the bow and arrow using only stone arrow points and not those made from the white man's metal. Additionally, all food cooked had to be from a fire made as their ancestors had done with a wooden bow and friction fire starter. *Little did Chief Iron Eagle realize that after sharing the Medicine Man's warnings with each of the warriors who were to accompany him on the special trip, one of the warriors had violated the instructions the Medicine Man had given the chief! As it turned out, the chief's very favorite food namely fresh venison and cornmeal mush had been stirred various times as it was cooking with a metal spoon! Stirred with a metal white man-made spoon because the chief, in order to not worry his wife about the dangers inherent in the forthcoming* trip, had not shared with her the Medicine Man's entire set of warnings about cooking with white man metal instruments... That he did realizing to obey the Medicine Man's warnings, he, the chief, would quietly and only selectively eat those foods his wife had prepared that conformed with The Great Spirit's warnings and therefore, not worry his wife about his forthcoming dangerous trip. A dangerous trip to the same country that both of her sons had made earlier in their lives and as a result, neither had returned...

In his great joy over being served his favorite meal of cooked cornmeal and fresh venison on the day of his departure, Chief Iron Eagle failed to heed the Medicine Man's warning when he forgot that his favorite meal was routinely stirred several times with a white man's metal spoon...

CHAPTER TEN

"CHIEF IRON EAGLE'S RIDE", "TOGIA'S" FINGER OF DEATH, THE METAL SPOON

"TURKEY WING" JACK JOHNSON nervously sat on his horse watching his three partners running their spring beaver trap line below, making sure they did not face any outside dangers. All morning long after he had awakened with a feeling that something bad was going to happen that day, he kept a sharp eye peeled just in case his earlier feelings came true. Then after he got bucked off his horse and landed on a rock pile wrenching his left shoulder, he figured that was what had been bothering him and dismissed other such negative thoughts for a while. However, an hour later such thoughts arose once again and kept dogging him as he took his position at the base of Whiskey Mountain, overlooking his partners Jim Peterson, "Mud Hen" McGurk and

Terry Knowland, tending their traps along the Green and a number of its adjacent beaver-filled waterways, skinning out their day's catches. But as he did, he finally found himself relaxing as he looked all around him at the natural beauty and quiet as only found on the American Frontier. Turkey Wing never tired over what Mother Nature had provided for him and he always tried to greet every day as if it was his last...

Turkey Wing never saw the flight of the arrow until the very instant it slammed into his right eye, exploded the eyeball, smashed through the bone of the skull, lodged deeply into his brain and spilled him from his horse! Moments later, Mud Hen, working along a large and heavily brushed-in beaver pond skinning a beaver noticed that his horse was very interested in something moving about in a nearby dense willow thicket. Fearing a possible grizzly bear might be in the willow thicket, Mud Hen dropped the beaver he had been skinning, removed his rifle from the saddle scabbard on his nearby riding horse and died within moments when a flint-tipped arrow point slammed into his throat! Grabbing the arrow's shaft sticking from his throat with both hands, he was for a few short moments aware of the sticky hot blood pouring from the tear in his throat, running through his fingers and spilling down the front of his buckskin shirt, as well as the extreme burning pain in his neck! Seconds later after landing on his knees in agony, he pitched forward and landed headfirst in a pool of his own blood, as his riding horse nervously smelling the scent of fresh blood, moved off a few yards and then commenced calmly feeding once again. Removing another dead beaver from his trap, Terry Knowland looked up with a big happy grin on his face over at where Mud Hen was supposed to be skinning out another previously caught beaver so he could show him his latest catch. Not seeing his friend Mud Hen standing and skinning where he was supposed to be, Terry nervously looked around him upon hearing a noise behind where he stood, just in time to see an Indian running right at him from his place of hiding behind a patch of willows with an upraised tomahawk! Standing there helplessly at the edge of the beaver pond with a dead beaver in his hands in terror, Terry never again moved until the tomahawk cleaved his skull to his neck, killing him instantly! Hearing a lot of unusual splashing in the beaver pond below him, Jim Peterson looked up from his trap setting duties just in time to see five mounted Indians riding up to the edge of the beaver pond in which he was working, raising all of their rifles and then seeing nothing but a large rolling cloud of white black powder smoke coming his way! Then only for a fleeting moment, Jim was aware of muddy beaver pond water closing over him, as five well-aimed lead slugs fired from close range tore into his chest area killing him instantly and spilling him into the beaver pond's deeper murky waters...

That evening after finally locating the four dead trappers' cabin, Chief Iron Eagle had the pleasure of killing the trappers' lone camp cook in surprise, as he bent over stirring a slow cooking pot of beans and rice meant for supper for the men still in the field who were running the group's trap line! That evening the eleven Northern Arapaho feasted on the white trappers' food, drank his whiskey and slept on the trappers' sleeping furs inside their cabin. After a breakfast of spitted venison removed earlier from the trappers' meat pole the next morning, Chief Iron Eagle's war party moved off down the Green trailing nine loaded riding and pack-horses from the dead trappers' camp carrying eight bundles of beaver 'Plus'! However before leaving the trappers' campsite, Iron Eagle saw to it that the five trappers' bodies were brought into their corral, tied to corral posts and burned at those stakes, as warnings to any other American fur trappers living and trapping in the area of the Green River... Suffice to say, Chief Iron Eagle's 'revenge ride' over the losses of his two sons was beginning to bear 'fruit' of the deadliest kind...

"Slim" Stevens sat on his horse close by his two beaver trapper companions keeping watch over his partners, "Coot" Carpenter and Darrel Ruggles. A short distance away, Coot was skinning a freshly caught beaver and off in the willows, Ruggles was relieving himself from a previous night's supper of spicy beans, rice and chunks of venison backstrap. Moments later and before he could do much of anything, Ruggles was cut down trying to run off across a sandbar in terror near where he had been taking a dump! That he tried doing with his pants hanging down below his knees, bare bottom hanging out in the wind and Scarred Wolf hot on his trail swinging his tomahawk from atop his fast-closing horse! Ruggles's head was exploded with one clean swipe from Scarred Wolf's lustily swung tomahawk split seconds later! That was when Scarred Wolf and his horse violently went down in a cloud of flying dust after Slim, seeing Ruggles running for his life, had shot Scarred Wolf's horse out from under him! However, Slim died moments later from three balls fired at him by more charging Indians storming out from their place of hiding in a dense willow patch from just yards away! Coot Carpenter on the other hand, ever the toughest man in that small group of trappers, dropped his beaver being skinned, grabbed his rifle off his nearby horse and shot and killed a hard-charging Indian coming his way with an upraised tomahawk from atop his racing horse! The impact of Coot's rifle bullet striking the on-rushing Indian in his chest flipped him immediately backwards over the horse's rump, landing his crumpled body onto the ground in an explosion of dust! Quickly grabbing his fellow trapper Slim Stevens's reserve rifle from off his nearby still-standing horse and turning, Coot died with an arrow and a rifle ball smashing into his chest before he could get another shot off!

Later upon finding the trappers' lean-to and their set of corrals by following the three trappers' backtracks, Iron Eagle and his remaining nine hungry men feasted on the dead trappers' foodstuffs. Somewhat later, the men slept in the trappers' sleeping furs that evening, after they had placed their dead fellow warrior atop a burial scaffold for his trip into the Upper World to meet with the Cloud People. The next morning after loading up the trappers' eight horses with their ten bundles of furs and saddling one of the trappers' horses to replace the one shot from under Scarred Wolf, the war party left camp and continued heading downstream on the Green on their hunt for any other trappers found 'not looking'. But not before they had tied the three dead trappers' bodies to corral posts and set them afire as warnings for all American trappers to leave the Green or suffer the same treatment! As Chief Iron Eagle and his fellow warriors rode away from the last group of dead trappers' campsite, he smiled. His trip to revenge the losses of his two sons in earlier battles with the hated trappers was going just as the chief's Medicine Man had predicted. He then realized if his 'ride' to remove the hated trappers continued with such successes, he and his warriors would soon be coming home loaded with many white man's valuable supplies and hailed as 'Great Warriors' by the members of his band. Leaning back in his saddle, Chief Iron Eagle looked forward to attacking any other groups of trappers he could find, because his Medicine Man's sacred vision had shown there would be many more successes, providing his earlier warnings against using any of the white man's implements before beginning such a 'Vision Quest' were strictly followed...

******

Ken McCloud, Duwayne Peepers, Jim Fagan, "Dirty" Dan McGee and Cliff Hostler sat on their sitting logs around their campfire come evening time after a hard day trapping. As they did, they watched with keen interest Peevis McGreen, their designated camp cook, working his suppertime magic around the hungry men's campfire. As Peevis bent over and poured a cup of coffee into Jim's held-out coffee cup, his two-gallon coffee pot EXPLODED!

BOOM – BOOM – BOOM – BOOM – BOOM – BOOM – BOOM! went seven quick unexpected rifle shots from the edge of darkness surrounding the trappers' campfire! Trappers Ken McCloud, Jim Fagan, and Cliff Hostler died as they were shot off their sitting logs around the trappers' campfire waiting for their supper to finish cooking and be served! Scalded Peevis McGreen in the meantime, ran screaming around and around and finally fell onto the ground by the campfire rolling around in pain! When the coffee pot of scalding hot coffee had been hit by an errant rifle bullet meant for Peevis, it had exploded all of its hot contents upward and all over McGreen's exposed hands, face, neck and head! Now he lay on the ground scalded all to hell and with both eyes almost blinded from being burned unexpectedly by the scalding hot brew! Peepers on the other hand, reached for his ever near at hand rifle and instantly died after being back shot from another rifle bullet fired from out of the darkness towards the trapper illuminated by the light of the fire! McGee hit the ground and rolled over behind a sitting log, then quickly rose to his feet, shot and killed Big Buffalo as he charged the trappers' campfire with an upraised tomahawk looking for the closest 'slow moving' trapper into which to sink the blade of his tomahawk and count coup! For his efforts in defending himself, McGee was shot in the belly with an arrow! Dropping his rifle and grabbing the arrow's shaft with both of his hands in pain, McGee stumbled and fell over backwards into the trappers' firepit! There he died in shock as he burned and bled to death!

By now, the remaining nine Indians in the war party swarmed around the trappers' campfire and with their sheath knives and tomahawks, made sure all the trappers were dead. That was except for Peevis McGreen, who was swarmed over and taken alive. An hour later, Peevis had recovered enough of his sight and was forced to finish cooking and feeding the Indians the trappers' supper. Once that chore was done, Chief Iron Eagle abruptly stood up, withdrew his tomahawk from his sash and smashed its blade into Peevis's face, and then the rest of the Indians, still upset over the loss of Big Buffalo, let Peevis just wiggle around on the ground and finally die a slow death from shock and bleeding to death from the tomahawk chop to his face!

That night the Indians spent another comfortable night in the dead trappers' cabin during a furious thunderstorm. The next morning after a breakfast of spitted moose meat from the trappers' meat pole, the cabin was looted and its beaver and wolf furs packed on the trappers' packhorses. Then once again, the six trappers' bodies were tied off onto corral poles and set afire as warnings to any other trappers trapping along the Green. Then Iron Eagle and his remaining eight Indians finished loading up the trappers' horses and with difficulty because of the size of their captive horse herd, began moving even further westward along the Green looking for more of the much-hated trappers. As they moved off from the last trappers' campsite, six dead trappers tied to corral posts briskly burned and trailing behind the group of Indians were 14 more horses carrying 28 bundles of beaver furs! However, back on a lone ridge in stark contrast to its surroundings, stood a burial scaffold holding Big Buffalo's body wrapped in a trapper's grizzly bear rug, as he began his journey into the Upper World making his way towards the rest of the Cloud People...

******

Swinging their string of riding and packhorses into their campsite led by Jack Jones and followed by Griz Peterson, Alvin Jaconetti and Billy Bob Randel, the four tired trappers headed for their horse corral. There they unsaddled their riding mounts, placed them in their hobbles and turned them loose to feed and water in the adjacent meadow. Then the three packhorses were led over to the men's cabin and unloaded. First in went several armloads of fresh beaver pelts followed by several large armloads of fresh willow branches to be used for the hooping. Last in went all the men's extra rifles from another pannier, carried along just so the men could have extra firepower in case they were attacked by superior numbers of hostile Indians while out running their trap line. Then those packhorses were also unpacked, hobbled and let out to graze and water with the rest of the trappers' horses as well.

In the meantime, Alvin walked over to his outside firepit and began building up his cooking fire. Then with the fire burning well, Alvin placed a large Dutch oven loaded with previously cooked pinto beans, red pepper flakes and dried wild onions near the flames so it could begin heating up so it would be hot and ready for part of the men's supper. Then Alvin headed over to his big wooden mixing bowl and made up a batch of biscuit dough so it would have time to rise. As he did that, Jones, Griz and Billy Bob began the laborious and messy work of de-fatting and hooping the men's daily catch of 18 beaver.

Soon the wonderful smell of boiling coffee, baking biscuits, spitted elk meat from the camp's meat pole and bubbling pinto beans graced the firepit area. Finally finished with the de-fatting and hooping of their beaver skins, Jack Jones, Griz and Billy Randel walked over to the creek and using handfuls of sand from the creek bottom, vigorously scrubbed their hands and arms to rid themselves of the oily beaver fat, bits of meat, fur, hair and sweat. Once fairly clean, the three men grabbed up their ever-present rifles after cleaning up in the creek and headed over to the cooking fire for their supper as Alvin continued making his final preparations for the men's hearty meal soon to be served.

Soon the only sounds heard around the trappers' campfire were those of crackling and burning wood, clanking of the cast iron being served from, and the men's sounds of pleasure over the taste of the food after another hard day's work running their trap line and processing the beaver furs. Following their supper and as Alvin began his supper clean-up duties, the other three men retired to the cabin and brought out their pipes, a canister of James River smoking tobacco and one of their flat kegs of rum. Soon all four of the men were sitting back on their sitting logs around the firepit, smoking their clay pipes and enjoying their cups of rum over the day's conversation regarding the running of their trap line and the funny event when Griz stepped into a muskrat hole, went into the water over his head and came out soaked and smelling of beaver pond mud.

That was when Alvin taking their almost empty coffee pot, dumped out the dregs and headed for the creek over by the corral to wash out the pot and fill it with fresh water for the morning's breakfast run. Standing back up with the two-gallon pot full of creek water, Alvin turned and found himself staring into the end of a rifle barrel pointed right at him from just a few feet away by an Indian standing by the corral! Slowly laying the coffee pot back down, Alvin found himself next being herded back to the outdoor firepit where he saw his three friends all standing up with their hands held high into the air! This after being surprised and surrounded by eight other heavily armed Indians with rifles pointed at their midsections and murderous looks on their faces! Additionally, a ninth and very distinguished-looking Indian just stood along his compatriots looking on. However, the look upon that ninth Indian's face, unarmed as he was, was murderous and savage-looking and meant to be clearly understood if ever there was any doubt as to the outcome of this situation…

Somehow, the men had let their guards down and were now being held captive by nine serious- looking Indians. As Alvin was returned to the firepit with the rest of his friends, he found himself looking at one of the Indians now holding his gaily tack-decorated "Togia" rifle and closely examining it. As it just so happened, the very same rifle he had picked up after the earlier Christmas Ambush Battle at the very campsite where Buck Snort, his men and Jack Jones's men had ambushed a number of Indians leaving the trappers' current cabin where they had slept for the night in order to avoid having to sleep out on the trail during a snowstorm. The same ambush of a number of Indians that had stolen all of the trappers' horses in the dead of night from the trappers' Osprey Nest Camp five miles downriver and after a hard two days of foot pursuit in the dead of winter, the trappers had finally caught up with the horse thieves. Then without further thought, the trappers had ambushed that band of Indians right at daylight and killed every one of them! The same Indians where Buck Snort had killed one of them who had been carrying the very highly tack-decorated rifle now being held and closely examined by a very serious and now horribly sinister-looking Indian! That same rifle now being held by the serious-looking Indian that Griz had identified as the one belonging to some sort of high-up Indian of importance based on all of the fine brass tack work on the stock and forearm. A rifle Griz had said was a Togia rifle that at one time might have belonged to a Northern Cheyenne Indian of some high importance. Then Alvin felt what was like a cold hand being placed upon his body over what he was remembering. A 'cold hand' because he re-membered that Griz had also said at the time the rifle had been picked up by him that he hoped its owner or the parent of the now dead owner, never found that rifle on him or anyone he knew. Because if such an important person had once owned that rifle, like the one carrying it the day he had been ambushed and killed by Buck Snort and that rifle's kin came along and found it in the hands of someone else, there would be hell to pay by its new owner... Then Alvin felt what he thought was that same 'cold hand' running over his body once again, when the Indian holding the rifle began looking intently at the four trappers with deadly and evil-looking eyes!

Alvin's heart 'froze' as the man holding the highly decorated Togia rifle then began looking at each and every trapper now being held captive with a look in his eyes that was nothing short of pure evil. Then the man holding the rifle spoke, saying in perfect English, "I am Chief Iron Eagle of the Wind River Band of Northern Arapaho. I speak the tongue of you white men because years ago when the "Black Robes" came through my country and village, they taught me to speak in the tongue of the white man."

Then there was a pause after saying those words in order for the meaning to be clearly understood by the trappers now being held as captives, that the man doing the talking was a person educated in the ways of a white man. Then Chief Iron Eagle slowly and with a sinister meaning, cocked back the hammer of the Togia rifle and then quietly asked, "Who does this rifle belong to?"

When Chief Iron Eagle spoke those cold words, his piercing black eyes fell upon each and every one of the trappers one at a time and when he looked at Alvin, Alvin found it hard to breathe because of a tightness now in his chest...

"I will ask one more time. Which of you trappers took this rifle before this night, when me and my warriors captured it and brought it back into the right hands?" coldly asked Chief Iron Eagle.

That time, not one of the trappers moved a hair or dared to even breathe. They all knew that rifle now belonged to Alvin after Buck Snort had killed its rightful owner in the Christmas Ambush Battle! However, not a single trapper moved or dared give away that information for fear over what might follow... Then Chief Iron Eagle once again looked very carefully into the eyes of each trapper as if looking for the answer he sought to his question. An answer sought because he knew the Togia rifle had at one time proudly belonged to his now dead young son Red Hawk, and there was no way his son would give away such a special and meaningful rifle. In short, Chief Iron Eagle figured someone had to kill his son Red Hawk, and only then would his son ever part with such a rifle that meant so much to him. Now that beautifully tack-decorated rifle was allowing Red Hawk to in essence 'return' from the dead, and allowing that whoever currently owned that rifle had the 'Togia Rifle Finger of Death' pointing right at him… But before Alvin could speak up and say anything, the 'Togia Rifle Finger of Death' POINTED and then spoke loudly…

BOOM! went the Togia rifle, as Chief Iron Eagle shot Jack Jones in the head being the closest trapper to him, killing him instantly! When he fired the weapon in surprise at Jones, every trapper jumped as did the rest of the Indians but upon recovery, not a single trapper said a thing or even looked at Alvin for fear of giving him away knowing what might be coming next to him if they identified their friend and fellow trapper as the rifle's current owner…

Then Chief Iron Eagle calmly began slowly reloading the Togia rifle with malice in his heart and saying not a single word. After finishing with the reloading of the rifle and cocking back the hammer once again, Chief Iron Eagle quietly asked, "Who is the owner of this rifle, the rifle from the hands of my dead son Red Hawk?"

With those cold words ringing cryptically through the night air, aside from the sounds of the crackling fire, the trappers' camp went silent. Alvin realized that what Griz had said the morning he had picked up the highly decorated and special rifle after the killing was done, 'about having hell to pay if the dead man's kin ever discovered what had happened to the rifle's owner', realized no truer words had ever been spoken... Not wanting any of his friends to pay the price that his friend Jack Jones had just paid, Alvin first said a few words to the "Almighty" to protect his soul. Then knowing what was coming, quickly drew his sheath knife, grabbed it by its homemade deer antler handle and hurled it with its heavy ten-inch blade right at Chief Iron Eagle's head! Accompanying the quickly thrown knife were Alvin's bellowed-out words ringing through the air as a warning to his surviving friends and fellow trappers to now make their 'moves', "THAT IS MY RIFLE, YOU KILLING SON-OF-A-BITCH!"

When Alvin hurled his ten-inch sheath knife at the threatening chief's head, the whole camp exploded into action realizing what was coming next! Seeing such quick movement coming from Alvin, the chief quickly jerked the Togia rifle up in defense in the path of what had just been hurled at him, only to have Alvin's heavy sheath knife slam blade-first deeply into the Togia's rifle stock with a loud "THUNK"! Had the chief not raised the rifle in such a defensive manner, Alvin's sheath knife would have struck him in the side of his head with such high impact energy, that it would have split his skull and killed him!

Whirling, the chief shot Alvin in the chest from just feet away with the Togia rifle, killing him outright! In the meantime, Griz, realizing they were all within moments of becoming 'dead men walking', quickly drew his sheath knife and plunged it into the ear of the surprised Indian standing right next to him during the wild explosion of events now taking place around him. When Griz's knife was plunged to its hilt out of desperation into the left ear of the Indian standing next to him, that man dropped like a man head shot from a rifle! Reaching out and grabbing that Indian's dropped rifle, Griz quickly cocked it, whirled and HAD HIS RIGHT EAR SHOT CLEAN OFF THE SIDE OF HIS HEAD BY ANOTHER INDIAN SHOOTING HIS RIFLE FROM THE HIP IN SURPRISE AT GRIZ'S QUICK MOVEMENT! Griz in turn, 'ear or no ear', staggered sideways from that bullet's impact ripping off his ear and then shot that Indian in the guts from just two feet away! Dropping his now-empty rifle and realizing he was soon to be killed by the other Indians scrambling about trying to get into the battle and get him in their sights, Griz sprinted off into the darkness, bleeding side of his face, throbbing ringing head and all… Then as Griz disappeared off into the darkness, the air around him was then immediately filled with rifle balls as the rest of the Indians got their act together and joined the battle shooting at him! Four rifle balls whistled through the air harmlessly at the rapidly fleeing Griz speeding his way through the brush as fast as his moccasin feet would carry him! However, two other bullets caught Billy Bob Randel square in his chest, tearing through his heart and lungs and dropping him like a stone! Then the only sounds heard around the trappers' campsite were those of metal rifle ramrods being jerked from their holders and hastily employed, as the Indians hurriedly reloaded their rifles before giving chase after a fast-fleeing personage named Griz...

That night, an angry Chief Iron Eagle had Alvin, Jack Jones and Billy Bob Randel burned to a crisp in the trappers' now more than blazing firepit! But figuring those trappers were the four responsible for his young son's death, he cut off all of the men's ears, noses, private parts and removed their tongues, so all of those trappers would wander in the afterlife because of their missing parts! Additionally, the chief had all of Alvin's fingers removed for being the one who had picked up and kept Red Hawk's Togia rifle after his son had been killed. The chief wrongly figured that with Alvin admitting the rifle was his, that he had been the one who had killed his son. He also figured the rifle had come back from the Spirit World and had 'fingered' Alvin as Red

Hawk's killer, when in reality all Alvin had been was a really good camp cook...

Somewhat later as the remaining seven living Indians sat around the firepit watching it consume the three bodies of the trappers and drinking the dead trappers' rum, Chief Iron Eagle began feeling a deep inner pain in his guts! He then began to realize his revenge ride along the Green to rid the area of white man trappers was in part, for some reason, failing. He had lost four of his best warriors from his war party and that alone, upon his return to his Wind River Band of Northern Arapaho Indians, would be viewed as a failure and result in his fall from power in disgrace as a chief. Additionally, he had been having those pangs of pain in his lower guts ever since the loss of his first warrior and it had only worsened as he kept losing more men! True, he had killed a number of the much-hated trappers and had collected many horses, their bundles of furs and the dead men's weapons to show for his efforts, but losing four of his best fighting men and warriors was simply a Northern Arapaho cultural disgrace!

The next morning only added fuel to his 'fire of disgrace'. He and his warriors had failed to find the one trapper who had escaped from the killing the evening before by smartly getting into the Green and having his tracks washed away as he had floated downstream making good his escape. That and now the pain in his inner guts felt like it was growing worse throughout the day, just as his Medicine Man had predicted would happen if the guidance received in his sacred vision was disrespected and not followed!

It was later the next afternoon after the two warriors killed in the shooting had been placed on burial scaffolds for their trip to the Upper World, when Chief Iron Eagle sat up abruptly like he had been shot while resting upon the dead trappers' sleeping furs. THAT WAS WHEN THE MEDICINE MAN'S WARNING ABOUT NO ONE EATING WITH WHITE MAN'S TOOLS TWO DAYS BEFORE THEY LEFT ON THEIR RAID REALLY BEGAN RINGING LOUDLY AND CLEARLY IN HIS MIND. SOMEONE HAD USED SOME OF THE WHITE MAN'S METAL BEFORE LEAVING AND THAT WAS WHY THEY HAD LOST SO MANY MEN AND HE FELT THE WAY HE DID PHYSICALLY! THEN WITH A COLDNESS RUNNING THROUGH HIS OWN BODY, IT FINALLY DAWNED ON HIM AFTER MUCH SEARCHING THOUGHT, THAT HE WAS THE GUILTY PARTY WHO HAD VIOLATED HIS OWN MEDICINE MAN'S CLEAR WARNINGS! WARNINGS HE HAD RECEIVED WHILE EXPERIENCING A VISION FROM THE GREAT SPIRIT!

HE THEN REALIZED THAT HIS FAVORITE CORNMEAL AND VENISON STEW THAT HE HAD FOR BREAKFAST ON THE DAY OF THEIR DEPARTURE WAS USUALLY STIRRED

BY HIS WIFE WITH A METAL SPOON! STIRRED WITH A METAL SPOON BECAUSE THE HOT CORNMEAL MANY TIMES STUCK TO THE BOTTOM OF THE CLAY POT IF NOT VIGOROUSLY STIRRED AND SCRAPED FROM THE BOTTOM OF THE COOKING POT DURING ITS LAST STAGES OF COOKING! IT NOW BECAME READILY APPARENT THAT HE HIMSELF WAS ULTIMATELY RESPONSIBLE FOR THE 'DEMONS' HE AND HIS MEN WERE SUFFERING BECAUSE HE HAD NOT HEEDED THE WARNINGS THE MEDICINE MAN HAD RECEIVED DURING HIS PERSONAL QUEST FOR A FAVORABLE VISION...

WITH THOSE THOUGHTS OF PERSONAL DREAD RUNNING THROUGH HIS MIND BECAUSE HE HAD VIOLATED THE INSTRUCTIONS RECEIVED FROM HIS MEDICINE MAN'S DREAMS, CHIEF IRON EAGLE STUBBORNLY CLUNG TO THE FEELING THAT HIS MAGIC WAS STILL STRONG ENOUGH BECAUSE THEY HAD OVERALL BEEN VERY SUCCESSFUL IN ALL OF THE HORSES AND FURS THEY HAD SEIZED. ALSO, THEY HAD KILLED A NUMBER OF THE MUCH-HATED AMERICAN WHITE FUR TRAPPERS, AS WELL AS HAD AVENGED RED HAWK'S KILLER AS THE ACQUISITION OF THE TOGIA RIFLE HAD PROVEN. WITH THOSE 'BULL-HEADED'

THOUGHTS FINALLY OVERRIDING HIS MEDICINE MAN'S WARNINGS, CHIEF IRON EAGLE FIGURED THEY WOULD PROCEED DOWNRIVER TO ONE MORE TRAPPERS' CAMP, KILL AND BURN THOSE INDIVIDUALS, THEN WITH THEIR VERY VALUABLE EXPANDED HORSE HERD PACKING ALL OF THE VALUABLE STOLEN FURS, RETURN HOME AND JUST PROCLAIM SUCCESS. SMILING OVER HIS PLAN AND IN LIGHT OF HIS SUCCESSES, HE LAY BACK DOWN ON THE DEAD TRAPPERS' SLEEPING FURS TO REST. HOWEVER, HE HAD NO MORE THAN LAID BACK DOWN WHEN HE HAD TO ROLL OVER AND VOMIT UP HIS BREAKFAST! THAT HE HAD TO DO SINCE HIS MEDICINE MAN'S CURSE COMING TRUE FROM HIS EARLIER VISIONS SEEKING SUCCESS ON HIS CHIEF'S REVENGE RIDE SOUTH INTO THE LANDS OF THE WHITE TRAPPERS, WAS STILL PHYSICALLY STIRRING STRONGLY WITHIN THE 'HEADSTRONG' CHIEF'S NOW SICKENED BODY...

******

Griz Peterson ran, stumbled, swam in the Green and crawled all night in his frantic efforts to put as much distance from Jones's old campsite where the rest of his friends had been killed by a raiding band of Northern Arapaho to the safety of the Osprey Nest Camp of trappers! By then his shot-off ear stump had crusted over with dried blood and stopped bleeding but that injury caused Griz great head pain every time he stumbled, fell or moved his head suddenly from side to side. But his determination and survival instincts were strong and he was bound and determined to safely make it to Buck Snort's Osprey Nest Camp, warn them about the dangers close at hand, re-arm himself and kill that Indian chief who had killed off his friends! That bitterness he felt over what had happened to his group of trappers continued to upwell in his being and drive him mile after mile towards Buck Snort's camp with the determination of a bull buffalo in rut after a cow buffalo in estrus...

"HELLO THE CAMP!" shouted Griz tiredly, as he rounded the timber below the Osprey Nest Camp and just about physically spent, stumbled his way up towards his friends' cabin.

Clem working around his firepit way before daylight that morning making the men's breakfast since he could not for some reason sleep, turned upon hearing the shout and seeing an exhausted and staggering Griz stumbling his way, realized something was bad wrong! Grabbing up his nearby rifle and shouting for Buck Snort and the rest of the trappers to respond to his warning call, Clem then ran down through their meadow to aid his badly exhausted friend from Jones's camp.

Moments later, an exhausted Griz stumbled into Clem's arms and then his spent legs collapsed under him! Soon, a heavily armed Buck Snort and company were surrounding an exhausted Griz and listening to his story of the death of their friends! Then Buck Snort, Griz and the rest of the trappers headed for their cabin and after making sure Griz was fed a good hearty breakfast, rested and totally re-armed, the trappers gathered around their firepit for a cup of rum and a council of war. Griz was able to let Buck Snort and company know that he figured they would be facing seven Northern Arapaho Indians within a day or so coming down from his old camp if they waited, but was able to provide nothing else regarding how to handle the deadly battle soon to come.

Buck Snort thought for a moment about how to meet the danger where they were outnumbered and the element of surprise was on the side of the attacking Indians. Then mad over what had happened to his friends at Jones's camp, Buck Snort came up with an idea of his own. After sharing that battle plan with the trappers, the men re-checked their powder and lead supplies and then were more than ready. About 30 minutes later, five very heavily armed trappers streamed out from the Osprey Nest Camp and headed upriver for Jones's campsite using the morning's darkness as one of their 'covers'.

However, the five trappers were careful to keep to the cover at the edge of the timber so if they ran into the seven remaining Indians coming their way, they would not be so visible, quickly detected and vulnerable to attack. And if lucky, the five trappers could attack the Indians shortly after daylight before they were ready and prepared for battle and Buck Snort figured that should even up the odds. However, par for the course when going into any kind of a highly emotional event, Buck Snort surely lived up to his name and the smells he created. But that made little difference to the rest of the men, because they knew not to worry. Not to worry because history had proven that in any kind of battle, Buck Snort, physiologically a creator of smells because of being poisoned early on in his life back at the orphanage, routinely fought to the death like a female mountain lion defending her kittens... That and being the excellent shooter that he was, he seldom missed whatever he was shooting at!

Shortly after the break of day, the hard-riding trappers arrived at a low ridge leading down to Jones's old campsite. There they were surprisingly confronted with the unexpected appearance of burial scaffolds recently constructed for the two dead Indians killed by Griz during the battle that occurred shortly after Jones's group had been captured by the Indians. Angered, Buck Snort rode up to the two burial scaffolds, threw a rope around the legs of the scaffolds and jerked both of them to the ground in a cloud of dust, flying bodies and buffalo robes. Then Buck Snort got an even better idea about how to handle their deadly Indian problem and with a lethal grin, set his plan into motion with the rest of the men. A deadly plan that if it worked, would play on the Indians' fear of the supernatural and once so distracted, would make killing them easier and almost guaranteed…

******

Chief Iron Eagle led his men out from Jones's old cabin site come late morning after an evening of drinking and headed for the nearby Green River, figuring he would travel down its length for about ten more miles and if no other trappers were discovered, return to their previous camp-site. There since there was no threat of trappers in country, remain for the evening and then taking all of their stolen horses and bundles of beaver furs, head back to the tribe's summer campsite in the Wind River Mountains. He had led his warriors no more than half a mile downstream when he saw that the burial scaffolds previously constructed the evening before for his two dead warriors, had either fallen down or been dragged down by the likes of a hungry grizzly bear or such. Realizing the cultural importance of his two warriors and their eternal journey, Chief Iron Eagle immediately turned his men towards the downed burial scaffolds so they could be once again constructed. That way, the two dead warriors could continue once again their journey into the Upper World in order to meet the rest of their ancestors, namely, the Cloud People.

Riding up to the downed scaffolds and still buffalo robe-wrapped warriors' bodies, Chief Iron Eagle could see that the two dead warriors remained rolled up in their burial dress. Mysteriously, they had not been eaten by any land predators and were still there all rolled up but just lying there on the ground after falling from the collapsed scaffolds. Ordering his men to dismount so they could rebuild the burial scaffolds, the men walked over and picketed their horses in the nearby outlying timber. As they did, they were careful not to utter the two dead warriors' names, which would cause them to continue wandering in the Lower World and slow their journey in meeting with their ancestors, the Cloud People. With that, the seven men walked over to the downed timbers and began rebuilding the burial scaffolds so the two dead warriors could once again be hoisted up onto the scaffold out of the way of the ground predators and resume their journey into the Upper World.

ALL OF A SUDDEN, THE TWO 'DEAD INDIANS' WRAPPED UP IN THEIR BUFFALO ROBES BUT OUT OF ACTUAL VIEW, BEGAN MOVING AND MAKING GROANING NOISES! CHIEF IRON EAGLE AND HIS MEN DROPPED EVERYTHING THEY WERE PREPARING TO DO AND IN TERROR OVER THE DEAD MEN COMING BACK TO LIFE, BROKE AND RAN FOR THEIR HORSES TIED OFF IN THE TIMBER! RUNNING, FALLING, STUMBLING

AND FEARING FOR THEIR LIVES BECAUSE OF THE TWO DEAD INDIANS SOMEHOW COMING BACK TO LIFE, CHIEF IRON EAGLE AND HIS FLEEING WARRIORS ALL OF A SUDDEN SLOWED THEIR RUNNING IN PANIC, IN AMAZEMENT! THERE BEFORE THEM EMERGING FROM THE TIMBER WHERE THEY HAD JUST TIED OFF THEIR HORSES WERE THREE VERY DETERMINED-LOOKING TRAPPERS WITH LEVELED RIFLES!

THEN ALL OF A SUDDEN, THREE WHITE CLOUDS OF BLACK POWDER SMOKE ROLLED OUT ACROSS THE PRAIRIE GRASSES AND ENVELOPED THE SEVEN PREVIOUSLY RUNNING FOR THEIR LIVES BUT NOW ALMOST STOPPED IN TOTAL PANIC OVER WHAT WAS NOW HAPPENING, INDIANS! INDIANS WHO JUST MOMENTS EARLIER BEGAN RUNNING FROM OBSERVED MOVEMENT AND SOUNDS COMING FROM WITHIN BUFFALO ROBES USED TO WRAP UP THEIR TWO DEAD FRIENDS KILLED THE EVENING BEFORE, TO NOW FACING THE DEADLY ENDS OF RIFLE BARRELS BEING WIELDED BY THREE VERY DETERMINED-LOOKING TRAPPERS WITH THE DISCERNIBLE LOOKS OF 'DEATH IN THE WIND' SPELLED CLEAR ACROSS THEIR FACES!

BOOM – BOOM – BOOM! WENT THE THREE TRAPPERS' RIFLES, SENDING

SPEEDING DEATH TOWARDS THE SEVEN NOW TERRIFIED INDIANS OVER WHAT THEY HAD JUST SEEN AND HEARD BACK AT THE BURIAL SCAFFOLDS AND WHAT THEY WERE NOW SEEING IN FRONT OF THEM! A SPLIT-SECOND LATER, CHIEF IRON EAGLE AND THREE REMAINING LIVING WARRIORS EMERGED THROUGH THE WHITE CLOUD OF BLACK POWDER SMOKE WITH UPRAISED TOMAHAWKS, NOW LUSTILY SINGING THEIR 'DEATH SONGS'! BEHIND THEM ON THE GROUND LAY THREE DEAD INDIANS WIGGLING THEIR LAST, KILLED BY THE THREE STRAIGHT-SHOOTING TRAPPERS' FIRST SERIES OF SHOTS FIRED FROM THEIR RIFLES...

DROPPING HIS RIFLE AND KEEPING HIS EYE ON THE CLOSEST INDIAN RUNNING RIGHT AT HIM LOUDLY SINGING HIS DEATH SONG, BUCK SNORT QUICKLY DREW HIS PISTOL FROM HIS SASH AND SHOT THE HARD-CHARGING INDIAN RIGHT IN THE FACE WHO WAS JUST SIX FEET AWAY WHEN THE BALL ENTERED HIS FOREHEAD! THE DEAD INDIAN'S BODY BEING SO CLOSE TO BUCK SNORT AND BEING CARRIED BY THE MAN'S RUNNING INERTIA, SLAMMED RIGHT INTO THE TRAPPER, CAUSING BOTH THE LIVING AND THE DEAD TO FLY THROUGH THE AIR BACKWARDS IN A JUMBLE OF TWO COLLIDING BODIES! SEEING THE

REMAINING TWO TRAPPERS IN FRONT OF THEM NOW HURRIEDLY WITHDRAWING THEIR DEADLY PISTOLS FROM THEIR SASHES AS WELL, THE REMAINING THREE INDIANS STOPPED THEIR CHARGE AS IF ON COMMAND, REALIZING TO CONTINUE MEANT THEY TOO WOULD SOON BE JOINING THE CLOUD PEOPLE! THEN ALL TOGETHER, THEY THREW THEIR TOMAHAWKS AT THE TWO STILL-STANDING TRAPPERS TO THEIR FRONT JUST AS BUCK SNORT BEGAN UNTANGLING HIMSELF FROM THE DEAD INDIAN LYING ON TOP OF HIM. THAT WAS WHEN THE DEAD INDIAN WAS ROLLED OVER ONTO HIS BACK AND BLOOD AND GRAY MATTER FLOWED FROM A BLUE-BLACK LOOKING .52 CALIBER BULLET HOLE IN HIS FOREHEAD... CHIEF IRON EAGLE NOW LAY QUIVERING HIS LAST AS HIS ESSENCE DRAINED OUT FROM THE HOLE IN HIS FOREHEAD SIGNIFYING THE LAST OF HIS REVENGE RIDE FOR HIS LOST SONS, RED HAWK AND WAR EAGLE... SIGNIFYING THE DRASTIC END OF THE ONCE GREAT CHIEF'S REVENGE RIDE, ALL OVER EATING WITH A METAL SPOON CONTRARY TO WHAT THE MEDICINE MAN'S SACRED VISION HAD SO INSTRUCTED, WHEN HE SHOULDN'T HAVE...

BUCK SNORT, NOW FINALLY UNTANGLED FROM THE NOW DEAD INDIAN HE HAD

'HEAD SHOT' JUST MOMENTS EARLIER, TOSSED HIS BODY OFF TO ONE SIDE. HE THEN STAGGERED UPWARD WITH HIS SECOND PISTOL NOW IN HAND, TOOK 'DEAD' AIM AND KILLED ONE OF THE THREE REMAINING AND NOW FLEEING IN TERROR INDIANS OVER WHAT WAS HAPPENING TO THEIR WAR PARTY! THE LAST TWO INDIANS FOUND THEMSELVES RUNNING BACK TOWARDS THE BURIAL SCAFFOLDS NOW IN ABJECT TERROR, ONLY TO DISCOVER THEIR FLEEING FOR COVER ON THE OTHER SIDE OF THEIR CURRENT BATTLEFIELD WAS FOR NAUGHT...

AS THE TWO REMAINING INDIANS FLED OUT ACROSS THE GRASSY SLOPE AWAY FROM THE THREE NOW-STANDING TRAPPERS HURRIEDLY RELOADING THEIR RIFLES BEHIND THEM, THE BUFFALO ROBES USED AS BURIAL SHROUDS ON THE TWO DEAD INDIANS PLACED UPON THE BURIAL SCAFFOLDS THE DAY BEFORE AND NOW LYING ON THE GROUND, WERE ALL OF A SUDDEN UNRAVELLED AND TOSSED ASIDE! THEN UP FROM THE 'DEAD' AROSE CLEM AND MUSKRAT WHO HAD BEEN CLEVERLY HIDING WRAPPED UP IN THE BURIAL ROBES AS PART OF BUCK SNORT'S BATTLE PLAN, KNOWING THE INDIANS' CULTURE WOULD NOT ALLOW THEM TO UNWRAP THEM AND LOOK INSIDE...

RISING TO THEIR FEET WITH THEIR RIFLES IN HAND, CLEM AND MUSKRAT SHOT DEAD THE LAST TWO FLEEING FOR THEIR LIVES INDIANS FROM CHIEF IRON EAGLE'S ORIGINAL WAR PARTY! TWO INDIANS WHO WERE NOW WAY MORE THAN TERRIFIED UPON SEEING TWO TRAPPERS RISING UP FROM OUT OF THE TWO BURIAL ROBES AND BEGIN SHOOTING AT THEM! WITH THE DEATHS OF THOSE LAST TWO INDIANS, ALL WAS NOW QUIET ACROSS THE PRAIRIE AS THE WHITE CLOUDS OF ACRID BLACK POWDER SMOKE SLOWLY DRIFTED OUT INTO NOTHINGNESS, AS HAD THE LIVES OF SEVEN KILLING "SONS-A-BITCHES", AS ALVIN HAD DESCRIBED CHIEF IRON EAGLE THE NIGHT BEFORE THE UNTIMELY 'TOGIA RIFLE FINGER OF DEATH' HAD TAKEN HIS LIFE…

WALKING OVER TO THE INDIAN HE HAD SHOT IN THE FACE JUST MOMENTS EARLIER WITH HIS PISTOL, BUCK SNORT OBSERVED A BEAUTIFUL GRIZZLY BEAR NECKLACE COMPRISED OF 20 LONG CLAWS AROUND THE DEAD INDIAN'S NECK. LIFTING UP THE BLOODY HEAD OF THE DEAD INDIAN, BUCK SNORT REMOVED THE NECKLACE AND WIPED THE BLOOD FROM ITS LONG CLAWS WITH SOME NEARBY GRASSES. LITTLE DID HE REALIZE AT THE TIME NOR DID HE CARE, BUT BUCK SNORT HAD JUST

SHOT AND KILLED CHIEF IRON EAGLE, THE 'TERROR OF THE TRAPPERS ALONG THE GREEN'! AGAIN, LITTLE DID HE ALSO KNOW HE HAD JUST KILLED THE FATHER TO RED HAWK, ANOTHER PREVIOUS KILLER OF AMERICAN FUR TRAPPERS WORKING THEIR TRAP LINES ALONG THE LENGTH OF THE GREEN RIVER. RED HAWK BEING THE SAME INDIAN FROM ANOTHER EARLIER WARRING BAND OF NORTHERN ARAPAHO THAT HE HAD LED BACK AT THE OSPREY NEST CAMP WHERE HE AND HIS MEN HAD BURNED ALIVE FOUR OF THE FIVE TRAPPERS THEY HAD CAPTURED AT THAT SITE… AND IRONY OF IRONIES, A CABIN SITE NOW CLAIMED AND OCCUPIED BY BUCK SNORT AND HIS BAND OF TRAPPERS WHO HAD JUST KILLED OFF THE LAST OF THE EVIL NORTHERN ARAPAHO 'SEED', CHIEF IRON EAGLE, OR SO THEY THOUGHT…

THEN BUCK SNORT HEARD WIND HORSE YELL AT HIM. TURNING AS HE HURRIEDLY RELOADED HIS PISTOL, BUCK SNORT WALKED OVER TO WHERE HE, WIND HORSE AND GRIZ PETERSON HAD HIDDEN EARLIER AS PART OF THEIR PLANNED AMBUSH THEY HAD SET UP FOR CHIEF IRON EAGLE AND HIS MEN. WHEN HE DID, IT WAS ONLY TO FIND GRIZ PETERSON DEAD FROM ONE OF THE THREE TOMAHAWKS HASTILY THROWN MOMENTS EARLIER AT THE

THREE TRAPPERS, SUNK DEEPLY INTO HIS TEMPLE! STANDING THERE IN RESPECTFUL SILENCE OVER THE BRAVE TRAPPER, BUCK SNORT JUST SHOOK HIS HEAD. HERE GRIZ HAD DONE EVERYTHING THAT HE COULD TO ESCAPE AND LATER WARN HIS FRIENDS IN ANOTHER TRAPPERS' CAMPSITE. THEN WITHOUT HESITATION EVEN THOUGH EXHAUSTED FROM HIS EARLIER ESCAPE ATTEMPT, HAD JOINED THE TRAPPERS HE HAD SAVED FROM SURPRISE NORTHERN ARAPAHO INDIAN ATTACK AND LED THEM BACK INTO HARM'S WAY WITHOUT HESITATION.

THEN BUCK SNORT THOUGHT DEEPLY TO HIMSELF AS HE STOOD OVER THE BODY OF GRIZ PETERSON, MOUNTAIN MAN, *THE FRONTIER IS A BEAUTIFUL AND YET DANGEROUS PLACE FOR ALL MEN BUT DAMN IT, WHY DOES IT ALWAYS SEEM TO TAKE ITS BEST "CHILDREN"?*

Later that afternoon, after he and his men had gathered up all of the dead Indians and piling all of them up into a nearby gully, burned them to a crisp as a warning to all other Indians to leave the fur trappers alone. Then the men buried what was left of Jack Jones, Griz Peterson, Alvin Jaconetti and Billy Bob Randel together in a common grave as the friends all of them had once been during better times. Then the trappers' gravesite was covered with large rocks over the burial mound so the wolves, badgers and grizzly bears would not dig them up and eat their remains.

Following that, Buck Snort and company gathered up their horses they had hidden back in the timber at the burial scaffold ambush site. However, when the trappers went to gather in the Indians' horses as well, Buck Snort found himself standing stock-still in surprise! There before his eyes stood the familiar pinto that had been Red Hawk's stolen buffalo horse and a horse that Buck Snort had subsequently purchased as an extra pack animal for his contingent of trappers back at the first Rendezvous! Finding himself taking a second look just to make sure he was seeing the same horse he thought he was, his suspicions were confirmed. There quietly stood the pinto looking at Buck Snort, showing the same degree of interest that the trapper was showing as he looked at the unusual animal... Shaking his head in disbelief over what he was seeing and realizing he now had another chance to make the unusual pinto his own personal riding horse and see what that got him, Buck Snort untied the animal. For a few seconds they both just looked at each other with a profound interest. Reaching over, unbuckling and grabbing his saddle off his old riding horse, Buck Snort tossed it onto the ground. Then taking his saddle blanket and shaking it off, he gently laid it over the broad back of the big pinto. As he did, the pinto only looked back at what was going on and then with almost a look of acceptance of its new owner, reached over by the corral's railing and pulled up a mouthful of grass and began quietly eating as if it too realized a new era was at hand with its new master... With the saddle being swung up and onto its back, the big pinto just kept eating more grass from around the corral as if 'he' was finally 'home'... Standing back and looking over the saddling procedure he had just accomplished with a satisfied smile, Buck Snort turned and got back to the rest of the business at hand.

Buck Snort and company gathered up all of Jones's horses, salvaged all of their gear and provisions from their old cabin and storage shed and packed them onto Jones's ten packhorses and four riding horses. Then the men removed 22 bundles of beaver *'Plus'* from Jones's cabin and packed them on the other packhorses as well. Finally, all seven of the Indians' riding horses were likewise secured for travel. Then sorrowful over the loss of their four trapper friends, Buck Snort and company headed back down the Green en route their own campsite at the Osprey Nest Camp but as they did, every man among them kept an eye 'peeled' looking for any further signs of trouble. Only this time, instead of riding his old bay, Buck Snort now found himself sitting comfortably in the saddle atop the powerful pinto he had always wondered about! And as Buck Snort rode and became familiar with his new horse of choice and the particular habits found in every horse, the animal moving powerfully and smartly under him did not disappoint…

The next day after a breakfast served up by Clem right at dawn, Buck Snort and company headed up onto a nearby timbered ridge and began cutting timber so the men could enlarge their current horse corral for their now well over 60 horse herd, not counting a number of Indian horses released earlier, as well as building a new storage shed to safely house and accommodate their huge pile of bundled beaver furs assumed from all of the dead Indian-killed trappers. That they had to do because back at Jack Jones's campsite, Buck Snort and company realized they were now richer than most trappers, thanks to Chief Iron Eagle and his dead warriors for stealing a large number of furs from the 18 trappers they had killed along the Green on the chief's revenge trip. 'Richer than most', because they were now the proud owners of 52 additional horses the Indians had taken from the 18 various trappers they had killed during Chief Iron Eagle's rampage along the Green to avenge his two lost sons, War Eagle and Red Hawk! Additionally, Buck Snort and company were also now the proud owners of an additional 68 bundles of beaver 'Plus' taken from all the dead trappers 'caught not looking' by Chief Iron Eagle during his rampage. That and in addition to the 24 bundles of furs they themselves had trapped and bundled during the fall and so far during the spring beaver trapping seasons! Now Buck Snort and company just had to find a way to get all of those furs and huge horse herd safely to the site of the upcoming 1826 Rendezvous so they could be sold... AT LEAST BUCK SNORT AND COMPANY DID NOT HAVE TO WORRY ABOUT THE DISASTROUS EFFECTS OF EATING FOOD PREPARED WITH A METAL SPOON, AS HAD BEEN PROPHESIED AND WARNED ABOUT BY CHIEF IRON EAGLE'S MEDICINE MAN IN A VISION RECEIVED FROM THE GREAT SPIRIT BEFORE HE HAD VENTURED SOUTH ON HIS REVENGE TRAPPER-KILLING RIDE...

For the next week, Buck Snort and company found themselves working from almost dawn to dawn. First they had to build a larger horse corral in order to house all of their horses and those they had acquired from Chief Iron Eagle's thievery. Once the larger horse corral was completed, the men transferred their labor efforts towards building a new storage shed in order to house all of the bundles of furs Chief Iron Eagle had stolen from all of the trappers he and his warriors had killed, plus their own 24 bundles of beaver furs accumulated to date! All of those labors were conducted in addition to the men running their spring trap line and de-fatting and hooping their daily catches of beaver as well!

And when they weren't trapping and such, the men were nightly using their tanned leather reserves to begin constructing makeshift pack-saddles for their horse herd so they could pack out all of their bundles of beaver *'Plus'*... Suffice to say, Buck Snort and his contingent of trappers would be more than ready for their long journey down to the 1826 Rendezvous and the following celebration among their old friends, since they were now running on about three hours of sleep nightly!

CHAPTER ELEVEN

THE 1826 RENDEZVOUS, FREE TRAPPERS, A FORTUNE IS MADE

BY EARLY SPRING, the beaver had moved out of their prime and with that, Buck Snort and company pulled their beaver traps completing the end of the spring trapping season of 1826. Then the work began in earnest making preparations for the long journey down to the distant 1826 Rendezvous site in Willow Valley near the present-day town of Hyrum, Utah, at a place previously named "Malachite's Big Hole". Day after day, the men made makeshift hobbles for each of their new horses with leather strapping, and continued assembling more new packsaddles from the remaining leather supplies and a 'passel' of new tanned hides produced from a number of elk taken, processed and tanned throughout the year by the trappers.

Then because of their extremely large horse herd and number of soon to be loaded packhorses in their caravan, the trappers realized they would be the target of every horse-poor Indian, hungry grizzly bear, wandering off horses or bands of Indians on the 'hunt' for weak or defenseless fur trappers heading for the Rendezvous loaded with valuable furs. With those thoughts in mind, Buck Snort and company decided to be more than prepared for trouble should such occasions arise while out on the trail. That they did because from their past experiences, nothing was guaranteed out on the American Frontier except hard work, adventure, hardship and death for those unfortunates who were not prepared…

For the next week, the four trappers disassembled every one of their firearms, cleaned out the black powder and lead fouling and reassembled them so they would be more than ready when needed. Then all of the trappers' 'possibles' bags were refilled with new greased wads, one-pound tins of extra powder and new flints, and all the powder horns were refilled from their stored lead tins of new and fresh supplies of powder kept in storage. Then over the next few evenings, a substantial number of their lead pigs were melted down using the fire in the fireplace as their lead-melting heat source and converted to a large number of lead balls for their rifles and pistols. Then a large number of those newly cast lead balls were also placed in every man's 'possibles' bag as well. Next, extra rifle scabbards were assembled from reserve buffalo leather stocks and fitted to both sides of each man's saddle, so each trapper in any kind of firefight or emergency given just half a chance and a little warning would have three rifles close at hand, along with two pistols carried in their sashes. While Muskrat, Buck Snort and Wind Horse were cutting, assembling and sewing together the needed rifle scabbards for each of the men until their fingers were almost raw from all of the needle work, Clem was made responsible for killing a number of deer from around their campsite and converting them into jerky for the trip through Indian country on the way to the much-anticipated Rendezvous. That way, the trappers while en route the Rendezvous would be able to keep the sounds of firing from their weapons for daily meat stocks to a minimum while in known hostile Indian country. And by so doing, not alerting any unsavory nearby characters any more than they had to, as to the closeness of a valuable trapper caravan ripe for the picking with only four trappers providing protection against any kinds of attacks. Lastly, everyone's packs and riding gear were closely examined and any worn leather or buckles repaired or replaced.

At the same time because of their experience as young men under the care and guidance from blacksmith Cliff Fulton when living at the orphanage, Buck Snort and Wind Horse had also been trained as skilled farriers and had taken to that trade like a 'western wood tick to the flank of a mule deer'. As such, they drew the detail of examining all of their shod livestock to make sure their horseshoes were tightened or if in need of replacement, were so cared for from their keg of replacement horseshoes. As for their number of unshod Indian horses, they were left as they were because of the limited number of horseshoes in their replacement keg. That the men did figuring the Indians' unshod horses had made it that far and a few more miles would hopefully not cause those stock animals any dangerous problems.

Each evening at the end of the day's labors, the four trappers met around their supper firepit and discussed any shortfalls discovered in their preparations and then finding any, someone was assigned to 'fill the gap' as was necessary. However, one evening, the discussion around the campfire turned deadly serious as to the extremely tired trappers' futures as Mountain Men. At the end of supper when the men had broken out their clay pipes and cups of rum from the last of their dwindling supplies, the issue of where to go trapping during the coming 1826 fall and 1827 spring trapping seasons arose.

Buck Snort, because of his now recognized and earned abilities as the group's leader even though he was the youngest among them, started off the coming year's trapping location selection conversations. Putting his cup of rum down, Buck Snort, long having thought out the group's coming trapping season's fortunes began by saying, "I think we all need to think about what is in our future as Mountain Men for the coming fall and spring beaver trapping seasons. I have long thought about this and here is what I would like to discuss and ultimately propose to you men for your consideration. We have a good and sound cabin here at this location with a fur and extra provision storage shed to match, along with a horse corral that is more than adequate for any size horse herd we may have need for in the future as well. We have not even begun to reduce the beaver number in this area and now without Jones's group upriver and trapping above our current trapping location, we are 'eating high on the hog' when it comes to beaver number and future outstanding places to run our trap lines. The game herds here are more than adequate as our food sources and since we have killed off a large number of local grizzlies, that problem seems to have pretty much gone away." (Author's Note: The North American grizzly bear has the lowest fecundity rate of any mammal in all of North America! In the great bear's case, from the time of one's birth until that specific bear just born produces another cub to breeding age, takes approximately TEN YEARS! TEN YEARS... Hence it was very possible for the fur trappers in this story to significantly reduce or eliminate a local troublesome grizzly bear population after a short period of time by overshooting!

At one time in North American history, there were estimated to be approximately 100,000 grizzly bears roaming the entire United States. Today, that species numbers only about several thousand in all of the United States, not counting Alaskan grizzlies! That being the case, the grizzly bear in the lower 48 states was placed under complete protection under federal law, namely the Endangered Species Act of 1973. In 2017, there began a REALLY serious movement to remove the grizzly bear from its federal protection and institute a limited hunting season for the great bear, low population number or not! That low number in mind, it is extremely important that state and federal conservation agencies not be politically motivated by local politics or 'stampeded' by cattle and sheep ranching interests or "KNOW-NOTHINGS" IN THE GOVERNMENT IN WASHINGTON, to cause the species to be further destroyed as a result of weakened federal laws, anemic enforcement or basically complete lack of protection. In the face of constantly increasing human pressures, it has now become critical that the remaining number of 'lower 48' grizzly bears does not drop below their natural genetic viability threshold of population number that allows THAT SPECIES to normally and biologically reproduce its own kind successfully and not go extinct.

It is this Author's OPINION, based on his 32 years of state and federal wildlife law enforcement experience protecting national and international wildlife species, including the great bear from 1981-1998 as the Fish and Wildlife Service's Special Agent in Charge of the Region 6 Division of Law Enforcement in the Rocky Mountain Region, that consideration must also be given to those Americans yet to come, so they can enjoy the great bear's presence and magnificence over the taste of a lamb chop dinner or some poorly thought-out political decision made in Washington during these politically unsettled times...

From 1981 until 1998 and my retirement, THE SERVICE'S DIVISION OF LAW ENFORCEMENT WITH GREAT ON THE GROUND COOPERATION FROM SERVICE CROSS-CREDENTIALED FISH AND GAME WARDENS FROM WYOMING AND MONTANA, NATIONAL PARK SERVICE RANGERS FROM MY EIGHT-STATE REGION OF RESPONSIBILITY, AS WELL AS LEVEL FOUR FOREST RANGERS, WITH FORWARD THINKING DIRECTION AND SUPPORT FROM SENIOR PROGRAM MANAGERS OF THOSE CONSERVATION AGENCIES, WE BROUGHT THE GREAT BEAR BACK FROM ITS DRASTICALLY REDUCED POPULATION NUMBER TO THAT OF A BIOLOGICALLY HEALTHY SPECIES. THAT WAS DONE WITH

THOUSANDS OF HOURS OF MANY-TIMES DANGEROUS BACK COUNTRY HORSEBACK PATROLS AT ALL HOURS OF THE DAY AND NIGHT PROVIDING LAW ENFORCEMENT PROTECTION FOR THE BEAR, AS WELL AS SUPPLYING CONSERVATION INFORMATION TO ALL BACK COUNTRY USERS ON THE HERITAGE VALUE OF SUCH A MAGNIFICENT SPECIES! I WOULD LIKE TO THINK THAT THOSE GRIZZLY BEAR POPULATION RECOVERY SUCCESSES DURING THAT TIME PERIOD, AS A RESULT OF THE GREAT PERSONAL SACRIFICES BY ALL OF THOSE DEDICATED OFFICERS AND HUNDREDS OF THOUSANDS OF DOLLARS OF STATE AND FEDERAL MONIES SPENT, WERE NOT DONE SO IN VAIN BUT WERE DONE FOR THE LOVE OF OUR COUNTRY, THOSE PEOPLE YET TO COME, AND THE RIGHT THING TO DO... WILDLIFE DIES WITHOUT MAKING A SOUND. THE ONLY VOICE IT HAS IS YOURS AND IF YOU ARE NOT SQUALLING IN ITS DEFENSE LIKE A 'SMASHED CAT', THEN YOU ARE PART OF THE PROBLEM... THINK AMERICA!)

Then Buck Snort stopped for a moment, took a burning limb from the fire and re-lit his now gone-out pipe. Seeing that he still had a more than attentive group, Buck Snort began once again with, "Let me see, where the dickens was I in my thoughts before my damn pipe went out?

Oh yeah, the critters, especially the wolves. We have more wolves in country than we can shake a stick at and as far as winter trapping another year for those excellent furbearers, I see that as another opportunity as well when it comes to enriching our successes as trappers. As for feed and water, we are blessed with more than ample supplies here in our meadow as well as in the creek running by our horse corral. So, that being said, that is not a concern. Our winters up to this time in our lives haven't been that bad, we have a more than an adequate wood supply that is close at hand and our cabin location is pretty much out of the way from the really bad northwest winter winds and really bad weather." Then once again, Buck Snort's pipe went out and with that he gave up, knocked the ash out in his hand and tossed the ashes towards the firepit.

Laying his pipe down on his sitting log, Buck Snort began once again with, "Now for the negatives as I can see them. We seem to have bad neighbors to our north in the form of those damn killing Northern Arapaho." Upon saying those words, Buck Snort heard a number of agreeing grumbles coming from his group and a nodding of their heads in agreement as well. "Anyway as I was saying, they are a real concern. However, the four of us have had pretty damn good luck in holding our own when push came to shove and as such, I say we stay here and meet any threat they are able to present during this coming year.

Then if they continue to be a threat and we remain their targets, I say at that time we visit this situation once again and decide what we want to do. But for now, I say we remain armed to the teeth, watch out for each other and stick closely by one another when we are working or out hunting. Then if those damn Northern Arapaho want a damn good fight, we damn sure give it to them and show them the same quarter they show us! After all we need to remember, this country belongs to the "Red Man" since he was here first and we are the intruders. But by damn it from what I have seen and experienced, this country is big enough for all of us to pursue our interests, so I say we continue on. And lastly, if we can get all of these furs, horses and firearms we have collected from all of our fights this year and sell them at the Rendezvous to other less well-off trappers or the friendly Indians, we all will be very rich men if we can just survive and make it back alive to civilization! With that in mind, we won't have to ever work again in our lives if we can safely get all of our goods to the Rendezvous, declare ourselves as Free Trappers for the higher prices that will bring for our furs and in doing so, manage to 'keep our hair'. If successful in those endeavors, after that, we can then spend what we have earned and enjoy the rest of our lives. Then like I said, after one more year and we all survive this here beaver trapping thing, I say we take a look at our 'hole cards', namely our Letters of Credit and our health. If we are as rich as I think we will be by then, we can call it quits, go back to our homes in Missouri, buy up some land, settle down and have a passel of kids to do our bidding without worrying about a speeding lead ball, a zipping arrow, a bad horse wreck, freezing to death, or dying from Clem's bad cooking..."

With those last words, there were smiles and a little laughter around the firepit, as the rest of the men drew their last 'drags' from their pipes, finished their cups of rum and then Muskrat stood up and cleared his throat so he could be heard. "Well, now that Buck Snort the 'blabbermouth' is all through, I will have my say. To date, Buck Snort has been true to his word, sound in his leadership and a friend to us all. I don't think he will lead us astray and with that said, I say we follow his suggestions and lead. Now, I am missing my beauty sleep and intend to wake up tomorrow better-looking than any of you other swamp rats will look, so good night."

With that said, Clem and Wind Horse also rose, knocked out the ash from their pipes into the firepit and with a nod and a wink, Wind Horse said, "Sounds good to us what we heard this night. From all that you have said, I dare say you have been giving it plenty of thought. Good night, My Friend and Brother." With that, Wind Horse and Clem headed for the cabin and their sleeping furs as well, not wanting to miss out on any of their beauty sleep either and come out tomorrow looking like 'swamp rats'...

******

"HELLO THE CAMP! FREE TRAPPERS COMING IN! DON'T SHOOT!" bellowed out Charlie Poke, as his caravan of six Free Trappers and their horses hove into view below the Osprey Nest Camp as they slow-walked into the campsite from the area along the Green.

Upon hearing those words, Clem whirled around in surprise from his breakfast-making duties and at the same time, remembering the previous evening's conversation led by Buck Snort about Indian troubles, grabbed his rifle off a nearby sitting log and prepared to defend himself against any threat if it became necessary.

"You won't need that "smoke stick", Friend. Me and my Free Trappers come in peace. We smelled the wood smoke clear down by the river and upon seeing your cabin, figured this here would be a good place to light down off these nags, warm ourselves and maybe be treated to a breakfast of sorts," continued Charlie Poke. Then he quietly led his riding horse on foot trailed by four fully loaded packhorses right into camp. Behind him rode five more heavily bearded trappers each trailing their own three fully loaded packhorses as well. Moments later as Buck Snort, Wind Horse and Muskrat stumbled out from their cabin upon hearing strange human voices with rifles in hand, they too observed six buckskin-clad strangers in various stages of 'dismount' moving in close to the firepit. Surrounding the six arriving strangers were a jumble of 25 riding and packhorses, all with heads now extended down eagerly looking for a bit of grass to eat. As the horses eagerly sought out any blades of grass, Buck Snort, ever the 'horse man' saw that all of the strangers' horses appeared to have 'been ridden hard and put away wet'... Realizing the six strangers had some sort of a reason for pushing their valuable horses so hard, Buck Snort held his tongue and waited for any such explanation if one was to be offered.

Still holding their rifles at the ready, Buck Snort and company walked up to the six strangers and then as Buck Snort extended his hand in friendship said, "This here man by our fire is our camp cook named Clem. This ugly one with the long hair is the one we call Muskrat, his close at hand friend standing on his right is called Wind Horse from the Omaha Tribe of Indians, and my handle is Buck Snort. And don't ask about my name because it is a long story. If we get into danger, you and your men will discover why I have been given such a 'handle' and now go by that 'moniker'."

Smiling over being treated all friendly like by the four strange trappers he and his men had just met, Poke said, "Good enough. I don't go by poking into one's name so that explanation will just have to wait. We all be Free Trappers and have been so for some time. We just spent our fall and spring beaver trapping just east of here in a place called the "Wind River" on the lands of the friendly Shoshoni Indians. This here man is called "Black James" who was a slave at one time and is our biggest eater, especially when it comes to putting away Dutch oven biscuits. Next to him are the brothers "Luke" with the one we call "Broken-Hand" and that 'moniker' should be obvious and his younger brother called "Jeff". Then the mangy-looking one to my right is called "Jim Jensen" and the man with the grizzly bear scars running clear across his ugly mug is known to his friends as "Scar Face Charlie". As for me, I go by Charlie Poke and am more or less the leader of this here 'brigade' of trappers. That about does it for the introductions and if you be so kind, we all have been riding hard and until recently just ahead of a nasty band of Northern Arapaho Indians most of the night. Fortunately, about five miles back we saw to it that they would no longer make life miserable for us or any other trapper types... I just hope what we left behind after we finished will be a reminder to any other Indians who foster like inclinations when it comes to causing us trappers any 'heartburn'."

Then hearing no comments regarding the trappers' recent run-in with the 'Sons of the Prairies', Charlie Poke continued by saying, "We sure could use some vittles if you boys would be a-willing to share. We dumped most of the last of our provisions in order to lighten up the loads we was a-carrying so we could outrun those damn Indians. Since then, we have not 'et' any too good. Now, none of us are cowards when it comes to work, so if you allow us to unsaddle and unpack our mounts so they can feed and water, we all would be willing to pitch in and give you a hand in making up something for the mess of us to eat," continued Poke with a friendly and hopeful grin.

Caught up by the strangers' total friendliness, Clem walked over to their cabin and soon reappeared carrying two more large Dutch ovens by their wire bails (handles). Then while Poke and his company of Free Trappers moved their stock over to the corrals and began unpacking them, Buck Snort and Wind Horse went over to their meat pole and with the two of them straining over the weight, let down a half-section of a previously killed young moose. Then with a number of cuts with their sheath knives, the two men soon had removed an entire backstrap and a number of thick steaks from the animal's fat-laden hindquarter. Meanwhile, Clem was busy mixing up his entire large wooden mixing bowl with flour, water, salt, and yeast for the small mountain of Dutch oven biscuits he figured would soon be needed to feed ten hungry men. That he did as Muskrat brought forth two one-gallon jugs of honey purchased at the first Rendezvous and set them by the fire to warm up so they would pour more easily over the biscuits. Then Clem took the one-gallon kettle full of previously cooked pinto beans and hung it over the fire on their cooking iron over just a mess of coals at one end of the firepit so the beans would warm up slowly and not burn. Then not 'missing a lick', Clem got out their last two-gallon sheet iron kettle, walked over to the creek and half-filled it with water. Shortly thereafter after picking through a mess of dry pinto beans in a gunnysack and removing the sticks, chaff and bits and pieces of mouse and white-footed woodrat dung, Clem dumped those clean beans into the kettle of water to soak for the men's coming supper. By then Muskrat had retrieved their extra one-gallon coffee pot from their cabin, filled it with creek water and hung it on a hook over the fire so it would boil and soon be made into a second pot of coffee for their group of now ten men. Then with Wind Horse's assistance, the two men loaded all of their metal meat skewers with chunks of the rich moose meat and set it to cooking around the fire for the huge breakfast soon to come. That they did after removing with the tips of their sheath knives all of the gray jay and Northern chickadee poop left on the meat by the previously feeding birds pecking at the scraps of fat as the animal carcass hung from the trappers' meat pole...

By then, Charlie Poke and his men had unpacked all of their mounts, hobbled them and set them loose to mingle and feed with Buck Snort's men's large herd of livestock. As he did, sharp-eyed Buck Snort noticed that several of Poke's horses were walking uneasily and looking closer, could see several loose shoes flopping on their hooves as the horses walked by. Being a good man with horses and an especially fine farrier after being trained by Cliff Fulton back at the orphanage, Buck Snort mentioned to Poke what he had just observed regarding the horses' hooves as they walked by on their way to the meadow in which to feed and water.

"You have a good eye for horseflesh, Buck Snort. Me and my men have not had any opportunity to run our livestock by a blacksmith for over two years of living out here along the Wind River. As to be expected, some have thrown their shoes and others have flat worn their shoes out," said Poke, as he watched some of his sorry-looking horseflesh amble off into the meadow to happily feed and water with Buck Snort's horses.

"Well, I will tell you what. From all looks and appearances, Clem is planning on you and your men spending the night right here at our camp so you and your men can rest up, get some chow down into your bellies as well as letting your horses catch up on eating some good grasses. That being the case, me and my men may be of some assistance to you and that of your horses. Wind Horse and I are both excellent farriers. Additionally, we still have what is left of a keg of brand new horseshoes that we have not used on all of our livestock and the tools needed to do what is needed doing. Being that you and your men could really use some help when it comes to taking care of your horses, what say you spend another day and let Wind Horse and me have at them horses with the remainder of the 'shoes' in that keg and our farrier tools so we can re-shoe those animals that need them?" asked Buck Snort with his characteristic smile spelled clear across his bearded face.

For the longest time, Poke just closely examined Buck Snort's face as if trying to figure him out, especially in light of his most generous and much-needed offer. An offer that was exceptional based on the fact that the men were still basically strangers, that horseshoes were like gold out on the Frontier and as such, each and every one of them were sold to those trappers needing them by the pound... Then Poke spoke up once again and this time, he surprised the hell out of Buck Snort and those of his group of fellow trappers standing around within earshot with his response.

"Buck Snort, me and my men have suffered long and hard while out here on the Frontier and during our earlier lives. All of my men are good Christian men. We all came from a small town near St. Louis called "Marthasville", where we was raised as kids and when the pox tore through the local communities some years back, we all lost our families, including Black

James who is a "Freed Man"! Not expecting such losses, me and my men all from the same Methodist Church family, found it very difficult not to curse God for what he done to us and our families. In fact we was so mad over our losses, we six distraught men sold our farms, teamed up and headed out into the wilderness to try and rebuild our lives once again. However, every damn man among us has run afoul of the Devil with the loss of our families first and then while out here individually running our trap lines and trying to start over. And yet, every damned one of us have been plucked from those many fires of Hell and surprisingly survived. Collectively, all of us have survived being shot at by Indians, attacked by grizzly bears, been involved in horse wrecks, have damned near drowned and froze to death, and have not had a single day go by when we often went to our sleeping furs cold, wet and hungry! Having said that, me and my men have come to realize that God did not abandon us during those many life trials but we early on, sure as 'God makes green apples', abandoned him! Yet he did not forsake any of us in our times of need and as a result of us growing up and realizing that, we all have come back to the fold 'as one of his sheep' and to this day are still being led by our Lord and Savior, Jesus Christ. And this we have done out here in this almost God-forsaken land by being good Christian men at every moment in time from sunrise to sunset!"

Then Poke paused in what he had been saying, realizing he had just surprised the dickens
out of his new friend by being so open regarding
their lives based on what he was seeing in Buck
Snort's amazed-looking facial expression. Then
'gathering up his skirts' on what more he had to
say, Poke began again. "So, you see, the good
Lord continues to watch over us sinners, and
you with your offer to help us and our horses in
our time of need, just goes to show what all of us
have learned over time while living out here on
the Frontier. God and goodliness is everywhere
out here from the sunrises and sunsets to the
good word spoken by a true friend, such as you
just uttered. You just have to look for it and it
appears we once again have been blessed and
found it... Buck Snort, you and yours have just
made lifelong friends whether you know it or not
with six, 'once we were lost and now we have
been found', Christian men. Yes, we will take
your and Wind Horse's offer up and welcome
your kind treatment being rendered to our valuable livestock. That being said and realizing after
looking at all of your livestock, just how in blazes
do you and your three men plan on getting all
of your horses to the Rendezvous without losing
the lot and your hair as well?" asked Poke with
an incredulous look upon his face.

Standing there stunned over what he had just
heard about the histories of the six strange trappers and their trials in a land when most every-

one kept their personal lives to themselves and now the rather obvious regarding their over 50 extra horses, Buck Snort, caught off guard with Poke's question, just stammered in total surprise without saying anything...

"Good," said Poke with a smile on his face. "Me and my men because of your generous Christian offer to shoe our badly in need of help horses, will help the four of you get all of your horses to the Rendezvous realizing the value they represent out here on the Frontier. And if me and my damn straight-shooting trappers and Christian men can't get that done for our new friends, then I damn sure will want to know the reason why..."

That evening, the ten new friends feasted on spitted moose meat, potted beans, a small mountain of Dutch oven biscuits and almost two gallons of coffee. Poke had been right. His men ate like there was no tomorrow and Black James alone ate nine hot out of the Dutch oven biscuits all smeared with gobs of rich honey! True to his word, Black James was an 'eager eater', as Buck Snort and his men watched on in amazement over the amount of food the giant of a black man could put away. In fact, it was a damn good thing that Buck Snort and company had half of a moose carcass hanging from their meat pole and thankfully, it only took Clem three minutes to bake up a new batch of Dutch oven biscuits once his ovens got hot, otherwise the men could just see Black James eating the biscuits, Dutch oven and everything else around it… Additionally, Buck Snort and company still had a storage shed not only full of bundles of beaver *'Plus'* but had a large amount of supplies brought back to their storage shed from all the Indian-killed trappers that would more than feed the ten men. Especially enough supplies to feed the six new men who had previously tossed most of their supplies in order to outrun the Northern Arapaho chasing them.

The next morning was more of the same. Poke's men ate like they hadn't eaten in days but they were worth every pound of food they managed to put away. Right after breakfast, Poke had been right about the work ethics found in his men. Jeff Luke and Broken-Hand Luke, without being asked, grabbed up their rifles and walked out into the nearby meadow now dotted with over 70 horses happily feeding. True to Mountain Man style, the two brothers stationed themselves where they could best watch over the horses and preclude any Indians from storming into the meadow and running off a number of the valuable animals. Following that, Charlie Poke and Jim Jensen asked where Buck Snort and company kept their axes and saws and were soon hard at work cutting up a nearby lightning-struck dead pine tree and splitting up the 'rounds' for fuel for the men's cooking fires.

As for Clem and Scar Face Charlie, they bonded

like a couple of kid brothers and set about making sure all of the men had more than enough to eat. As they did, Scar Face Charlie relayed to Clem how he had gotten that huge scar clear across his face and was missing one ear because of a grizzly bear's surprise attack. It seemed before the story was finished, walking up onto a grizzly bear sleeping in his day bed more times than not, could cost a surprised fur trapper an ear and a nice rip of flesh from off the face... However, that wasn't the only problem that happened that day as Scar Face Charlie had been heading off into the brush to take a big dump when he had walked right up onto the sleeping bear. After the attack and the rest of his trapper buddies had killed the bear, patched him up and sewed back the flesh over his missing ear, it seems they had also discovered that Scar Face Charlie in his extreme fear over being attacked, had messed in his buckskin pants BIG TIME when the bear had risen up and attacked... Lastly Muskrat, Black James, Buck Snort and Wind Horse went into the meadow and separated out small numbers of Charlie Polk's horses with horseshoe problems. Those were brought back to Buck Snort's corral and there throughout the next four days, every one of Charlie's horses had their hooves cleaned, worn-out horseshoes removed, hooves trimmed and new horseshoes attached. As it turned out, every horseshoe remaining in Buck Snort's keg of shoes was used except two! Then Clem and Scar

Face Charlie got out their nails and hammered the two horseshoes over the cabin doorway for good luck.

As it turned out, Charlie Polk and company stayed a lot longer than just for supper as had been surmised earlier. The two groups of men got together and decided they would travel as one group down to the next Rendezvous site that had been decided upon by the trappers at the first Rendezvous. That decision was made by the group of trappers for several reasons. Because of Buck Snort's generosity in shoeing Charlie's herd of horses, Charlie and his men had decided the Christian thing to do was to assist Buck Snort's group of trappers to the Rendezvous because of their large and almost unmanageable huge herd of Indians' and trappers' horses. That plus the men not only liked each other's company but for the protection the ten trappers derived from traveling all together as well.

So for the next week, the ten men made preparations for the long and dangerous trip to the southwest and the location of the 1826 Rendezvous located in Willow Valley near current-day Hyrum, Utah, at a place named Malachite's Big Hole. First on the list, Buck Snort and company had to locate a dry and sandy ground location near their current campsite whereby they could build a 'cache' so they could leave those articles they did not need in order to make the lengthy trip. That they did because Buck Snort had convinced his men the best thing to do was to return to their current campsite and spend their next fall and spring beaver trapping seasons in that location. After two days locating, digging up, providing interior roof supports and lining a 'proper' cache with grasses gathered from along the creek so the stored provisions would not get moldy or wetted, the extra gear and provisions not needed for the trip to the Rendezvous and other implements were stored underground. As it turned out, not only did the men have a jumble of their own gear to store underground but almost an entire year's worth of provisions and implements gathered up from Jack Jones's encampment after the Northern Arapaho had killed three of the trappers in camp and a fourth one in a subsequent battle. And being that Jones and company had purchased enough supplies for a whole year, what Buck Snort and company had gathered up after the battle was almost enough to carry them through another year by itself without reprovisioning! Then the very large cache site was thoroughly covered up and hidden from casual view by any Indians passing by, smelled out by hungry grizzly bears or just discovered by curious wolves upon seeing the ground covering the cache site had been altered slightly.

Come the chosen morning set for departure to the Rendezvous site, all ten men were up way before daylight. Up way before daylight because the men had so many horses to saddle and pack before they could depart. As Clem and Scar Face Charlie tended to their breakfast fires and 'makings', the remaining eight men tended to the pack and riding horse preparations for the trip ahead. Partway through the horse-packing preparations, the men adjourned for their breakfasts and then it was back to their packing preparations. Finally by noon, the men had loaded all of their bundles of furs, cooking implements, provisions, sleeping furs, and the like.

Then for the next 14 days of slow travel, the men headed out and down along the Green River. Then ultimately leaving the Green, the trappers headed to the southwest into Willow Valley, near the current-day town of Hyrum, Utah. (Author's Note: "History" is not exactly sure if the 1826 Rendezvous site was actually held near Hyrum or Cove, Utah. The Author has chosen Hyrum in this story because it is easier to locate on a map so the reader can follow the story's progress. However, the actual location was clearly within the physical territorial limits of Old Mexico during that time period.) Upon leaving the Green River, the men were treated to a special change in their diets. BUFFALO were now found in abundance and being the favorite meat of Mountain Men, the men feasted every night and morning upon delicious-tasting buffalo meat instead of having to eat the usual elk, deer and moose meat!

Finally riding into the south end of the scenic Willow Valley along the "Blacksmith Fork River" now led by Charlie Poke, who knew the way having previously trapped in that area only a little further to the west, the men quickly spotted an inviting-looking grove of cottonwoods. Shortly thereafter they headed for and set up their camp under the shade of the cottonwood trees and alongside a small stream. Then the work began once again as the men separated out their bundles of furs and other packed items into two basic campsites alongside one another. Then after Clem and Scar Face Charlie had scampered around gathering up every loose stick of wood they could find, they then scraped out the needed firepit and set up their cooking area. As they did, Buck Snort, Wind Horse and Charlie Poke, along with two now unloaded packhorses headed out to find the nearest herd of buffalo before they were spooked out of the country by all the other arriving trappers and friendly Indians, seemingly quietly melting into the area from every point of the compass.

Well, that quietness of arrival was for everyone except for the Wind River Band of Shoshoni Indians. They could be heard coming from a long way away. Heard with their arrival were the many happy sounds of men, women and children talking and laughing, numerous barking dogs and a large dust cloud accompanying and 'announcing' the arrival of the Indians' entire horse herd and encampment! Soon there was an even larger dust cloud forming on the northern edge of the Rendezvous site as the Indians set up their large encampment, barking dogs, milling horses watched over by small boys and all... Within the hour after their arrival found large hunting parties going forth so they could kill enough buffalo for their entire encampment's meals.

Four hours later the three trappers who had left earlier on a buffalo hunt returned to their campsite with both horses' panniers fully loaded with bloody and dripping fresh buffalo meat. Then the scramble was on as the two Luke brothers headed off for a nearby stand of pine timber with axes in hand. An hour later they returned dragging a long pine pole behind their horses. Shortly thereafter, the ten trappers had erected a stout as all get-out camp's meat pole and soon quarters of the fresh buffalo were gently swinging in the wind cooling out and forming a glaze on the great-tasting meat soon to come.

Shortly thereafter, the men's campsite smelled of boiling coffee, spitted buffalo meat merrily cooking away over an open fire along with the smell of Clem's Dutch oven biscuits. Just as the rest of the group of buffalo hunters finished hobbling all of their riding and packhorses so they could be better controlled around other arriving trappers' horses, Scar Face Charlie let out a yell that supper was ready. Suffice to say, Scar Face Charlie did not have to let everyone know that supper was ready a second time... In fact,

Black James stood there first in line waiting to be served with his characteristic smile running almost from ear to ear knowing what was soon to grace his plate and palate. Within scant moments of letting the men know that supper was ready, all that one could hear around that campsite were the sounds of wood burning in the firepits, the clanking of Dutch oven lids being lifted so fresh baked biscuits could be retrieved from the Dutches, additional buffalo meat sputtering over the open flame, along with the happy sounds of hungry men doing what they liked doing best, namely eating their favorite meat from the buffalo...

The next morning as Clem and Scar Face Charlie prepared the men's breakfast, the rest of the men checked their horse herd making sure the horses' hobbles were still secure and that none of their horses had wandered off and gotten mixed up with those of other trappers or the now more incoming streams of friendly Shoshoni Indians looking for a good camping and horse-grazing site, so they could subsequently trade their furs and secure for their women the white man's much-desired goods.

For the next eight days of May, in between a number of cold and wet spring storms, the trappers and friendly Indians made the most of a number of 'happy to be there' celebrations. At first the celebrations started off slowly as the trappers and Indians wandered about looking for old friends and avoiding enemies. Then as more and more trappers and Indians streamed into the large and getting crowded campsite, the celebrations grew more diverse, noisy and long-winded. There were many get-togethers of old friends to see who had 'gone under' and reacquaint each other with those who had managed to live through another 'sunrise' and 'keep their hair'. Evening meals were shared with other arriving trappers as were numerous hunting trips in order to keep fed the increasing number of meat-hungry men. Soon the days as well as the evenings grew more and more rowdy and noisy as the men anxiously awaited the arrival of the pack strings coming from faraway St. Louis bringing the much-needed supplies. And hopefully this Rendezvous unlike the Rendezvous held in 1825, great supplies of rum and whiskey! (Author's Note: General Ashley in 1825 at the first Rendezvous, had by oversight, forgotten to include in his long list of needed supplies for the trappers any rum or whiskey! That was the LAST time any supplier at the Rendezvous forgot to bring the much-desired rum and whiskey supplies…)

Finally from trappers' campsites at the edge of the Rendezvous location, a lot of yellin' and hellin' was heard! General Ashley on May the 25th hove into view from his long 78-day trip clear from St. Louis bringing the trappers and Indians their much-needed provisions. Almost from horizon to horizon, General Ashley's heavily loaded mule and horse pack strings numbering over 300 animals and their 30 herders streamed into the Rendezvous site amidst many cheers and yells of excitement. Then once General Ashley set up his camp, he held off setting up for business wanting to make sure he did not begin trading until most everyone had arrived bringing their valuable furs, hides and peltries.

(Author's Note: General Ashley, the man largely responsible for creating the Rendezvous system of trade, gambled greatly on the system he had created. At great personal expense, he had purchased many thousands of dollars' worth of supplies, arranged for huge pack trains to bring those supplies across thousands of miles of wild and dangerous territory, fought off Indian attacks, forded swollen rivers and finally arrived at a previously selected location out in the middle of nowhere on the Frontier. There he traded his supplies for valuable furs and then upon completion of the trading, headed back many thousands of miles to places like St. Louis in order to sell and recoup his huge and risky investment.

That General Ashley and eventually others did because by the 1500's, beaver were essentially extinct throughout Europe. The fur trade in Europe was driven by the Europeans' demand for furs and skins of all types. That was because the standard of living was higher and increasing, as was the demand for clothing that was fashionable, comfortable and warmer. Textile manufacturing in that day and age produced clothing that was rough, course and limited in colors. Whereas clothing made from furs and hides was soft, warm and durable. Collateral with the increasing demand for clothing that was warm, durable and comfortable was the initiation and expansion of a rich furbearing industry in North America. With a full-blown expansion and exploration ongoing in America and a fur demand in Europe that could hardly be satisfied, the market for American furs of all kinds exploded and the North American fur trade era was off and running.)

Finally realizing that most all of the trappers and friendly Indians who wanted to trade their furs for his goods had finally arrived and figuring he would need another 70 or so days to be able to return safely weather-wise to St. Louis, General Ashley opened up his trade for business. That he did figuring he needed to arrive back in St. Louis no later than the month of September. September being the usual last month of good weather before the winter storms roared throughout the western part of the country. With General Ashley realizing how many days of travel back to civilization he was facing and not wanting to do so during the winter months, had his traders lay out their wares for business at the 1826 Rendezvous site!

Come the first morning of trading in one's furs and peltries for the coming years' worth of supplies, General Ashley sent 'criers' throughout the settlement of trappers and Indians announcing the beginning of the highly anticipated event! Instantly, there was a mad scramble to round up one's horses, load them with the furs, hides and peltries to be traded and race to where the fur buyers and graders were gathered to begin the much-anticipated event! At Buck Snort and Charlie Poke's camp, the ten trappers in an orderly fashion began packing up all of their furs to be traded. Once everyone had helped everyone else get all of their horses packed, off went a team of trappers to conduct the business of trade. However, there were also men left back in their camp to make sure their horses, extra firearms and remaining provisions did not 'wander' off into the hands of those trappers or Indians from other camps who were 'light fingered'!

Moving into a line of trappers waiting their turn to trade in their furs, Buck Snort, Wind Horse, Charlie Poke and Scar Face Charlie just visited with several friends while they waited. With six graders and sorters working the line of trappers, it wasn't long before Charlie Poke moved up to General Ashley's sorters and graders. As he did, General Ashley recognizing Buck Snort, walked back into the line of trappers waiting their turn for his graders and sorters to examine each man's catch.

"Good Morning, Buck Snort and Wind Horse. I see that the two of you kept your hair for another year," said General Ashley, and then he stopped speaking as his eyes swept down the long line of heavily packed horses obviously belonging to Buck Snort and Wind Horse. Stepping out from the long line of horses, the General counted by using his finger pointing at each horse and when he finished counting 32 horses, his eyes just swung back to those of Buck Snort with a look of disbelief spelled clear across his face. Then the General said, "What the hell is going on, Buck Snort? All 32 of those horses can't all belong to you and your men. What the hell is going on?" said Ashley, speaking now in clipped tones of words not really believing what he was seeing.

"General, all of those horses and the furs they are packing belong to me and my men. They came as a result of me and my men having to kill off a mess of Northern Arapaho who were killing trappers up and down the Green River and stealing all of their furs. We put a stop to that killing and since the original owners of those furs were all dead, we took their furs as ours and wish to trade them in along with the rest of our own furs and pelts...," said Buck Snort, as his eyes never left those of the still looking on in disbelief, General.

"Well, Hell, Buck Snort. That will amount to a bundle of money at $3 per 'Plus'," said Ashley, as his eyes almost 'read nothing but dollar signs'!

"I have been meaning to speak to you about that, General," said Buck Snort, now also speaking in 'clipped' tones himself. "Me and my men have served under you for the time required under our original contracts that all of us signed with you and Major Henry. The way we see it, none of us are any longer bound by those earlier contracts as company trappers, and now we all wish to be considered as "Free Trappers", and paid accordingly," said Buck Snort, whose 'determined looking' eyes never left those of General Ashley's!

For the longest time, both men just looked at each other like a 'hungry robin would look at a worm in the springtime'…

"Well, Buck Snort, now that you mention it, you are correct. Your company contract and those of the rest of your party of trappers have expired as well. That said, you and your group of trappers are no longer bound by the contract's original language regarding being paid 'halves' as a "Company Trapper" for your catches. But you and your men will still be bound to pay the prices I have set on my goods because of all the risks I have taken in just getting them safely here," said General Ashley, as his eyes continued 'hungrily' looking up and down at Buck Snort's long line of heavily laden horses… Horses that the General knew carried many thousands of dollars in valuable furs once he got them into his hands and later sold them back in St. Louis at a major fur house for even higher prices.

"That being understood, me and my men also wish to sell most of the horseflesh you are seeing in this long line of horses, as well as a number of fine firearms we took from the hands of those murdering damn Northern Arapaho if you would be interested," said Buck Snort, full well knowing that the General's company always had need for extra horses and firearms.

"That will be a deal," said Ashley, as his eyes once again looked 'hungrily' at the long line of well-cared for horseflesh quietly standing in line waiting to be unpacked so they could go off and 'put on the feed bag'.

Then Buck Snort stuck out his hand for the General to shake confirming the deal. Without any hesitation at all, General Ashley's hand shot out and he shook Buck Snort's hand as if he was pumping a water pump handle in his excitement over making such a huge deal. True, he had to purchase Buck Snort's beaver *'Plus'* for $6 apiece at Free Trapper rates instead of just $3 per *'Plus'* at Company Trapper prices, but he could still make a profit once he got all of those furs back in St. Louis and a rather nice one!

Then the General turned saying to a near at hand fur grader, "Carl, I want you to personally take this next trapper's line of furs. You grade them fairly and they are to receive $6 for all of their Made Beaver and $4.50 for the smaller or lesser-graded ones." Then the General turned saying, "Bring me your horseflesh three days hence after the rush by the other trappers to sell their furs has died down somewhat. Swing them by where we have set up our blacksmiths to tend to other horses in need and they will be doing the grading, buying and selling based on age, condition and temperament."

With those words, the General hurriedly left Buck Snort and Wind Horse to go and tend to an argument between several other trappers and another one of the General's teams of sorters and graders.

By late in the day, General Ashley had purchased Buck Snort's 92 bundles of beaver 'Plus', most of which had been graded out as Made Beaver (adult), numbering 5,543, for a total of $33,120! They then also received an additional $4,050 for their wolf pelts and lastly, $1,400 for their 14 grizzly bear rugs! When the business portion of the deal involving furs and pelts was totaled, Buck Snort and company received a company Letter of Credit from General Ashley totaling $38,570, making Buck Snort's trappers rich men! And they still had a rather large horse herd to sell to the General in three days when the push to sell one's furs had died down somewhat, as well as 40 flintlock rifles, 15 pistols and one Togia rifle... Later when General Ashley had signed the Letter of Credit and handed it over to Buck Snort, the trapper glanced at it, folded up the document, walked over to his riding horse and placed it into his saddlebag along with his other Letters of Credit received in transactions from the years before. Then Buck Snort and Wind

Horse gathered up their horse herd and slowly herded them back to their campsite so they could tell the rest of their company they were now rich men...

Three days later, Buck Snort and company rounded up the number of dead trappers' horses and those from the dead Indians and moved them over to the area where General Ashley had set up a number of blacksmiths and farriers to serve the trappers' and Indians' horse-related needs. Keeping out a total of 15 of the best horses for themselves, including Buck Snort's pinto 'Buffalo Horse', the men presented 52 horses to the lead blacksmith to examine and offer prices based on a per animal basis. Six hours later, Buck Snort walked over to his big pinto, opened up his saddlebag and placed another Letter of Credit therein totaling $4,800! That figure added to the men's previous Letter of Credit of $38,570, totaled $43,370! When Buck Snort announced what the final total of their Letters of Credit amounted to, namely $43,370, the men were hopping around and squalling in joy like sandhill cranes during their spring mating season... Like their leader Buck Snort had promised, they were all rich men! (Author's Note: For comparison, in that day and age, a working man made around $400 per year for his labors!)

And Buck Snort and his company still had 40 flintlock rifles, 15 single shot horse pistols and one Togia rifle to sell. So, on the way back to their camp, the four men split up and hitting different trapper and Indian encampments, put out the word that they had a passel of good rifles and pistols for sale over at their encampment in case anyone needed a new one or extra firearms. That evening, amidst the noise of celebrations going on around them, Buck Snort's camp was visited many times by a number of trappers and an even larger number of Shoshoni Indians all in the need of better rifles and pistols. After those trappers and Indians needing new firearms had traded beaver *'Plus'* for their weapons of choice, Buck Snort had in turn traded those beaver skins received for those firearms back to General Ashley for another Letter of Credit amounting to $822.50. Buck Snort did not factor that Letter of Credit in on their total because he planned on using that amount to purchase the provisions they would need for the coming trapping seasons, few as they would need. Figuring in the fact that his group of trappers still had a cache site back at their cabin loaded mostly with Jack Jones's annual provisions originally for four men, he figured they would be very selective in their coming purchases. But they would still make sure their supplies of expensive rum would be more than adequate when facing the Frontier's cold nights… Like he had advised his fellow trappers earlier, they were still very rich men as long as they could 'keep their hair'. And they would remain so, especially when they factored into their current Letters of Credit what they would earn during the coming 1826 fall beaver trapping season and that of the 1827 spring beaver trapping season as well... However, Buck Snort and company had one small problem. Throughout their sales of rifles and pistols, no one, especially the Shoshoni warriors, after looking at the gaily decorated Togia rifle, wanted what they were now calling once they learned of its 'story', the "Ghost Rifle"!

Then to make sure they got to purchase all of the supplies they would need for the coming year, Buck Snort and company headed for that part of the Rendezvous site set aside for displaying and selling the available wares that General Ashley had brought that one would need for another year afield. There after discussing among themselves the supplies they still possessed back at the cache site, figured out what they would need and with Clem doing the shopping and the rest of the men chiming in on their personal wants, selected out and made ready for purchasing those still-needed supplies.

First on their list were six eight-pound lead tins of rifle powder and four four-pound lead tins of pistol powder, 100 pounds of lead pigs, eight flat wooden kegs of Fourth Proof Rum, eight lead tins of powdered yeast (for making biscuits and cobbler crusts), five 50-pound bags of green coffee beans, eight 50-pound bags of flour, two 50-pound bags of rice, four 50-pound bags of pinto beans, two 50-pound bags of dried apple slices (cobblers), four 50-pound bags of brown sugar cones, a 20-pound sack of hard candy, one keg of horseshoes, one 50-pound keg of nail spikes, leather strapping (saddle/packsaddle repairs), two 20-pound bags of flints, two dozen fire starters (easily lost or broken), four heavy duty files for axes and shovels, a new 4'-long single buck saw, one sack of assorted buckles, new wide brimmed hats for each man, two new capotes for each man, eight woolen blankets for sleeping or making new capotes, a new saddle for Clem, two dozen socks for each man, new gloves for each man, moccasin-making leather, four new leather-working awls, two skinning knives with the bevel on one side, ten bottles of castor, six tins of bag balm, a 20-pound tin of cinnamon, four large whetstones, and on it went until the men figured with what they had back in their cache and what they were purchasing, they would have more than enough for the four men for over a year if it became necessary. As it turned out, with their Letter of Credit from the sale of all the firearms they had compiled after their run-ins with the Indians and from the dead trappers, there was enough credit left over for three more kegs of rum, eight carrots of chewing/smoking tobacco and eight new clay pipes because they were easily lost or broken…

That afternoon the men arrived back at their stack of goods and provisions left under the care of Ashley's men and soon all was loaded upon their packhorses. About then General Ashley arrived and wished the men well for the coming trapping seasons and shared several cups of company rum with them as well. It was then that Buck Snort got an idea and after a quick ride back to their encampment and return, presented the Togia rifle to General Ashley as a sign of respect... (Author's Note: The next day, General Ashley was approached by Mountain Men Jedediah Smith, William Sublette and David Jackson and after extensive discussion, sold out his company that he co-founded, a company named "The Ashley-Henry Fur Trade Company", 'lock, stock and barrel'. The three Mountain Men, new owners of the old Ashley company, promptly named their new company, "The Rocky Mountain Fur Company", which went on to become a giant in the fur trade business in the following years of the trade... General Ashley went on to return to St. Louis and sold his furs for many thousands of dollars. General William Henry Ashley (1778-1838), during his lifetime was a miner, land speculator, territorial militia officer, frontiersman, trapper, fur trader, U.S. Congressman (1831-34), and first Lt. Governor of Missouri (1820-24). Upon death, he was buried atop an Indian burial mound. The Togia Rifle or "Ghost Rifle" as it was called by Indians leery of its bloody past and presented to General Ashley by Buck Snort as a gift of friendship, has been lost to American history… However, there are a number of examples of such similarly tack-decorated rifles in a number of modern-day museums.)

That evening as Clem and Scar Face Charlie busied themselves around the cooking pits preparing the trappers' suppers, a discussion was being held regarding the men's return to their trapping grounds. That discussion went on into the night long after supper had been eaten and a number of additional cups of rum consumed. Finally it was decided the two groups of trappers would spend one more week at the Rendezvous site in celebration and then they would leave the day after and head back to their trapping grounds along the Green and Wind Rivers. In so doing, the decision was made that the two groups of trappers would travel together for the company and protection it offered against any hostile Indian attacks.

For the next week, the Rendezvous celebrations 'swirled around' the trappers like muddy river water as singing, shooting, horse racing, wrestling contests and many communal meals were held among their old and newly made friends as well. Being Free Trappers, Buck Snort and company made sure they visited the many Shoshoni women known for their talents at making beautifully tanned bighorn leather shirts that were heavily beaded and flashy looking. In fact, Buck Snort found himself visiting one beautiful and young Shoshoni woman, daughter to Wind

River Band Chief White Eagle, several times! Buck Snort could not get over her beauty and engaging ways when he was in her presence as she worked at form fitting several heavily beaded buckskin shirts for him. After several visits and purchases of beautifully beaded buckskin shirts, the beautiful young Shoshoni woman finally shared her name with Buck Snort. After asking her name several times, the young Shoshoni woman finally quietly said that her name was "Chenoa", which in her language meant "White Dove". The whole time that Chenoa was talking to Buck Snort, a white fur trapper, she, out of respect, kept her beautiful eyes cast downward in accordance with her culture. About then, Shoshoni Chief White Eagle strode into the tipi and all discussion between Buck Snort and Chenoa ceased. However, the fitting work on his latest beaded buckskin shirt progressed without a word being spoken and just gestures made on her part when Buck Snort needed to hold out an arm for measurement or the like...

The next day, Buck Snort visited Chenoa's tipi, picked up his newly beaded buckskin shirt and left six Made Beaver *'Plus'* as payment. However, later that afternoon, found Buck Snort once again at the trader's campsite purchasing several strings of red and blue glass beads and a bolt of bright vermillion cloth. Then mounting and spurring his pinto, Buck Snort headed for Shoshoni Chief White Eagle's tipi with his gifts of red and blue glass beads and a bolt of vermillion cloth for Chenoa as a gift of thanks for all the beautiful work she had done making him several beaded shirts. That and another opportunity for him to get better acquainted with Chenoa! However, when Buck Snort arrived at Chief White Eagle's encampment, he found it abandoned! Asking around, Buck Snort discovered that Chief White Eagle had left early that morning and was returning to his summer encampment in the Wind River Mountains... Downcast, Buck Snort collected up his glass beads and bolt of cherished red vermillion, mounted his horse and slowly rode back to his encampment. As he rode back to his encampment, Buck Snort physically felt like something wonderful had been lifted up and removed from his body...

Chapter Twelve

MUSKRAT'S MOOSE MADNESS, "WINTER BEAR" UP ON THE GREEN...

TWO DAYS LATER, Buck Snort and company along with Charlie Poke's band of trappers saddled their riding horses, packed their packhorses and left the 1826 Rendezvous site for their trapping destinations along the Green River and up along the Wind River. However before leaving, the trappers had discovered that the evening before a meeting had been held by a number of the trappers and it had been decided that a location called "Sweet Lake" or "Bear Lake" in current-day Utah would be the 'home' for the 1827 Rendezvous. That was IF the two teams of trappers decided to return instead of quitting the fur trapping business and upon taking their fall and spring furs, heading for St. Louis to sell their furs and retire from the business. (Author's

Note: Research into the American fur trade has revealed that most trappers lasted approximately 2.7 years trapping out on the Frontier before they died, were killed or gave up fur trapping and returned to the civilized world.)

For the next ten days without event, Buck Snort and Charlie Poke's trappers left the current-day State of Utah which was then in Mexico Territory, traveled northeasterly across the Green River Valley and into the Rocky Mountains. Being that they weren't pushing an additional herd of 50-plus horses as they had been when coming to the Rendezvous, they were able to make it back to the Osprey Nest Camp of Buck Snort and company in just ten days instead of the 14 it took them to make it to the site of the second Rendezvous. Once there, Charlie Poke's trappers held up for several days resting and letting their horses put on the 'feed bag' in preparation for the remainder of their long and hard trip further to the northwest across the Wind River Mountains to their previous old campsite and beaver trapping grounds along the Wind River.

However, true to Charlie's word about his men being good Christians and possessing a good work ethic, they worked together with Buck Snort's trappers putting up their friends' winter wood supply, spending a day on a big game hunt when they collectively killed six elk, nine mule deer and a moose. The meat from those animals was then brought back into Buck Snort's campsite, hung from their meat poles for daily meals, or deboned and the meat processed into thin strips and put onto the meat smoking racks for processing into jerky used during the winter months. As for the valuable hides from those animals, they were de-fatted, stretched and the tanning process begun so their valuable leather could be used somewhere along the line. Thanks to the help from Charlie's men, Buck Snort's company of trappers were already way ahead of the coming winter months' work and the rapidly advancing beaver trapping season. Lastly, the entire crew of trappers dug up the cache site, removed all of the goods stored underground and placed them into their cabin and storage shed for safekeeping away from the coming bad weather. Then during the several evenings Buck Snort and Charlie's men were together, they broke out their rum supply and saw to it that everyone was more than 'relaxed' come time for everyone to head to their sleeping furs for a night's rest after their hard day's work.

Then to Buck Snort's surprise that first evening they were back in camp and after eating a huge meal to satisfy the needs of the hardworking men, Charlie Poke spoke up by saying, "How much longer do you and your men plan on trapping out here on this Frontier? After all, you and your men, after selling off all of those furs, extra horses and firearms, should be pretty near set for life back in the civilized world in Missouri if you so choose."

"I don't know," said Buck Snort after being asked a question neither he nor his men had really discussed. "It's going to depend on our health, our success as trappers and if those damn Northern Arapaho leave us alone or constantly make our living out here dangerous as sin," said Buck Snort slowly, having been caught off guard by the direction, tone and tenor of Charlie's question.

"Well, you can't stay out here forever. If you try and do that, you are more than likely going to end up as a bear scat out on the hillside, wiggling your last with a bevy of arrows sticking out from your moth-eaten carcass, rolled over upon and busted up by a bumble-footed horse, freeze to death or just plain damn starve," said Charlie Poke, as he stared into the campfire with kind of a funny faraway look plastered clear across his heavily bearded face.

"What are you saying, Charlie?" asked Buck Snort, as he took another pull on his pipe and let the rich-tasting smoke slowly swirl away from his face and upward into the constant cloud of now-fleeing mosquitoes that always seemed to be present and hovering around each of the trappers around the campfire come the cool evenings.

"Buck Snort, me and the boys have been talking among ourselves lately whenever we get a quiet moment together and the time to think about our futures as trappers. Just look at the six of us. Me and Jeff Luke are so stove up from wading around in those damn icy cold winter and early spring waters setting our beaver traps, that it takes the two of us almost an hour each morning just to warm up our rheumatism by a fire so we can walk or even mount up into our saddles. Scar Face Charlie has only one eye that works really well after that damn bear attack, and he still has nightmares at night about having his head in the mouth of that damn old grizzly bear afore we killed it as it was a-squeezing his head until he figured it would explode! As for Jim Jensen, he still is carrying a stone arrowhead in his groin from a battle we had with the Sioux years back, and he is saying that arrow point is not getting any better but hurting him a lot more, jabbing at his insides when he is riding in a horse's saddle all day long. In fact, he is now noticing it is hard to piss without passing blood! Black James is complaining more and more about not being with people who look like him or being able to feel the soft skin and warmth of a loved one lying alongside of him come the cool nights. And lastly, Broken-Hand Luke is finding that his bad hand is getting worse by the month. So much so that it is causing a lot of numbness moving further and further up his arm, clear to his shoulder. Besides, he is finding it harder and harder to quick-load his rifle in battle and is afraid the day is coming when he will only be able to get one shot off in battle and then he will be an easy kill by a tomahawk-wielding "War Hoop" as he tries reloading with just his one good hand!"

For the longest time after detailing the physical, emotional and mental woes his men were feeling as a result of living the hard life out on the Frontier and not having the best luck, Charlie Poke just looked into the crackling fire like he was looking for some answers contained within the dancing flames. Then Charlie said, "I think this is our last year beaver trapping over on the Wind River. Thankfully we are among an Indian people who respect us whites and work with us on a daily basis. And to be quite frank with you, it is getting harder and harder for me and the boys to keep our hands off those damn pretty Shoshoni women at the end of a day's hard work. And if we try to get any closer to them damn pretty women, I feel we will wear out our welcome and either be asked to leave or be run off by their young bucks who want those women for themselves!" (Author's Note: The Mountain Men to a man, according to research, considered the Shoshoni women the most beautiful of all of the Indian women encountered out on the Frontier. Hence the high number of Mountain Men, according to numerous research documents reviewed by the Author, who married into the Shoshoni Nation of People and lived out their lives as a tribal member. That plus the Shoshoni peoples, ever since the days of the Lewis and Clark Expedition, had been friendly to most whites, which made for an easy living arrangement among the tribal members if the whites so chose.)

Upon hearing those words from Charlie Poke, Buck Snort felt an almost physical feeling moving throughout his body. Then without uttering a single word regarding the issue with the beautiful Shoshoni women, his mind flooded back to his brief and wonderful earlier encounter with Chenoa and his later efforts to bring her some prized gifts coveted among many Indian women. It was only then that he realized he did in fact miss some of what the civilized world had to offer. Then Buck Snort's mind spun back to what Charlie Poke had said about the wealth he and his men had accumulated and what they might be going to do with it…

Then physically shaking his head as if to rid those thoughts he had from his mind, Charlie began speaking to Buck Snort once again. "Buck Snort, me and the boys have amassed a pretty good nest egg after our four years of successful beaver and winter wolf trapping as well. That in mind, me and the boys have come to the conclusion that come the spring of this coming year when the beaver go out of their prime, if all of us are still alive, we are going to pull up our stakes, return to St. Louis, sell our furs and redeem our Letters of Credit. The only concern that we have is to do that, we must traverse through the lands of those damn dreaded Arikara Indians. Ever since they lost their most beloved chief to a white man's disease, they have been on the warpath with all white men. True, there are the six of us and right fair shots we be, but there is always that stray arrow or bullet clearing any of us from our saddles and then what do we have… I am kind of hoping that the six of us run across a number of other trappers who want to return to St. Louis at the same time. If we do, we will join up with them and with a larger group be able to safely cross the lands of those killing sons-a-bitches. That being said, maybe we can send one of our own over to your camp come the end of spring trapping to see if you fellas want to throw in with us and then we would have ten good men to attempt such a dangerous journey through the land of the Arikara and the Sioux. If that could be done, then the six of us plan on settling down on a piece of good bottomland somewhere in Missouri, seek out some wives who will have a bunch of us broken-down and crotchety bastards and try and enjoy what we have left of our lives as farmers and ranchers," quietly said Charlie Poke. Then once again his eyes returned to the campfire as if looking in the flames for any questions or answers he may have overlooked…

With that, Buck Snort rose, walked back to the cabin and brought forth one of their flat kegs of rum and made sure everyone around the fire that evening had a full cup of the fiery rum 'for what ailed them'… Then he made sure his cup was filled as well, as his eyes sought out the flames for its answers as to what he had been feeling when Shoshoni women had been mentioned by Charlie

Poke, as well as the possibility of joining up with his bunch of trappers and together riding down to St. Louis through hostile Indian country... Later that night lying there in his sleeping furs with Dog quietly snoring alongside him, the thoughts of Chenoa flooded through his mind and then thoughts of heading south through South Pass to St. Louis and what would be his life thereafter. It was then that he saw beautiful Chenoa walking towards him in a bighorn skirt covered with elk ivories and then she reached out just as she got to Buck Snort, as sleep drifted over him and a world of darkness closed around and over him...

The next morning after a hearty breakfast of spitted moose backstrap, Clem's special Dutch oven biscuits filled with plumped-up raisins and brown sugar, coffee as stout 'as an angry mule's kick' and one of Clem's Dutch oven apple cobblers made from dried and previously soaked apple slices, the two teams of trappers separated company after wishing each other 'safe travels'...

Standing there at the edge of their meadow and watching Charlie Poke and company ride out of sight, Buck Snort turned and just shook his head. Shook his head over the conversation he and Charlie had the night before about Shoshoni women, leaving for St. Louis by the end of the spring beaver trapping season and then settling down in Missouri. Then shaking those thoughts from his mind, Buck Snort said, "Let us mount up. We have a full day's work lying ahead of us so let's get going. We aren't catching a damn thing unless we are up to our hind ends in cold water and pulling Made Beaver from the jaws of our traps."

Somewhat later that morning, Dog led the trapper caravan out from their campsite as he always did. Following Dog was Buck Snort atop his big pinto and behind him trailed Wind Horse and Clem close by. As for Wind Horse and Clem, they trailed three heavily loaded packhorses carrying panniers loaded with 30 St. Louis-style beaver traps weighing five pounds each, 30 dried wooden anchor poles, axes, shovels, hammers and bottles of castor to be used as a lure and attractant for any curious beaver. However, one of the three packhorses carried two panniers loaded with eight fully loaded rifles just in case the group ran into a large number of hostiles who were spoiling for a fight. Because if a superior number of Indians showed up full of fight, they damn sure were going to get one because between the panniers full of loaded rifles and the personal firearms the trappers were carrying, many 'someones' would die that day...

Heading upstream on the Green, the trappers soon arrived at a place they had designated earlier as the 'jumping off place' for their fall beaver trapping line. Without a spoken word, Buck Snort and Wind Horse dismounted and left their horses to graze nearby under the watchful eyes of Clem. Walking forward along the waterways, both men's experienced eyes soon discovered evidence of freshly used beaver slides and then had the heavy five-pound beaver traps thrust into their hands by an equally experienced Clem acting as an assistant to the actual beaver trappers. In the meantime, Muskrat rode his horse off a short distance from the trappers and positioned himself atop his horse so he could watch over his much-exposed friends along the Green and in its adjacent waterways and be in a good position to offer protection against 'man or beast' should the occasion arise...

Within the next two hours, Buck Snort and Wind Horse had expertly set 20 of their 30 carried beaver traps and then because of the heavy number of beaver and their extensive evidence of living throughout the waterways, set no more traps figuring they had set enough to keep all of the men busy come pelt-processing time at the end of each day. With that work accomplished, the four trappers moved off into a nearby grove of aspen trees, let their horses graze and sat on the ground relaxing and discussing the day's events. Come early afternoon, the men mounted up and 'ran' their previously set trap line removing beaver already caught and because of the heavy beaver number in evidence, reset their traps in the same areas once again. As that was going on, Clem, with his lightning-fast skinning knife with the bevel only on one side to prevent unnecessary cuts through the valuable skin, quickly skinned out their day's greasy catch of eleven beaver caught using only 20 traps…

Then the men headed for a rather extensive patch of willows and began cutting hooping-sized limbs for the pelt-stretching process to come along with the de-fatting once the men arrived back at their cabin. Walking through a dense patch of willows with his arms already wrapped around a huge bundle of freshly cut willow boughs, ALL OF A SUDDEN A HUGE GOLDEN-TAN MOUND OF SOMETHING IMMEDIATELY ROSE RIGHT UP IN FRONT OF BUCK SNORT! "URRRGH-URRRRRGHHH!" ROARED A MONSTER IN SIZE GRIZZLY BEAR JUST DISTURBED FROM ITS DEEP SLEEP IN ITS DAY BED! A DAY BED BUCK SNORT HAD ALMOST STEPPED DIRECTLY INTO AS HE LUMBERED CLUMSILY THROUGH THE WILLOW PATCH CARRYING HIS BUNDLE OF PREVIOUSLY CUT BOUGHS…

THROWING HIS ARMLOAD OF WILLOW BOUGHS INTO THE AIR IN PANIC, A THOROUGHLY FRIGHTENED BUCK SNORT STANDING ONLY SIX FEET AWAY FROM A THOROUGHLY PISSED-OFF AND SURPRISED MONSTER IN SIZE GRIZZLY BEAR STANDING TEN FEET TALL, TURNED TO RUN! HOWEVER, HE WAS NOT QUICK ENOUGH AS THE GREAT BEAR REACHED OUT AND BIT DOWN ON BUCK SNORT'S HIND END, JERKED HIM BACKWARDS AND

THEN GAVE THE NOW GRAVELY INJURED BUCK SNORT A VIOLENT HEAD TOSS INTO AN EVEN DENSER PATCH OF WILLOWS!

BUCK SNORT MANAGED A CROSS BETWEEN A GURGLE AND A SCREAM AS THE BEAR'S HUGE CANINE TEETH BIT THROUGH AND TORE A LARGE CHUNK OF FLESH FROM BUCK SNORT'S BUTTOCKS, WHEN HE HAD BEEN VIOLENTLY TOSSED OFF TO ONE SIDE! WHEN THAT HAPPENED, BUCK SNORT LEFT A FOUR-POUND CHUNK OF HIS BEHIND IN THE BEAR'S JAWS NEVER TO BE SEEN AGAIN! THEN THE BEAR BURST THROUGH THE DENSE WILLOW THICKET, GRABBED THE LYING FACE DOWN BUCK SNORT BY HIS SHOULDERS AND ONCE AGAIN VICIOUSLY LIFTED UP THE HELPLESS TRAPPER! THEN ONCE AGAIN, IT HEAD TOSSED BUCK SNORT UP ONTO THE GRASSY KNOLL ADJACENT THE WILLOW PATCH! CRASHING THROUGH THE WILLOWS SENDING THE TRAPPERS' HORSES RUNNING IN EXTREME FRIGHT, THE BEAR BURST OUT ONTO SOLID GROUND AND CHARGED A BADLY WOUNDED BUCK SNORT TRYING TO REACH ONE OF HIS PISTOLS. ROLLING OVER ON HIS BADLY DAMAGED BACK AND RUMP, BUCK SNORT MANAGED TO SHOOT THE CLOSE AT HAND CHARGING BEAR IN HIS CHEST WHICH ONLY FURTHER ENRAGED THE ANIMAL!

TWO MORE QUICK LUNGES AND THE BEAR WAS ONCE AGAIN UPON BUCK SNORT AND BITING DOWN UPON HIS CHEST, LIFTED THE TRAPPER UPWARD AND HEAD TOSSED HIM OFF TO ONE SIDE JUST AS DOG BLEW INTO THE SIDE OF THE BEAR'S HEAD AND BIT DOWN WITH ALL HIS MIGHT! WITH THAT DISTRACTION, THE BEAR STOOD UP AND GRABBING THE FURIOUSLY BITING DOG WITH BOTH PAWS, BIT DOWN ON THE DOG'S FRONT CHEST AND THEN DROPPED THE HAPLESS AND NOW HOWLING OUT IN PAIN ANIMAL AT ITS FEET! DROPPING BACK DOWN ON ALL FOURS, THE BEAR WENT TO ADMINISTER THE KILLING BITE INTO THE BARELY MOVING BUCK SNORT, ONLY TO HAVE THREE .52 CALIBER RIFLE BALLS SLAM INTO ITS SHOULDERS AND NECK FROM JUST FEET AWAY!

SCREAMING OUT IN PAIN, THE GREAT BEAR UNSTEADILY ROSE UPON ITS HIND LEGS TO ITS FULL TEN FEET IN HEIGHT, TURNED AND FACED THREE TRAPPERS HURRIEDLY TRYING TO RELOAD THEIR RIFLES. ROARING IN PAIN OUT THROUGH ITS NOW BLOODY AND FOAM-FROTHED MOUTH, THE BEAR BEGAN WALKING ON ITS HIND LEGS TOWARDS THE THREE TRAPPERS NOW RAPIDLY DROPPING THEIR RIFLES AND GRABBING THEIR PISTOLS! AS THEY DID, A BROWN BLUR ONCE AGAIN

CHARGED THROUGH THE BATTLE SCENE AND GRABBED THE BEAR BY ITS RUMP AND BIT DOWN HARD ONCE AGAIN! "URRRRRGH!" ROARED THE BEAR, AS IT TURNED TO FIGHT OFF A FIRMLY CLAMPED UPON ITS TENDER BOTTOM, MADLY BITING DOG!

POW-POW-POW-POW-POW-POW! WENT THE SOUNDS OF SIX PISTOLS BEING FIRED SIMULTANEOUSLY FROM JUST FEET AWAY INTO THE HUGE HULK OF A BADLY BLEEDING BEAR NOW SAVAGELY ROARING OUT OF ITS MIND IN PAIN OVER BEING STRUCK SIX TIMES…

DROPPINGTOTHEGROUNDONALLFOURS AND WHIRLING AROUND AND AROUND TRYING TO GET AT THE DOG SAVAGELY BITING ITS MALE PARTS, THE BEAR MADE A FATAL MISTAKE. THE BEAR SHOULD HAVE BEEN MORE WORRIED ABOUT WIND HORSE THAN A LOWLY DOG BITING AT ITS MASCULINITY… WIND HORSE RAN RIGHT UP TO THE DISTRACTED BEAR WITH A DOG NOW MORE THAN FIRMLY CLAMPED ON ITS TENDER MALE PARTS AND WHEN THE BEAR SENSED THE DANGER OF A CLOSE AT HAND HUMAN, TURNED TO ATTACK THE PERCEIVED THREAT FROM THAT SECTOR…

WHEN THE BEAR QUICKLY TURNED, IT DISCOVERED A PISTOL BEING THRUST INTO ITS GAPING MOUTH AND WHEN

IT INSTINCTIVELY WENT TO BITE DOWN ON WIND HORSE'S HAND HOLDING THE PISTOL, AN EXPLOSION ENDED THE DRAMA OCCURRING OUT ON THE GRASSY KNOLL ADJACENT TO THE GREAT BEAR'S DAY BED! WHEN WIND HORSE PULLED THE TRIGGER ON THE PISTOL HE HAD BRAVELY THRUST INTO THE BEAR'S GAPING MOUTH, THE HUGE LEAD BALL ROARED DOWN ITS SHORT BARREL AND BLEW THROUGH THE SPINE HOLDING THE BEAR'S HEAD UPRIGHT. AS THE PISTOL BALL BLEW THROUGH THE BEAR'S SPINE AND OUT THE BACK OF ITS NECK, THE BEAR DROPPED AWAY TO THE GROUND STILL IN THE BITING AND MAULING JAWS OF DOG AND MOVED NO MORE…

Surprisingly, the only horse still standing around the battle site anywhere near the bear was a pinto with ears laid back and steadfastly standing next to an inert Buck Snort, snorting and ready to do battle with bared teeth! It took Wind Horse some long moments in time to get Buck Snort's Buffalo Horse quieted down and secured. Later as the trappers began walking towards their camp since their horses had already headed for their corrals, that found Wind Horse atop the pinto holding a badly bleeding Buck Snort in the saddle with him and balancing a badly wounded Dog in front of Buck Snort, with Clem and Muskrat on either side of the horse making sure neither man nor dog fell off as they slowly walked back towards their campsite.

An hour later found a badly drunk Buck Snort filled with as much rum as he could hold, lying face down on their kitchen table inside the trappers' cabin. There he lay stark-assed naked and oblivious to his world of pain with Clem washing his badly torn shoulders, ripped chest area and missing cheeks from his badly bitten-off hind end clean of all bear vomit, dirt and coagulated blood with warm water and shaving soap! Once wiped clean, Wind Horse sloshed liberal doses of their rum over the badly damaged parts of Buck Snort's body until he passed out from the alcohol-burning pain on the damaged tissue. Then Clem and Wind Horse wiped off the excess of that liquid. Then with a leather sewing needle and thread, Clem, the group's Frontier Doctor began sewing closed the gaping holes in the man's bottom, chest and shoulders area! Finished with Buck Snort, Dog was also washed off with the men's shaving soap and warm water and then sewn up without a whimper as well... Then as Clem fixed supper, Muskrat and Wind Horse de-fatted and hooped the beaver 'Plus' and later after supper had been eaten, the men took turns with cool rags dipped in creek water and placed over the tissue-damaged areas, waited and watched over a now feverish Buck Snort and Dog all night.

The next day with Clem washing off Buck

Snort's naked body as he lay on his sleeping furs, he also tended to Dog as well, who refused to leave Buck Snort's sleeping furs. As Clem tended to the wounded ones, Muskrat and Wind Horse did double duty, ran the trap line and processed the steady flow of harvested beaver furs come nightly...

It took another ten days before Buck Snort's daily soap and water baths were concluded once his fever broke and he began eating Clem's cooking once again. However, Dog seemed to heal up faster, between his licking of his wounds and Clem's washing him off with warm shaving soap and water. And as he did, Dog never left Buck Snort's side except to go to the bathroom, drink or eat. Then it was another six days before Buck Snort could mount the big pinto because he had suffered so much muscle damage to his shoulders, especially when the bear had bitten down on those muscle masses and had violently head tossed him, ripping them asunder. Additionally, a triple thick beaver skin blanket had to be made which allowed Buck Snort to ride his pinto horse bareback once again, but it wasn't until almost the end of the fall beaver trapping season that he could ride somewhat comfortably because of his very sore bottom with all of its missing meaty parts. And without those muscle masses acting as extra padding, sitting atop a horse or its saddle on the bony hip bones made for an uncomfortable ride...

Finally the day arrived towards the end of the fall beaver trapping season when Buck Snort and Dog could once again join the beaver trapping team on a regular basis. And like before when the trapping team finally formed up again, out went their 30 traps that time in order to catch as many beaver as they could because of the reduced catch they had previously suffered because of Buck Snort's serious injuries. Serious injuries and being one trap-setting trapper shy on a daily basis. That they did because to date, they had only caught and processed 189 beaver throughout the entire fall beaver trapping season!

By day two of the remainder of the fall beaver trapping season, things were pretty much back to normal once again. However, because of missing so much muscle mass from his bottom, Buck Snort found it difficult to move easily when he found himself stomping through deep, foot-clutching mud normally found in the old beaver ponds. But hard work soon overcame most of the men's problems and the beaver 'Plus' once again flowed and crowded the men's cabin and their nearby storage shed. And once again now that things were somewhat back to normal as well as during his 'downtime' healing up, Buck Snort had time to think over Charlie Poke's suggestion that they all ride south come the end of the spring beaver trapping season, return to St. Louis and settle down in Missouri. But that was as far as Charlie Poke's suggestion went...

One November morning as the men arranged themselves throughout the marsh trapping beaver as they normally did when they were racing against 'Old Man Winter' and breaking the thin ice in order to set their beaver traps, the water's cold was felt most deeply. As they did, Buck Snort could more than feel the effects on his badly damaged bottom whenever the icy waters slapped up against the injured tissue but he managed to carry his share of the load, realizing he soon would not be facing trapping under such conditions once the waters froze making trap setting difficult. Then he could have some more time in which to heal up during the winter months with less wading around in the freezing cold waters and that he was looking forward to.

"OOOOOGHHH – OOOOGHHH!" WENT THE SOUNDS OF A BULL MOOSE BELLOWING IN A MARSHY AREA CLOSE TO WHERE MUSKRAT SAT QUIETLY IN HIS SADDLE WATCHING OVER HIS FELLOW TRAPPERS. UPON HEARING THE BULL MOOSE BELLOWING SO CLOSE AT HAND AND NOW SMELLING HIS URINE-SPRAYED BODY, MUSKRAT FOUND HIMSELF SHIFTING HIS WEIGHT AROUND IN HIS SADDLE QUICKLY AS HE CHANGED POSITIONS SO HE COULD WATCH THE AREA MORE CLOSELY. THAT HE DID AS THE BULL MOOSE CONTINUED HIS CHALLENGING BELLOWS AND FEELING HIS NOW UNEASY HORSE CONSTANTLY

SHIFTING ITS WEIGHT UNDER HIM FEARING IT WAS ABOUT TO BE MOUNTED BY THE MOOSE... BY NOW, MUSKRAT'S HORSE WAS CONSTANTLY SHIFTING ITS WEIGHT FROM ITS FRONT TO BACK FEET NERVOUSLY, AS IT TOO NOW REALLY FELT THE NEARNESS OF THE MOOSE OF WHICH IT WAS DEATHLY AFRAID...

"CRASH-CRASH-CRASH!" CAME THE SOUNDS AS THE BULL MOOSE IN RUT AND STILL UNSEEN IN THE NEARBY DENSE BRUSH OF THE MARSH, BEGAN THRASHING HIS GREAT ANTLERS THROUGH THE BRUSH IN FAKE COMBAT, AS IF GETTING READY TO DO BATTLE WITH AN 'UNSEEN OPPONENT' UPON NOW SMELLING THE NEARBY HORSE!

Muskrat realizing a bull moose deep in rut was nothing to mess around with, shifted his weight in the saddle one more time and then set his heels to his horse's flanks so the both of them could move away from the danger a bull moose deep in rut represented. As he did, he kept his eyes on the now seen moving and being violently thrashed brush from whence came all of the loud bellowing and 'brush-fighting' the irritated bull moose was engaged in...

"CRASH-CRASH-CRASH!" EXPLODED THE BRUSH ONLY NEARER THAT TIME AND WITH THAT, MUSKRAT SPURRED HIS HORSE SO THEY COULD MOVE OUT FROM THE AREA. HOWEVER, HE WAS TOO LATE!

558 | TERRY GROSZ

BURSTING OUT FROM THE DENSE WILLOW
BRUSH ASSOCIATED WITH THE BEAVER
PONDS, A HUGE BULL MOOSE WITH SEVEN-
FOOT WIDE ANTLERS BURST FROM COVER
AND IMMEDIATELY UPON SEEING MUSKRAT
SITTING UPON HIS HORSE, LOWERED HIS
HEAD AND FROM TEN FEET AWAY, MADE A
FULL BLOWN CHARGE! MUSKRAT'S HORSE,
UPON SEEING THE CHARGING MOOSE FROM
JUST NOW MERE FEET AWAY, BEGAN TRYING
TO BUCK MUSKRAT FROM THE SADDLE SO IT
COULD ESCAPE...

"KA-THUMP!" WENT THE MOOSE'S
LOWERED ANTLERS INTO THE RIGHT SIDE OF
MUSKRAT'S BUCKING HORSE, KNOCKING IT
AND MUSKRAT TO THE GROUND IN A FLYING
JUMBLE OF BROKEN HORSE'S LEGS, A HORSE
SCREAMING OUT IN PAIN OVER SUFFERING
A NUMBER OF BROKEN RIBS PUNCTURING
HIS LUNGS, AND THE LIGHTS WENT OUT FOR
MUSKRAT, AS AN ANTLER 'PRONG' SLAMMED
INTO THE SIDE OF HIS HEAD!

Buck Snort upon hearing the irritated bellowing
from a nearby moose motioned for Wind Horse who
was setting a trap just 20 or so feet away, to leave the
beaver pond out of concern as did he. Then Buck
Snort and Wind Horse saw the moose burst from
the brush and with lowered antlers in a full blown
charge, plow into the side of Muskrat and his riding
horse, sending both slamming onto the ground!

Running like the wind at his nearby pinto,

Buck Snort leapt onto his thickly padded beaver skin riding blanket, jerked his rifle from its scabbard and kicked his horse in the flanks all in one practiced motion as they took off running for Muskrat and his downed horse! With Wind Horse right behind Buck Snort on his horse, the two men rode right up to the enraged moose still goring and mauling Muskrat's downed and now dying horse! Upon seeing such a scene, both men were shocked because somewhere underneath all of the moose's lowered head and antler mass lay their friend Muskrat! Spurring his unafraid pinto right up to the heaving flanks of the engaged and enraged moose, Buck Snort leaned over and stuck the end of the barrel of his rifle against the maddened moose's head showing only reddened eyes surrounded by the whites of its eyes and pulled the trigger of his rifle. **BOOM!** went Buck Snort's rifle and simultaneously, the 1,500-pound moose dropped like any kind of a large head shot animal immediately to the ground and moved no more!

Then Buck Snort and Wind Horse bailed off their horses and both men grabbed the huge mass of antlers and jerked them up and off the limp body of Muskrat whose right leg was still pinned underneath the body of his now dead horse! About then Clem rode up and between the three men, managed to drag the moose's body off the horse and pull Muskrat's out-cold body from under his now dead horse as well. Then as Clem the trappers' 'Frontier Doctor' tended to Muskrat, Wind Horse and Buck Snort unstrapped and removed Muskrat's horse's saddle and bridle and left the two dead animals where they fell as supper and several other meals for the grizzly bears, wolves, coyotes, ravens and anyone else whose 'big guts had eaten the little guts' they were so hungry...

Finally after splashing a lot of icy cold beaver pond water on Muskrat's bloody head where he had been 'speared' by an antler prong, he finally came around. However, he had a huge, blood-filled swelling on the side of his head and after carefully loading Muskrat upon Clem's horse, those two headed for their cabin where Clem could lay his friend out on his sleeping furs and tend to him and the lump on the side of his head as best as he could.

With Clem leaving bodily supporting Muskrat in his saddle, Buck Snort and Wind Horse decided they had enough bad luck for the day. With that and the oncoming winter weather and snows arriving any day, the two men pulled all of their remaining beaver traps and called their fall beaver trapping season over with just 223 total pelts being trapped and hooped throughout that period of time...

Arriving back at their camp just as the first snowflakes of the season began lightly falling, Buck Snort and Wind Horse unsaddled their horses and removed their panniers. They then hobbled their animals and let them loose so they could graze during the day's last hours of day-light along with the rest of their horses being let out from the corral as well. Then after storing all of their riding and packing gear under tarps by their corral and placing their beaver traps in their storage shed, the two men headed straight for their cabin to see how their friend Muskrat was doing.

Slipping inside the cabin, the men found Clem bent over the fire in their fireplace tend-ing to a pot full of beans. A quick look over at where Muskrat normally slept found the trap-per quietly sleeping with a large gray wrap of cloth wrapped around his still swollen and most likely sore head. Then Clem advised the two trappers that Muskrat had more than likely suf-fered a concussion and would be out of it for a few days. Plus, he had lanced the bloody lump on the side of his head and figured it would be a day or two before Muskrat would feel like 'cut-ting any wood or breaking any horses'... But since they had finished their fall beaver trapping season and brought in all of their trapping gear and had it stowed away under some tarps and wolf trapping was still about a month away, he felt that would give Muskrat time to heal up and be ready for the wolf trapping season that was to follow.

True to 'Frontier Doctor' Clem's prediction, all Muskrat did for the next three days was sleep and eat a little elk stew and then sleep some more.

However, when Muskrat was awake, the rest of the trappers saw that he was still unsteady on his feet, had trouble looking at any kind of light be it sunlight or the light from the fireplace, had fits of dizzy spells and had apparently injured his back so badly that he found even ordinary walking painful. That the men found problematic, especially when it came to Muskrat's awkward walking around inside the cabin and a declared pain in his lower back that made any kind of heavy lifting extremely painful.

After about two weeks of watching over Muskrat, his vision cleared as did his headaches, his aversion to bright light faded but his sharp back pains persisted. It soon became apparent that Muskrat could mount his new horse that had replaced his dead one with some difficulty and long rides were painful by the end of the day. And thankfully, the men had purchased five more flat kegs of rum than they normally did and a cup of rum was found to be very helpful to Muskrat in the pain-killing department just prior to going to his sleeping furs or riding his horse through rough country. However, the men soon discovered that Muskrat could ride with some difficulty, was rather limited in his lifting abilities especially any weight greater than his saddle, could load and shoot as good as he ever could, but use of his tomahawk in any kind of physical battle however was out of the question because of his painful back.

So the other three men made sure they saddled Muskrat's horse every time they went anywhere to lessen his back pain or causing even more intense back pain. Because of Muskrat's inability for physical combat, the trappers just got rid of his tomahawk. They then just outfitted him with two sash pistols and two additional pistols carried alongside of his saddle in pistol scabbards loaded with buck and ball in case of any close at hand fights between 'man or beast'. Lastly, the men made sure they carried a small jug of rum for him every time they ventured forth to help lessen any back pain he might have and made him always the one on horseback watching over the others in what they did since he was still their best shooter. Other than that, just like Buck Snort, the two men adapted their new weaknesses around their remaining strengths and life went on with just a little more thought as to how much longer they could subsist on the Frontier they loved so much as viable Mountain Men doing what they dearly loved…

Finally the deep of winter arrived and the men decided it was now time to begin running their wolf traps in order to catch those animals with the densest of furs. There was about a foot of fresh snow on the ground, 'the frost was now always on the pumpkin', wolf packs could be heard almost around the clock hunting for their next meals, and the men made sure that four of their wolf traps were set adjacent their horse meadow where the horses would not find them but the clever wolves with their wonderful senses of smell could...just in case...

Making final preparations for their wolf trapping season, the men cut a small mountain of wood and stacked it near their cabin for easy access, especially when they came in late at night and almost half-frozen from the weather. Then all four of the men set to casting bullets for their pistols and rifles and disassembling their primary weapons, cleaning out the lead and black powder fouling found within and then reassembling them so they would be ready for what was coming. Following those chores, the men's wolf traps were pulled from their storage shed, smoked over their jerky-making meat racks and placed in panniers ready for transport into the back country. Clem then cleaned out the men's 'possibles' bags one evening under candlelight, added new greased wadding and placed additional flints therein along with supplies of fresh jerky, new fire starters and a small jug of rum for Muskrat in case his back gave him fits. Lastly, Clem saw to it that new pistol and rifle powders were removed from their airtight lead canisters and that fresh powder was transferred into the men's pistol and rifle powder horns that they carried daily. As Clem attended to the above duties, Wind Horse made sure their tomahawks and sheath knives had their blades 'freshened' and Buck Snort and Wind Horse made sure the horses selected for the wolf trapping details and their horseshoes were ready to go. Not wanting to get caught flat-footed by the weather, the men checked all of their warmest winter clothing supplies and made sure if caught out in a surprise snowstorm, they could remain warm if they had to stay out overnight under the stars. Then Clem and Wind Horse saw to it that four buffalo robes were placed into several of the panniers in case if they were caught out overnight, they could stay warm and up off the cold and snow-covered ground.

The next morning Clem fed all of the men a Mountain Man's breakfast of coffee stout enough to stagger a bull buffalo in rut, spitted elk steaks cooked medium rare, Dutch oven biscuits loaded with plumped up raisins, cinnamon and brown sugar, followed up with warm honey to drizzle over the biscuit fare... Suffice to say, if anyone messed with Clem after that feed, they had better bring two rifles and a lot of powder and shot...

Heading out in sub-zero weather under clear blue skies a day later, Buck Snort led the way with his canine 'helper' happily trotting alongside the pinto. A 'Buffalo Horse' that had now accepted the raggedy-looking dog as an equal and the dog the pinto as well... Trailing Buck Snort was Wind Horse leading two packhorses carrying panniers loaded with buffalo skin ground cloths, tarps, sleeping furs, an ax and a jug of rum for Muskrat. Behind him came Clem trailing two horses, one toting two panniers carrying fully loaded extra rifles and the other with empty panniers for carrying any freshly caught wolf skins. Last trailed Muskrat with a big grin on his face and now mostly recovered except for his injured back after his run-in with a bull moose without an ounce of sense when it came to doing battle with the heavily armed trappers...

In order to break in the trappers and their horses for the cold weather work and dangerous riding that came with riding in the snow and frequent icy conditions underneath, the trappers stayed to their long, wind-swept ridges running down to the Green and set out a number of their wolf traps. That plus the herds of elk and deer were staying to the wind-swept ridges and sagebrush flats as well, making the discovery and killing of a number of them for bait stations to be used for the trap settings as easy as pulling a trigger. After a long day and only one horse wreck when Buck Snort's pinto hoof-slid on an ice-covered small log covered up by the freshly fallen snows, causing the horse to slip, lose its footing and roll in the snow! However, every man was riding with just the toes of his winter moccasins in the stirrups so if his horse fell, the foot could be easily and quickly extracted, allowing the rider to quickly step free from the falling horse and hit the ground running without injury to either party.

Soon, a number of elk and deer had been

slaughtered, opened up and their intestines spread around the traps, hoping with the smell of death hanging heavy in the air, it would invite to 'dinner' any hungry wolf 'wearing' a nice dark brown coat. As it turned out over the next two months, the weather remained bitter cold and as a result, the trapping of wolves could not have been any better! Soon the men's cabin was fairly littered with hanging and drying wolf hides as another 61 found themselves stacked up in the men's storage shed awaiting their final ride to the next Rendezvous!

Then finally moving later into the fringes of timber, Buck Snort employed a trick an old trapper had taught him back while at the Rendezvous. The 'trapping trick' taught to him had been so simple, that when it came to fooling the ever-clever and intelligent wolves it was almost too good to be true.

Stepping off his pinto early one morning, Buck Snort remembered the old trapper's wolf trapping trick and without saying anything to his partners when it came to trap setting time, Buck Snort 'pulled the wool over the eyes of his comrades'... Walking into the deep timber after Clem had opened up a large cow elk and after removing the backstraps for the trappers' suppers, Buck Snort employed the just-learned 'wolf trapping trick'. Removing his tomahawk and cutting down a number of spruce boughs, Buck Snort returned to the elk kill and wolf trapping site. Then without saying a single word, Buck Snort took the wolf trap to be used and began rubbing the spruce boughs all over the wolf trap until some of the plant's oils were smeared over the metal. Then careful to hold the trap with some spruce boughs so the human scent would not be transferred to that trap, set the trap and drove its trap chain anchor into the partially frozen soil. Then taking the spruce boughs, Buck Snort once again carefully dragged the boughs over the now carefully hidden in the snow, trap. Finally scattering the boughs about, Buck Snort walked off from the area, mounted his faithful horse and the trappers left the trap site. This Buck Snort did six more times with their remaining wolf traps. The next day, the amazed trappers found seven freshly trapped wolves in their spruce 'treated' traps and only three wolves caught in their other seven un-treated traps. After that, all of their wolf traps were set accordingly... By the end of their wolf trapping season, the trappers discovered that using the 'spruce bough' method of trapping in conjunction with the partially gutted elk and deer baits, they had caught another 43 beautiful wolves and their peltries!

Then the weather broke warm around the first of December. When it did, Clem soon found himself itching to get back outside to his outdoor firepits and get the sounds and smells of spitted meats filling the air with biscuits and boiling coffee smells wafting throughout the campsite instead of that of the strong smelling drying wolf hides inside the confines of their cabin. A visit to their meat pole hanging heavy with moose and elk soon graced Clem's cooking rods and with raised biscuit dough from inside their warm cabin and bear oil in the bottom of his two Dutch ovens, Clem bent over and began making his hand-shaped specialty biscuits from the warm and yeasty-smelling biscuit dough loaded with plumped up raisins, cinnamon and chunks of brown sugar. Soon, the cooking air around Clem's outdoor cooking fires smelled of pinewood smoke and the heavenly smell of all of the goodies being cooked about...

"URRRGH-URRRGHHH!" bellowed a savage and starving winter bear as it charged right into the cooking pit area and in so doing, knocked Clem into his wooden bowl of biscuit making dough! "URRRRGH-URRRRGH!" BELLOWED OUT THE WINTER BEAR AS IT THEN SAVAGELY MAULED CLEM ALONG THE EDGE OF THE FIREPIT, IGNORING THE FIRE'S FLAMES AND KNOCKING THE COOKING RODS ASUNDER! WHEN THAT HAPPENED AND EVEN THOUGH STUNNED BY THE BEAR'S SAVAGE ATTACK FROM BEHIND, CLEM MANAGED TO SCAMPER OUT FROM THE EDGE OF THE FIRE AND COLLAPSE ON THE FAR SIDE OF THE FIREPIT WITH THE 500-POUND STARVING WINTER BEAR CHASING AND SLAMMING DOWN RIGHT

ON TOP OF HIM! REACHING DOWN, THE BEAR GRABBED CLEM BY THE LOWER PART OF HIS FACE, JERKED HIM UPWARDS CLEAR OFF THE GROUND AND IN THE PROCESS, KNOCKED THE COFFEE POT AND TWO DUTCH OVENS 'BANGING AND CLANKING' ALL OVER THE PLACE!

Buck Snort, hearing all of the most unusual banging and clanking sounds coming from the outside the cabin, walked over and opened up the cabin's front door only to see a huge grizzly bear in the process of biting down on Clem's face and hearing his muffled screams! Bellowing out a warning to the rest of the men in the cabin, Buck Snort grabbed their ever-present extra rifle stacked alongside their front door just for such emergencies if the cabin was being stormed by Indians, cocked the hammer, drew a quick bead on the bear that was careful to miss Clem, and pulled the trigger!

BOOM! WENT THE RIFLE, AS THE HEAVY .52 CALIBER LEAD SLUG TORE THROUGH THE BEAR'S HEAVING GUTS AS IT, IN ITS WEAKENED CONDITION, TRIED LIFTING CLEM UP OFF THE GROUND ONCE AGAIN BY ITS HOLD ON THE TRAPPER'S FACE WITH ITS JAWS! TOSSING THE NOW EMPTY RIFLE ASIDE, BUCK SNORT TORE OUT FROM THE CABIN AND RUNNING RIGHT UP TO THE SIDE OF THE NOW REALLY MADDENED AND GUTSHOT BEAR AS IT CONTINUED

TEARING AT CLEM'S HEAD AND FACE, GRABBED A DOUBLE-BITTED AX FROM A NEARBY STUMP AND SWINGING IT FOR ALL ITS WORTH, BROUGHT THE BLADE DOWN UPON THE BEAR'S BACK, SEVERING THE ANIMAL'S SPINE!

BOOM – BOOM! WENT TWO MORE SHOTS FROM THE CABIN AS WIND HORSE AND MUSKRAT SHOT THEIR BULLETS SO THEY WOULD PASS RIGHT BY AN AX-SWINGING BUCK SNORT AND LODGED THEIR BULLETS INTO THE BEAR'S SIDE AND SHOULDER AS WELL! WITH THE ARRIVAL OF THOSE TWO HEAVY RIFLE BALLS INTO THE BEAR, THE ANIMAL NOW IN SAVAGE FURY, REACHED OUT AND BIT THE AX HANDLE INTO TWO PIECES AND WITH A VIOLENT TOSS OF ITS HEAD, SENT BUCK SNORT AND HIS PART OF THE AX HANDLE FLYING INTO THE NOW MUCH-VISITED FIREPIT AS WELL!

BUCK SNORT'S STAY IN THE BLAZING CAMPFIRE HOWEVER WAS SHORT-LIVED, AS A NOW CRAZY IN THE HEAD BUCK SNORT OVER THE VIOLENT ATTACK BEING CARRIED OUT UPON HIS DEAR FRIEND, JUMPED OUT FROM THE FIRE CARRYING A 'FLURRY' OF SPARKS WITH HIM... HE THEN DREW HIS TEN-INCH SHEATH KNIFE AND JUMPED UPON THE HEAVING AND NOW CRIPPLED AND DYING BEAR'S BACK! THEN RISING UP FROM HIS MOUNTED POSITION

ON THE BACK OF THE DYING BEAR, RAISED UP HIS KNIFE NOW BEING HELD IN BOTH HANDS AND VIOLENTLY SLAMMED ITS LONG BLADE RIGHT UP TO ITS HANDLE! WHEN HE DID, HIS RAZOR SHARP BLADE SLICED BETWEEN THE BEAR'S RIBS AND PLUNGED DEEPLY INTO THE BEAR'S HEART AND ONE LUNG!

WITH THAT FINAL ACT, THE BEAR SIGHED, VOMITED A RUSH OF FOUL SMELLING DIGESTIVE JUICES FROM ITS STARVED BEING AND SLUMPED OVER CLEM IN DEATH... THAT RUSH OF VOMIT ONTO CLEM'S BADLY PUNCTURED AND BLEEDING FACE CAUSED HIM TO VOMIT AS WELL, JUST AS WIND HORSE, CLEAR FULL OF ADRENALINE, BODILY JERKED CLEM OUT FROM UNDER THE BEAR! THEN OTHER THAN CLEM'S GAGGING UP VOMIT AFTER BEING SAVAGELY BITTEN IN THE FACE, THE REST OF THE MEN JERKED HIM AWAY FROM THE BEAR AND QUICKLY DRAGGED HIS BADLY DAMAGED BODY BACK INTO THEIR CABIN...

With blood from Clem's facial wounds spurting every which way and Clem vomiting bodily fluids as well, the cabin's floor was soon a stinking and slippery mess. However, Muskrat soon had some gray cloth used to normally patch up the men's winter clothing, torn off in strips and soon Clem's head and face looked like he was part-Egyptian mummy of old... With that and still feeling an inner rage like he had never felt before having such a close friend being attacked by a grizzly bear that should have been in hibernation, Buck Snort took a shovel full of cold ashes from the fireplace and began sprinkling them on the floor to soak up the slippery fluids splashed about. Well, that and living up to his namesake, stunk up the men's cabin something fierce as a result of his old orphanage affliction caused by being poisoned by some of the older boys living there who did not like him...

Then as Muskrat fussed over his long-time friend trying to stem the flow of blood from Clem's face and wiping off the excess fluids so he could better see the damage that had been inflicted, Wind Horse and Buck Snort headed outside. By now, the horses in the nearby corral smelled not only the odor of fresh blood and death but that of a grizzly bear and were reacting accordingly! Not wanting a corral full of crazy-acting horses to go nuts and break free from their confines, Buck Snort and Wind Horse began dragging the dead bear with difficulty around behind their cabin and up onto the hillside so it would be out of sight and its rank smell reduced.

"What the hell is a grizzly bear doing here at our campsite instead of being in a cave somewhere hibernating?" asked Buck Snort, as he began dragging a mess of limbs and brush over the top of the bear so its carcass could be burned.

"My father before he drowned spoke of such things," said Wind Horse, as he too dragged a number of limbs and brush over top of the bear's carcass and then with a fire steel, started a fire so they could start burning the bear's carcass up, reduce its attraction as a food source from the wolves and help calm down their nervous and excited horses over the fresh smell of a much-dreaded and feared predator.

"What did your father have to say about such things? After all, this bear should have been in hibernation months ago and not out running around in the dead of winter looking for some-thing to eat," said Buck Snort, as he tossed more tree limbs over the bear's now burning carcass.

"My father spoke of such a bear that he called a "Winter Bear." Apparently some bears are not able to eat enough food in the fall so they can go into hibernation when it is time and survive not being able to eat for so many months. As such, they are doomed to roam around in the winter months trying to get enough food to eat so the animal can store up enough fat so it can in fact still hibernate and not die in its cave from starvation. He also told me that such a bear can be identified just like this one by being so skinny and when they attack, because they are so hungry, they are extremely vicious and will eat anything they can get their teeth around! That is why the bear attacked Clem without any fear of a blazing fire. It was starving and being in such poor condition, feared no man and had we not intervened, the bear would have eaten Clem and then probably tried eating us and our horses as well. It is a good thing, My Brother, you took such action when you did. From what I saw of Clem's face, he is going to be really scarred up the rest of his life with all of those bite marks all over his face, missing an ear and part of his nose as well. Now that we have this fire going and are burning up this damn old bear so our horses don't go crazy with fear, I think we best get back inside and see what we can do for Clem," continued Wind Horse. After adding more limbs and some of their cut and split winter wood supplies to the fire, the grizzly bear was left to the flames. The next morning upon examination of their 'bonfire' work, other than the largest of the bear's bones, the rest would soon disappear under the ravages of time and thus the winter bear became just a bad memory and an ugly face left upon the trappers' camp-designated cook, namely that of Clem…

CHAPTER THIRTEEN

"CHARLIE LEFT HAND", A BAD SMELL, "KAYA", FRONTIER GRACE!

AFTER WAITING MANY MONTHS for his brother Chief Iron Eagle, to return from his sacred 'Vision Quest' along the Green River to avenge the loss of his two sons because of white trappers and with no return, brother Charlie Left Hand decided he would now act to avenge the now almost certain loss of his only brother. Seeking spiritual help from his Northern Arapaho Band's Medicine Man and after a "Sweat", the two men visited the spiritual world seeking advice and counsel from The Great Spirit over the matter of a revenge trip to bring atonement from the white trappers for killing what had to be Charlie Left Hand's only brother and chief.

After so doing and under the further guidance

of the Medicine Man, Charlie Left Hand was advised to contact a selected number of his band's most spiritually powerful men and gifted warriors. Selected for his 'Vision Quest' to avenge the loss of a gifted and most respected Northern Arapaho Chief and a number of his band's most talented warriors, Charlie Left Hand settled on the following warriors as directed by the band's Medicine Man. Selected was "Two Moons", a gifted tracker and shooter. Another man selected for Charlie Left Hand's 'Vision Quest' was a man named "Prairie Dog", who was reputed to see what lay ahead when most warriors were blinded by everyday life. Another Medicine Man's suggestion was that of two brothers who were reputed to be the fiercest warriors of the band named "Medicine Dog" and "Wolf". Last to be selected for the very special 'Vision Quest' was a warrior who only had one eye. However, his remaining eye was reputed to be like that of a golden eagle and could see things happening at great distances. That warrior was a man named after his 'eagle-like' abilities, "Kicking Bird."

Because of the unexplained loss of Chief Iron Eagle and his warriors, Charlie Left Hand's Medicine Man required this selected group of warriors to fast for a week, bathe every day and afterwards wipe off their bodies daily with ashes from a sacred fire made from the big sage brush. Lastly, the Medicine Man suggested that the selected men eat the heart from a buffalo as the only meat eaten for a whole week when fasting in order to gain that animal's stamina, spirit and ability to withstand going long days without water or food.

The only information that the select group of warriors possessed was that their great chief had gone south to the area the white men called the Green River. And those men who more than likely had killed the chief and his men could be positively identified because they would be in possession of the white pinto and spirit horse that the chief's son Red Hawk, had coveted as his Buffalo Horse. And it had been the horse Chief Iron Eagle had been riding when he left on his 'Vision Quest' many months earlier. Without further delay, Charlie Left Hand and his select group of warriors, after spending a week performing many rituals and sacred ceremonies, left right at daylight on the eighth day after having been 'bathed' in the sacred smoke of the Medicine Man's big sage fire...

For the next five days, Charlie Left Hand's men slowly made their way south from their encampment until they arrived along the Green River. Right away they came upon four fur trappers living in several tipis obviously made by their enemy the Sioux Indians, and decorated accordingly. Staying out of sight, Charlie Left Hand's men spent the afternoon quietly watching the four men making sure they became familiar with the trappers and their four Indian women's habits and movements around their camp. As they soon deduced from their clothing and speech, the warriors figured the four men were from the Hudson's Bay Fur Company and their women were speaking in the tongue of their hated enemy, the Sioux! The warriors decided they would spend the rest of that afternoon watching the trappers and their women in order to make sure there were no more trappers from the camp still afield spring trapping beaver.

Not seeing any sign of the pinto horse that Chief Iron Eagle had been riding or seeing any other men arriving in camp but realizing the four hated white men were spring beaver trapping on the land of the Northern Arapaho and were in the company of four Sioux women, they made plans for a deadly night attack. That night when the men and their women were gathered around their campfire together fixing supper, Charlie Left Hand and his five men set their trap. Coming in from two sides so his warriors would not be caught in a deadly cross-fire once the shooting started, Charlie Left Hand waited until his men had quietly moved into position. Then using the call from that of a great horned owl, Charlie Left Hand gave out the bird's three-note call letting his men know he was ready for the attack. Instantly, upon hearing the three-note call of the great horned owl, the four Sioux women in the trappers' camp stopped what they were doing and looked all around in alarm. Charlie

Left Hand from his hidden position in nearby trees just smiled, knowing that some bands of the Sioux Indians felt that upon hearing the call from such a bird, that meant culturally someone was going to die!

As for the four trappers waiting around the campfire to be served by the Sioux women after they had de-fatted and hooped their beaver catch of the day and aware of their women's cultural fear upon hearing the call from such an owl, just roared with laughter upon seeing the women's immediate change in their dispositions. That laughter immediately stopped when five rifle shots roared out from the darkness, and the four trappers sitting around the fire using their saddles as chairs, plunged forward in unison upon being squarely hit in their backs and sides by the five accurate-shooting Northern Arapaho Indians hiding in the darkness!

Instantly, the four Sioux women scattered like quail being chased by a hawk and in so doing, quickly ran into the capturing arms of Charlie Left Hand and his five warriors. Twenty minutes later, all four of the unfortunate Sioux women had been stripped of their clothing and were being brutally raped and sodomized by six sex-hungry men again, again and again… After two hours of being gang-raped over and over again and being 'passed around' by the six Northern Arapaho acting like emotionally sex-starved ani-mals after the 'high' they had just experienced in the killing, it was over! Then upon Charlie Left Hand's verbal command when his men's animal lusts appeared to be totally satisfied, the four exhausted Sioux women, historical enemies of the Northern Arapaho, simultaneously had their throats cut in squirting splashes of blood!

Then the Northern Arapaho men scalped all of the trappers and also cut off their trigger fingers, ears and noses and tossed those parts into the campfire. Following that, Charlie Left Hand had Kicking Bird and Wolf walk back to where all of the Northern Arapaho men's horses had been hidden and brought into camp, as the rest of his men began looting the four dead trappers' camp. First to be looted was the trappers' lean-to where kegs of rum, gunpowder, foodstuffs, eight tightly packed bundles of beaver furs, and several extra rifles and pistols were happily discovered. That was especially so when the kegs of rum were discovered and brought forth and its fiery liquid began flowing. Then as Medicine Dog and Two Moons began spooning out the dead trappers' stew and sharing the previously made Dutch oven biscuits around the campfire, Prairie Dog, who had continued exploring the contents from the tipis, let out a yell of excitement!

When he had yelled, his five compatriots, fearing an attack from other unseen trappers coming into their camp, made mad dashes for their rifles sitting or lying nearby! Then out came Prairie Dog pushing a beautiful, tall and long-haired

Indian woman whose hands were bound! As Prairie Dog pushed the young and very beautiful Indian woman out into the light of the campfire, the men could see that the woman looked all of the men right in the eyes with a fierce look of independence, pride and total lack of fear. Walking her into the light of the campfire so the men could see her better, they were quietly surprised over the woman's lithe body, her calm countenance and the look of fierce determination in her beautiful dark eyes. To a man, they all recognized that the woman now their prisoner was from a family of class and high status, like that from a very powerful chief... But no matter her class or high level of defiance, she was Charlie Left Hand's prisoner for him to do with as he pleased and he knew she was the one soon to 'please' him!

Then the other men began feeling a desire forming in each of their loins upon looking at such a beautiful woman. However, fortunately for the Indian woman standing there in front of the six of them, spending two hours having their way physically with the four now dead Sioux women for the last two hours left only a mental not physical desire for spending some intimate time with this new beauty...

"Take her back and leave her where you found her. Just make sure she is also bound by her legs as well so she cannot run off and escape," said Charlie Left Hand. "I will deal with her later but not tonight and none of you are to touch her until I have finished with her," he continued with a look in his eyes that was all too meaning...

Leaving Wolf behind the next morning to guard their prisoner and watch over the dead trappers' camp, Charlie Left Hand took the remainder of his men upstream looking for more trappers, especially the one with the 'telltale' white pinto. However as they did, all they discovered were burned-out and previously looted trappers' cabins as a result of Chief Iron Eagle's earlier predations before he had been killed. Arriving back at the four dead Hudson's Bay trappers' camp later in the afternoon, the five warriors tiredly dismounted and immediately got into the supply of the dead trappers' rum once again.

After more than several cups of rum, Charlie Left Hand told Wolf to bring him the woman prisoner, all to the jeers and knowing laughter by the rest of his now evil-thinking men. After Wolf had untied her, he pushed the woman out from where she had been lying in the lean-to and over to where Charlie Left Hand, who was standing by the campfire with a leer of lust spreading across his face.

"What is your name, My Beauty?" he asked as he reached out, pulled her into him and then shoved his right hand down the front of her heavily beaded buckskin shirt and onto the nipple and fullness of her left breast...

WHOOOMP! went her right knee deeply into

Charlie Left Hand's groin in an instant, dropping him to the ground in a curled-up fetal position, howling in abject pain!

"OOOOOHHH, OOOOHHH!" loudly groaned Charlie incessantly, as he rolled around and around on the ground like a gutshot prairie dog, as the unknown woman looked down upon the man with defiance and contempt in her eyes at a man who just moments earlier was figuring on having his way sexually with her! Then her dark eyes of defiance swept across the other men's eyes as if challenging each and every of them...

That was when the unknown but defiant woman was violently knocked to the ground by Medicine Dog from a blow alongside her head with his coup stick! "If you don't want more of the same, I suggest you do what our leader desires of you," growled Medicine Dog, as he looked down upon the almost knocked-senseless woman lying at his feet!

Lying there bleeding from her head wound after being knocked viciously alongside her face, the woman managed to glare back up at Medicine Dog with a look only meant to kill if she somehow had her way, the means and opportunity...

Then Charlie Left Hand after slowly regaining his feet somewhat unsteadily after being kneed in the groin reached down and grabbed a chunk of firewood. Then he commenced beating the defiant woman about her shoulders, head, breasts and groin area until he had to stop from his maddened state because of exhaustion! "Take her back and tie her up!" said Charlie Left Hand, with a voice literally dripping with the venom of the thoughts racing through his mind.

Two Moons and Prairie Dog lifted up the now unconscious woman from off the ground, dropping huge droplets of blood along the way as she was carried back to her lean-to, only to lay bleeding and bruised from the beating she had just endured from her tormentor! Never having seen Charlie Left Hand beat a helpless woman so badly before, the rest of his warriors just quietly went about their camp duties in disgust with a now great loss of respect for the man leading them on this 'Vision Quest'…

Charlie Left Hand, for his part in the beating of the woman, just sat on a sitting log rubbing his manhood badly damaged from an earlier blow administered by the beautiful woman… beautifully…

The next day the five warriors led by Charlie Left Hand, led a trapper's horse carrying a badly beaten woman, seven more horses heavily packed with the four dead Hudson's Bay fur trappers' supplies, three trappers' riding horses and eight bundles of furs, headed now south along the Green looking for any signs of white spring beaver trappers with a large pinto horse, after finding no more trappers further north along the Green. A telltale pinto horse which had last been seen being ridden by Chief Iron Eagle, now suspected of being killed by unknown white trappers... After an hour of cautious travel staying mostly out of sight as they headed downstream on the Green, Charlie Left Hand held up his hand for his caravan of warriors to stop. This he did as he saw Two Moons, the group's best tracker, sent out earlier to look over the area for any more trappers, riding like the wind was on his tail carrying a devil and heading towards them!

Reining up his lathered-up horse alongside that of his chief in a flying cloud of dust, Two Moons said, "There is a trappers' cabin located just a short ways below us. I just saw the trappers coming back from running their beaver trap line and there are four of them, and ONE OF THE TRAPPERS IS RIDING A LARGE PINTO HORSE THAT LOOKS LIKE THE ONE CHIEF IRON EAGLE WAS RIDING BEFORE HE DISAPPEARED ON HIS 'VISION QUEST'!"

With those encouraging words running like a bolt of lightning through the group, all of the warriors were physically moved over the thought of a soon to be coming deadly battle! One in which they would soon be able to put the mysterious disappearance of their Chief Iron Eagle to rest once and for all time...

Upon hearing those words, Charlie Left Hand turned in his saddle and pointing over to a finger of timber said, "Let us head for those trees and make our camp. Then later tonight, we can move in on the four trappers when they are sleeping or in their cabin and avenge what they did to my brother and put this whole matter to rest once and for all time!"

Moments later, the six Northern Arapaho warriors had moved into the timber and made their camp alongside a small creek. There they unloaded all of their horses and let them graze within the dense timber alongside the creek so they would be out of sight. Then with all thoughts of being 'pleasured' by the beautiful Indian woman forgotten for the moment, Charlie Left Hand and his men bedded down so they could rest up before finally confronting the trappers and the ones who had more than likely killed his brother. However, before the men bedded down for a late afternoon sleep, they 'hog-tied' their woman prisoner so she could not escape while the men were sleeping. Then after eating some of the jerky they had discovered back at the four dead Hudson's Bay trappers' camp, the six warriors wrapped themselves up in their sleeping furs and drifted off to sleep.

******

Riding back into their camp, the four trappers dismounted, unsaddled and unpacked their horses. Then their animals were turned out to graze and water in the nearby meadow. Then Wind Horse opened up the gate to their corral and let the rest of their horses out so they could feed and water as well with the other stock. In the meantime, Clem, still healing up after being mauled and almost killed by a savage winter bear, hobbled around his beloved campfire setting the coffee pot over the building flames to boil and slowly, still feeling the effects of his recent mauling by the winter bear, began making supper preparations. Then Clem walked over to their nearby stream, filled up a bean pot with water and headed back to his firepit where he began picking through a sack of pinto beans removing the chaff, animal droppings, dirt, and unfit to eat beans. Once he had a small mound of clean beans assembled on a hand towel, they were placed into the bean pot partially filled with water and thoroughly washed. Then taking the bean pot back to the creek, the dirty water was drained off, the pot refilled with clean water and brought back to the firepit. With that, he made a trip over to their meat pole, cut off several large chunks of hindquarter, cubed the meat and after removing any bird poop found on the meat left behind by small feeding birds, placed the chunk-meat into the bean pot to slow cook as well. Then into the pot went several handfuls of rice and a heavy dose of black pepper, cut-up dried wild onions, red pepper flakes and salt. That pot was then placed over the end of the firepit where it would not burn but would slow cook over the next few hours before supper. Removing a sack of sliced and dried apple slices, numerous handfuls of those dried slices were placed into a pot of water along with a small mound of raisins so they could plump up and be used later in a cobbler. Then into his wooden mixing bowl went the water, yeast, flour and salt which was mixed into dough and then set alongside the fire so it would have time to 'rise' before he began making biscuits and his apple cobbler crust. Next it was off to his meat pole once again where Clem cut off, trimmed and brought four large moose steaks over to his cooking table by the fire. Those were heavily salted, peppered and placed on spitting irons and made ready for roasting over the fire. Following that, into one of his Dutch ovens went a small mountain of green coffee beans which were then roasted over the fire. After they had cooled, Clem saw to it that they were crushed and ready for his style of 'stout as an angry mule's kick' coffee soon to come. Minutes later after several handfuls of crushed coffee beans found their way into the boiling pot, the air around the campfire came alive with its aromatic smells. Standing up and surveying his efforts around the campfire, Clem thought to himself, *no God-damned bear is going to take anything away from this camp cook...*

In the meantime as Clem continued puttering around his firepit making supper, Wind Horse and Buck Snort unloaded the horses' panniers. Twelve fresh beaver pelts were removed and taken into the cabin where they could be defatted, scraped of all meat scraps and hooped so they could begin the drying process. In the meantime, Muskrat removed all of the trappers' extra rifles carried as extra protection against Indian attacks from one of the panniers and took them into the cabin for safekeeping. As was usual, Dog hung around his other pal, Clem, looking for any unused, bird poop-covered meat scraps tossed his way… Plus it allowed him to sleep near the warm fire after a long morning exploring the prairie, mountains and beaver pond areas as the trappers 'ran' their trap line.

As the sun began setting, Wind Horse and Buck Snort brought in their horses, curried down the horses ridden or packed doing the day's work along their trap line and then shut the corral gate. About then Clem let everyone know that his supper was ready and soon around the trappers' fire the only sounds heard were those of a crackling fire, spitting meat sizzling away, the clanking of metal plates, cups, forks and knives, and the happy sounds hungry men make when feasting away around a campfire with their 'brotherhood'…

As Clem cleaned up after the supper had been served and eaten, the rest of the men broke out their clay pipes and cups of rum, sat back and talked about "Cabbages and Kings"… That was when Buck Snort brought forth a rather large 'something' wrapped up in a piece of tanned deer hide and when Clem had finished with the dishes, he was asked to come over to where Muskrat, Buck Snort and Wind Horse were sitting on their sitting logs around the campfire with big expectant and knowing grins on their faces...

Then Buck Snort stood up and cleared his throat so all could see that he had a presentation to make. Immediately it got quiet around the firepit as Buck Snort began by saying, "Gentlemen, since we only have one person in our group who has tangled with a grizzly bear and lived, I thought it only fitting that such a person be so recognized. So, Clem, if you would stand and be recognized I would appreciate it."

With that request hanging in the evening air along with the usual hordes of mosquitoes found around a trappers' firepit, Clem stood with a puzzled look on his badly disfigured and still-healing face. A disfigured face missing a nose, one ear and covered with many deep and ugly scars that came with having one's head inside that of a grizzly bear's mouth, just before it was shot, stabbed, axed and killed... That was when Buck Snort let the deerskin holding 'something' open up in his hand, revealing a magnificent 20-claw grizzly bear necklace! A grizzly bear claw necklace taken from around the neck of a dead Chief Iron Eagle after Buck Snort had killed him in the fight back at the burial ground battle site near the Jones's cabin...

Upon seeing the dazzling 6"-long claw necklace being unfolded in the deerskin in the dancing light of the firepit, its magic and meaning was not lost on the man almost killed by a starving grizzly bear. Its magic and meaning was also not lost on Clem over the respect that Buck Snort, Muskrat and Wind Horse were paying him as a hardy Mountain Man either...

Then all of a sudden, Buck Snort took the necklace and draped its claw-clattering magnificence over Clem's head and around his neck. All of a sudden, Clem found his hands wrapped around the surprise gift being draped around his neck that was so full of the meaning of life and having such friends in that life... He soon found his eyes filling with tears of joy and his heart filling with pride over such a gift. Moments later found all four trappers, Mountain Men and dear friends one and all, in each other's arms laughing and crying with joy over that moment in time...

******

Lying in the bushes quietly hidden from the trappers' view or that of the large dog they had in their camp, Northern Arapaho warrior Two Moons watched the four Mountain Men eating their supper. He lay there alone because his leader Charlie Left Hand, after hearing Two Moons's report on what he had seen, including that of the presence of a very large dog in the trappers' camp, had decided that Two Moons, his best tracker, return to the trappers' camp alone. That way the dog would hopefully not scent the presence of a lone warrior and if the trappers were not warned, they would be easier to capture and kill if not winded and warned by their dog. And since Two Moons's presence had not been discovered by the trappers' dog, Charlie Left Hand's clever battle plan was bearing fruit. Also, when Two Moons had quietly slipped up and into the trappers' camp earlier and had hidden nearby so he could observe what was going on, his heart had been rewarded. When slipping by the trappers' horse corral, he once again had observed the large pinto in that corral. The one and same horse Chief Iron Eagle had ridden earlier in his 'Vision Quest' to return to the land south of their camp and that of the white man trappers along the Green River. He now had confirmation that the four trappers were the ones who had more than likely killed their great chief, especially in light of the presence of the pinto now being ridden earlier by one of the trappers.

Then Two Moons's eyes had been rewarded with another bit of supporting evidence that the four trappers now being watched were the killers of Chief Iron Eagle. Lying there hidden and watching the trappers, Two Moons with his own eyes had seen one of the trappers presenting a large grizzly bear necklace to the trapper whose face was badly scarred. THE ONE AND SAME GRIZZLY BEAR NECKLACE TWO MOONS HIMSELF HAD PRESENTED TO CHIEF IRON EAGLE AFTER THE TWO OF THEM HAD KILLED THE SAME KIND OF BEAR RAIDING THEIR HORSE HERD MONTHS EARLIER! THE ONE AND SAME NECKLACE THAT

TWO MOONS HAD HIS WIFE CONSTRUCT AS A GIFT FOR HIS BELOVED CHIEF AND THE ONE AND SAME HE HAD PERSONALLY PRESENTED TO THE CHIEF FOR HIS BRAVERY WHEN THE GREAT BEAR HAD BEEN SURPRISED AND KILLED BY THE TWO OF THEM AS IT HAD FEASTED UPON ONE OF THEIR TRIBAL MEMBER'S HORSES...

Upon seeing the presentation of the necklace to the trapper with the badly scarred face, Two Moons could hardly lay still over that discovery! However, he continued lying there in thick cover until the trappers had left their campfire, gone to the bathroom for the evening and then went inside their cabin. Now that the trappers and their dog had left, Two Moons quietly rose from his place of hiding and headed back to Charlie Left Hand's hidden camp so he could tell him the good news about this being the group of trappers who had more than likely killed his brother based upon one of the trappers possessing the chief's pinto. That and even more importantly, seeing the very necklace that he himself had personally presented to Chief Iron Eagle after the two of them had killed the great bear as it raided their tribe's horse herd and had killed one of their horses!

Sneaking back by way of the trappers' horse corral, Two Moons was surprised to find that the chief's old pinto horse was very disturbed by his nearness and continued snorting his apparent displeasure over Two Moons's presence by loudly stomping its feet in anger and lowering its ears looking to bite as he sneaked by. With the horse's apparent displeasure over having Two Moons so close and making so much noise, Two Moons decided they would sneak up to the trappers' cabin from the side of the cabin away from the horses' corral in order not to alert the trappers inside of their close presence once the rest of his band had arrived. Then picking up a horse turd out of meanness, Two Moons bounced the dropping off the snorting and foot-stomping horse's head in spite and then disappeared into the darkness on his way back to his camp. Little did Two Moons realize that little bit of animosity on his part with the thrown horse turd would soon come home to roost, if the pinto had his way...

******

Inside the cabin under the light from several beeswax candles and that from the fireplace, the trappers all admired the 'grizzly bear necklace's outstanding badge of courage' now being proudly worn around Clem's neck. That called for another cup of rum and soon the four men were deep in happy conversation over the day's successful trapping, their great supper and the presentation of Clem's 'badge of courage'...

About then, Buck Snort stopped mid-sentence in what he had been saying to Clem and just listened. Seconds later he finished his sentence,

but continued listening 'out of his other ear'...
Then excusing his person saying, "He had to
go and 'get rid' of some of the rum previously
drunk in celebration over the day's events,"
he picked up his rifle and walked out into the
darkness surrounding the cabin. As he did, Dog
brush-blocked Buck Snort alongside his right leg
and was out the door with him as he always did.
With that show of the dog's loyalty, Buck Snort
just had to smile. With that, he reached down
and petted Dog behind his ears as he went by...

Now outside the protective walls of their
cabin, Buck Snort always amazed himself after
having lived in the wilderness a few years discovering just how his senses had sharpened. As a
Mountain Man, he realized that to survive out on
the Frontier, one had better listen, look and sense
what was going on around him, otherwise he
could end up as a 'bear scat'... Tonight he found
was no different the very second he stepped
outside the cabin. Immediately he found himself
straining his eyes in the darkness in order to see
better, was listening to every sound that 'approached' his ears and searched the air he was
breathing in for any smell that may warn him
of close at hand danger, like that of the close at
hand presence of a grizzly bear.

Right off, he sensed what he had heard earlier
while in the cabin, that from his horse's hoof-
stomping behavior, something had upset his
very intelligent Buffalo Horse! The animal, smart

beyond his years, was nervously foot-stomping and snorting as if to clear his nostrils of a scent of nearby danger. Shifting his rifle to his shooting hand and peering deeply into the darkness surrounding the horses' corral sensing maybe a grizzly bear was close at hand, found him quietly drawing in large draughts of air searching for the oftentimes rancid smell of a close at hand bear. Not picking up any smells of bear, Buck Snort hopped over the corral fence and walked over to his horse which was walking over to him as well and plainly in an agitated state. With that, the pinto walked up to Buck Snort and placed its great head onto the trapper's shoulder as if by so doing, that would rid the area of danger. Petting the horse's neck and trying to comfort the animal, Buck Snort could see the animal needed even more attention…

Walking over and laying his rifle against the corral rail, Buck Snort looped his strong right arm over the great horse's shoulders only to find him still trembling and foot-stomping out of agitation. "Here, Big Fella," said Buck Snort, "It's alright and I don't see or smell any bear nearby so it is OK." Then figuring maybe a good currying down would calm his horse over what was bothering him, Buck Snort walked over to a barrel near the corral rail holding a number of curry combs and retrieved one. Walking back, he began currying down his horse because that always seemed to calm the animal down, so curry him he did…

******

Two Moons slipped back into Charlie Left Hand's camp lit by the light from a small camp-fire. There he met his fellow warriors all stand-ing around waiting for his return after scouting out the trappers' nearby campsite.

"The trappers are all inside their cabin and celebrating. The good news is Chief Iron Eagle's pinto horse is in the trappers' corral, and I saw one of the trappers give Chief Iron Eagle's spe-cial grizzly bear claw necklace that he always proudly wore around his neck to a trapper with a badly scarred face. These are the trappers who killed your brother and our great chief!" said Two Moons excitedly.

"THEN WE GO!" said Charlie Left Hand. "And we take this woman with us. I full well intend on capturing all of the trappers alive and torturing them in front of this woman. Maybe then she will realize what a great warrior I am and then let me bed her without resistance. However if she refuses my advances this next time, then I will take her anyway on one of the trappers' sleeping furs, then let all of you who want to take her as well! Then I will kill her and leave her with the rest of the dead trappers. As our rewards, we will stay in their cabin this night, eat their food, drink their rum and take their horses and furs, and burn down their cabin tomorrow with them in it as a warning to any other white trappers who want to trespass in the sacred country of our ancestors! Now we go because I have waited long enough to avenge the death of my brother and tonight The Great Spirit has smiled upon us," said Charlie Left Hand with a deadly cold determination-sounding tone and tenor in his voice.

With that and with Two Moons advising they needed to approach the cabin from the far side of the trappers' horse corral so those horses would not give their arrival away, the men gathered up their gear. Then following Two Moons, the small war party walked and led their horses towards the hated trappers' cabin and their eventual capture, torture and killing that was to follow.

******

Buck Snort continued currying down his Buffalo Horse, while all the time talking gently to him and trying to comfort and calm him down. During that time, Muskrat opened up the cabin door and yelled out, "Buck Snort, are you alright? Sure seems like you are taking a long time to take a piss."

"No, I am fine. I am just out here currying my horse and calming him down," replied Buck Snort.

With those words of assurance, Muskrat shut the cabin door as Buck Snort continued working with his horse. About 20 minutes later, Buck Snort realized with his much better night vision now that he had been outside for a while, that his horse was intently watching the trappers' cabin and now ignoring him. About then, Buck Snort felt Dog rub up against his right leg and let out a low rumbling growl! Looking down at Dog and realizing he was looking in the same direction that Buck Snort's pinto was looking, he began looking intently at the cabin as his Frontier senses of survival were now kicking in! When he did, he saw several darkened figures quietly walking up to the front door of their cabin, momentarily bunch up and then bursting into the cabin amidst much yelling and hearing a single shot being fired! When that occurred and the cabin door had been flung wide open, the cabin's dim light from the candles and fireplace flooded out into the nighttime! Just for an instant, Buck Snort saw a number of Indians quickly push into the cabin, followed by much yelling and heard a single shot being fired, and then even more yelling filling the air!

Grabbing up his rifle and leaping over the corral's rails, Buck Snort took off running for the cabin with Dog close by his side! About then, Two Moons realizing there was one trapper missing and he presented a very real danger, turned and pushed through the rest of the warriors bunched up inside the cabin waving their rifles around in the direction of the three trappers now backed up against the back wall! Pushing his way through the cluster of warriors back towards the open front door area, Two Moons stepped outside looking for the missing trapper and the potential danger that represented. That was when Two Moons received a face full of dog with a mouthful of violently slashing teeth that could only be generated by a 60-pound furious flying through the air dog protecting his now close at hand and charging into the deadly fight, master!

Letting out a scream in fright and now in intense pain, Two Moons dropped his rifle and because of the dog's impact slamming into his head, was bodily thrown backwards inside the cabin and onto the backs of his five surprised fellow warriors! Medicine Dog, feeling Two Moons's bodily impact against his back, quickly turned and upon seeing the attacking dog, realized what had happened. With that and being bunched up with the other warriors and unable to quickly use his long-barreled rifle, he quickly drew his tomahawk and cleaved the dog's skull with its blade! In so doing, Medicine Dog killed the attacking animal instantly! Unfortunately for Two Moons, the violent impact of Medicine Dog's emotionally charged tomahawk striking the dog's skull, went clear through the animal's head, past his jaws and into Two Moons's forehead, killing him instantly as well...

With the surprise and violent arrival of Dog onto Two Moons's face, ALL HELL BROKE LOOSE! THE ATTACKING DOG GAVE THE TRAPPERS THE SURPRISE MOMENT THEY NEEDED... WITH THAT, THEY ALL QUICKLY WENT FOR THEIR RIFLES LYING NEARBY

AGAINST THE CABIN WALLS AND PISTOLS IN THEIR SASHES. DURING THAT MICRO-INSTANT ALL OF THE ATTACKING INDIANS WERE DISTRACTED. MICRO-SECONDS LATER, THE INSIDE OF THE CABIN WAS FILLED TO THE CEILING WITH CLOUDS OF WHITE BLACK POWDER SMOKE FILLING THE AIR FROM ALL OF THE TRAPPERS' QUICKLY FIRED WEAPONS! WITH THAT "THUNDERCLAP" OF SO MANY RIFLES AND PISTOLS BEING FIRED BY BOTH SIDES, EVERYONE'S EARS VIOLENTLY RANG WITH ALL THE NOISE GENERATED FROM ALL OF THE SIMULTANEOUS SHOOTING IN SUCH CLOSE CONFINES WITHIN THE CABIN!

BECAUSE THE INDIANS WERE SO SURPRISED AND DISTRACTED BY DOG'S ATTACK FROM BEHIND ONTO TWO MOONS'S FACE AND HIS TERRIFYING SCREAMS, THEIR RIFLES WERE STILL POINTED EVERY WHICH WAY IN THE INITIAL STAGES OF THEIR ATTACK INSIDE THE TRAPPERS' CABIN GETTING READY TO BEGIN SHOOTING AT EVERYTHING THAT MOVED! ADDITIONALLY, SINCE THE INDIANS WERE ALL CLUSTERED TOGETHER JUST INSIDE THE OPEN FRONT DOOR OF THE CABIN WITH RIFLES POINTED BOTH TO THE FRONT FACING THE SURPRISED TRAPPERS AND NOW WHIPPED AROUND BACKWARDS TOWARDS THE ATTACKING

DOG, THEY SUFFERED THE WORST BECAUSE OF THEIR INDECISIONS!

MEDICINE DOG DIED NEXT WHEN BUCK SNORT SHOT HIM THROUGH THE THROAT WITH HIS RIFLE FROM FOUR FEET AWAY WHEN HE SAW WHAT THAT INDIAN HAD DONE TO HIS DOG! HE BLED VERY LITTLE BECAUSE A SOLID SHEET OF FLAME FROM THE END OF BUCK SNORT'S RIFLE CAUTERIZED THE BULLET'S ENTRY POINT INTO HIS THROAT! HOWEVER, THE HEAVY .52 CALIBER BALL OF SOFT AND QUICKLY EXPANDING LEAD MADE SURE THAT LIVING BEING NEVER AGAIN DREW A BREATH OF AIR!

COWARDLY WOLF DIED NEXT IN THE CONFUSED HAIL OF FLYING LEAD... IN CHARGE OF THE CAPTURED WOMAN, HE HAD PUSHED HER THROUGH THE TRAPPERS' CABIN DOOR OPENING WHEN THE INITIAL ATTACK HAD STARTED. AS SUCH, SHE WAS PUSHED INTO THE DIRECT LINE OF FIRE COMING FROM THE NOW FULL OF FIGHT TRAPPERS! WITHIN SECONDS AFTER BEING FORCED TO THE FRONT OF THE ATTACKING INDIANS WHERE THE TRAPPERS' FOCUS OF FIRING WAS DIRECTED, SHE WAS SHOT THROUGH THE POINT OF HER SHOULDER AND DROPPED TO THE FLOOR IN AN INSTANT! BUCK SNORT, HAVING THE COWARDLY

WOLF'S HEAD FILLING HIS SIGHTS, FELLED HIM WITH HIS FIRST PISTOL SHOT OF BUCK AND BALL TO THE BACK OF HIS HEAD! HIT FROM SO MANY LEAD PELLETS FROM SUCH CLOSE RANGE SPEWED THE ENTIRE KITCHEN AREA OF THE CABIN WITH RED BLOOD AND GRAY MATTER!

UPON SEEING THE RED AND GRAY SPEW OF WOLF'S ESSENCE SPRAYING THROUGHOUT THE CABIN'S EATING AREA MERE SECONDS LATER, WIND HORSE, SEEING AN INDIAN WOMAN PUSHED INTO THE FOREFRONT OF BATTLE AND FIGURING SHE WAS A NON-COMBATANT, PULLED HIS SHEATH KNIFE, YELLED TO GET HER ATTENTION AND THEN TOSSED HER HIS LONG-BLADED KNIFE TO BE USED IN HER DEFENSE…

THEN BUCK SNORT TOOK A BULLET INTO THE POINT OF HIS LEFT SHOULDER, MORE THAN LIKELY FIRED BY ONE OF THE TRAPPERS, ALL OF WHOM WERE NOW FURIOUSLY FIRING BACK AT THE MASS OF ATTACKING AND BUNCHED-UP AND MILLING INDIANS IN THE CABIN'S DOORWAY! KNOCKED BACKWARDS INTO THE DOOR JAMB FROM THAT BULLET'S IMPACT, BUCK SNORT NOW FULL OF ADRENALINE, QUICKLY RECOVERED FROM HIS NON-MORTAL BUCK AND BALL WOUND INTO THE POINT OF HIS LEFT SHOULDER.

QUICKLY DRAWING HIS SECOND PISTOL, BUCK SNORT FILLED HIS FRONT SIGHT WITH KICKING BIRD'S FACE WHICH WAS STILL FULL OF ABJECT SURPRISE OVER WHAT WAS EXPLODING ALL AROUND HIM... WHEN HE DID, IT WAS ONLY TO HAVE THE FRONT OF HIS FACE HEAVILY SPLATTERED WITH THAT INDIAN'S BRAINS, AFTER HAVING JUST BEEN SHOT BY ANOTHER TRAPPER AT SUCH CLOSE QUARTERS! WITHOUT A THOUGHT OVER WHAT HAD JUST OCCURRED BECAUSE OF THE HEAT OF BATTLE, BUCK SNORT QUICKLY WIPED HIS EYES FREE OF THE WARM AND STICKY GRAY MATTER WITH THE SLEEVE OF HIS BUCKSKIN SHIRT SO HE COULD ONCE AGAIN SEE TO SHOOT...

NEXT TO DIE WAS THE BIGGEST COWARD OF ALL, NAMELY CHARLIE LEFT HAND! AIMING HIS PISTOL IN THAT MAN'S DIRECTION IN ORDER TO HEAD SHOOT HIM, BUCK SNORT SAW CHARLIE LEFT HAND, WHO WAS STILL TO HIS FRONT, ALL OF A SUDDEN LET OUT A LOUD SCREAM AND QUICKLY BEND OVER AND GRAB AT HIS LOWER EXTREMITIES! THAT WAS WHEN BUCK SNORT SAW THE INDIAN WOMAN WHO WAS LYING ON THE FLOOR AND NOT DEAD, WITH A LONG-BLADED SHEATH KNIFE SHE HAD GOTTEN FROM WIND HORSE, SLAM THE BLADE DOWN ONTO THE TOP OF

CHARLIE LEFT HAND'S FOOT, PINNING IT TO THE CABIN'S WOODEN FLOOR... THAT WAS WHEN CHARLIE LEFT HAND HAD LET OUT A SCREAM OF INTENSE PAIN AS THE KNIFE'S SHARP BLADE PENETRATED DOWN THROUGH HIS ENTIRE FOOT, ONLY TO HAVE THAT SCREAM CUT SHORT WHEN THE INDIAN WOMAN PULLED THE KNIFE FROM HIS FOOT AND WHILE IN HIS BENT-OVER POSITION TRYING TO GRAB HIS BADLY INJURED FOOT, HAD THE WOMAN'S SHEATH KNIFE THRUST DEEPLY UPWARDS INTO HIS GROIN AREA! HIS SCREAM OVER THAT WOUND WAS THEN CUT SHORT WHEN ANOTHER BULLET FIRED FROM THE TRAPPERS INTO THE CLOUD OF BLACK POWDER SMOKE AND AIMED IN THE DIRECTION OF THAT SCREAM, ENTERED THE TOP OF HIS HEAD, KILLING HIM INSTANTLY! LAST TO DIE WAS PRAIRIE DOG, WHO UPON SEEING A NUMBER OF HIS FRIENDS DYING BEFORE HIS EYES, RAISED HIS TOMAHAWK AND STORMED INTO THE CLOUD OF BLACK POWDER SMOKE IN THE DIRECTION OF THE THREE TRAPPERS. TWO QUICK PISTOL SHOTS PRETTY WELL CONFIRMED WHAT HAPPENED NEXT TO PRAIRIE DOG... UNFORTUNATELY, HE DID NOT HAVE ENOUGH TIME TO SING HIS DEATH SONG...

Then Buck Snort heard Wind Horse call out,

"Buck Snort, are you alright? Answer me, damn you! I can smell the terrible smells you make when you are emotionally aroused, so you must still be alive and somewhere inside this here stinking, smoke-filled cabin..."

It was then that Buck Snort, remembering how he got his name because he could release clouds of foul-smelling gasses when under stress after being poisoned at the orphanage, could now smell himself over the acrid smells of freshly fired black powder and the sickly sweet smell of fresh blood and chunks of gray matter, LOTS OF IT!

"Yeah, I am alright. I will stand over here by the door until this damn smoke clears so I can see what still needs to be done," said Buck Snort hurriedly reloading his pistol. "You alright, Wind Horse?" asked Buck Snort.

"No, I was hit in the side and am bleeding like a stuck hog. But I think I will be alright if I can get to some wrapping cloth. I don't think any of my guts are busted up so that is a good thing, but I sure have one hell of a long flesh wound on my side!" yelled Wind Horse.

"Are any of those bastards still alive?" shouted Wind Horse still under the emotion of the moment.

"I don't think so. But now that I am reloaded, I will check to see what we have left alive. How is Clem? Is he alright because I can't see from all of this damn smoke filling the cabin," asked Buck

Snort, with deep concern sounding in the tone and tenor of his voice, as he began coming down from his killing moment in time.

"I am alright, I think. I took a round in the leg but it didn't break any bones so I think I will be alright if I can stop it from bleeding!" yelled Clem. "But dammit all to hell, the ear that that damn grizzly bear did not get when it tried eating me was shot clear off by one of those damn Indians. I know their culture does not allow anyone who is missing any of their body parts to travel into their Upper World. Well, you can bet before all of this is said and done, I will be cutting off every one of those bastards' ears so they can't get into their Upper World because one of those son-of-a-bitches just shot off my last good ear... And by dammit, that was my best-looking ear too!" said Clem, which drew a smile from Buck Snort, full well knowing from the strength of Clem's voice and how he bellowed his displeasure over having lost his last ear, that he was going to be alright...

By then the black powder smoke in the cabin caused by so many rifles and pistols being fired in such close quarters was beginning to drift out the front door and now that Wind Horse had opened up a window, the cross draft was helping clear out the remaining smoky atmosphere. Moments later as the smoke cleared further and now leaning against the front door jamb, Buck Snort could see a standing Wind Horse with some gray cloth showing blood soaking through from his side wound. Then there was Clem with a thigh wound but it appeared to be just a flesh wound that was bleeding like hell through his fingers as he attempted to stem the flow. Then Buck Snort's heart froze! There was his friend Muskrat standing by their kitchen table with his face held down and he was furiously bleeding from his head! Then Muskrat looked up and Buck Snort's heart damned near stopped over what he saw! Muskrat had been shot through the open mouth and out the side of his face and was bleeding furiously from the side of his face!

Seeing that and taking one more close look at the pile of dead Indians strewn about the inside of their cabin and seeing no movement from any of them other than the Indian woman who was attempting to stand, Buck Snort jumped over a chair and walked over to Muskrat. Helping him to sit down by their kitchen table, Buck Snort could see that when shot, Muskrat fortunately had his mouth wide open, probably yelling. That being the case when hit, the bullet had gone clear through Muskrat's open mouth and out the side of his cheek, just below his ear! If that ball had been one inch higher or one inch lower, it would have slammed into his jaw and teeth and exploded inside his mouth! Had that happened, such a wound more than likely have killed him causing him to bleed out...

Then Buck Snort saw that his friend Wind

Horse was starting to wobble from his loss of blood and going into shock! With that, he walked over and steadied Wind Horse over to the kitchen table and had him sit down. Then pulling his wrap aside a bit, he could see that the bullet had gouged out a large chunk of soft tissue and muscle from Wind Horse's side but fortunately had not hit and exploded against a rib... Just as Buck Snort started to push more cloth wrapping into the deep wound to slow the bleeding, he felt a soft hand on his good shoulder gently pushing him off to the side. When he felt the softness of that hand, Buck Snort looked over at whose hand had been placed onto his shoulder and for a moment, had to catch his breath...

Buck Snort found himself looking into the most beautiful set of dark as night eyes he had ever seen! Well, the second prettiest set of beautiful dark eyes. The first he had seen of the same type of beauty was when he had visited the Shoshoni woman back at the Rendezvous making him some fancy Free Trapper shirts. The same woman he had tried to get close to because of his interest in her, only to have the entry of her gruff-looking father the chief into their tipi. That unexpected entry stopped all further conversation between the white man trapper and the young and beautiful Shoshoni woman...

Then with a smile even though she was bleeding from a shallow flesh wound on her left shoulder, the Indian woman said quietly, "My name is "Kaya" or "Turtle Woman" of the Wind River Shoshoni. Move, so I can help your friend and stop his bleeding before he bleeds to death."

Almost in shock over hearing such a soft purring voice and looking into such deeply beautiful eyes from so close and still in emotional shock over all the killing he had just experienced and done, Buck Snort finally found himself doing as he had been told. Then he happened to look over at his friend Wind Horse and saw the pure amazement and deep surprise over what he was seeing happening with the young woman named Kaya as well. In fact, Wind Horse said with a big grin of pleasure, "Buck Snort, have I died and gone to the Upper World or the white man's Heaven?"

Then Kaya, after taking a quick look at Wind Horse's wound, looked over at Buck Snort saying in a strong and commanding voice, "I need some heavy cloth, needle, thread, rum and some bear grease." For the longest time, Buck Snort just stood there almost in shock once again upon hearing a woman's voice, until Kaya had to repeat herself so he would get his 'tail end' in gear.

That was when Buck Snort caught himself and then set his carcass into motion… Soon he had returned with a bolt of gray cloth, a cup of rum, a large leather-sewing needle, a small pot of Clem's used for cooking bear grease, and a spool of red thread held in his mouth because his hands were already full of the other requested items.

Soon Kaya was gently washing out Wind Horse's wound with rum and when she had the bleeding pretty much halted, bathed the area in bear grease and sewed up his wound just 'slicker than cow slobbers'! Then without another word, Kaya had Muskrat sit down and after bathing his face with warm soap and water, dry shaved the damaged side of his face with his ever-sharp sheath knife, washed out the exit wound and sewed it shut as well. Then Kaya had Clem sit down at the kitchen table, drop his buckskins and patched up his thigh wound as well. Then it was Buck Snort's turn and soon under the expert caring hand of Kaya, had his shoulder wound sewn up 'slicker than a whistle' and smelling of bear grease like everyone else as well.

Finally sitting down at the kitchen table and needing attention herself, Buck Snort poured more hot water into a pan and headed for Kaya's side so he could patch up her shoulder flesh wound. That was when Buck Snort got surprised! When he went to pull down part of Kaya's buckskin shirt exposing her shoulder and one breast, she took her hands and placing them on his, gently removed them from her bloody shirt. Then looking over at Wind Horse, Kaya made a move with her hand letting him know he was the one she had selected to pull down her shirt exposing her breast and patch up her shoulder wound… Realizing what Kaya wanted done and figuring she had selected him because he himself was an

Indian, Wind Horse moved over to her side and then looked at his trapper friends with a 'look' meant for all of them to find something else to do in their cabin beside looking on...

Sensing what Wind Horse and Kaya desired, namely some privacy, Buck Snort and Clem supporting Muskrat, walked him outside the cabin and sat him down on a sitting log. Then Clem hobbled around and built a fire in the outside firepit as Buck Snort, the least wounded of the trappers, bodily hauled the Indian dead from their cabin one at a time and with his pinto and a rope, dragged their bodies down to the Green and dumped them into its waters. When he returned after dumping the last of the dead, he found Kaya wearing one of his clean and heavily beaded fancy Shoshoni shirts sitting on a sitting log by the fire washing out her bloody shirt in a pail of water like it was an everyday event. Sitting alongside Kaya was Wind Horse and the two of them were visiting like they were long-lost brother and sister...

Then Buck Snort took Dog on his final ride on the back of the pinto up behind their cabin and buried him amidst many free-flowing tears over a ratty-looking dog that had taken a liking to him and had never once let him down... Even the pinto seemed to sense the loss of Dog and kept standing by the burial mound looking down and smelling the fresh mound of dirt as if looking for his 'friend' to appear and once again run along his side and play with him...

While Clem and Kaya fixed breakfast, Buck Snort and the pinto backtracked the trail the Indians had left back to where they had left their horses before sneaking up and into the trappers' cabin. Shortly thereafter, Buck Snort returned trailing and herding the six Indians' horses and eleven other horses once belonging to the dead trappers still loaded with provisions and bundles of beaver pelts. After finishing breakfast, the 'walking wounded' trappers unpacked the horses, hobbled them and turned them out with the rest of the trappers' horses. Then after hauling in all of the dead trappers' supplies, cooking implements and bundles of beaver pelts into their cabin for safekeeping, the men rearranged their cabin with sleeping furs, buffalo robes and the like inside their cabin. That they did so Kaya would have her own part of the cabin and private place to live, since she now appeared to want to remain with the men since she had nowhere else to go, having been captured early on in life by the Sioux and then later on, traded to the Hudson's Bay now long-dead fur trappers...

With that in mind, Wind Horse moving somewhat slowly because of his side wound and Buck Snort removed four of their tanned buffalo hides from their storage shed and brought them into the cabin. Then the two men still mindful of their painful but not mortal wounds, slowly hung and nailed the buffalo skins from the ceiling rafters at the north end of their cabin and in essence, made a 'buffalo skin walled-off room' for Kaya so she could have some privacy. All the while they made Kaya her own place within the cabin, the men were aware of the number of smiles that came their way over the considerate way they were treating and not physically or sexually abusing her...

Then Clem reminded everyone with his familiar bellow that breakfast was ready and if they didn't come and eat it, he was going to throw it out. He didn't have to call everyone twice as the men 'made merry' around the cooking fires with a hearty breakfast, obviously glad to still be alive. As they did, they noticed that Kaya assisted Clem, who was still too stove up from his wounds to serve breakfast as well as cook it. Then while Clem and his 'new hand' Kaya cleaned up, Muskrat, Wind Horse and Buck Snort, still having a trap line to run, slowly saddled up the men's riding and packhorses with a fair amount of grimacing for the day's work soon to be done because of their still-draining wounds. However, Wind Horse saw to it that Kaya had her 'pick of the litter' when it came to selecting her own new riding horse from the four dead trappers' and Charlie Left Hand's riding stock. Picking out a nice looking bay, Wind Horse saw to it that she had a good saddle from the dead men's supplies and adjusted it so she could comfortably ride along with the men. This he did because he was in no way leaving Kaya alone back at their cabin while the men went out trapping. Especially now since he was just getting to know her and discovered that he was having strange and un-usual feelings for her...

An hour later due to all the injuries being suf-fered by the wounded men, they finally shuffled out from their camp in order to run their spring beaver trap line. However, that day was sadly different. That day the men rode from camp without Dog trotting alongside the men or hap-pily leading the way. No one said anything about his absence but it was apparent that Dog was no longer with the men and even Buck Snort's pinto kept looking back for the dog to come trotting along... In fact, it took the group of trappers the next several weeks to get over the fact that they no longer had Dog as an equal partner when they rode from camp each morning to check their trap lines...

That morning after the battle with Charlie Left Hand's warriors, the trappers' caravan had dras-tically changed. As usual, Buck Snort rode in the lead as they headed for their trap line. Behind him now rode Wind Horse and Kaya, each trail-ing two packhorses... Two of the packhorses now carried a wealth of firearms in each of their panniers gathered up after the fight in case the trappers ran into more of the 'Charlie Left Hand ilk'... Trailing Wind Horse and now Kaya, were Muskrat and Clem, ever the guards against being attacked from the rear as they rode out to their trapping site or while they were working on the ground on-site.

Then once at their trap line, Buck Snort and Wind Horse stripped down and got into their leggings so they could run the trapping portion of the trap line in the water and mud. Now after Clem had given Kaya several lessons on how to properly skin a beaver, those skinning and assistant to the two trappers' duties fell on her shoulders. Then Clem rode off and joined Muskrat on horseback still painfully standing guard duty a short distance away. This change was made because both men were good shooters and Muskrat still needed help getting into his saddle after dismounting to go to the bathroom. So Clem happily drew those duties for his life-long buffalo-hunting friend.

But that left a weakness on the trapping site without Clem being close at hand as a protector and one that Wind Horse gladly volunteered to remedy. Shortly thereafter, Wind Horse had taken the time to teach Kaya to load and accurately shoot both a rifle and pistol. That way once she learned, she could be the first line of defense to Buck Snort and Wind Horse doing all of the trapping, because the trappers were not able to also carry along their bulky rifles to protect themselves while in the marsh's waters and moving around in the mud hauling 40-50 pound beaver around.

Every day after running the men's trap lines

until Kaya became proficient, Wind Horse and Kaya would adjoin to the meadow back by their camp and there Wind Horse would provide daily instruction on how to load both rifles and pistols and accurately shoot both firearms. The rest of the trappers noticed that at first Wind Horse and Kaya acted more like brother and sister and then as time went along, that relationship, to the rest of the trappers' delight, was becoming more than that...MUCH MORE! It was as if a kind of 'Frontier Grace' had descended upon the four trappers...

However, that change in trapping team assignments soon bore fruit. As it soon turned out, Kaya, after Clem's instructions on the proper techniques in skinning a beaver, turned out to be an excellent skinner! Additionally, Kaya soon became a crack rifle and pistol shooter under Wind Horse's personal and professional methods of instruction in the use and care of firearms and her 'guard' duties...

Then there were additional changes in the trappers' camp because of Kaya. Every day right at sunrise, Kaya attended to each trappers' wounds until they were healed-up and back to normal. That also included once the wounds were healed, the careful but painful removal of the thread binding the wounds. Then Kaya was found every day at Clem's side like a younger sister learning from the master on how to cook and properly spice the trappers' meals the way they preferred. Soon, Kaya and Clem were like brother and sister, much to the satisfaction of the rest of the trappers as well...

Then one day, Buck Snort sat Kaya down at the kitchen table in their cabin and brought forth bolts of gray and red vermillion cloth, several beautiful white, tanned bighorn sheep hides, tanned deerskins and a number of river otter and beaver skins. Then Buck Snort told Kaya that she no longer had just one outfit of still blood-stained clothing to wear. She now had all the needles, thread, hides and tanned pelts needed to make everything from new moccasins to much-needed heavy winter clothing. Upon hearing what Buck Snort had to say and wanted her to do, Kaya jumped up and gave Buck Snort a big hug and a kiss. However, the kiss was placed on his cheek and not the kind of kiss that she occasionally offered to Wind Horse... Soon, Kaya turned out being the best-dressed person in camp and all of her "brothers" made sure she lacked for nothing, and Lord help him if anyone mishandled or tried messing with her...

One month later, the beaver came out of prime, the men pulled their traps and headed for their camp at the close of the 1827 spring beaver trapping season. Other than the distressing loss of Dog, it had been a good year, especially with having Kaya at the men's sides. Looking over their successes, the men discovered that they had 104 prime wolf pelts in their storage shed, along with 223 fall beaver pelts and 497 spring beaver pelts in their possession, for a total catch of 720 mostly Made Beaver pelts! Additionally they had acquired eleven horses from the four dead Hudson's Bay trappers and another six horses from Charlie Left Hand's now dead band of Indians, and had only lost one of their group's original horses to Muskrat's earlier moose attack. Lastly, they had acquired an additional ten rifles and eight pistols from the dead trappers and Indians! The way Buck Snort and company figured it, they were now even richer men than they had been the year before, once all of the pelts, extra horses and firearms were sold!

But as the men sat around their campfire one night discussing their year, they now found themselves for the first time discussing the negatives of Frontier life as well, especially in light of their accumulating physical disabilities. Disabilities such as the time Buck Snort had stepped on a sleeping monster grizzly bear in its day bed and had suffered a loss of much of his arm and shoulder strength from the savage attack, not to mention the loss of most of his hind end mass of tissue, which caused him a lot of physical misery come the cold winter months or after long days' rides in the saddle. As for Muskrat, it was well known around the camp that Muskrat had challenged a bull moose in rut and had not only lost the full use of his now badly damaged back but had lost his best riding horse as well. And as a result, had great difficulty just getting up into a horse's saddle and found his back was causing him pain if he stepped wrong or fell. Clem, well there was Clem. He had decided to take on a winter bear and having come out second best, even his beloved mother would not recognize him now without having any ears or a respectably sized nose... The only man walking about and not a member of the 'walking wounded' was Wind Horse. And as it now seemed, he had discovered by chance the love of his life and had, unlike many of his comrades, been 'Graced by the Frontier' and not battle-scarred...

After discussing their successes and problems, Buck Snort got up from his sitting log around the campfire, walked back to the cabin and moments later, he returned with a keg of rum under one arm and a handful of metal drinking cups... For the rest of that evening, the four men for the very first time discussed what their future should be and what they hoped to accomplish with the remainder of their lives, physically altered as they were. Should they stay and brave the odds found out on the Frontier or should they take their furs, head for St. Louis and with their Letters of Credit, cash them in and then retire to the good lands found in the State of Missouri, settle down and raise families.

Missing throughout most of the men's conversations was the input from their friend and fellow trapper, Wind Horse. He was always a quiet man but that day when such challenging conversations were flying back and forth, he was unusually quiet. Unusually quiet because he loved what the life on the Frontier could bring with its daily adventures but now he found that with what was developing between himself and Kaya, things were changing, drastically... To force her to continue living this kind of life-style, Wind Horse found it to be unfair. Unfair because his relationship to date with Kaya had disclosed that as a young girl out berry hunting with a bunch of other women from her tribe, she had been ambushed by a number of Sioux warriors. Many of her group had been killed and she along with a number of other young girls had been captured and taken away back to the land of the Sioux. There she had been mistreated as a slave by the Sioux women, made to do the worst of things in order to just survive, including suffering through numerous rapes by many younger sexually predatory Sioux men. She had lost two children as a result of those rapes and in their recent conversations about their lives to be, let Wind Horse know that she would now fight to the death if ever confronted with more of what she had already endured... As such, Wind Horse found his heart filled with happiness every time he was around her and now, was not inclined to continue exposing her to what could happen to a beautiful woman out on the Frontier if something was to happen to him where he couldn't protect her, or her other protectors in the trapper family couldn't and she was once again captured...

That plus he now had his friends sitting around the fire who were trying to figure out what to do with the rest of their highly physically altered lives as well. True, they were rich men but the allure of the wilds out on the Frontier was a very strong pull indeed. And as such having been through so much with his dear friend and 'brother' Buck Snort, he was reluctant to just up and abandon him as well. Hence the quandary that Wind Horse now found himself in as the evening's discussions on what their future lives would bring continued on late into the night...

Rising early the next morning, Kaya headed out the front door of their cabin with Clem in order to get the cooking fires going and begin making breakfast for the rest of the men. After taking care of a call of nature, she washed up and then headed over to the firepit and began putting more wood on the fire so they could have the right kinds of coals in order to make Clem's much highly favored style of Dutch oven biscuits. Walking over to where Clem was mixing up a mess of dough, Kaya began helping him with the biscuit making duties as she always did.

"HELLO THE CAMP! FRIENDLY FREE TRAPPERS COMING IN!" shouted a voice from one of two fur trappers heading up from the Green River on their horses and coming towards their campsite.

Kaya not wanting to take any chances having been captured and abused by Hudson's Bay trappers before, reached over and hefted her rifle from up off her sitting log. She then felt the comforting hand of Clem, almost a father figure now, being laid against hers letting her know everything was alright.

"HELLO CHARLIE, COME ON IN, LIGHT DOWN AND TAKE A LOAD OFF THEM DAMN FLEA BAGS THE TWO OF YOU ARE CALLING HORSES!" bellowed Clem right back.

Soon there was much handshaking, backslapping and joshing each other, as Kaya stood there still armed with her rifle just in case things 'went south' with the two strangers.

Then the other three trappers tumbled out from the cabin where they had been casting up a small mountain of lead balls and soon the entire campsite was a swirl of talking, laughter, mingled with a fair amount of joshing each other. However, just as soon as the making merry among the friends subsided somewhat, Wind Horse was quick to introduce Kaya as the newest member of their group to the appreciative nods of the two strangers. He then went on to let the men know about the battle and how she had fought as well. Those words from the much-respected Wind Horse now really brought smiles and nods of appreciation and respect from the two strangers…

"BREAKFAST IS READY," said Clem, as he and Kaya began serving the men hot Dutch oven biscuits, spitted elk meat, beans and coffee. For the next hour or so, between mouthfuls of food and discussion, the visiting trappers had a lot to say to their friends. Then when breakfast was done, Buck Snort brought out one of their last kegs of rum and with cupfuls all around, the discussions really 'flew' back and forth as a result of the fiery liquid. Especially since the visiting trappers had come all that way to the Green in order to see if Buck Snort and company wished to call the fur trapping business quits and head south with Charlie Poke's crew for St. Louis. There they would trade in their furs, claim what they had coming on their previous Letters of Credit and then get on with their lives as citizen farmers and ranchers in the great State of Missouri.

Soon the talk turned to what Buck Snort and company had saved up over their years of trapping and what that would buy the men back in Missouri in the way of a land purchase so they could start over in a less dangerous trade. Then the talks shifted to the physical well-beings of not only Buck Snort and company but the physical problems all of Charlie Poke's men were saddled with. As the words flew back and forth, Kaya now finished with her duties helping Clem, sat on one of the sitting logs and just listened to what the trappers had to say in the way of justifying staying in the fur trade on the Frontier, or leaving it for a more gentle and less dangerous lifestyle in a place called the State of Missouri.

That was when Kaya caught Wind Horse looking at her like he had never looked at her before. Seeing that look, Kaya got up, walked over to Wind Horse, placed her hand on his shoulder and with a nod of her head, walked off to the cabin. Moments later, Wind Horse and Kaya found themselves in the cabin where it was quiet so they could talk quietly among themselves. It was then that Kaya said, "Wind Horse, I know you are in love with this life and I love many aspects of it as well. However, I look at Buck Snort, Muskrat and Clem and all of them are busted up because of what the Frontier has done to them. I do not want that for them, us or any children we may have if you and I decide to remain together. If I have a vote, I would like to go to this white man place called St. Louis, sell our furs and see if we can still have a good life without me having to carry a gun and watch out for man or beast trying to kill, capture or eat the two us. But, know that I will go wherever my man decides to go and make a good home for him and our children and now I have spoken."

With that, Kaya got up, walked out back to the men in full discussions around the firepit and began refilling the men's cups with more rum. Later that evening around the firepit after supper, Buck Snort and company, after much discussion over leaving or staying, finally decided to take a vote as to whether they stayed or left the fur trade and the Frontier they loved so much. A vote on whether the men continued living on the Frontier and facing its challenges and unforeseen dangers as trappers, or returned safely back to Missouri and took up their lives as farmers or ranchers. Whether the men could walk away from such Frontier splendor and live a life without having to face the unknown every day they survived. As the talk ebbed and flowed over staying or leaving, it was obvious a life on the Frontier had a very strong hold on the inner beings of all of the men gathered around the campfire that evening…

The next morning, with the help of Charlie Poke and Broken-Hand Luke, Buck Snort and company began breaking camp and preparing for a long trip with Poke back over part of the Rocky Mountains to Charlie's camp located along the Wind River. There the two groups of men totaling a force of ten heavily armed trappers would head south along the Wind River to the Sweetwater River through a place called South Pass, and then to points south and east eventually leading to St. Louis and a new life…

Two days later found Buck Snort and company being led by trapper Charlie Poke over the Rocky Mountains towards the southeast to Charlie's camp located near the Wind River… Five days of uneventful travel through the beauty of the Rocky Mountains led the trappers' caravan to Charlie Poke's campsite along the Wind River and in and among Chief Bear Hunter's Wind

River Band of Northern Shoshoni. There they would plan for the next surprising adventure in their and Kaya's lives.

Chapter Fourteen

"CHENOA", "SAKEYA" AND FRONTIER GRACE

AS CHARLIE LED THE LONG STRING of fur trappers, extra horses and their heavily loaded packhorses right through Northern Shoshoni Chief Bear Hunter's camp of tipis, they were met with numerous barking dogs, excited little children running about the caravan, warriors standing outside their tipis waving to their friend Charlie Poke and beautifully dressed Shoshoni Indian women standing about quietly and demurely looking on at the long stream of just-arriving white men fur trappers.

Charlie and Broken-Hand Luke led the impressive caravan followed by Buck Snort riding his big pinto trailing a number of fully loaded packhorses. Behind him rode Wind Horse and Kaya also leading a number of heavily loaded packhorses. Last in the impressive string of fur trappers rode Muskrat and Clem also leading two long strings of heavily loaded packhorses and extra riding horses taken from Charlie Left Hand and his warriors. By now, with all the barking dogs and noisy and excited children running about, the majority of Chief Bear Hunter's band were now out from their tipis and looking on because such a large number of heavily armed arriving fur trappers represented quite a Frontier spectacle in their village!

ALL OF A SUDDEN, KAYA BAILED OFF HER HORSE AND RAN SCREAMING AND CRYING INTO THE CROWD OF SHOSHONI MEN, WOMEN AND CHILDREN SURROUNDING THE ARRIVING CARAVAN OF FUR TRAPPERS! WHEN SHE DID, THE SURPRISED CROWD OF SHOSHONI QUICKLY PARTED AS KAYA TORE THROUGH THE HORDE OF ONLOOKERS STANDING AMONG THEIR BUFFALO SKIN TIPIS WATCHING ON. AS SHE DID, TRAILED BY A NUMBER OF BARKING AND CHASING DOGS, KAYA RAN RIGHT INTO THE ARMS OF A YOUNG SHOSHONI WOMAN WHO ALL OF A SUDDEN WAS RUNNING RIGHT AT KAYA, SCREAMING AND CRYING ALL THE WAY TOWARDS HER AS WELL…

For the longest time, the two Shoshoni women after meeting, just laughed and cried as they hugged and danced their way around in circles of great joy. In the meantime, the horde of Shoshoni onlookers had closed ranks around the two obviously very happy and excited women and just noisily looked on in wonder over the surprise spectacle suddenly taking place in their normally quiet village.

Then the crowd of noisy onlookers grew deathly quiet as their great chief, Chief Bear Hunter, strode briskly into the circle of onlookers and right up to the two women still dancing around in circles, now holding each other's hands as they laughed and cried at the same time. THEN ALL OF A SUDDEN, THE TWO VERY HAPPY SHOSHONI WOMEN BROKE APART AND RAN RIGHT INTO THE OPEN ARMS OF THE GREAT CHIEF WITH SUCH ENERGY, THAT THE THREE OF THEM WERE SPILLED OVER BACKWARDS ONTO THE MUDDY GROUND! THAT WAS DONE AMIDST A GROAN OF SURPRISE AND EMBARRASSMENT AMONG THE BAND OF INDIAN ONLOOKERS WHO HAD NOW FORMED A LARGE CIRCLE OF HUMANITY AROUND THEIR HIGHLY RESPECTED CHIEF AND THE TWO YOUNG WOMEN WHO APPEARED TO HAVE JUST GONE CRAZY!

In the meantime, Charlie Poke and Buck Snort had halted the fur trappers' caravan and just sat there on their horses in utter shock and surprise over what they were seeing! ESPECIALLY WHEN THE CHIEF AND THE TWO WOMEN

ACTING ALL CRAZY-LIKE AROSE AND BEGAN DANCING AROUND WITHIN THE CIRCLE OF STILL LOOKING-ON AMAZED BAND OF SHOSHONI, CRYING AND YELLING OUT IN OBVIOUS INTENSE JOY …

By now, the huge and getting larger crowd of interested Shoshoni Indians were as silent as a 'mouse pissin' on a ball of cotton' over the antics of their much respected chief, his very much-loved and normally reserved daughter and that of a strange Indian woman wearing the clothing of a Sioux Indian. A Sioux Indian woman who was the sworn enemy of the Northern Shoshoni, now locked up in the arms of their great chief and his daughter…

Finally realizing what the previous spectacle must have looked like to his surprised band of Shoshoni still gathered around and looking on, Chief Bear Hunter stopped what he was doing and raised his right arm and hand high into the air so all could see in order to get the attention of the onlookers. He then in a very loud and happy tone and tenor of voice said, "My People… Welcome back if you will my youngest and previously captured years ago daughter "Sakeya", who I just learned had been renamed Kaya by the Sioux! The daughter I lost years ago when she was out berry picking with others of my band and was captured by a band of Sioux warriors and taken into their ranks as a slave woman. She tells me that she was badly treated by our common enemy the Sioux, and lived her last ten years among the Sioux as a slave woman to all in her band of captors. She has also told me that the trappers got into a fight with her captors, killed all of them, took her into their group as one of them and now treat her as an equal or like a long-lost sister."

Then looking over at the long string of horses and trappers quietly sitting and standing off to one side, the chief realized the people responsible for bringing his daughter back according to his daughter Sakeya, were in his midst! Without another word, the chief strode through the crowd of still-surprised onlookers as they respectfully parted to let him pass, as he headed directly towards the still amazed onlooking trappers, watching to see what he was going to do.

"Hello, Charlie, my friend! I see that you have brought me back my younger daughter," said Chief Bear Hunter, as he pumped Charlie's hand who was still sitting on his horse, up and down in welcome like he was using it to pump water from a well. That the chief did, not realizing Charlie had nothing to do with getting his long-lost and now found daughter safely back! Realizing the chief had mistakenly figured that Charlie and his band of trappers were responsible for his daughter's safe return, he turned to make things right.

"Chief Bear Hunter, the men responsible for saving your younger daughter and then caring for her as if she was one of theirs, are sitting behind me there on their horses. I had nothing to do with the fight they got into with the captors of your long-lost daughter. However, they are friends of mine and I would like you to meet them," said a very happy Charlie Poke over the fact that Buck Snort and his fellow trappers had treated the chief's beautiful daughter so well, had not 'bedded' her against her will and unknowingly had brought her back into the camp of the much-respected and very powerful Shoshoni chief...

With those words of correction and Charlie's subsequent dismount, he walked the great chief back among Buck Snort and company and introduced every one of them to the chief. However, when Charlie got to Wind Horse, another surprise awaited not only him but all of the rest of the trappers as well.

All of a sudden, Kaya, now using her Shoshoni name of Sakeya, broke into the ranks of the trappers and their horse herd. Then reaching out, she pulled Wind Horse over to where her father stood and introduced him. When she did, she made sure her father and great Shoshoni chief realized it was Wind Horse who had saved her back in the battle with his thrown sheath knife to protect herself from Charlie Left Hand, and now she proudly proclaimed she and Wind Horse, "Wished to become one!"

With that introduction followed by her revelation about Wind Horse becoming her husband, the great chief just stood there 'stock-still' and stunned over the events quickly swirling around him like a 'dust devil out on the prairie'! Here it was just a few short moments earlier he discovered that he had his daughter back from the much-hated Sioux and now she was favoring the white man trapper who had helped her defend herself in battle, as her husband-to-be... For a long moment, the chief just stood there in shock. In shock after discovering he now had his long-lost daughter back only to have her proudly proclaim she wished to marry one of the trappers... Then before the chief could respond, something else happened that took his breath away over what was happening as well...

STANDING THERE QUIETLY HOLDING SAKEYA'S HAND WAS HER OLDER SISTER, THE BEAUTIFUL "CHENOA". The same woman who had made Buck Snort his beautiful beaded shirts back at the 1826 Rendezvous! The one and same woman whose beautiful dark eyes had captured Buck Snort's attention and heart as one of the most beautiful women he had ever seen! The same Shoshoni woman, that when her father the chief had entered their tipi, all conversation just begun between Buck Snort and Chenoa, immediately ceased. The one and same woman that Buck Snort had fallen so hard for, that he went back to the Rendezvous traders and bought her a very expensive bolt of vermillion red cloth to present to her. The one and same

Shoshoni Indian woman who when he had returned with the bolt of red cloth, found that she
and the rest of her band of Shoshoni had pulled
up stakes and had just left to return to their home
campsite in the Wind River Mountains...

AND NOW, HERE WAS THAT SAME
WOMAN, AND SHE WAS CASTING
CAREFUL LOOKS AT BUCK SNORT AS HE
SAT THERE MAGNIFICENTLY ATOP HIS
LARGE PINTO HORSE... AND BUCK SNORT
WAS CASTING MANY NOT SO CAREFUL
LOOKS BACK AT THE WOMAN CALLED
CHENOA WHO WAS RELATED TO KAYA,
AS SHE HAD BEEN NAMED BY THE SIOUX
WHEN THEY HAD CAPTURED HER. THAT
WAS WHEN CHIEF BEAR HUNTER CAUGHT
BUCK SNORT LOOKING INTENTLY AT
HIS LAST REMAINING DAUGHTER AND
WHEN HE DID AND FIGURED OUT WHY,
IMMEDIATELY AND CURTLY DISMISSED
BOTH CHENOA AND SAKEYA AND WITHIN
SECONDS, BOTH WOMEN DISAPPEARED
INTO THE CROWD OF SHOSHONI AS FAST
AS A 'ROCKY MOUNTAIN WHISPER IN THE
WIND'...

Then Chief Bear Hunter spoke up saying,
"Charlie Poke, my good friend, you and the rest
of your trappers shall celebrate with me and my
people this evening over the return of my youngest daughter safely from the hands of the Sioux.
You shall bring nothing but your presence and

'big hungers' and my people will celebrate with us the return of one of my own as well." With that, the chief turned, said something to one of his warriors who soon sped off to gather up more warriors for a buffalo hunt to come and then just as quickly as he had arrived, he disappeared back into the crowd of his people in order to be with his daughters...

That abrupt leaving by the chief left Wind Horse wondering what the hell had just happened... But a subsequent special look and a nod of Charlie's head indicated it best to hold his questions until they all were at Charlie's campsite and out of earshot of the chief. That he did for fear of unnecessarily riling up the Northern Shoshoni Indians over the return of the chief's daughter, only to lose both of them to the trappers! That Charlie did because he knew of the fighting reputation of the Shoshoni warriors when all riled up. And somehow walking off with the great chief's daughters had the potential to cause a lot of 'rile'...

A half-hour later and the fur trappers had arrived at Charlie's cabin and horse corrals. There they unsaddled and unpacked their horses, hobbled them and let them out into the nearby meadow with the rest of Charlie's horses so they could feed and water. Then to avoid loss due to critters or weather, all of the trappers' supplies and bundles of furs were brought into Charlie's larger cabin for safe storage. It was then that Wind

Horse approached Charlie over what appeared to be the loss of the love of his life and what to do about it. Charlie advised they all had best wait until the celebration dinner and then figure out what they were to do, but he counseled Wind Horse to remain calm, because Charlie felt Chief Bear Hunter was a good, fair and just man. And a man who had just gotten his long-lost daughter back, so best let him get used to the wonderful gift and then if the time was right and the Gods are with you, then you cautiously approach the man and see if he will let his beloved kin run off with a smelly fur trapper...

That was when Buck Snort approached Charlie and filled him in on his experience with the chief's older daughter at the 1826 Rendezvous site and his now more than just a passing interest in her. When he did, Charlie just tilted his head back and roared with laughter till the tears rolled from his eyes.

"What the hell do you find that is so funny?" asked Buck Snort, somewhat pissed over what Charlie had found that was so funny over his desire to get to know the chief's older daughter better and the predicament that now had placed her somewhat out of reach...

"The chief only has two daughters and three sons. If you two think he is going to give either of his only daughters up so easily you are both sadly mistaken. He is a good man but he is all business when it comes to his kids, so we best tread lightly when approaching him regarding this subject of the two of you seriously running off with his daughters. But tonight might be the time to approach that issue, especially when you fellas are going to contribute one of your last kegs of rum for the occasion if you want to have any chance of loosening him up and then running off with his daughters. Especially in light of the fact that we all were planning on heading south to St. Louis a few days from now, getting out of the fur business forever and you two desiring to take his daughters away from him more than likely forever... And in order to do that, take his daughters through dangerous Arikara and Sioux Indian country! Now I know there will the ten of us trappers to protect ourselves when we move south and we all are damn good shooters. But if those damn bloodthirsty Arikara hit us with 50 or 60 warriors, we may not make it to the next sunrise. And if you are lucky enough to pry the chief's daughters out from his loving arms and we get hit hard by the Arikara or the Sioux, those women will pay a heavy price, especially when the tenth or eleventh 'Buck' rises up off of them after they have been gang-raped that many times! Just saying," said Charlie Poke, full well knowing what serious challenges his two friends might be facing. Realizing Charlie spoke the truth, both Wind Horse and Buck Snort let the issue slide...but for just a while...

That evening, the trappers streamed back into

Chief Bear Hunter's campsite only to smell many good things cooking and finding the Shoshoni people dressed up in their finest for the celebration they were coming to join. Dismounting, the trappers were guided over to a large seating area where two whole cow buffalo, quartered up as they were, were being slowly turned on two huge spits over the fire's coals. As expected, the keg of rum that Buck Snort had brought went over well, especially with the special warrior cast cooking the two buffalo for their special guests.

Then after the ten guest trappers had been seated, out walked Chief Bear Hunter, flanked by his wife "Berry Picking Woman", three strapping strong-looking sons named "Elk Killer, "Eagle Man" and "Fast Antelope", with Chenoa and Sakeya now using her Shoshoni name, beautifully dressed in pure white, tanned bighorn sheepskins fully adorned with elk ivories and red and blue glass beads. Moments later upon seeing Sakeya walking towards him dressed up in such finery, Wind Horse found it hard to breathe. Then when Sakeya slid her hand into his in front of her onlooking band of Shoshoni people, Wind Horse felt his heart rate quickening and dared hardly to breathe over what was happening in front of so many…

"Do not worry, Wind Horse," whispered Sakeya. "I told my father about me being 'taken' many times by the Sioux and the two children produced from such happenings. My father was very mad over hearing those words and swore he would kill the next ten Sioux that he would meet for 'spoiling me in the eyes of the young men of our tribe'..." Then in front of those Shoshoni assembled for the celebration, Sakeya stood up on her toes and kissed Wind Horse! When she did, a moaning sound of disbelief and surprise all of a sudden rippled through the crowd, as the look upon the chief's face over what had just occurred remained impassive!

Moments later, Chief Bear Hunter raised his right hand to get the attention of his people. When the crowd noise had died down over seeing Sakeya's outward show of affection for Wind Horse, Chief Bear Hunter said in a clear and loud voice, "Today I got my long-lost daughter back from her life of captivity with the Sioux. As such and since the trapper who saved her in the recent battle between the Northern Arapaho and the fur trappers is here, I have decided I will honor her wishes to be with the fur trapper man forever as his wife. Now let us hear no more whispers of this matter that I have been hearing about my daughter being 'taken' by many Sioux while in captivity. In our tribe because of that 'taking', she is now considered unclean and as such, will be unable to marry one of our own People. Therefore, she is released to select her own husband and as all of you have seen this evening, she has 'spoken' with the physical act of a kiss on the lips of the man of her choice. Now, let all of us celebrate the safe return of my daughter and her selection of a good and powerful man to live with her forever..." With those words, the chief seemed to wash his hands of the Shoshoni cultur- ally unclean problem Sakeya carried because of her unfortunate captivity with the Sioux. Soon the celebration of her return was in full swing as well as that of her choice of life to come. In so doing, Wind Horse's heart was 'filled' and that of Buck Snort, having seen no outward sign of affection from Chenoa that evening or overt sup- port from the chief, felt his heart sink...

However, while sitting alongside Charlie Poke, Buck Snort noticed that when Chenoa came by ladling out food into the men's bowls, she seemed to 'fish around' every time she came by Buck Snort for the best tasting morsels of food and then placed them demurely into his dish... At the same time, Charlie also noticed that the pair of saddlebags Buck Snort always carried along with him wherever he traveled, always laid by his side. Then he noticed that Buck Snort seemed to be shuffling around in one of those saddlebags when the beautiful Chenoa came by once again with more food for the trappers. When she did, Buck Snort removed a tanned deerskin bag from one side of his saddlebag, opened it up and removed a beautiful red and blue glass-beaded necklace he had purchased at the 1826 Rendezvous, made in a country called Italy. Then standing up clearly in front of the gathered crowd of those celebrating, he bravely placed the beautiful necklace around Chenoa's neck and then sat down like nothing out of the ordinary had just occurred...

For a moment Chenoa just stood there and then putting down the kettle she had been carrying and dishing food from, she ran her fingers along the triple strand of beautiful Italian glass beads. Then catching herself, she quickly picked up the kettle and its ladle and moved onto serving the rest of the trapper guests like nothing out of the ordinary had just occurred. But something out of the ordinary had just occurred and Chief Bear Hunter and his wife, along with the rest of his band, had indeed noticed...

After the celebration and for the next week, Charlie Poke's trapper campsite was a whirlwind of human activity. With the realization that the men were facing a 60-70 day trip across hostile Indian lands to their south and east in order to arrive at their destination in St. Louis, the trappers made sure once they were en route, they could sustain as well as protect themselves the entire way. Right off Clem and Broken-Hand Luke, the two designated camp cooks, went through all of their supplies, provisions and cooking essentials, eliminating what they would not need and keeping just the bare essentials for feeding such a large number of men along such a trip. That way, their horses would not be loaded with extra equipment or provisions for which there was no further need. As they continued making such equipment and provisions selections, daily trips were made to Chief Bear Hunter's camp and those cooking implements and provisions not needed for the trip were in turn traded for numerous Indian tanned deerskins. Those tanned deerskins in turn, were then wrapped around the valuable bundles of beaver and wolf furs for the long transport south so they would not be dirtied or damaged while on the journey.

Then as several of the trappers ventured forth on a daily basis hunting deer, elk and buffalo, meat from those animals was processed into jerky for the long trip, as well as cooked and served daily for the hardworking trappers' daily meals. Collaterally, Buck Snort and Wind Horse spent the better part of the week disassembling every rifle and pistol in camp. Those then had all of their lead and black powder fouling and residue removed and were then oiled with bear grease and reassembled. When that necessary firearms care was completed, it was discovered the trappers had enough weapons between the two groups of men so that each trapper would be armed with two pistols carried in their sashes and two rifles as well. Of those two rifles carried by each trapper, one would be carried in hand and the other in a scabbard on each of the men's riding horses. Additionally, there still were ten pistols and nine rifles left over and those would be carried on the various packhorses scattered throughout the pack train in case unusual emergencies arose and the need for extra firearms became a necessity. That in mind, the trappers made the needed number of extra rifle scabbards from tanned deerskins.

Then come the evenings, the men found themselves bagging up their freshly made jerky for the trip as well as casting up a large mountain of rifle and pistol balls in case the Arikara and Sioux, whose lands the men would be crossing, got a little testy and wanted to see who was the better shooter... Once all of the weaponry had been inspected and made ready to go, Wind Horse and Buck Snort saw to it that the entire herd of riding and packhorses had all of their hooves inspected and those needing horseshoe adjustment or replacing were fixed from Buck Snort's last keg of horseshoes.

However, each evening while bringing Chief Bear Hunter and his people equipment, provisions and leather goods for distribution that the trappers would not need for their trip to St. Louis, Wind Horse and Buck Snort took some time and were allowed to spend a few moments with Sakeya and finally after several requests, Buck Snort was even allowed by the very protective chief and father to spend some time with Chenoa! Mostly the two men were just allowed to take long walks with the two women and in every instance, according to strict Shoshoni customs, a member of their family walked along with the two couples. And as it turned out, in every instance, the chief delegated two of his big strapping hunks of men sons to make sure Buck Snort and Wind Horse did not cross any cultural lines and by so doing, that kept the two ladies in line as well...

During those visits, Wind Horse discovered that the chief had now changed his mind and was having second thoughts over letting Sakeya leave with Wind Horse as had he earlier advised would be allowed. And as Buck Snort quickly discovered, there was no way the chief was ever going to consider letting Chenoa marry outside his band! Even though Buck Snort and Chenoa had begun to fall in love with each other during the short period of time they had been allowed together, that situation he had chosen to ignore. And every time Chenoa had approached her father about taking Buck Snort as her man, he had stubbornly refused saying, "No, she was to only marry within her own culture so he could have many grandsons and granddaughters for me and Berry Picking Woman to enjoy in our later years!"

As the days sped by and the ten trappers moved closer and closer to their departure date set for leaving to go across country to St. Louis, the great chief seemed to dig in his heels even deeper when it came to letting either of his two daughters marry outside his clan of people. And that was with Chenoa telling him there were no young men in the band that she wished to marry. That her heart had now settled upon Buck Snort and no one else! Then Buck Snort came up with an idea. Figuring in everything that they needed for the trip, including extra packhorses and riding horses in case some of their livestock were stolen by Indians, eaten by a grizzly bear or the like, they still had seven more horses than they needed to carry everything south to St. Louis... And it just so happened that those seven extra horses they had no need for had once belonged to Charlie Left Hand and his band of now-dead Northern Arapaho warriors...

One evening, Chief Bear Hunter heard a number of horses being driven up to the front of his tipi and then nervously stomping around. Stepping outside to see what the hell was going on, since he had not authorized any of his warriors to leave during their main buffalo hunting season so there would be food a-plenty for winter for his Wind River Band, he saw Wind Horse sitting there on his horse. Behind Wind Horse was Buck Snort herding the seven extra horses the trappers did not need for their long and dangerous trip through Indian country to the white man's city of St. Louis.

"Chief Bear Hunter. I have come with horses to trade for the hand of your younger daughter, Sakeya! I offer all seven for her hand if you will allow it," said Wind Horse with his heart up in his throat over what the crusty old chief might decide!

Chief Bear Hunter said nothing but one could tell from the look on his face after hearing those words, that he liked the idea of acquiring seven more horses. Especially in light of the actions from his stubborn daughter who had been hounding him every night about him letting her go with the one that she loved... Walking around the horses and realizing they were all of fine stock, the chief just stood there thinking. Then all of a sudden, Sakeya bolted out from his tipi and ran over to the side of Wind Horse! Wind Horse did not even dare move for fear of really making the old chief madder than a hornet so he held his tongue over her bold actions. Then Wind Horse got reinforcements. Out from the chief's tipi streamed Chenoa and the chief's wife, Berry Picking Woman! Berry Picking Woman strode over to the side of her husband and then pulling his head closer to her lips, she whispered something to her husband.

Then the chief with a funny look on his face said, "I will take your offer for these seven fine-looking horses and you can have my daughter since she is bound and determined to 'lay with you' or cut her wrists or hair in shame over my actions not to let her leave with you." With that, the chief called forth his three sons and they happily took the horses from Buck Snort and began leading them over to where the chief kept his small herd of horses from mixing with those of the rest of the members of his band.

Then the chief turned and looking Buck Snort in his eyes said, "However with you, my daughter Chenoa will continue to live with me and Berry Picking Woman until she decides to marry a member of her own people, and that is final!"

Upon hearing those words, Chenoa burst out into tears and fled back into the chief's tipi followed by her mother, who gave her husband the chief, a look that could kill had it been from 'the flight of an arrow'... With those words, Chief Bear Hunter whirled on his moccasins and also retreated back into his tipi to the sounds of much wailing, arguing and crying coming from inside the buffalo hide structure...

Upon seeing those actions, Buck Snort rode his horse up alongside that of his 'brother' Wind Horse saying, "Let us go before he changes his mind. You can come back tomorrow, pick up Sakeya and her things and leave with the rest of us when we leave in two days. There is no use for me to try any more at having Chenoa go with us because the chief has made that pretty easy for me to understand his feelings regarding this matter. She is not leaving and I don't favor having an arrow driven through me if I try to take her by force," said Buck Snort sadly. And with those words, Buck Snort turned his big pinto and the two of them quietly walked back to Charlie Poke's campsite.

Two days later way before daylight, found the ten trappers and Sakeya up fixing breakfast, loading the packhorses and saddling those horses to be ridden by the trappers. Since Charlie Poke knew the way back down to St. Louis and had been on that long and dangerous trail once before, he was chosen as the right man to lead the multiple horse caravan of valuable furs and the like all the way to St. Louis. As the men finished loading all of the horses and finished their breakfast, Charlie made one more trip around and through his cabin making sure they had not left anything of value. Then riding up to the head of the long caravan of quietly waiting trappers and horses, he took one more look all around the area he had called home for two years, turned in his saddle and with a wave of his hand, the men streamed out from his old campsite and headed for the lowest pass in the Rockies, a place named South Pass. Then from there, head for the nearby Sweetwater River and then south and east through the lands of the dreaded Arikara and Sioux.

By late morning, the fur trappers' caravan was strung out and in a comfortable gait as they headed to the south and east towards South Pass. ALL OF A SUDDEN ONE COULD HEAR THE RUMBLE OF A LOT OF HORSES IN THE DISTANCE COMING THEIR WAY! TURNING IN HIS SADDLE AND LOOKING IN THE DIRECTION FROM WHENCE WAS COMING THE SOUNDS OF THUNDERING HORSES' HOOVES, ALL CHARLIE COULD SEE WAS A

LARGE CLOUD OF DUST BEING STIRRED UP! REALIZING THEY HAD BEEN SPOTTED AND WERE DANGEROUSLY OUT IN THE OPEN TO INDIAN ATTACK, CHARLIE QUICKLY SIGNALED WITH HIS HAND FOR THE MEN TO PICK UP THEIR PACE AND HEAD FOR A SMALL GULLY LYING IMMEDIATELY TO THEIR SOUTHEAST. THIS THEY DID BECAUSE BEING IN INDIAN TERRITORY AND LEADING A VERY VALUABLE FUR CARAVAN, THEY MADE AN EASY AND INVITING TARGET! BY NOW, THE CARAVAN OF RIDING AND PACKHORSES WAS IN FULL GALLOP AND A QUICK LOOK BEHIND REVEALED OVER 100 INDIANS ACROSS THE HORIZON RIDING HARD TOWARDS THEM AND FAST!

DROPPING OVER THE EDGE OF THE SMALL GULLY, CHARLIE SWUNG THE MEN INTO A DEFENSIVE POSITION FACING THE ONCOMING HORDE OF INDIANS AND HERDED THE VALUABLE PACKHORSES INTO THE BOTTOM OF THE GULLY SO THEY WOULD NOT BE STAMPEDED BY THE ONCOMING HARD-CHARGING INDIANS! THEN AS THE MEN NERVOUSLY FINGERED THEIR RIFLES, THEY MADE SURE THEIR EXTRA WEAPONS WERE NEAR AT HAND AND AWAITED THEIR FAST ONCOMING FATE... A FATE THAT WOULD SOON BE EASILY DECIDED BECAUSE FROM THE LOOKS OF IT, THE TRAPPERS WERE EASILY

OUTNUMBERED BY AT LEAST TEN TO ONE!

"HOLD IT! HOLD IT! HOLD IT!" YELLED CHARLIE, AS HE ALL OF A SUDDEN RODE HIS HORSE BACK OVER THE LIP OF THE GULLY NOW HOLDING ALL OF HIS HORSES AND MEN. ACROSS THE SAGEBRUSH FLAT RODE THE 100 OR SO INDIANS AND IN FRONT OF THE ONCOMING HORDE RODE CHIEF BEAR HUNTER...

RIDING HIS LATHERED-UP HORSE RIGHT UP TO CHARLIE POKE, THE CHIEF RAISED HIS RIGHT HAND IN THE SIGN OF PEACE AND THEN SAT BACK DOWN IN HIS SADDLE AND JUST LOOKED INTO THE EYES OF HIS FRIEND CHARLIE, WHOSE EYES WERE QUESTIONING WHY THEY HAD BEEN INTERCEPTED BY HIS BAND OF SUPPOSEDLY FRIENDLY INDIANS...

"Charlie, I have come in peace. I am bringing ten of my best warriors including my three sons, Fast Antelope, Elk Killer and Eagle Man. I have had a change of heart... Between my wife and eldest daughter and The Great Spirit or "Tam Apo" (Our Father) talking to me, I have changed my mind ABOUT MY DAUGHTER AND ONE OF YOUR FUR TRAPPERS!" Then turning in his saddle, the chief waved his hand and all of sudden coming forward through the ranks of his Indians were his three sons leading four heavily loaded packhorses and on another horse with a smile as wide as the Mighty Missouri was long, rode beautiful Chenoa!

Then the chief said, "Tam Apo has changed my hardened heart and wanted me to bring my last daughter and give her to the trapper you call Buck Snort! He is to take her and 'lay' with her and bring me many grandsons and granddaughters... I have looked into his eyes and sensed what is in his heart and after talking with Tam Apo, give her willingly to the trapper. I have also brought ten of my best warriors including my three sons to help you safely travel through the lands of the Arikara and Sioux. It is my hope that all of you can safely travel through those lands and that my ten best warriors return safely to my People as well. Now go and may Tam Apo ride with you and yours to this white man place called St. Louis," said the chief with tears openly running down the cheeks of his face, followed with a wave of his lowered right hand in an 'away' gesture.

Sitting on his horse not far from where the chief and Charlie sat talking, Buck Snort could hardly believe his ears or what he was seeing! Chenoa would soon be his! Then he truly realized that The Great Spirit had also smiled upon him! Especially so when he could see Chenoa and her horses being led over to where he sat upon his steed, with a smile also as wide as the Missouri River was long...

The last thing any of the trappers saw of the great chief, Chief Bear Hunter of the Wind River Band of Shoshoni Indians, was he and his men lined up in a long line on the horizon watching the trappers, their furs and the 'loves of their lives' riding alongside, finally disappearing into that vastness known as the Great American Frontier...

CHAPTER FIFTEEN

ST. LOUIS-BOUND, TROUBLE, TIME TO SAY 'GOOD-BYE'

FOR THE NEXT 15 DAYS after crossing through the South Pass and riding alongside the Sweetwater River, the trappers and their Shoshoni escort travelled safely across parts of the Frontier through huge herds of buffalo, elk, deer, numerous packs of wolves and the occasional band of bighorn sheep.

Each day of travel to the south and east found the long caravan of fur trappers strung out single file, surrounded by the ten Shoshoni outriders providing protection as well as extra sets of eyes watching the countryside for any signs of danger. Then come evening time after finding a shelter of trees along a water source, the trappers made camp. When they did, all of their horses were unpacked and let out to graze and water until darkness overcame the land. Then the valuable livestock was brought into the center of the trappers' campsite, picketed on a long rope picket line and hobbled against any kind of easy or surprise Indian thievery during the dark of the night.

In the meantime, Clem, Broken-Hand Luke, Chenoa and Sakeya made camp on a daily basis, built campfires, gathered in wood and water and with a constant supply of fresh elk or buffalo from the nearby herds supplied by the Indian outriders, along with coffee and biscuits, provided the basic meals for the hardworking men moving the pack string and providing outrider protections. Every day of travel, the trapper and Indian caravan observed numerous bands of Indians out hunting buffalo for their winter meat supplies but because of the obvious large number of defenders of the valuable caravan, the men were not bothered. But, those groups of Indians spotted every day, did in fact closely watch...

Then Clem ever the camp cook and by then tuned into the likes and dislikes of his eating fraternity, started making sure his hardworking men and two women were well fed. Every night after supper had been served and the dishes cleaned up, Clem and his fellow cooks would go to work on preparing for the next day's meals. First with some of the fresh meat left over from the daily kill of elk or buffalo, Broken-Hand Luke, the two women and Clem would cut up the fresh meat into chunks and set it over the cooking irons in cast iron pots to 'stew' away. Then into another large cooking pot full of warm water would go a small mountain of beans and rice to soak and fluff up. Two hours later found Clem mixing the previously cooked meat chunks, beans and rice together and set over the fire's coals to further slow cook, so the men would have a meat-heavy and hearty stew ready for part of their breakfast meal. Then with another pot of raisins also 'fluffing up' in warm water so the men would have raisins in their biscuits come morning and with the addition of brown sugar scraped off from sugar cones into the biscuit dough, the men would soon have a breakfast with Clem's special Dutch oven biscuits, hot coffee and meat-heavy stew to help carry the men through the day with only jerky for their noonday meal. Then come suppertime, large chunks of buffalo (the men's favorite), biscuits, coffee and a Dutch oven and apple slices 'bake' would round out the men's supper. As it turned out, Buck Snort and company had knives, plates, cups and spoons for ten, as did Charlie Poke and his company of men. So, having enough eating crockery and utensils for 20, pretty well and luckily fit the complement of men now heading for St. Louis and suffice to say, the men and two women 'made hay' over their daily offering...

Then come every morning, Clem, Broken-Hand Luke and the two women were up early so the men could have a hearty breakfast. And as it turned out, that gave the men time to take care of their calls of nature and then the real work began for the day. Every day each of the horses had to be inspected for any kinds of sores caused by the packs or saddles rubbing the horse's skin raw. Then to help the horses in their labors, every animal was also curried down and any further pack or saddle sores discovered were summarily treated with bag balm to reduce the injured areas. Then and only then, all of the horses were watered, saddled and packed. That usually took the men from before daylight until around ten in the morning before all of the horses were saddled and packed ready for travel. Then breakfast was served and just as soon as the men had eaten, everything was cleaned up, put away and packed for the day's coming travels.

Then the caravan, barring any horse wrecks or other problems such as those caused by grizzly bears or hostile Indians, the pack train kept on the trail until just before dusk. As most of the outriders located a camping spot for the night that was out of sight and near a water source, several of the Indians would down a buffalo or elk, butcher the animal where it fell and then head for camp with the travelers' meat for their evening meal and later breakfast 'stew'. Then as the animals were unsaddled or unpacked, inspected for any kinds of pack or saddle sores and let loose so they could feed and water under the guard of at least four men, the cook crew would be hard at work making supper for the night and making preparations for the next morning's meal as well.

After bringing in the horses right at nightfall and letting them water one last time, the men would then picket the horses inside their camp-site to preclude any horses 'up and walking off' in the hands of Indians and then hobbled them so they could not be easily stampeded off. Finally, the men and women would prepare for sleeping under any trees found that evening and four men would be selected to keep the camp-fire going all night, keeping the coffee boiling as well as providing guard duty so the rest of the crew could safely sleep. Then every four hours, another team of four men would be roused from their sleeping furs to provide guard duty and the previous crew would crawl under their sleeping furs so they could get some welcome sleep before the following morning's duties.

With the arrival of day 17 out on the trail and still heading along the Sweetwater River towards where Charlie figured he and company would at some point in time run into the North Platte River, a 'usual' for the prairie during the heat of summer arose. Finally hitting the trail in typical summer heat out on the prairie around eleven o'clock on that particular day, Elk Killer confronted Charlie and the two appeared to be in deep conversation and looking skyward back towards the northwest. Soon they broke off their conversation and with that, the group formed up into their usual formation so they could safely travel. However, by around three in the afternoon in oppressive prairie heat, just as Elk Killer had predicted, Charlie and the company of travelers observed a thin line of ominous blue-black rolling ugly clouds forming from out of the northwest along the horizon and heading in their direction as they traveled out across the open prairie.

About then Buck Snort rode up after seeing the same saying, "Charlie, we have a bad-looking thunderstorm coming right at us from out of the northwest! I think we best head for some kind of cover knowing what the summer thunderstorms can be like out here on this prairie."

"Yeah, I know. Elk Killer and I have been watching it for over the last hour or so and like you, I feel we best get off these horses and head for some timber down in a gully for the protection that can offer us in the event we get into a lightning storm," said Charlie to Buck Snort, as he nervously kept watching the rolling black clouds coming their way portending an oncoming violent thunderstorm. And from all appearances, the oncoming thunderstorm was rapidly bearing down upon the men and their animals…
About then, the rolling ominous sounds of far-off thunder could be heard and it wasn't just once in a while but almost a constant rumbling sound, heralding a vicious lightning storm was on its way as well and soon! For the next few moments

the men just sat there on their horses watching the rapidly forming line of black clouds heading their way. Then with his arm, Charlie waved in the Shoshoni Indian outriders…

"I say we head for that long line of cottonwoods dead ahead of us and make an early camp. That way we can prepare for the rains that follow and be out of the way from any stray lightning bolt coming our ways while out here on this damn open prairie," said Buck Snort.

Before Charlie could respond, Black James came riding up to the two men trailing his string of pack-horses and just looking ahead like nothing was out of the ordinary said, "Boss, don't look to our north just now so they don't know we have seen them, but there are six men on horses sneaking in behind our incoming outriders on their horses and they don't appear to be any of our group of travelers."

"I saw them as well earlier traveling along that long line of ridgelines to our north," said Buck Snort. "I don't think they are any of ours either and as such, I asked Fast Antelope some time back if he could quietly scout them out and let me know if they are friendly, or 'Bucks' out looking for fur trappers not watching their behinds so they can make off with a mess of our horseflesh and what they are carrying! I have yet to have Fast Antelope return so in order to not let them know they have been spotted, I say we go about our business, head for that string of cottonwood trees and 'hole up' there for the night before we get blown off our horses by lightning or drowned by the rains that are fast coming for sure. In fact, I can now smell the moisture in the air as we sit here talking among ourselves," continued Buck Snort.

About an hour later amidst many much closer, low gathering rain clouds, the line of trappers and their Indian escort made their way into a long line of tall cottonwoods with a small creek running through the tree-lined gully bottom they now 'happily called home'.

There in the dense grove of cottonwoods and bushes of buffalo berries in a big hurry, the men quickly unloaded their packhorses and tightly stacked their packs under the heavy leaf foliage of the cottonwoods for protection from the rain they knew was coming. By then, everyone could hear the faraway constant rumbling of thunder and the smell of moisture now hanging heavy in the air, as did the now oppressive heat boiling up from off the vast plains. Then as the men quickly ran rope picket lines from tree to tree and doubled their horses' hobbles before picketing them so they couldn't easily stampede off or be stolen, other trappers dragged out their tanned buffalo hides and used them to cover up the now exposed and valuable packs and roped them down. Then the rush was on to lay out everyone's sleeping furs under the heavy canopy of trees and under numerous buffalo hides, in order for everyone to have a dry place in which to sleep once the rapidly oncoming rains were upon them. As the men hurriedly dragged all of their saddles under some additional buffalo hides so they would remain dry, Clem ran around and saw to it that everyone had a small bag of jerky for their supper that evening because of the oncoming heavy rainstorm which would make cooking on an open fire impossible.

Just getting the last horse double hobbled and picketed found the air overhead already laced with dangerous bolts of lightning! Some of those bolts were observed striking and killing nearby running herds of buffalo also now trying to get away from the impending danger! Then as if ordered 'from above', lightning bolts and heavy rains swept out across the prairie like heavy walls of water draining down from the Heavens in sheets! As everyone scampered for their sleeping furs and buffalo hide coverings, the first deluges of rain fell upon the trappers and their Indian protectors in a wall of cold, large raindrops and hail the size of deer turds!

WHAM—BAM—BOOOM! thundered the bolts of lightning splitting the air, as they zipped across the now running and panicked herds of elk and buffalo running every which way across the prairie and now thundering into the nearby tree-lined gullies in which the trappers now cowered! That they did, as the sharp smell of ozone laced the airways and the smell of burning buffalo flesh and cottonwood leaves now filled the airways as well. Then the smell of lightning-singed buffalo hair could be smelled as the animals thundered into the cottonwood gully the trappers and their Indian counterparts were nervously trying to hide in and survive what Mother Nature was dishing out! Then the sweet smell of burned blood could now also be smelled as buffalo stampeded into the cottonwood gully, and bolts of lightning snapped and swirled around their now bluish-cast horns from all the electricity in the air and formed electric arcs from upraised tail to tail as the buffalo poured into the cottonwood grove in total panic!

BOOM – BOOM – BOOM – BOOM – BOOM! bellowed the trappers' rifles as they killed buffalo after panicked buffalo pushing into the trappers' sleeping area and where they had stacked their bundles of packs, scattering the panicked animals now every which way in 'the face and fury of rifle fire'! Then when the trappers' rifles had been emptied and there was no way to reload them in the now driving rains, the **POW-POW-POW-POW!** sounds of pistols being used at close-in ranges to keep the panicked buffalo from pushing their way through the trappers' camp and causing human injury filled the air!

By now, darkness had slipped onto the prairies only backlit by the constant brilliant flashes of lightning striking unfortunate buffalo within the now milling herds, as well as unfortunate cottonwoods 'unable' to avoid the white-hot bolts of electricity striking and boiling away the sap under the bark of the trees being struck!

Holding his rifle at port arms, Buck Snort stood in among a small clump of closely grouped cottonwoods that were too close for buffalo to run through, protecting a terrified Chenoa lying at his feet near the base of a large tree. THEN BUCK SNORT REALIZED THAT FAST ANTELOPE HAD STILL NOT GOTTEN BACK TO HIM WITH ANY INFORMATION ON THE GROUP OF INDIAN OUTRIDERS THAT BUCK SNORT HAD SEEN EARLIER A RIDGELINE OVER! Standing a terrified Chenoa up alongside a large cottonwood and wrapping her in a buffalo hide, Buck Snort handed her one of his pistols and told her to stay right there and not move because the terrified buffalo crowding into the protection of the cottonwoods could not get to her because of the close-in trees surrounding where she stood. Then grabbing up his rifle and with a feeling that all was not well, in addition to the near at hand terrified buffalo and bolts of lightning 'stitching' their way through the cottonwoods, Buck Snort began walking down the picket line holding all of their valuable horses. Fortunately the trappers had stacked most of their packs at or near the picket line so most of the buffalo could not get through and push the terrified horses away from their tie-downs.

As bolt after bolt of lightning illuminated the countryside just about every second and the thundering noises overhead in the center of the fast-moving storm almost deafened anyone nearby, Buck Snort continued carefully walking down the horses' picket line. As he did and with a bad feeling that something other than the storm was 'in the air', he slowly walked along the picket line and carefully watched along the line of horses every time the lightning illuminated everything under the canopy of cottonwoods in which they had been picketed.

BOOM—BAM—BOOM! went the thunder as the bolts laced across the sky and then all of a sudden Buck Snort saw what had been bothering him. That last bolt of lightning struck a cottonwood tree not far from him and when it did blowing limbs and bark everywhere as the strike lit up the area, he saw three Indians running from under the tree just struck with lightning with their hands held over their heads as if to provide some sort of protection!

AND THE INDIANS BUCK SNORT HAD JUST SEEN WERE NOT DRESSED LIKE THE TEN SHOSHONI INDIANS CHIEF BEAR HUNTER HAD DISPATCHED ALONG TO PROTECT HIS TRAPPER FRIENDS AND DAUGHTERS! MOVING CAREFULLY DOWN ALONG THE PICKET LINE IN THE DARKNESS TOWARDS THE THREE STRANGE INDIANS HE HAD JUST SEEN, BUCK SNORT WAITED FOR THE LIGHT FROM THE NEXT LIGHTNING BOLT HE KNEW WOULD SOON

BE COMING. **BOOM!** WHEN IT DID, THAT BOLT OF LIGHTNING ILLUMINATED THOSE SAME THREE INDIANS HE HAD OBSERVED EARLIER, ONLY NOW THEY WERE AMONG THE HORSES' PICKET LINE AND APPEARED TO BE ATTEMPTING TO STEAL A NUMBER OF THE TRAPPERS' VALUABLE HORSES WHILE USING THE OVERHEAD STORM AS A COVER IN ORDER TO DO SO!

NOW QUICKLY MOVING DOWN THE PICKET LINE TOWARDS WHERE HE HAD LAST SEEN THE THREE INDIANS TRYING TO UNTIE THE HORSES, BUCK SNORT WAS THANKFUL THAT HE HAD INSTRUCTED ALL OF THE TRAPPERS TO MAKE SURE EACH HORSE WAS DOUBLE HOBBLED AND ALSO TIED WITH TWO KNOTS WHERE THEY WERE TIED OFF ONTO THE PICKET LINE TO PRECLUDE EASY KNOT UNTYING BY SOMEONE WHO DID NOT BELONG...

WHAM! WENT ANOTHER CLOSE AT HAND BOLT OF LIGHTNING AND WHEN ITS BRILLIANT LIGHT LIT UP THE AREA, BUCK SNORT FOUND HIMSELF STANDING RIGHT BEHIND AN INDIAN FRANTICALLY TRYING TO CUT LOOSE A HORSE. BUCK SNORT'S TOMAHAWK 'CHOP' CUT SHORT THAT INDIAN'S ATTEMPT TO STEAL A TRAPPER'S HORSE BUT IN THAT BOLT OF LIGHTNING, BUCK SNORT ALSO SAW THE TWO OTHER CLOSE AT HAND INDIANS CUTTING

HORSES LOOSE AS WELL, JUST BEFORE HE HAD KILLED THE CLOSEST INDIAN TO HIM!

PICTURING IN HIS MIND WHERE HE HAD LAST SEEN THE OTHER TWO INDIANS ATTEMPTING TO CUT SOME HORSES LOOSE, BUCK SNORT MOVED IN CLOSER TO WHERE THEY HAD BEEN STANDING AND WHEN THE NEXT BOLT WENT OFF OVERHEAD AND A TREMENDOUS THUNDERCLAP FOLLOWED, IT DROWNED OUT THE SOUND OF A PISTOL BEING SHOT INTO THE BACK OF THE SECOND INDIAN FROM JUST TWO FEET AWAY! DROPPING HIS NOW EMPTY PISTOL, BUCK SNORT COCKED THE HAMMER ON HIS FLINTLOCK RIFLE PRAYING ALL THE WHILE IT WOULD FIRE IN ALL OF THE HEAVY RAINS THAT WERE FALLING, AND AIMED WHERE HE FIGURED THE NEXT INDIAN WOULD BE STANDING COME THE NEXT LIGHTNING FLASH. WHEN MOTHER NATURE SAW TO IT THAT HE GOT ANOTHER BOLT OF LIGHTNING ILLUMINATING THE SUSPECT AREA FOR JUST A SPLIT-SECOND, BUCK SNORT FIRED FROM JUST FEET AWAY INTO THE BACK OF THE THIRD INDIAN WITH THE ROPE FROM A HORSE IN HAND AND BENT OVER TRYING TO RELEASE THE ANIMAL'S HOBBLES!

The next bolt of lightning illuminated Buck Snort retying a horse back onto its picket line while an unknown Indian wiggled away his last movements on "Mother Earth" at the trapper's feet! Then as the main fury of the fast-moving storm overhead kept roaring across the prairie, its receding illuminating flashes of light showed no more Indians trying to use the storm for cover to aid them in the stealing of the trappers' and Shoshonis' horses. With that last flash of light, Indians were nowhere to be seen... Then careful not to scare Chenoa and get a pistol blast in his face, Buck Snort just remained near her so he could protect her if necessary and waited until daylight finally allowed all of the trappers to crawl out from under their wet buffalo hides and see a thoroughly soaked Buck Snort standing guard in the middle of their horses' picket line with three dead, later identified by the Shoshoni Indians, as Sioux Indians! When little Chenoa saw what had happened, she was thankful as to why Tam Apo or The Great Spirit of the Northern Shoshoni People, had made sure her father released her so she would be cared for the rest of her life by such a great trapper and brave white man...

The next day the trappers remained hidden in their cottonwoods looking for any more horse-stealing Sioux Indians. None were ever seen again and FAST ANTELOPE WAS NEVER AGAIN SEEN AS WELL! It was assumed that he had been discovered by the Sioux spying on them and then was caught and killed by them! Then not wanting to brave the storm's fury, all but three of the group of Sioux seen by Black

James and Buck Snort had returned to their camp. However, three of their kind attempted to steal some of the trappers' valuable horses using the cover of the height of the storm, only to fall to the fast-thinking Buck Snort and his unerring aim with tomahawk and firearm... Truly, Tam Apo had smiled upon Buck Snort as well... And he realized that even more every time little Chenoa wrapped her arms around him and gave him a kiss!

Days later the trappers and their Shoshoni Indian escort reached the North Platte River and there Charlie and Buck Snort decided they would rest up the men and their horses for several days before heading onward to the next 'milestone' in their travels, namely the Missouri River and home of the dreaded Arikara Indian Nation, hater of all white men and fierce 'Sons of the Prairies'...

One evening during their travels days later after supper had been had, Charlie gathered in all of the men and their Indian escort around the campfire. There he informed the men that if he remembered his earlier travels coming into this country years earlier as a trapper, that they were only a day or so away from reaching the Missouri River. Then once there, they would follow that river south until it reached the Mississippi River and then they would follow that river all the way down to St. Louis and then they would be home. With those words of 'final destination' hanging 'heavy' in the air, there were smiles all around on the faces of the trappers and questions of wonder as to what lay ahead on the faces of the Shoshoni in the white man's great city of St. Louis...

However, continued Charlie, now that they were in the country of the dreaded Arikara Indians, Indians who hated the white man trappers and their historic enemy the Shoshoni, they would have to change their travel plans. No longer since they were such a large group could they expect to safely travel during daylight hours without being seen and attacked. They would now have to travel at night by the light of the moon, utilizing their horses' ability to see the trail when traveling at night along the edge of the Missouri River until they were away from the land of the deadly Arikara. (Author's Note: Today, the once great and fierce Arikara Indian Nation of Peoples, reduced in number from numerous white man diseases and almost constant warfare, has been consolidated with the Hidatsa and Mandan Indian Nations on the Fort Berthold Indian Reservation in north-central North Dakota. Today they are federally recognized as The Three Affiliated Tribes.) Then come daylight, the group would 'hole' up somewhere out of sight along the Missouri's densely brushed river bottom, sleep during the daylight hours and travel nightly until they were safely within the lands of Wind Horse and his People, the friendly Omahas. Then since they would also be out of

the land of the Sioux, they could once again safely travel during daylight hours and make better
time getting into St. Louis. Following those general plans and then accompanied with several
cups of the last of their rum supplies, the men
discussed their nighttime travel procedures until
sleep overcame the tired travelers. Somewhat
later with guards posted and no nighttime fire
to give away their location, the rest of the group
slept in shifts.

So for the next four weeks in order to avoid
any run-ins with the dreaded Arikara, Charlie
and Buck Snort led their groups of trappers and
Shoshoni Indians through the lands of the 'Sons
of the Prairies' traveling at night and 'holing up'
during daylight hours. Being that such a drastic
change had to be made, the Shoshoni Indian escort was now kept in closer to the trappers' fur
caravan and Clem and his people had to make
related changes as well when it came to cooking
for the group. In order to feed the group, a single
buffalo would be killed right at dusk and shot only
by the best shooter so a number of shots would
not be used to kill a single animal. Then as the
rest of the group headed for the Missouri River's
densely brushed bottoms for their evening stay,
the buffalo would be hurriedly quartered and
then that small group of hunters would head for
the camp, careful to hide any evidence of their
shod horses' hoofprints trail as much as possible.

Then Clem and company of cooks would see

to it that they maintained only the smallest of cooking fires made from the driest of wood to keep the smoke column down. That they did in order to feed the 21 people in their group, but still provide the best meals that they could so the hardworking group could function without alerting any nearby Indians of the trappers' and Shoshonis' cooking fires. However throughout the following weeks of travel under such conditions, Clem and company made sure everyone had his Dutch oven biscuits, hot coffee and spitted buffalo for all of the meals that he and his crew cooked, 'come rain or shine'.

******

Leaving their Sioux Indian encampment early one morning to go and remove juvenile golden eagles from their nests located along the bluffs of the Missouri River before they fledged for their valuable spotted tail feathers, "Bull Buffalo's" first-born son "Chaska", met up with his teenage friends sitting on their horses impatiently waiting for him. Then with much laughter and bantering back and forth, "Fire Maker", "Strong Boy", "Achak", "Spirit" and "Ahanu" sprinted their horses down towards the river in order to see which of them had the fastest horse. However before they got there, a small herd of buffalo returning from watering in the river interfered with the horse race, scattering the boys' horses and buffalo alike to the four winds.

Laughing and regrouping, the boys trotted

their horses south along the Missouri until an hour or so later they arrived at a series of high bluffs along the waterway known for their golden eagle nesting sites. Somewhat later, the boys had arrived at their first golden eagle nest site holding three young eaglets almost ready to fledge. After crawling down the side of the cliffs and shooting the three young eagles with their bows and arrows while the eaglets' parents flew around the nest-invaders screeching their alarms, the boys later back on top of the bluffs examined their prizes. Then the boys cut off the bird's wings, removed their tail fans, cut off their feet and removed the eaglets' heads. Then since none of the boys had eaten any breakfast, they cooked and ate the birds' livers and hearts in order to gain the birds' magical powers of sight and fierceness. Then carefully wrapping the feathered items into a tanned deerskin brought along for care of the feathered items, items to be used in making dance bustles, coup sticks, headdresses and the like, they were packed on the back of one of the boys' horses. That accomplished, the six boys headed further downriver to another cliff nesting site where they had observed two more young eaglets about ready to fledge.

That time Achak and Spirit descended the cliff face and killed one of the eaglets standing on the nest protesting their presence. Then Spirit shot the remaining eaglet which flopped off the narrow ledge where its parents had built their nest and fell flopping with the arrow in its body a hundred feet or so into the brush below growing alongside the river. With that Achak brought the dead bird up to the rest of the waiting boys as Spirit carefully descended the cliff face and once below the nest site, surrounded by all of the cast feathers, droppings and remnants of dead prey that had fallen from the cliffside nest site, retrieved the now dead eaglet.

Turning to climb back up to his friends with his beautifully feathered prize, Spirit all of a sudden smelled wood smoke! Realizing that was a most unusual place for someone to camp or build a fire, his 20,000 years of Native American survival senses kicked in. Laying the dead eaglet under a rock so the ever-present ravens and magpies would not disturb the carcass, he began sneaking through the dense brush along the river for about 60 yards when all of a sudden he froze in surprise and wonder!

There below where he stood along the cliff face, Spirit spotted several strings of horses tied to picket lines, mounds of bundles of furs like white men trappers he had seen in his village packed on their packhorses, several small campfires being tended by two Indian women and several white men, and then several more strings of horses picketed so they would not be readily seen in the dense brush. About then, Spirit smelled cooking meat along with the faint smell of burning wood! Now more than fully alert, Spirit dropped onto all fours and began crawling even closer into what appeared to be a camp full of the much-hated white man trappers! Soon, Spirit counted at least twelve white men fur trappers and a number of Indians of unknown origin! Then the nearby sound of a snapping stick caused Spirit to freeze, as he observed an unknown Indian walking through the brush coming his way! Stopping only a few yards away, Spirit saw the approaching Indian drop his breechclout and leggings and begin having a noisy bowel movement just yards away from the boy who was now hardly daring to even breathe! In fact, he was so close to the Indian tending to his call of nature that he could now smell the bowel movement...

Moments later, the Indian of unknown origin used a handful of brush and leaves to wipe his behind, rose up, pulled up his breechclout and leggings and walked back towards the small campfires. Once there, he sat down by the fire and began quietly talking with one of the beautiful Indian women working around the fires making what appeared to be food soon to be eaten. Not wanting to be discovered, Spirit slowly rose up off his belly and began quietly crawling backwards until he felt it safe to rise and leave the area hurriedly on foot before being detected.

About 20 minutes later and all out of breath from climbing the sloping cliff face with all the strength and endurance he possessed, he fell gasping for breath by the rest of his friends still dismembering the eaglet. Chaska, being the oldest at age 20, realized that something was dead wrong and with a wave of his hand, all the rest of the boys quit jabbering and just looked at their friend Spirit, lying there on the ground gasping for his breath! Moments later, Spirit got his story out and immediately all the boys were surprised over what they were hearing from their friend. That was all except for Chaska…

Chaska had a look upon his face that none of his friends had ever seen before. That look was one of extreme excitement, joy and a spirit of adventure splashed clear across it that almost scared the rest of the boys looking on in disbelief over the physical change they were seeing in their friend! Then Chaska made a 'come hither' gesture with his hand that meant for all of the boys to move in closer so they all could talk without being overheard by the number of men camped below…

"What Spirit has just seen is a gift from The Great Spirit to all of us! The Great Spirit has chosen all of us this morning to show the rest of our tribe that we all are not only warriors but great warriors as well! What Spirit has seen here this morning will allow all of us to take it upon ourselves to perform a 'Vision Quest' of the highest degree. He has chosen us to go forth on this 'Vision Quest', sneak into the fur trappers' camp, steal their valuable horses and count coup not only upon our enemies but those from a different tribe as well! The Great Spirit is asking all of us to walk away from being just mere boys, but to become warriors of the highest order this day and bring great joy and blessings upon not only us but that of our families and ancestors as well."

By now, Chaska's great enthusiasm over an idea of a 'Vision Quest' had spread to all of the young men! In essence, the earlier trip to collect the sacred feathers from the golden eagles and after eating pieces of the great birds' hearts and livers, had obviously blessed and brought great honor to each and every of them! Then if they were able to sneak into the trappers' camp, steal their horses and ride out with not only those horses but great honor for their counted coup as well, would make all of them great warriors in the eyes of their families, friends and ancestors!

Soon the young men, armed with just their bows and arrows, were plotting on just how they could sneak into the trappers' campsite, steal their valuable horses and escape as the young warriors they were now fast becoming... By now, each young man thought of himself as great as the bird whose parts he had consumed earlier in the day and now possessed the powers of the great golden eagle as well...

Soon, the six of them had sneaked up to the very edges of the fur trappers' campsite and lying out along a long brushy ridgeline, were making their plans on how to sneak into camp, steal the horses and leave without being detected. As they planned such a dangerous adventure, all of the boys realized that The Great Spirit was riding with them that morning! This they realized because one by one, all of the trappers were going to sleep, apparently so they could leave in the darkness and disappear to wherever they were going. That point was fast made when the last man had crawled under his sleeping furs and now the only sounds coming from the trappers' campsite was that of men snoring as they slept, as only men will do when they have worked hard and are planning on continuing to do so once again after it had gotten dark! Upon seeing that last trapper roll up into a grizzly bear robe and within moments move no more, sent ripples of not only excitement but the needed courage to do what they were now planning! And that excitement and ripple of encouragement now physically surged through the young men lying there watching the scene unfolding below, realizing all of the trappers and Indians were now in deep sleep... That excitement over what was to come was increased when each of the young Indian men let their eyes 'feast' upon all of the valuable horseflesh picketed below and now unguarded, as the trappers and their Indian friends slept throughout the brush-covered riverbank!

Sneaking silently into the trappers' campsite about an hour or so later on foot, all six of the young Indian 'warriors to be' had decorated themselves with muddy stripes drawn across their faces giving every one of them a fierce 'warrior' look. Additionally, every boy had now dismembered the tails and wings of the golden eagles killed earlier in the day and taking those sacred and powerful feathers, had adorned those feathers throughout their long braids, as well as had woven a number of them into parts of their clothing for the sacred power the eagle feathers had brought to such an adventure…

Cautiously sneaking into the sleeping trappers' campsite in a line abreast, one quiet footstep at a time with their bow and arrows held at the ready, the young warriors carefully approached a line of horses tied off on a picket rope. Horses which were now all quietly looking at the line of unknown young men slowly sneaking in their direction with interest, as if they were coming to take the horses for a ride. As the young 'warriors' sneaked closer and closer, not a single horse let out a call or warning noise associated with alarm.

In fact one of the horses, a rather large pinto, was watching the line of cautious young Indian men approaching the horses with extreme interest. Years earlier, that same horse, that large pinto, had been carefully selected by a young Indian man like those now slowly approaching, and eventually had trained it as a Buffalo Horse. And that young Indian looking like some of those young men now approaching the picket line of horses, had cared for the large pinto and eventually became its kind master. Those days the large pinto horse remembered all too well as if they were only yesterday, and the joys of those

days with such a young Indian man began happily spinning through its mind. Maybe this was
more of the same with a young Indian man as a
master. Who knew?

Carefully and quietly, the young Indian men
reached the line of picketed horses and every
horse on that line had not raised any alarm but
only looked on with interest as the young men
began quietly untying each of the horses and rubbing their necks and noses. Then Spirit, full of the
'Vision Quest' he was now undertaking and was
being shown the way by The Great Spirit, carefully slipped the hobbles from the horse he had
selected as his prize. Then with a big grin, Spirit
looked over at his close friend Chaska, who now
had his arms around the big pinto's neck and
was actually showing a degree of love in the face
of extreme danger to the big magnificent horse
who appeared to be showing his love in return
for the young Indian man as well.

Then quietly leaping upon the back of a large
bay horse standing alongside the pinto, a horse
that he had untied and also previously removed
its hobbles, Chaska slowly and quietly began riding away from the picket line. As Chaska slowly
headed out from the camp with a beautiful bay
horse under him and trailing the large pinto
which would show those looking on back at his
camp what a great warrior he was, he got the
surprise of his short life! Looking back, Chaska,
leader of the group riding a large beautiful bay

and trailing the pinto, saw the rest of his friends all strung out and riding upon the horses they each had chosen from the trappers' picket line and had released as well.

Then with a 'whoop' of joy and conquest, Chaska let out his triumphant yell meant to arouse the sleeping trappers and was immediately jerked backwards from off his bay by the reins he was holding leading the large pinto he was trailing! The pinto had long recognized the look and smell of the man riding the horse to his front were not those of his much-beloved master, Buck Snort... And as such after starting to be taken away from the camp where he knew he belonged, jerked his massive head backwards, pulling Chaska over the rump of the bay and onto the ground with a hard sounding "WHUMP"!

STUNNED FOR JUST A MOMENT AND REALIZING HIS POORLY THOUGHT-OUT YELL HAD ALERTED THE TRAPPERS IN CAMP, CHASKA JUMPED UP AND GRABBED THE REINS OF THE BAY HE HAD BEEN RIDING EARLIER BEFORE BEING JERKED OFF BACKWARDS. LUNGING UPWARDS ONTO THE BACK OF THE BAY AS THE LARGE PINTO JUST STOOD THERE LOOKING ON, CHASKA TOOK A .52 CALIBER BULLET FROM BUCK SNORT'S RIFLE INTO THE BACK OF HIS HEAD, TURNING HIS BAY AND THE PINTO STANDING CLOSE AT HAND A PINKISH-RED IN COLOR! **BOOM!**

BUCK SNORT'S SOUND OF SHOOTING WAS IMMEDIATELY FOLLOWED BY A NUMBER OF FAST SHOTS BEING FIRED BY THE FAST-WAKING TRAPPERS AND SHOSHONIS, DROPPING FIRE MAKER WITH A SHOT INTO HIS THROAT, STRONG BOY WITH A HEART SHOT, ACHAK WITH A SHOT TO HIS CHEST, SPIRIT WITH A BULLET INTO HIS BACK AS HE ATTEMPTED TO RIDE OFF ON THE HORSE HE WAS STEALING, AND AHANU WITH A MISSED HEAD SHOT THAT DROPPED LOW AND BLEW OFF HIS ENTIRE LOWER JAW!

By the time the white clouds of black powder smoke had cleared from the trappers' campsite, the men were up and hard at work. Charlie and a number of his men dragged off the dead boys' bodies and threw them into the swiftly flowing Missouri River for disposal. Meanwhile, Buck Snort and Wind Horse backtracked the six Indian boys and located their tied-off horses some 100 yards away. There they removed their saddles and bridles, removed their deerskin full of dead eagle parts and slapped their horses on their rumps so they would run off. Then they hauled all the boys' riding gear and the deerskin full of eagle parts over to the Missouri River and disposed of those items into the muddy flowing waters as well.

Then because of all of the shots being fired at the horse thieves which would more than likely bring unwanted local Indian attention, the trappers' camp was immediately cleaned up, all the horses packed and several hours later found the trappers moving downstream in broad daylight as they stayed along the river's shoreline riding in and out from the dense brush fields trying to remain hidden as best as possible. That they did until dusk and then out onto the open prairie and riding at night, the trappers with just jerky for a meal rode hard all night putting many miles between them and the recent killing field.

Finally halting their travel along the Missouri River many miles below where Chaska and the rest of his boyhood friends finished their first and only 'Vision Quest', the trappers holed up deep in the brush. After unpacking and unsaddling all of their livestock, Buck Snort and Wind Horse accompanied the very hungry horses out onto the nearby prairie and let them feed and water all night. In the meantime, Clem and company set up their camp, set out their sleeping furs under the trees in case of a late day thunderstorm and then set up their packs in a defensive circle around those sleeping furs just in case some Sioux Indians managed to cross their shod horses' trail or had managed to trail the trappers all the way from their previous kill site to where they had currently holed up.

The next morning right at daylight, Buck Snort and Wind Horse brought in all of the trappers' livestock and tied them off on a previously laid out set of picket lines. Then after eating breakfast with the rest of the men and women, Buck Snort and Wind Horse went to the sleeping areas set out for the two of them, and soon the men were soundly sleeping after their all-night vigil with the "two loves of their lives" watching the horses feed ...

As for the rest of the camp, the trappers set up defensive positions and stayed in camp the entire day without the benefit of any campfires or cooked meals just in case they had been trailed that far by grieving parents of the six now-dead boys. Still fearing being successfully trailed by the dead boys' families of warriors, the horses were packed, camp broken and once again, the trappers and their Indian escort rode all night south along the Missouri River as they headed for the relative safety of the junction of the Missouri and Mississippi Rivers.

Sitting on their horses and overlooking several small white men communities spread out across the rich farmlands below and with the mighty Mississippi River flowing off to the south, the trappers realized they were safely home back in civilization. With that realization, there was much happy shouting, backslapping and hand-shaking among the men, trapper and Indian alike. That evening among a number of farm-houses and cultivated lands, Charlie and company along with Buck Snort and company made camp alongside a small stream. There the men set up their final campsite on the Frontier and after another supper prepared by Clem, Chenoa, Sakeya and Broken-Hand of venison from a deer just shot, hot coffee, and Dutch oven biscuits, the men and the ever-present horde of mosquitoes sat around a huge campfire and laughed, shared tales from their earlier lives and finished the last of their rum. As for Chenoa and Sakeya, they sat quietly by the fire wondering what kind of a life they would have living in and among a strange race of people called 'white men'...

That evening as the stars overhead glistened, no one worried about being ambushed by the 'Sons of the Prairies' or a hungry grizzly bear. Then as the night lengthened and thoughts of home began surfacing in the trappers' minds, it was apparent with only the sounds of a crackling campfire that it had come time to 'turn their backs' and say 'Good-bye' to what had been an exciting and deadly life out on the Frontier... But in those 'Good-byes' to the Frontier, their loyal Shoshoni protectors and possibly Charlie Poke and his fellow trappers, there lay a coming surprise! As for the two Shoshoni women who had chosen an unknown life with the 'loves of their lives', it would not be 'Good-bye' but 'Hello' to the life that now lay ahead...

Chapter Sixteen

GOING FROM "HELL" TO "HEAVEN"

THE FOLLOWING DAY, after some confusion as to the location of the Rocky Mountain Fur Company's fur house, the trappers finally arrived at their destination in St. Louis. There the much-surprised Fur House Manager found himself looking out across a large herd of horses carrying dozens of bundles of furs, gaily decorated numbers of Indian men, two beautiful Indian women and ten obvious Mountain Men identified by their buckskin dress, browned skin from the effects of many long days of exposure in the sun and determined looks. Then Fur House Manager David Hagar found himself confronted by two of the Mountain Men asking if he was the one to talk with regarding sorting, grading and purchasing a number of their beaver *Plus'* and wolf skins.

Hagar, amazed at the jumble of men and heavily packed horses carrying so many bundles of furs, advised he was the man to see, and soon Buck Snort and Poke's men and horses were led inside the huge fur house. Within minutes they were soon being swarmed over by a large number of fur company graders and sorters. There Poke and company and Buck Snort and company had their furs graded, sorted and prices settled upon. As for Buck Snort and company, they sold their 104 prime wolf skins for $10,400, and their 720 Made Beaver *'Plus'* at $7 each for a sum of $5,040, for a total princely sum of $15,440!

When Buck Snort's company saw those figures, there was much whooping and hollering in the fur house over being paid so much for all of their hard work! So much for Mountain Prices not being paid for their lot of furs this time... Then the men's eyes got even bigger when Buck Snort went to his saddlebags and brought forth all of his earlier years' Letters of Credit they had earned from previous sales of their furs, weapons and horses at Fort Henry or the Rendezvous.

When Fur House Manager Hagar was handed all of those previous Letters of Credit, his eyes flew wide open once he had shuffled through that handful of documents! Then without a single word, Hagar walked over to his fur desk and began ciphering all the Letter of Credit documents for a final tally. As he did, a profound silence settled in among Buck Snort, Muskrat, Clem and Wind Horse, as they waited for a final tally representing their many years of hard work. As for Chenoa and Sakeya, not realizing their future was being ciphered and at stake, they just in typical Indian fashion, quietly waited. Shuffling the Letters of Credit in order, Fur House Manager Hagar ciphered out loud, "1823 Letter of Credit, $5,010; 1824 Letter of Credit, $11,755; 1825 Letter of Credit, $5,146.50; 1826 Letter of Credit, $43,370; and your fur balance for this year of our Lord 1827, $15,440. That comes to a total of $80,721.50! WOW! You men have just about broken the bank! If you will wait for a few minutes, I will have to have my boss sign off on this newest Letter of Credit. But no two ways about it, all of you men are rich beyond your wildest dreams…!"

Upon hearing that figure, Buck Snort and company began yellin' and hellin' and dancing in a circle on the fur-grading platform like a bunch of schoolkids. As for their women seeing such an outward display of emotion and not realizing what had just happened, just shook their heads over the antics of the men they had chosen for their husbands-to-be… Later when Hagar's boss arrived with the men's current Letter of Credit on the Merchant's First Bank of St. Louis, he shook the hands of all four men present. Then Buck Snort had to ask for directions so they knew where to go, deposit their Letters of Credit and withdraw some spending money for when they were in town for food, lodging and a celebration to follow.

About half an hour later, their Letters of Credit had been deposited into the Merchant's First Bank and with a 'possibles' bag full of heavy Spanish silver dollars, the entire contingent of trappers and Indians headed out onto the streets of St. Louis on a mission. As they did, the men could not help but be amused over the antics of their Indian friends. It was as if the Indians, never having been in a big white man's city before, found their heads were on swivels as they gawked at every sight the city had to offer...

Then with Charlie Poke's crew in hand, the men got directions to the nearest livery and eatery. Soon their horses had been checked into a livery so they could be fed and watered, and then the men walked down the streets of St. Louis until they came to a large eatery with a huge sign overhead advertising, "ALL YOU CAN EAT -- $1.00 — MA SYLVIA'S HOUSE — NO RIFLES ALLOWED INSIDE — WIPE YOUR FEET!" With the smell of great food emanating from inside and flowing out the eatery's swinging doors, with a whoop and a holler, the men placed their rifles against the front side of the building as the sign advised and then trooped inside, ready to put a hurt on the vittles being served inside.

"GET THEM DAMN STINKING INJUNS OUT OF HERE!" bellowed a large man sitting at a table full of what appeared to be dockworkers at the back of Ma Sylvia's dining room.

What the man had yelled at first surprised

Buck Snort and then pissed him off! Since he had stacked his rifle up along the outside wall of the eatery as the overhead sign had advised next to a rather large man named Thomas Davis, whose job it was to act as a bouncer and make sure no one ran off with anyone's rifle other than his own, he found himself almost 'naked'... However, being a man of principles and what he figured was a good Christian, he ignored the ignorant dockworker and seated himself down at a rather large empty table with Poke's crew and the rest of the Shoshoni Indians.

The next thing Buck Snort discovered was a rather large and burly man smelling of sour whiskey and possessing the body odor of a bull moose in rut standing alongside and glaring down at him. "Say, Mister, didn't you hear me tellin' you to get those damn smelly Injuns out of here!"

"These are my friends, if you don't mind," said Buck Snort, looking up into the pockmark-faced burly looking dockworker weighing in around 300 pounds and proud of it from the way he carried himself.

"My name is Mike Fink. I am the toughest alligator wrestlin', ass kickin' son-of-a-bitch on this here river and don't take kindly to any snivelin', stinking Mountain Man dressed in the skins of animals. Now get your stinkin' Injuns out of this here eatery or me and my friends will see to it that none of you will be eatin' nothin' but milk and bread after we kick your'n teeth down your cotton-pickin' throats," continued Fink as he glowered down at Buck Snort and his table of Mountain Men and Indians.

About then Buck Snort saw a dozen or so burly dockworkers rise up from their table at the end of the eatery and begin clomping down the hardwood floors of the dining hall coming towards him as if to back up what "River Man" Mike Fink was demanding! That was when Mike, all of a sudden, spit a large spew of tobacco juice down onto Buck Snort's hands that he had placed in front of where he was sitting at the dining room table waiting to be served…! When that happened, Buck Snort felt a rage roaring up inside of his being like a tornado. There was no way he had ever been so treated and by being so treated, 'the savage beast' inside of his being was forcing its way to the surface… "Hell was a-coming on a Black Horse!"

"Well, you spineless shit, whatcha goin' to do about it?" bellowed Mike Fink, in a now almost silent as a tomb eatery that just moments earlier was a dining room filled with 50 or so diners enjoying themselves having lunch.

"WHOOMP!" Buck Snort's left fist drove deep into Mike Fink's groin and man parts, sending him screaming like a banshee to the floor in agony! In a second, here came a dozen or so of Fink's fellow burly dockworkers making a run at Buck Snort's table as if to enforce Mike's earlier order and settle up with the buckskin-clad Mountain Man who had the audacity to do what he had just done to Fink! Then in a second, they all slid to a stop and raised their hands as all of them found their burly crowd facing 20 drawn and fully cocked horse pistols just pulled from the Mountain Men's sashes and leveled at the once oncoming men...

"ALRIGHT, ALRIGHT, YOU DAMN MEN! PUT DOWN THOSE PISTOLS AND YOU DOCKMEN RETURN TO YOUR TABLE OR I WILL LET THESE MOUNTAIN MEN HAVE AT YOU WITH ALL OF THOSE HAND CANNONS!" yelled Sheriff Dickens, who just happened to be having lunch just a few tables away. Then equally burly Sheriff Dickens slowly rose up from his dining table and walked over to Mike Fink, who was still rolling around on the eatery hardwood floor like an alligator had a hold of his man parts and was in the process of REALLY clamping down!

"You, Men, grab up this bastard and get him the hell out of here afore I throw the whole damn bunch of you whiskey soaked son-of-a-bitches into my jail and leave you there until you stink up the place worse than you are stinking up Ma Sylvia's eating establishment!" growled the sheriff.

Seconds later, the herd of dockworkers who had already finished up their meals, gathered up a still-groaning Mike Fink and hauled him out from the local eatery before the sheriff let the straight-shooting Mountain Men loose with their horse pistols. Then Sheriff Dickens walked over to the table full of Mountain Men and Shoshoni Indians obviously to have his piece with them as well. Then all of a sudden, his face lit up and he began grinning like a pig in a newfound bucket of slop...

"Well, I will be damned! Vince Toni, is that you, Man?" blurted out the sheriff upon getting a better look at the man who had just bested Mike Fink, river bully!

"Yes Sir, Sheriff. It's me just back from beaver trapping out on the Frontier here with my friends. Looks like you came along at the right time because my friends and I were not leaving until we had our lunch. I am sorry it had to come to that confrontation, but we meant no one any harm or disrespect. We just arrived back in town after three months on the trail and just wanted something to eat, that's all," replied Buck Snort, as he stuck out his hand in greeting his old family friend from his childhood days. The one and same sheriff who had sent him to the local orphanage after his folks had died in their house fire. Sent him to the orphanage because he was under 16 and state law required all homeless children to go to an orphanage until they aged out at 16 years of age.

"Well, I will be damned! It is you and man, have you ever grown up. Damn, last time I saw you, you were nothing but a snot-nosed scrawny kid wanting out of that damn old hellhole and dirty orphanage run by Cal Jenkins that I had to by law stick you into. Then the next thing I knowed, you were up and gone out somewhere onto the Frontier as one of Ashley's 100 fur trappers. And now you are back and by dammit, you sure look good," said Sheriff Dickens with a welcoming grin.

"Sheriff, let me introduce you to my friends," said Buck Snort, who then just moments later had introduced the old sheriff to his table full of fellow fur trappers, Indian guards and the two women.

"Mind if I join you, Folks?" asked the sheriff and then without being asked to, just did so on his own. Soon everyone at the table was gabbing away as trays and trays of good old fashioned home cooking was delivered to their table. After about an hour of talking and eating the sheriff asked, "What are you plans, Vince, now that you are home and do you plan on staying? I could sure use a damn good deputy if you would be a-willing," he continued.

"Don't rightly know what all of us have planned but yes, we are home for good. We just quit the fur trapping business and this is our first day back in town. So right now, we need to find a good place to sleep, get a bath, get out of these smelly buckskins and purchase some good old fashioned American clothing and then tomorrow, we will get together and try and decide what the hell we all will do," said Buck Snort.

"I have an idea. Old dirty and mean as a snake Cal Jenkins has just up and died. To my way of thinkin', Cal ran what I would call a 'hellhole' of an orphanage doing to those kids what no man should have ever done. However, there wasn't much any of us could do because that was the only orphanage in the entire county and if any of you kids ever said anything about the treatment old Cal dished out, we found that person either dead for some reason or badly beaten. Like I said, the way Cal ran that orphanage it was a "Hellhole far from Heaven"! Anyway, he left no one, course no one would have him and as a result, the old orphanage is going to be auctioned off pretty soon in order to pay his bills. Say, Washington County still needs a good orphanage. How about since you came from there, you take it over and run it like the "Heaven it needs to be for kids"? It is still a good 1,000-acre producing farm, the building is sound, just needs some paint and maybe a new roof, and the manager of the orphanage gets paid by the county for each kid that is housed there," said the sheriff with a hopeful look upon his face.

Upon hearing that information, Buck Snort felt something almost physical happening to his insides and he just looked long and hard at the old sheriff. He couldn't put his finger on it, but something had just been aroused within his being when the old sheriff had uttered those words about the orphanage needing someone to buy it and run it and the farm like they needed to be. Then for some reason, Buck Snort chanced a look over at Wind Horse and found him looking back with the most unusual piercing look he had ever seen on Wind Horse's face, EVER!

"Well, I have business to do down at the jail. Think about it, Vince. The old orphanage could use a good man to run that place properly and you just might be the man to do it if you had the money to buy that old place out," said the sheriff as he got up, excused himself and headed out the door.

For the longest time after the sheriff had left the table, the group of men and women just nursed their drinks and picked at their plates of food and then Buck Snort said, "Well, we got things to do down at Lisa's Emporium, so we best get cracking."

Earlier while out on the trail en route St. Louis, Buck Snort and company had discussed what they could do for the ever-faithful Indians who had traveled all the way down to St. Louis as their extra protectors. It finally had been decided to give them seven horses taken from Charlie Left Hand's bunch and before they returned, take them to Lisa's Emporium, load them up with provisions and then send them back to their Wind River Tribe in the Rocky Mountains so they could give them to the chief and his people in gratitude for their service. So for the rest of that first day in the city, Buck Snort and company spent the day with the nine remaining Shoshoni men purchasing provisions that their band back in the Wind River Mountains could use. That done and with fully loaded packhorses, the nine Shoshoni wanted to leave right away and head home because they had been on the trail for three months already. With that, the men said their 'Good-byes' along with their thanks, as the two sisters said their tearful 'Good-byes' to their brothers and fellow tribal members as well. Then they were gone heading off after the setting sun and whatever life was to bring to those nine faithful warriors.

The next morning found the four trappers and the two Shoshoni women back at Ma Sylvia's for breakfast. They were alone that morning because Charlie Poke and his men were elsewhere looking around for what they might do with the rest of their lives and somehow stay together if at all possible. However, that turned into one of the most memorable breakfasts EVER! Apparently the four men had been thinking most of the night among themselves about what the sheriff had said about what they had planned for their lives now that they were back home. Surprisingly, the orphanage and its farm becoming available for purchase and operation seemed to be a thought running through their minds they could not shake...

Sitting down at the breakfast table, Wind Horse began the group's conversation with a surprising observation. "Buck Snort, yesterday when you were confronted with that giant of a man named Fink and it got dangerous, YOU NEVER MADE A SMELL! I think being home has done something to you and your system, as well as your loving relationship with Chenoa. I think you are healed from whatever happened to you back at the orphanage and now you are back to your old self before being poisoned."

With those factual words out, Muskrat jumped right into the conversation backing up Wind Horse over his powers of observation about Buck Snort, and reminded everyone about Native Americans like Wind Horse and their powers of observation and decision making being so accurate. Then Clem quietly said, "I too noticed there was no smell associated with the danger that Fink fellow presented yesterday and as such, I now propose we call Buck Snort by his given name and hereinafter, he will be known to all of us by his given name, Vince Toni…" Then after all the name-change support had been uttered around the table with much happiness, the discussions became unusually silent once again as if more was to come.

Then the next surprise came from Muskrat who brought up the sheriff's discussion about the orphanage. "I lay awake in bed most of last night thinking about what the sheriff said yesterday about the orphanage becoming available for purchase. And to me, it made sense for us to do it. We certainly now have the money to do so, thanks to those beaver and wolves who gave up their lives and hides so we could become rich. We all came home looking for a new life and I think here it is! I am just from the stock of an illiterate farmer and can only sign my name with an "X". But, crippled up as I am, I am still a good farmer at heart. And since this orphanage has 1,000 acres of good bottomland and is already a working farm, I could see myself supporting buying the place and working the farm as the orphanage's farm manager. From that job, I could get back into farming as well as teach the young men at the orphanage how to become good farmers!"

Then Clem spoke up saying, "That goes double for me too on what Muskrat said. I am a damn good cook. I could see me as the orphanage's full-time cook if that would please the rest of you. If we bought that place and I had my choice, I would like to be that head cook for the rest of my life. Plus like Muskrat, I too could teach others on how to cook as a profession." Then having had his say, Clem, the man among the four men who seldom said much, just went back to his food and listened to what the rest of the men had to say since he had just said his piece…

Then Wind Horse said with a smile on his face, "Like the rest of my brothers, I too laid awake in bed most of last night thinking about what the sheriff said. I could see myself helping to run that orphanage and farm, especially working in the foundry and blacksmith shop. After all, Vince, we both were pretty good farriers and workers in metal as Cliff had taught us. With our metal-working expertise, we could help run that farm if maybe Muskrat was to oversee its overall farming operations, Clem did all the cooking and you and me ran the foundry. I am just saying…"

Looking at his brothers looking at him, Vince just had to smile. He like the others had been figuring out a way they all could stay together, all work together and make the orphanage a good home for themselves and their wives and any of their own kids that came along, as well as for the county's homeless kids dumped into that system. Both he and Wind Horse had come from there and understood what it represented. Then Vince said, "Just imagine what the four of us could do not only for ourselves in creating our new home but in creating a good home situation to those kids who have no home or anyone to turn to. We could be those people and it would give a stable home life for Chenoa and Sakeya, who could also work with any girls who would be dumped into that system as well…"

Then it grew silent around the table. "What say we all take a trip out to the orphanage this afternoon, look things over and then decide what we are to do with the rest of our lives," said Vince.

That afternoon, the men and women rode out to the orphanage and began looking the farm over. Riding around the landed area under the plow, Muskrat got really excited. "This is damn good-looking bottomland. There is no way this land won't support the six of us, any kids we might have and any kids who are dumped into the orphanage."

Then later back at the orphanage, the men and women walked through the buildings and found they needed cleaning, painting, a new roof, new beds and the kitchen needed a complete re-make. Seeing all of that only excited the men even more over the possibility of taking over the facility and giving it new life and leadership.

Then the surprise of the afternoon reared its head with a bellowed-out challenge, "WHAT THE HELL DO YOU PEOPLE THINK YOU ARE DOING? THIS IS A COUNTY ORPHANAGE AND IS OFF LIMITS TO FOLKS JUST WANDERING AROUND!" said an older but still full of spunk Cliff Fulton, as he exited the foundry building on the orphanage property.

Moments later, Cliff found himself wrapped up in the arms of Wind Horse and Vince Toni for a most happy and joyful reunion! Then later with Cliff introduced to Muskrat and Clem along with Wind Horse and Vince's choices to be their wives, the old-home gathering got even more joyful! That evening with Cliff in tow, the group feasted at a very high class eatery back in St.

Louis where they continued getting acquainted once again and for the first time with Muskrat, Clem and the two ladies. Cliff turned out to be more than excited over the prospect of having the men and ex-fur trappers buy the old orphanage and get it back into living and operating shape, along with the farm and foundry. That evening also found all of the men in concert over buying the place and in so doing, being made a final home for the four of them. And by so doing, allowing the four of them and their wives to live out the rest of their lives in peace as well as would Cliff Fulton, the man who had generously given the two kids from the orphanage their start in trapping, if Vince and Wind Horse had their druthers…

Come the day of the auction, Vince, representing his group of ladies and ex-fur trappers was able to purchase the farm and facility for just $5,500! Then the work began as roofers, carpenters and local businesses were brought in and with fur monies banked in the Merchant's First Bank, brought the grand old lady of the farm and orphanage back to its 'fighting self' along with a new name, heretofore to be called "The Beaver Trappers' Orphanage"…

Then to Vince's group's surprise, two farms adjacent to the orphanage grounds were purchased by Charlie Poke's crew of worn-out old beaver trappers and a very happy reunion was had by all concerned! Especially when later, under Muskrat's expert direction as a farmer, all three farms found themselves working together when it came to using, teaching and training a large number of young men dumped into the orphanage system, to become very good farmers.

Then when a number of young women and more young men found themselves in the orphanage system as a result of a deadly, fast-spreading measles epidemic in the St. Louis area wiping out a number of families, a need existed for a women's home as well as one for the boys. A year later after new housing construction was completed, a women's and men's orphanage was now in existence. In the meantime, Clem found himself overwhelmed as the cook for both men's and women's facilities, and began a separate training program for young cooks which was soon coupled with homemaker training programs for the young women under the guidance and direction of Chenoa and Sakeya...

Lastly, Vince and company remodeled and expanded the orphanage's foundry. The business of making traps for furbearers soon dropped off as the fur industry changed because the beaver were almost eliminated and the social demand went from that of beaver hats to that of those made from silk worms from China... But with the demand for agricultural products in the area because of the nearness of the ever-expanding city of St. Louis, the need for making farming implements and other related metal products gave all the business that Vince, Wind Horse and an aging Cliff Fulton could handle in their newly renovated foundry... And again, many young men were introduced to iron-working training programs and soon became proficient in the metal business throughout the area thanks to Cliff, Vince and Wind Horse's expertise and training.

One late afternoon months later, found Vince, Muskrat, Clem and Wind Horse on the orphanage's covered front porch sitting in wicker rocking chairs, smoking their clay pipes full of James River smoking tobacco and drinking cups of Fourth Proof rum purchased from Manuel Lisa's Emporium in St. Louis. The afternoon air was warm, there were no mosquitoes and each man had just finished a hard day's work in the kitchen, field and foundry doing what they now loved doing. Shortly thereafter, they were joined by Chenoa and Sakeya, who had just finished teaching a sewing class for the orphanage's young ladies. However, those were the only ladies on the porch because Clem and Muskrat never married.

As the afternoon conversation waned and one could almost tell the men's minds had somehow collectively drifted back to their younger more adventurous days beaver trapping on the Frontier along the Bighorn and Green Rivers in the beautiful Rocky Mountains, trying to hang onto their horses and 'hair', Vince said quietly, "Well, Gentlemen, we have turned this place from "Hell" into "Heaven" and now for us, "Summer Is Gone", but here we are together and finally home at last..."

(Author's Note: In 1918 during the deadly great American flu pandemic that took so many lives, the Washington County orphanage, loaded with many homeless children because of deaths in their families from the killer flu, burned to the ground! The local sheriff figured the fire was started by some the boys at the orphanage smoking in their bedrooms at night in violation of orphanage rules... However by then, "The Old Guard" had gone the way of the beaver, buffalo, grizzly bear and the 'Sons of the Prairie' in the "Old West"...)

A Look At Curse of the Spanish Gold

(THE MOUNTAIN MEN BOOK 2)

BY TERRY GROSZ

IN 1829, JACOB AND MARTIN left Kentucky to become Mountain Men, trappers of the Rocky Mountains. The rugged mountains that lay beyond America's frontier remained mostly unexplored. In those days, when beaver were plentiful and the buffalo roamed freely, the killing was good. The two young men would also find that life would be hardscrabble in the high frontier. They would face grizzly bears and hostile Indians. And they would risk horse wrecks and mountain storms to trade their furs each year at "rendezvous." *Curse of the Spanish Gold* is the story of two adventurers who lived hard in the earliest days of the Wild West.

Available now from Terry Grosz and Wolfpack Publishing.

ABOUT THE AUTHOR

TERRY GROSZ was born in 1941, in Toppenish, Washington. He graduated from Quincy High School in 1959, and attended Humboldt State College where he earned his Bachelor of Science Degree in Wildlife Management in 1964, and his Master of Science Degree in 1966. He was a California State Fish and Game Warden from 1966 until 1970, based first in Eureka, California, and then in Colusa, California, in the Northern Sacramento Valley. He then joined the U.S. Fish and Wildlife Service in 1970, first serving in California as a U.S. Game Management Agent and later as a Special Agent until 1974. In 1974, he was promoted to a Senior Resident Agent position over the States of North and South Dakota where he served until 1976. In 1976, he was promoted to a Senior Special Agent position and was transferred to Washington, DC, where he served as the Endangered Species Desk Officer and Foreign Liaison Officer until 1979. In 1979, he was transferred to Minneapolis, Minnesota, where he served as the Assistant Special Agent in Charge until 1981. In 1981, Terry was promoted and transferred to Denver, Colorado, as the Special Agent in Charge over the wildlife resource-rich eight-state region of the Service's Region 6, encompassing over 750,000 square miles in the States of North Dakota, South Dakota, Nebraska, Kansas, Montana, Wyoming, Colorado, and Utah. He retired from the U.S. Fish and Wildlife Service in 1998, after a 32-year career in state and federal wildlife law enforcement.

In 1999, Terry began his second career as a writer, with the publishing of his first wildlife law enforcement true-life adventures book titled, "WILDLIFE WARS", which won him a National Outdoor Book Award in the Nature and Environment category. He has since had 13 additional wildlife law enforcement adventure books published, titled, *For Love of Wildness, Defending Our Wildlife Heritage, A Sword For Mother Nature, No Safe Refuge, The Thin Green Line, Genesis Of A Duck Cop, Slaughter In The Sacramento Valley,*

Wildlife On The Edge, Wildlife's Quiet War, Wildlife Dies Without Making A Sound (volumes 1 and 2), and *Flowers and Tombstones Of A Conservation Officer* (volumes 1 and 2).

In addition to this current book titled, "BUCK SNORT" TONI AND "WIND HORSE", MOUNTAIN MEN, Terry has written eleven additional Mountain Man and Western historical novels titled, *Crossed Arrows; Curse Of The Spanish Gold; The Saga Of Harlan Waugh, Mountain Man; The Adventures Of The Brothers Dent, Mountain Men; The Adventures Of Hatchet Jack, Mountain Man; The Adventurous Life Of Tom "Iron Hand" Warren, Mountain Man; Josiah Pike; Hell Or High Water; Elliott "Bear Scat" Sutta, Mountain Man; The Saga Of The Barnes' Clan, Mountain Men;* and *"Four Scalps" Ofer Tal, Mountain Man.*

Additionally, Terry has a two-hour movie film credit on the reality-based TV series of "Animal Planet" titled, "WILDLIFE WARS", filmed in 2003 and released nationwide, based on a number of Terry's true-life wildlife law enforcement adventures involving his very active career as a state and federal wildlife officer.

Terry has earned many awards and honors during his lengthy career, including the U.S. Fish and Wildlife Service's Meritorious Service Award in 1996—Recognized as one of "The Top

Ten" employees of the U.S. Fish and Wildlife Service under Service Director Frank Dunkle, for which he received a $5,000 bonus—The first federal employee to be honored with the "Guy Bradley Award" presented by the National Fish and Wildlife Foundation in 1989 for outstanding excellence in the field of wildlife law enforcement—Colorado Conservationist of the Year Award in 1984—The Conservation Achievement Award for Law Enforcement from the National Wildlife Federation in 1995 (the first such law enforcement officer so honored by that organization)—Special Achievement Award for Law Enforcement Excellence from the U.S. Department of Justice in 1998—Distinguished Alumnus Award, College of Natural Resources, Humboldt State University, 1995—Humboldt State University Distinguished Alumnus Award, 2008—Distinguished Achievement Award from the Native American Fish and Wildlife Society, 1992—Received the U.S. Fish and Wildlife Service's highest annual performance ratings under five different senior level supervisors from 1983-1998—Unity College in Maine awarded Terry an Honorary Doctorate Degree in Environmental Stewardship in 2002.

Terry resides in Evergreen, Colorado, with the Co-Author of his life, Donna, whose heart he won and was his high school Sweetheart and now Bride of 55 years and counting…

Find more great titles by Terry Grosz and Wolfpack Publishing at:

http://wolfpackpublishing.com/terry grosz/

www.ingramcontent.com/pod-product-compliance
Lightning Source LLC
Chambersburg PA
CBHW020604040726
47498CB00003B/622